I Only Have Fangs for You

I Only Have Fangs for You

KATHY LOVE

BRAVA

KENSINGTON PUBLISHING CORP.
http://www.kensingtonbooks.com

BRAVA BOOKS are published by

Kensington Publishing Corp.
850 Third Avenue
New York, NY 10022

All Kensington titles, imprints and distributed lines are available at special quantity discounts for bulk purchases for sales promotion, premiums, fund-raising, educational or institutional use.

Special book excerpts or customized printings can also be created to fit specific needs. For details, write or phone the office of the Kensington Special Sales Manager: Kensington Publishing Corp., 850 Third Avenue, New York, NY 10022. Attn. Special Sales Department. Phone: 1-800-221-2647.

Brava and the B logo Reg. U.S. Pat. & TM Off.

ISBN 0-7582-1135-X

First Kensington Trade Paperback Printing: December 2006
10 9 8 7 6 5 4 3 2 1

Printed in the United States of America

For my readers, who have embraced the Young Brothers and all their undead quirks.

Acknowledgments

Thank you to the Tarts!
As always, your support is greatly appreciated.

Thank you, Julie, Chris, and Lisa
for the last minute read-throughs,
the brilliant advice, and just being there.
You are the best!

Thanks, Mom and Dad
for all your help with everything
and your constant encouragement.

Thank you, Bill and Mary Ellen
for all your help.

Thank you, Cindy, Guinness, and Nellie.
You were wonderful entertainment to Emily
and a great help to me.

Todd, I really needed you on this one,
and you were there.
Thank you and I love you.

And all my love to Emily.

Chapter 1

"Has anyone ever told you that you have a beautiful neck?"

Sebastian pressed his lips to the neck in question. The bare skin just below the woman's earlobe was warm and wonderfully scented, and just like that, his fangs lengthened. But he repressed the hunger and smiled slightly as he felt the woman startle. She leapt away and spun to see who was taking such liberties. Her outraged expression dissolved into a slow, pleased grin.

"Sebastian," she breathed, unconsciously tilting her head so her silky blond locks fell back over her shoulder, exposing more of her lovely neck and collarbone. The tiny pulse at the base of her throat quickened, a rapid, delighted flutter under her tanned skin. Her eyes roamed over him with appreciation.

Sebastian grinned. He could always count on Hannah to be very welcoming. And he needed Hannah's sort of welcome tonight. After the week he'd had, he deserved a very, very welcoming Hannah.

He frowned slightly. Her name *was* Hannah, wasn't it? Or was it Anna?

Sure, they had spent a few nights together in the past, but really, there had been very little talking involved. And they had met here, in the nightclub, with the mobs of patrons and the loud, pulsating dance music—it was an easy mistake, right? Hannah. Anna. An honest mix-up.

In his mind, he suddenly saw his brothers' disapproving looks. Rhys with his censorious frown, and Christian with that condescending arch of his eyebrow.

Sebastian refocused on Hannah—well, probably Hannah. Her name didn't matter, not for what he had in mind. Although, he did catch himself studying her, estimating her age, even though he knew she was old enough to be here at the club. But after being called home from his vacation (if anyone could call time spent with his preachy brothers a vacation) because the cops had been tipped off that Carfax Abbey, his nightclub, was serving minors, he felt the need to be more cautious. Even though it was an utterly ridiculous accusation.

Of course, he couldn't very well tell the police that his club had never served a minor because the men carding at the door were actually preternatural creatures. And preternatural creatures were absolutely great at sniffing out underage partygoers. Minors always gave off a specific and strong vibe. Youth, nervousness, and excitement. Hard to miss and easy to turn away.

Fortunately, the police decided the accusation was unfounded without that information. With that problem solved, he was now ready to focus on more pleasurable things. He needed that. Between the NYPD, and his brothers, he needed some fun.

He also needed to reaffirm himself. To reaffirm that his existence was just fine the way it was, despite his brothers' opinions to the contrary. He was single, he was undead, and he was damned happy about both.

He grinned at Hannah.

"Hi there, Han . . . darling." Maybe it was better to avoid names, though.

Probably-Hannah's smile widened, her eyes narrowing with a predatory hunger that would put any vampire to shame. She stepped back to him, pressing her breasts against his arm as she leaned in to speak.

"Sebastian, I missed you."

He sighed at the sensation of her body against his. Oh yeah, Probably-Hannah was definitely the right place to start reaffirming. He didn't have that confused.

"Where have you been? I couldn't find you the last time I was here."

"You were looking for me? When?" he asked, making sure his voice dripped with disappointment.

"Last Saturday."

He could have guessed that. Probably-Hannah was one of his club's many regulars. Repeat mortal customers who his vampire patrons labeled "Fang Freaks." Mortals who returned to his nightclub over and over in hopes of hooking up with a preternatural being. Of course, the mortals didn't understand that was what kept them coming back, nor did they understand the source of their addiction. They just knew that what happened here didn't happen anywhere else.

Sebastian glanced over Probably-Hannah's shoulder to see a group of women watching him.

He smiled. They each responded with some form of invitation: a tempting smile, a coy bat of the lashes, an enticing shift of their bodies that readily said, "Here I am."

He breathed in deeply. Damn, it *was* good to be a vampire. *And* the owner of one of the most popular nightclubs in Manhattan. This is where he ruled, where he had control. And his possibilities were so open. But for tonight, he'd made his choice. He might not remember if she was Hannah or Anna, but Sebastian hadn't forgotten this woman's reaction to him or her taste on his tongue. His body responded, his fangs distending just a bit.

"Care to dance?" He motioned to the dance area, where muted red and purple lights glowed under the frosted flooring.

She nodded, twining her arms around his and falling into step beside him.

Carfax Abbey, a name taken from his favorite novel, *Dracula* (of course), was busy tonight. As he stepped into the throng of gyrating dancers, he was overwhelmed by the scent of mortals, warm and musky with a heady undertone of sweet rustiness. Mingling with that was the impression of other preternatural beings. Their presence made the air vibrate as if the molecules and atoms were agitated by their very existence. The sensation was as exciting as the humans' scents, but not quite as alluring.

He pulled the lovely blonde against him and began to move with the sultry beat of the music. Her arms came up to snake around his neck, her fingers toying with his hair. Her eyes locked with his as she followed his movements instinctively. Their bodies pressed tight together. A delicious friction.

"I love this song," she said, her lips grazing his ear as she spoke over the music. "I love how you dance."

He pulled her tighter, more interested in enjoying her body than her small talk. Which could explain the uncertainty on her name.

He dropped his nose to her hair, smelling the fruity perfume of her shampoo and the sweet scent thrumming just beneath the surface of her smooth skin. Maybe one more dance, then he would invite her to his apartment upstairs over the club.

Tonight he was edgy. His hunger barely contained. Sex and feeding were his two favorite pastimes, but this evening his body literally ached for both.

"Hannah, you found him."

Ha! He'd been right; it was Hannah.

He turned his head to see an auburn-haired beauty in a black-and-red brocade corset and a very tight, very small, black leather skirt. A pair of black boots came up over her knees.

Sebastian started to speak, but paused. He'd slept with her, too, hadn't he? What was her name? Alex? Alice? Elise? Damn.

"Yes, I did find him. See, Sebastian, you've been very, very missed."

The new woman, whose name definitely did start with a vowel, smiled widely and nodded. "Very missed."

"Sebastian Young!" Another woman with exotic dark eyes and long black hair joined them. "Where have you been?"

She stepped between the two women and hugged him.

Now, he did know this woman's name. "Hello, Leah."

The dark-haired woman pulled back and smiled admonishingly. "Gia, love."

"Right. Right. Gia."

"So, Sebastian, why have you been so scarce lately?" The redhead touched his arm as she spoke.

"I had some family commitments I needed to attend to," he said. Actually, it had been more like family torments. He loved his brothers, but they were newly reformed and utterly fang-whipped. In other words, dead dull.

Not that they'd ever been that much fun anyway.

Which was why he was here. "But enough boring talk. Let me get you beautiful women drinks."

He herded them toward the bar, his thoughts already on the delights that lay ahead for the night.

The entire length of the bar was lined up a couple rows deep with waiting patrons as two of his bartenders, Nadine and Ferdinand, rushed to fill drink orders. He strolled to the end, which was left clear for the cocktail servers to pick up their orders.

The area was empty, except for one waitress, a rather ordinary-looking woman with her black hair pulled into two messy ponytails/knots on the top of her head and plastic-rimmed glasses. At first he thought she was a mortal, which surprised him, because it was standard club policy to avoid hiring humans. Then as he got closer, he realized she was actually a preternatural. A vampiress.

He frowned, regarding her in disbelief. This creature was a vampire? The vibe radiating from her wasn't as obvious as it was with most vamps. In fact it was quite faint, but it was definitely there.

He studied her, realizing her faint preternatural vibration wasn't the only thing strange about her. Not all vampires were beautiful, but they were all striking in some way. This vampiress had nothing remarkable about her. Not looks, grace, style. She truly was plain. The only thing unusual about her was her skin, which was the palest he'd ever seen. Even for a vampire.

As he came to a stop near her, she cast him a wary glance, then rushed to pick up her drink tray, nearly toppling over a few of the glasses in her haste. Without another look, she scurried toward the booths in the corner of the club.

Sebastian frowned, watching her briefly before Nadine's voice drew his attention away.

"What can I get you tonight, boss?" she asked, a smirking grin on her full, burgundy-glossed lips.

Calling him boss was their joke. At six feet tall, not many people were Nadine's boss. Add that she was a werewolf, and no one was. That being said, she was his best employee and one of his closest friends.

He gestured with his head in the direction of the waitress. "She's new. Did you hire her?"

Nadine nodded. "Wilhelmina? Yes."

"Wilhelmina?" Sebastian grimaced, he should have guessed she would have an odd name. "You've got to be kidding?"

"She's fine. She needs this job," Nadine said. "And not all of us can be as unnaturally perfect as you."

Sebastian laughed. Nadine knew she was just as unnaturally perfect as he was. It went with the territory of being preternatural. He glanced back to the new waitress.

She cleared a table, fumbling with an empty glass. She did

manage to catch it by the stem just before the goblet hit the floor and shattered.

Okay, that usually went with the territory. Now he wasn't so sure.

"So what can I get you?" Nadine asked again.

"I'd like to get these ladies a round of drinks," he said, nodding to the trio, who giggled and twittered behind him.

Nadine raised a perfect, arced, black brow, then chuckled and shook her head. "Only three?"

Sebastian smiled. She loved to give him a hard time about his women—or rather the amount of them. "Yes, three. I'll wait for mine."

"Mmm, mmm, mmm." Nadine shook her head again. "Well, I guess you have been away for awhile."

"Yes," he agreed. He had. And the way the hunger was gnawing at him tonight, he had no doubts that he could satisfy all three of these ladies. Maybe more than once.

He turned back to them. They beamed at him, excitement and anticipation in their eyes.

"So," he smiled slowly, "what would you ladies like to do this evening?"

Wilhelmina set the tray on the bar as she blew a strand of hair out of her eyes. Then she tugged at the snug waitress uniform, an Asian-inspired black brocade dress with a mandarin collar. The uniform covered her from neck to knee, well mid-thigh anyway, but she still felt barely covered.

"Busy night, eh?" Nadine said, sliding a drink down the bar to Ferdinand before turning back to Wilhelmina.

"Yes, I'm afraid I'm not very fast either," Wilhelmina admitted. Being a bit of a recluse, she'd thought the crowds and the noise would be the hardest part of working in a nightclub. She'd never been able to handle crowds. She hadn't expected the actual job of cocktail waitress to be such hard work. While focusing on her drink orders and the carrying tray helped to keep the crowd from overwhelming her, it was distracting from her real reason for being here.

She handed Nadine a slip with a dozen or so drinks listed. Nadine nodded and hurried off. Wilhelmina fiddled with the strap of her high-heeled maryjanes, another part of the uniform that she wasn't accustomed to wearing. It was little wonder she was slow.

High heels, she shook her head. So impractical.

Taking a breath, she used the small break to survey the club. Vampires, werewolves, other shapeshifters of various breeds mingled and danced with mortals. And the mortals didn't have any idea.

She watched one female vampire take the hand of a mortal male and lead him to the exit. Wilhelmina's first instinct was to run after the mortal and tell him what would happen if he left with the vampiress. But she knew from past experience that approach wouldn't do any good. She'd tried it several times before, and all she ever received for her efforts was a look that stated that the human thought she was a loon. Oh, and there was also the one time that a mortal had threatened to have her arrested. Even now, she shivered at that idea. She definitely wanted to avoid that.

No, chasing them down and telling them the truth wasn't the way to protect mortals.

Someday she hoped vampires and mortals could live truly together, without vampires having to hide and without humans being little more than a source of food and entertainment. That was the hope of all the vampires, shapeshifters, and other creatures that were involved in the Society of Preternaturals. But the only way that dream was going to be achieved was to end all the legends and myths about supernatural beings. Thus preternatural creatures couldn't continue to act like the monsters of folklore. They had to realize their actions were propagating these myths.

She watched the couple exit the club, feeling mildly ill and saddened. She wanted to do more to help these mortals. And thus to help the vampires too, of course. Unfortunately, real change was often a slow process. Think globally, act locally. Which brought her back to why she was here.

Scanning the huge club, she assessed the layout of the place again. She studied the large upper level with its tables and private booths. Then her gaze dropped to the dance floor mobbed with dancers. She hoped her plan would work better than her first one. And she hoped it wasn't too dangerous. Her intent was to protect mortal lives not to find a non-preternatural way to harm them.

Then she noticed him. Even in the sea of very pretty humans and stunning preternaturals, he stood out. Tall and lean in his stylish designer clothing with his intense eyes and pouty lips, Sebastian Young was the poster child for unnaturally beautiful vampires. The only thing that didn't quite fit was his hair. Instead of black like the images of Dracula or other gothic undeads, his hair was mussed and blond like a surfer—or maybe an Abercrombie & Fitch model.

She had heard that he was a gorgeous creature, but even with that knowledge, she hadn't been prepared for her first sighting of him earlier this evening. When he'd approached the bar with his entourage of mortal women, she'd actually been physically stunned by his beauty.

Wilhelmina considered herself very practical and hard to impress, so she hated to admit it, but he was impressive. It was little wonder mortals couldn't resist him.

He now danced with one of the women he'd been with at the bar. He held the blond woman against him, her back pressed to his front. Wilhelmina watched as his hands caressed the mortal through the thin material of her dress, stroking upward, moving slowly over her belly, then up her ribcage to stop just under the curve of her full breasts.

Wilhelmina swallowed, telling herself to look away. Yet she couldn't tear her gaze from him, and what he was doing. He nuzzled his cheek against the woman's silky hair as his hands moved back down over her midriff. His pouty lips parted as he pressed them to the curve of her bare shoulder. His tongue tasted her golden skin.

Wilhelmina's own lips parted as she breathed in a sharp breath.

"He's something, isn't he?"

Wilhelmina jumped, then glanced guiltily at Nadine.

"Wh—who?"

Nadine smiled, obviously not believing Wilhelmina's attempt to sound unaware of who she referred to.

"Our employer," Nadine clarified anyway. "The one you were eyeing as if he were good enough to eat."

"I was not." Wilhelmina frowned. That was ludicrous.

Again Nadine didn't seem convinced. Her smile widened further, her teeth gleaming white against her lovely, dark skin.

"I will have to introduce you." She glanced to where he danced with the lovely blonde. "Later, though. I'd say he's busy for the night. You know, after being away."

Wilhelmina glanced back, too. Another woman joined them on the dance floor, her hands slipping around him from behind so he was sandwiched between the two women.

"Very busy," Nadine said, with a wry, yet almost fond chuckle. She began to place drinks on Wilhelmina's tray.

Wilhelmina watched the antics of the dancing threesome for a moment longer, then determinedly picked up the tray.

So she'd finally seen *the* Sebastian Young. She knew she would eventually, and she wasn't going to be shaken by his presence. The goal was to stay focused on why she was here. Why she had picked this nightclub and this vampire. Sebastian Young disgusted her. He was everything she despised in a vampire.

And she planned to destroy him.

Chapter 2

Wilhelmina delivered her tray of drinks before slipping into the backroom. Given what she intended to do, it seemed a little silly to worry about the patrons getting their cocktails. But she needed to appear like a good employee. She couldn't afford to get fired. If this attempt didn't work, she still needed to stay here. For her sabotage to work, she had to have access to the internal workings of Carfax Abbey.

Carfax Abbey. Even the name of the club was pompous. The lair of the world's most legendary vampire. Did Sebastian consider himself as legendary? From all that she had heard about him, she didn't doubt it. The Society said his hunger was insatiable. He was a real threat.

She crept farther into the storage room, pausing occasionally to listen. She couldn't hear anyone near, but she knew she would still have to act quickly. She looked up at the ceiling. Every six feet or so, a silver sprinkler head jutted down from the drywall.

She headed to the back of the room, where a large metal barrel was used to store recycling. Carefully, she lifted the barrel and positioned it under one of the sprinklers. Then she scurried back to where she'd stashed some broken-down beer boxes and other cardboard behind cases of liquor. She placed it in the metal drum and rummaged through her pocket for a small box of matches.

Sliding it open, she paused, staring at the matches, the head of each matchstick red like droplets of blood in her hand.

What was she doing? She couldn't go through with this. She didn't want to hurt anyone. She just wanted to protect the humans who naively came here thinking the club was nothing more than a happening nightspot.

But maybe this wasn't the way to do it.

She closed the box and started to slip it back into her dress, when the graphic on the front caught her attention. *Carfax Abbey* scrawled in raised red lettering like swirls of blood across the cover.

She thought of Sebastian and all the things she'd heard about him. His misuse of mortal women. His insatiable hunger. His arrogance.

She opened the matches again. She was doing the right thing. For the right reasons. Sebastian Young needed to be stopped.

She swiped the match across the striker. It flared, and before she could think better of it, she held the flame to the cardboard in the barrel. The thick paper was surprisingly slow to ignite. And surprisingly smoky, too. But eventually it began to burn in earnest.

She stepped back, watching and hoping the sprinkler above the feeble blaze got hot enough before the smoke set off the fire alarms. A smoke alarm would just delay the vampires' amusement for the night. She wanted a real interruption. Gushing water and the damage created by the deluge was bound to suspend the nightclub's nefarious activities for quite a while.

Wilhelmina crept over to the door and checked to make sure no one was coming because of the smell. The smoke had become thick enough for humans to smell, never mind someone with preternatural senses. But from what she could see from her limited angle, everyone was still busy drinking and dancing and socializing.

A loud pop drew her attention back to the fire. She hurried to the metal barrel. Flames rose high above the top of the drum, but it was still well-contained. Thankfully. She wanted the nightclub closed; she didn't want it burned to the ground. Nadine had told her that Sebastian, his brother and his brother's wife lived above the club. Her intent wasn't to hurt them.

She could feel the heat of the burning cardboard now, and the smoke had lessened. All she had to do was wait.

She didn't have to wait long. Within a few seconds, the sprinkler over the barrel began to spray an umbrella of water.

Joyful laughter bubbled up inside of her. This time, she'd done it. She'd saved the mortals at the club. They wouldn't experience the brutal bloodlust of a vampire. Not tonight.

She listened, expecting to hear the squeals of the patrons as water poured down on them. The abrupt silence of the dance music. The pounding of hundreds of feet racing for the exit, but she heard none of that.

Instead she heard a sharp, irritated voice demand, "What the hell is going on?"

Wilhelmina spun around, her high heels slipping in the water that had begun to pool around her feet. Before she could catch herself, she fell flat onto her bottom in the puddle, the sprinkler showering cold water down over her.

Sebastian stared at the soaked woman seated in a growing pool of water. Not exactly how he'd imagined a woman falling at his feet tonight. And frankly, he wasn't too thrilled to be pulled away from the women he *had* been expecting to fall at his feet. But when he'd gone to the bar to order another round of drinks, he'd smelled smoke. He'd followed the scent to this—odd scene. His new waitress on the floor, drenched, near a smoldering recycling barrel.

"What the hell happened here?"

The vampiress—Wilhelmina—braced her hands on the floor and started to lever herself up. Sebastian reached forward to help her, but she jerked her arm out of his hold. The movement caused her feet to slip out from under her again, and she returned to the puddle with a loud plop.

"Are you all right?" he asked, crouching down so he was at eye level with her.

She peered at him through water-splattered glasses and a tangle of wet, black hair that had escaped her interesting hairstyle. The two knots on the top of her head, which had looked a bit like horns, now drooped and looked more like floppy dog ears.

Sebastian would have smiled at the image she created, if he hadn't let his gaze drop from her bedraggled hair to her body. The silky brocade of her uniform adhered to her figure, revealing every slope and curve. The hemline, already short by his own design, clung to the tops of her pale thighs, perilously close to revealing far more.

"Here, let me help you up," he insisted more gruffly than he'd intended. He stepped into the spray, water saturating his shirt, but he managed to capture her elbow. This time, she allowed him to help her. She slipped once as she tried to get her footing. Finally she managed to stand.

The new position didn't help as much as he hoped it would. The silk-like fabric still remained plastered to her skin, perfectly displaying the roundness of her breasts, peaked with pointy, taut nipples. The hemline clung and created a V at the junction of her legs.

He stared at the alluring sight until the erection in his pants pulsed, far more sobering than the cold water still splattering down on him. He immediately released his hold on her arm.

This was crazy. They were both standing in a rapidly growing puddle, gaping at each other. And he was actually feeling attracted to this strange, wet waitress.

"Holy shit." Nadine's statement finally seemed to break the spell formed between himself and the new waitress.

Sebastian spun around to see both Nadine and Ferdinand

peering in the doorway. He stepped out of the fountain of water and swiped a hand through his soaked hair.

"I knew I smelled smoke," Ferdinand said.

"What happened?" Nadine asked.

"I have no idea," Sebastian said, then frowned at Wilhelmina. "What *did* happen?"

"I . . ." Wilhelmina stepped out of the spray too. She shivered and then thankfully crossed her arms over her chest, concealing those taut nipples.

Sebastian gritted his teeth. Why was he even thinking about that? His storage room was flooding, for God's sake.

"I . . ." She shivered again, and her gaze strayed to the puddle spreading slowly toward boxes of expensive bourbon. "I . . . was sneaking a cigarette, and I guess it accidentally caught the paper in the can on fire."

"You smoke?" Nadine asked.

Wilhelmina shifted, hugging herself tighter. "Um, yeah. Sometimes."

Sebastian frowned at the shivering woman. Something didn't seem right. But then he disregarded the thought. His senses were still on high alert from the visit from the police. Besides, from what he'd seen so far, everything about this woman didn't seem right.

"Ferdinand, there is a water valve for this room in the back corridor near the bathroom. Switch it off," Sebastian said. "It should be labeled."

Ferdinand nodded and disappeared out of the doorway.

"Come on," Sebastian said, holding out his hand to Wilhelmina. "You need to get dried off."

Wilhelmina stared at his hand as if she expected it to leap out and bite her.

"What—what about the rest of the bar?" She nibbled her bottom lip.

Sebastian's gaze dropped to her mouth, watching the action for a moment, noticing how red her lips looked. Red and very soft. Then he frowned, irritated that he found the sight oddly fascinating. "What about it?"

"Aren't the sprinklers going off all over the club?"

"Ah," he said, understanding her concern. "No. Sprinkler systems are designed to only trigger the heads that sense a rise in temperature. The rest of the club is fine."

"Oh," she said, her lips turning down at the corners in an expression that seemed to imply disappointment, but Sebastian couldn't be sure.

Before he could consider it further, the sprinkler stopped, making the room oddly quiet, even with the dance music blaring in the main room.

Sebastian wiggled the fingers of the hand he still held out to her. "Come on. Let's get dried off."

She hesitated, regarding him with wide, wary eyes behind her water-dotted lens. Then she nodded. But she still didn't accept his hand as she fell into step beside him.

God, she was so stupid. Why hadn't she realized that setting off the sprinkler would only trigger the one near the fire? She should have known that!

"Just down here."

Wilhelmina stopped fixating on her own stupidity and turned her attention to the man walking slightly ahead of her. Sebastian's stylish green shirt was now rumpled and wet, clinging to his broad shoulders and muscular back. His pants were equally drenched and outlined the curve of his tight, little . . . She immediately lifted her gaze from his perfect rear end and instead focused on the soggy, suctioning sound of his expensive shoes as he strode down the hall.

"Here we are," he said, glancing back at her and then gesturing to a large freight elevator. He lifted the metal gate that served as the door and waited for her to step in.

She glanced at the small enclosure, anxiety filling her. "Wh—where are we going?"

"Upstairs to my apartment."

She stepped back. "Why?"

Did he want to get her alone to exact some wicked punishment on her? Her skin tingled at the idea, and she told herself it was fear. Absolutely fear.

But instead of laughing evilly and informing her of his dastardly plans, he smiled in a lopsided way and said, "Because that's where I keep my towels."

When she just stared at him, he pushed the elevator gate higher and gestured with his head. "Please get in. Even if you don't mind wet clothes, I'd like to change mine."

She hesitated just a moment longer, then stepped inside. Sebastian dropped the gate and pressed the black button labeled with a white number three. The elevator shuddered to life.

Although the elevator was large by, well, elevator standards, Wilhelmina felt like the enclosure was closing in on her. Sebastian, while on the other side of the space, wasn't helping matters. His large body seemed to eat up the distance between them.

She watched him from the corner of her eyes, his presence unnerving, more unnerving than the enclosed quarters. She again noticed the way his damp clothes adhered to his muscles. The way his mussed hair curled, golden in the subdued light.

She grimaced, forcing her gaze to the metal flooring. *Of course, he's unnerving*. Because of all the terrible things she'd heard about the man, she told herself. Although as her skin tingled again, she wasn't sure if that was totally true.

After what seemed like ages, the elevator jerked to a stop and Sebastian lifted the metal grating. Wilhelmina stepped past him, giving him a wide berth, into another hallway that looked similar to the back halls of the nightclub—unpainted drywall and metal ductwork along the ceiling. The only difference was that at the end of this hall was a heavy, ornate, wooden door and beyond that Sebastian's apartment.

Again, she considered just telling him she was fine and taking the elevator back down to the club. She knew better than to get into a situation where she was alone with him. Then Sebastian offered her another lopsided smile, and for some reason, she didn't leave. Instead she followed him through the doorway.

She didn't understand why she followed him. There was nothing to be gained from going to his place. No reason to see if she could find more ideas for sabotage from his personal space. After all, because of her ignorance about the workings of sprinkler systems, she wasn't going to be employed at Carfax Abbey much longer. Her second attempt at sabotage, another failure.

Actually this attempt was an utter disaster.

Sebastian twisted the doorknob and stepped aside to allow her in. The door opened into an entryway with dark hardwood floors and burgundy walls. She paused again, her senses telling her this was dangerous. She shouldn't be alone with this vampire. He was untrustworthy and potentially very dangerous.

Then she recalled that Sebastian lived with his brother, Rhys. She knew of him from Dr. Fowler, the scientist whose foundation had proved the truth about preternatural beings. Rhys had become a believer in Fowler's teachings. She knew he could be trusted. In fact, maybe getting to know him and his mate would be a way to put a stop to his brother's biting ways. They must disapprove of his behavior, too.

Sebastian led her through a small kitchen to a spacious living room. This room also had dark hardwood floors and was decorated in a deep plum color with oversized gray furniture and heavy wooden end tables. The walls were lined with shelves full of books, and a gray marble fireplace created the focal point of the room.

Wilhelmina was surprised. It was hardly the place where she would have expected the infamous Sebastian Young to spend his time. She pictured a place of seduction. Not coziness and warmth.

This had to be his brother's influence. She concentrated,

trying to sense other presences in the apartment. She couldn't detect any.

"Doesn't your brother live with you?" she asked.

"Rhys lives in the apartment above this. I used to live up there too, but once he married his wife, Jane, I thought I should give them their space. I had this place built about six months ago."

He'd had the apartment built like this for himself? She gaped around. Where were the mirrored ceilings? Not that a vampire would likely have mirrors. But where was the shag carpeting? The low, colored, recessed lighting? The piped-in porn music?

Then the realization that she was alone with him hit her. A shiver ran down her spine. Cozy or not, what if he did bring her up here to do something nefarious? Surely, he was furious about the flooded backroom. Surely, he was going to chastise her in some way.

She stepped back from him, her eyes on the door. If she remained calm, she could likely make it back to the hallway and the elevator before he caught her. She glanced at him, noting his long legs and lean muscles. Maybe she could. Maybe.

But rather than approach her with a villainous glint in his intense golden eyes, he strode away from her and opened another heavy wooden door on the other side of the room.

"Here's the bathroom, if you'd like to dry off."

Although there didn't seem to be anything menacing about his offer, she still regarded him uneasily.

He flipped on the light and pushed the door wide. "See, it's a bathroom. Really."

She nodded, feeling a little foolish, then slowly crossed the room. The bathroom was also large with a separate shower and whirlpool bathtub. But that was the only decadent luxury in the room. The décor was gray marble, both functional and stylish.

He crossed to a closet near the shower. She stood near the

bathroom door, watching him. He pulled out a towel, then he strolled toward her.

Ha! Here we go. Now he was going to suggest she undress or something equally rude and offensive. She shivered, another tingle shimmying over her flesh.

He simply held the plain white towel out to her.

"Here you go. And help yourself to anything you want."

He grabbed a towel for himself and headed toward the door.

"Wait," she said more sharply than she intended, her voice echoing off the tile. He paused and turned back to her, arching an eyebrow.

"Aren't—aren't you going to fire me?" she asked, her voice now much softer, and irritatingly to herself, a little shaky.

Sebastian shook his head. "No. Accidents happen." He offered her another smile and left the room.

Wilhelmina remained motionless, the towel held loosely in her hand. She couldn't believe it. He wasn't going to fire her. Her plans for him and Carfax Abbey weren't thwarted.

She wondered why she didn't feel more pleased.

Chapter 3

"Oh my God! What happened?"

Wilhelmina stepped into her apartment and dropped her purse on the floor. She brushed her still damp hair from her face, and toed off her wet shoes before answering her roommate, Lizzie.

Lizzie sat on the sofa, a huge platter of nachos balanced on her lap. Her long legs curled under her, her glossy amber hair loose around her shoulders. As usual, she looked lovely, making Wilhelmina all the more aware of her drowned-rat impersonation.

"Well," she stated, "I set off a sprinkler."

Lizzie set the nachos on the coffee table and leaned forward, excitement lighting her pale blue eyes. "You did?" Then she paused. "Wait, *a* sprinkler?"

Wilhelmina nodded and held up a single finger.

"Why? What happened?"

Wilhelmina flopped into a chair that took up a majority of one corner of the small room. She ignored the fact that her dress was dampening the chenille cushions.

"Apparently when you light a fire under a sprinkler only that sprinkler goes off, not all of them."

"Well, they all go off in the movies."

"I know," Wilhelmina agreed, still disgruntled about the

whole fiasco and her trust in cinematic truth. "And, unfortunately, it gets worse."

Lizzie paused, a nacho dripping with cheese and meat halfway to her mouth.

"Not only did I set off only the one sprinkler, but I slipped and fell into the water. In front of him."

"Oh no." But Wilhelmina couldn't help noticing that Lizzie didn't seem surprised.

Then Lizzie's pale eyes lit up. "Super-Fang's back?"

Wilhelmina frowned at the nickname Lizzie had given Sebastian. Granted she didn't know his real name or the name of the club. Only registered members knew that information. Which, given how dangerous Sebastian was, seemed a little self-defeating. Not to mention Lizzie could probably hold her own with the vampire. Still, she had the feeling her roommate wasn't taking Wilhelmina's mission seriously.

"Yes, he returned to deal with the police investigation on the accusation that Carfax Abbey was serving minors."

"That was a good one," Lizzie said. "I thought that one would work."

Wilhelmina nodded. So had she. She sighed. "So all my sabotage attempts have managed to do so far is lure the nefarious vampire back to his club to witness me falling in the small flood I created." She sighed. "That ought to stop his evil ways."

Lizzie shook her head, giving her a sympathetic smile. She popped the nacho into her mouth and chewed thoughtfully.

Wilhelmina watched her, wishing she could drown her sorrows with a little binge-eating.

"Well, it sounds like you made a good attempt," Lizzie said as she munched another nacho, and then she uncurled from the sofa, her impossibly long legs elegant even in jeans. "And he didn't fire you."

She picked up the platter and headed toward the kitchen before she spun back to her. "He didn't fire you, did he?"

"No," Wilhelmina said, still unsure how she felt about that surprising fact.

"That's good, right?" Lizzie gave her an encouraging smile and disappeared into the kitchen. Wilhelmina closed her eyes and let her head fall against the back of the chair.

She appreciated Lizzie's support especially since she knew her new roommate thought that Wilhelmina's involvement with the Society was a bit out there. But her sympathetic smiles only managed to make Wilhelmina feel more like a failure.

She knew Lizzie was only being supportive because she was a friend. She never asked for many details, although she had tried to help with sabotage ideas. Lizzie seemed to like the idea of that, even though Lizzie thought most of the work the Society of Preternaturals did was silly. She wasn't for the integration of preternatural creatures. She wanted a cure for them. That was where her energy was focused. Her research.

But until, or even if, a cure was found, Wilhelmina felt that she had to help mortals any way she could. Even if it meant sabotaging one preternatural hotspot at a time.

Wilhelmina shivered, even though her bloodless skin didn't register the coldness of her damp clothing as it would have if she were human. But she'd been shivering since she'd gotten wet, since she'd . . .

An image of Carfax Abbey's owner appeared behind her closed lids. In some ways, he'd been exactly what she imagined, and in others . . . in others, he'd been very different. Like his unexpected reaction to the water damage. He'd handled the whole debacle with an easygoing amusement that she hadn't expected in an arrogant, dissolute, and wicked vampire. He'd even helped mop up the water himself. Although he had still looked every inch the decadent vampire doing it.

That was another reaction she hadn't anticipated—her fascination with his physical appearance. She'd encountered many beautiful vampires in her existence, and she'd been fully prepared for Sebastian's good looks. Or at least she'd thought so. And still she'd found herself watching him throughout the remainder of her shift, which he'd actually cut short, sending her home because she didn't have any other dry clothes to put on. She hadn't expected that from the infamous vampire either. Consideration.

She opened her eyes. She couldn't let his laid-back manner fool her. That was part of his charm, part of his lure, used to disguise the monster underneath.

"So what about the club owner?" Lizzie called from the kitchen. "Was he all that the Society had made him out to be?"

Wilhelmina frowned. Sometimes she really hated Lizzie's animalistic ability to guess her train of thought. Wilhelmina didn't want anyone picking up the feelings stirring inside her at the moment. Surprising notions about how intriguing she'd found the owner.

No, no, no! She only found him interesting because he was her opponent, her nemesis. She was wise to study him. And she was equally as wise to remember that he was beautiful and mesmerizing in just the same way a flame was to a moth.

Let's face it, the moth never made out well in that attraction. She knew that firsthand.

"Well?" Lizzie asked again as she re-entered the room, a large glass of iced tea in one hand and three packages of Twinkies in the other.

Wilhelmina shook her head. If Lizzie were human, she'd weigh three hundred pounds. But then, if she were human, she wouldn't have an enormous appetite. Lycanthropes really could pack it away.

Lizzie sank onto the sofa and arched a dark brow at Wilhelmina. "So? What was Super-Fang like?"

Wilhelmina frowned, another image of Sebastian appearing in her head. His golden eyes and lopsided smile.

"Dangerous. Very, very dangerous."

Lizzie nodded as she took a large bite of her snack cake. "So what's the next plan of attack?"

Wilhelmina sighed, and for just a moment, she considered putting an end to this crazy idea. But she couldn't let herself do that. She believed in what she was doing. She just needed to remain determined. She would see Carfax Abbey closed down. Unfortunately, she'd used her two best plans, and they'd both failed.

"I don't know," she finally admitted.

"What about the idea to empty all the vodka and gin bottles and fill them with water?"

Wilhelmina winced. Had she actually thought that would stop the club's business?

"No. That won't work."

"You could also replace all the whiskey and bourbon with tea," Lizzie said, raising the glass of amber-colored liquid to demonstrate before taking a sip.

"I don't think that would do much, except cost him some money."

"Probably not," Lizzie agreed, then she smiled slyly. "But it would be sort of fun."

"What if I put something in the beer that would make the human patrons sick?" Wilhelmina suggested.

Lizzie shook her head. "No. Food poisoning is a dicey proposition. Humans are fragile, and you wouldn't want to mortally injure the ones you're trying to save."

Wilhelmina nodded. That was true.

They both fell silent as they considered other possibilities.

"You know," Lizzie finally said, "I'd just go into the club before it's opened and burn the place to the ground. That would certainly stop him."

Wilhelmina shook her head. Lizzie had been right when she'd said that Wilhelmina didn't want to hurt anyone. She didn't. She wanted to stop what happened at the club, but she didn't want to do anything that would truly hurt someone. She wasn't a radical who believed that sometimes violence was the means to an end. Although some of the members of the Society did feel that way. She just wanted mortals to be safe from sadistic, self-serving vampires. She wished there had been someone out there who'd done the same for her.

"Okay," Lizzie agreed, "no burning to the ground. Let me think." She ripped open another package of Twinkies.

Wilhelmina watched her, trying to think of something that would cause the club to be closed down for longer than an evening. Fire was out. Water damage was out—too much fire needed. Tampering with the liquor, ineffectual. Food poisoning—too dangerous. What did that leave?

"I've got it," Wilhelmina said, suddenly. "Health inspectors."

Lizzie nodded, looking impressed. "Yes, that could work. If you did it right."

Wilhelmina grinned. Oh, she'd do it right. This time her plan would definitely work.

Sebastian strode through the nightclub, nodding to several of the club's employees as he passed. They were busy with their sidework, getting ready for another hectic night. He scanned the large room for dark hair and black-rimmed glasses, but didn't see either. The new waitress wasn't in yet, or maybe it was her night off. Or better yet, maybe she'd quit.

"Where's the new girl?" he asked Nadine, keeping his voice casual as he slid onto a bar stool.

Nadine glanced at him, then picked up a bundle of napkins. "She'll be in any minute."

"So what's the deal with her?"

Nadine didn't look up from where she crouched behind the bar, restocking the shelves. "What do you mean?"

"She's—odd."

Nadine rose, crumpled up the empty wrapper from the

napkins and tossed it down the bar into a gray plastic trash can.

"She is," Nadine agreed. "But she's harmless."

"When she's not starting fires in the backroom, that is."

"That was an accident."

Sebastian nodded, but knew he didn't look convinced. There had been something about the new waitress's behavior that still didn't seem right to him. It was almost as if she'd been disappointed when he'd assured her the rest of the nightclub was fine. And then in his apartment, she'd been downright afraid of him.

He supposed he could chalk up her fear to the fact that she'd fully expected to be fired, which many other business owners would have done. He wondered why he hadn't.

"You said that she needs this position," Sebastian said. "Why? What's her story?"

Nadine ladled maraschino cherries from a large jar into a metal serving tray. "I don't know much about her. She's pretty quiet."

"Then how do you know—" Sebastian started, but his head bartender silenced him with a sharp flash of her dark eyes.

"I just get the vibe that she needs this job," she stated. "There's something . . . desperate about her."

Sebastian couldn't disagree with that. At the very least, there was something desperately strange about her. He started to say so when Nadine's next comment stopped him.

"She seems lost."

Sebastian paused. Hadn't that been what he'd sensed about her, too? He just hadn't been able to label it as Nadine had. But there was something anxious and almost lost about her. She was unlike any vampire he'd encountered, and running this club, he'd met many. He had to admit that she made him curious.

And other than being a little accident-prone, she was obviously not dangerous. In fact, aside from her strangeness, she was rather unexceptionable. Another peculiar trait for a vampiress. Vampires were nothing if not noticeable. She wasn't.

Except when wet, he amended. She'd definitely been noticeable then. The image of her sitting in that puddle, dress hiked up to the tops of her pale thighs, appeared in his mind again.

He gritted his teeth, annoyed with himself. He wasn't irritated with himself for noticing. After all, that's what he did. He *always* noticed women. It was the fact that the image was still so clear in his mind, and kept replaying. He'd seen far more provocative displays of skin from far more beautiful women, yet something about—what was her name?

Wilhelmina.

He grimaced. But something about Wilhelmina had captured his attention. Again and again over the course of last evening, and again tonight.

He'd obviously been depriving himself. Time with his holier-than-thou brothers really did cramp his style. And last night, the sprinkler incident had put a damper (no pun intended) on his plans. By the time he was finished cleaning up the backroom, he'd decided just to head up to his apartment to relax. Alone. He'd been too preoccupied: with who could have called the cops about serving minors, and then as much as he hated to admit it, Wilhelmina. He'd thought about her more than the damned cops.

He sighed, turning his thoughts to the threesome of women he'd turned away. That had been stupid. He wouldn't still feel so uneasy if he'd spent last night feeding his hunger and burned off his extra tension with them. Maybe they'd be back tonight and he could make up for his bad behavior. They would forgive him. Women always did.

Again, the new waitress popped into his head. Except for her, maybe. She definitely didn't respond to him like most women, whether vampiress or female human. Even Nadine was more receptive to his charm—and Nadine was one tough she-wolf.

Nadine's a wolf, understanding dawning on him. That had to be why Nadine was championing the weird waitress. Wolves were protective by nature.

"Nadine, I appreciate your decision, but I'm not sure she's cut out for a job here. I mean look at Greta." He gestured to the leggy blonde, leaning on the end of the bar chatting with Crystal, a curvy brunette. "And Crystal. Our cocktail waitresses are part of the allure of the place. They are supposed to be a draw for the patrons."

"Give her a chance. This is where she needs to be," Nadine said, certainty in her husky voice.

Sebastian studied his right-hand woman and friend. Finally, he nodded. Nadine was a good judge of character, another trait of werewolves. Animal instincts and all that. And he'd trusted her for years with all his hiring. It didn't make much sense to question her now.

Still, while there was something that intrigued him about the vampiress, there was something that made him uncomfortable as well. His gut told him he should bypass Nadine's opinion and give the little waitress her walking papers.

"Hi, Wilhelmina," he heard Greta greet the waitress in question.

Sebastian glanced down the bar to see her rush into the club. Her hair was again knotted in that peculiar, messy, hornlike hairstyle and her black plastic-framed glasses slipped down to the tip of her nose. She scurried in a graceless way, the large knapsack on her back causing her to stoop forward, making her look like a hunchback.

"Hi," she murmured to the blonde as she hurried past.

As she approached, she hesitated slightly when her eyes met his. Then as she started forward again, the toe of her left foot caught on one of the nearly nonexistent grooves in the marble flooring. She tripped forward but managed to catch herself on the back of a bar stool before she fell.

Sebastian started to stand to make sure she was okay, but before he could rise, she scampered past him toward the employee lounge.

"Wilhelmina," he called, turning his bar stool in her direction.

He'd expected her to be reluctant to speak to him, but instead she spun to face him.

"Y-yes," she said, her gaze darting from him to Nadine and then back to him again.

"Are you okay?" he asked. As in his apartment, he got the vibration that she was scared.

"Yes," she said quickly. "I—I just need to call my roommate before my shift starts. I—I forgot to tell her—something."

Just then her knapsack shifted, and she reached a hand to one of the straps to secure it. She backed away from them. "I, um, I need to make that call."

She continued to back away a few more steps, then turned and literally fled into the small lounge.

Sebastian glanced at Nadine. "I hope you are right about her."

Nadine gave him a bemused look that stated she currently had her doubts as well. "Me too."

Chapter 4

Wilhelmina rushed into the employee lounge, a relieved sigh escaping her as she saw the room was empty. Thank God. She started to sag back against the wall, her heart pounding and her knees weak. But at the last moment, just as her back would have connected, squeezing the backpack between herself and the wallboard, she caught herself.

Pushing straight, she reached for the straps of the pack and eased it off her shoulders. She placed the large sack on the floor, watching as the nylon rippled and undulated like a living thing. Of course, the creatures inside were alive. And judging from the squeaks and clawing, they were also more than a little upset. The woman at the pet store had looked a little upset, too, when Wilhelmina had asked to buy all of their rats, and then had stuck them in her knapsack. Oh well. This had to be done.

"Sorry guys," she murmured to the bag, "but you can't be any more distressed than I am."

The last person she'd expected to be in the bar was Sebastian. She'd just assumed that the *great* Sebastian Young didn't make an appearance until the place was bustling with his next round of human victims. After all, that was the importance of the nightclub for him, wasn't it?

Wilhelmina hadn't expected him to be sitting right there at the bar, watching her with those intense, golden eyes.

She'd been prepared for the rest of the waitstaff, and how quickly she was going to have to race through the bar, so they didn't sense the animals in her backpack. She'd almost blown it when she'd seen Sebastian and their eyes met. It was a sheer miracle that she managed to keep her footing when she'd tripped. And then he'd called her, and she'd been certain that he'd sensed the rats. But he hadn't. Her hope that the waterproofed knapsack would buy her a little time had worked. The scent of the rodents hadn't easily filtered through the rubberized material.

But she knew she didn't have much more time. The werewolves' sense of smell was very keen. She needed to get this done, fast.

Creeping back to the doorway, she looked both ways to make sure no one, especially Sebastian, was around. The coast was clear. She ducked back into the lounge and hurried over to the backpack.

As she unzipped the nylon, a fountain of rats sprang from the growing gap. They scrambled over each other and over her hands, their little claws scratching her skin in their desperation to escape.

"Sorry guys," she whispered again. "But you're free now. Scurry wherever you like."

The dozen or so rats seemed to take her at her word and scuttled away, heading to the corners of the room rather than exposing themselves to the middle. She watched them for a second, feeling a strange connection to them. She'd lived much the same way for most of her life. Clinging to the edges, trying to remain unnoticed. Never exposing herself to the world. That was how she'd survived.

But she was putting herself out there now. She rose suddenly feeling less nervous and more positive that this was the right thing to do. The brave and strong and honorable thing to do.

She unzipped the side pocket of her bag and pulled out her cell phone. The number for the New York health department, which she'd gotten before she left her apartment, appeared in her call list. Arrowing down to it, she hit *Send* and the phone began to ring.

"Hey, there."

She nearly dropped the phone as she quickly flipped the cover shut, just as a faint hello sounded on the other end. Trying to appear calm, she turned to look at the speaker, knowing exactly who owned that deliciously velvety voice. Sebastian leaned in the doorway, watching her with a troubled frown.

"Hi," he said, his voice oddly soothing. "Are you sure you're all right?"

She blinked at him, again stunned that anyone, preternatural or not, could look that dazzling. And combined with that voice. . . . She blinked again.

Sebastian's frown deepened, and he stepped into the room. She shifted, realizing she'd been staring. For how long, she didn't know. Long enough for him to sense the rats? Had they had time to scurry away?

She glanced down at the bag, which was unzipped and wide open in the middle of the floor. She didn't want him questioning her about the now empty pack. Returning her eyes to his, she hoped he didn't follow her glance. His intense eyes were locked on her face, watching her.

Taking what she hoped was a subtle sidestep, she positioned herself in front of the knapsack. With her heel, she nudged it under a chair. The zipper clanged on the metal of the chair leg, and for a moment, she feared it was one of the rats squeaking. Before the cause of the sound registered, she raised a hand to her mouth and coughed loudly, dramatically.

Sebastian stepped even closer, reaching out a hand to pound her on the back, but she jerked away, falling rather unceremoniously onto the chair under which she'd just hidden the bag.

"I'm fine," she assured him quickly, wanting him to leave. She was afraid the rats weren't dispersed enough and could still be detected. Not to mention, she was too aware of how close his body was to hers. His leg practically brushed her bare knee. She gave their near touch a sidelong glance, then forced herself to meet those intense eyes of his.

"I'm fine," she said again, pressing a hand to her chest. "Um, allergies." Then she offered him a forced smile. "I—I really must make that call." She held up the cell phone, still clasped in her other hand.

He studied her, but this time there was an emotion she didn't quite understand in his eyes. And for a split second, she could have sworn his gaze had dropped to her lips. Of course, he was probably noting that her smile was labored. She was quickly discovering she could never make a living as an actress.

Then his golden eyes narrowed and before she could think to react, he reached forward and caught her hand.

"What happened?"

She glanced down at his finger stroking over her skin, and it took her a moment to realize he was tracing the faint marks from the rat's claws on her pale skin.

"Oh that," she said, searching for some excuse, but her mind couldn't focus on anything but the slightly roughened pads of his fingertips like suede on her skin.

"They look like cat scratches," he said, looking back up to her eyes.

"They are," she said, immediately grasping his excuse. "I—I have a cat."

Sebastian raised an eyebrow to that. "Cats and vampires don't mix. We freak them out." His fingers caressed the small welts again. "But I guess you've learned that."

"Yes," she said again, forcing another smile. Or at least she thought it was a smile. She couldn't be sure, since she couldn't seem to focus on anything but him. And his fingers.

Finally, she managed to gather her thoughts enough to ease her hand away from his. He allowed the withdrawal, although his eyes still held hers.

"Are you sure you are okay?"

She nodded. "I just need to make that call. It—it's a really important call."

He regarded her closely, and she had the feeling that he didn't believe her.

"And private, too," she added, hoping that would get him to leave.

He didn't move for a second, but then nodded. "Okay."

He crossed the room, stopping in the doorway to look at her again. His mouth parted, as if he planned to say something else, but then he just nodded and left the room.

Wilhelmina blew out the breath that she didn't even realize she'd been holding. She sagged back against the chair, the tingling in her body nearly overwhelming. She remained that way, boneless, her mind numbed, unable to do anything for a moment. Then she lifted the cell phone and flipped the cover up. Her fingers shook as she arrowed down to the right number.

"Hello," she responded to the voice on the other end. Her voice was breathy, but determined. "I need to report a health code violation, and I think someone needs to be sent right away. Carfax Abbey is overrun with rats. Yes. Yes."

She gave the woman on the other end the address.

"Thank you."

She hit the *End* button, her hands still trembling. She'd done it, the right thing.

And in the nick of time, too. Sebastian Young had just proved how dangerous he was—and not just to mortals, but to her as well.

"Have you ever heard of a vampire having allergies?" Sebastian asked his sister-in law, Jane. She looked up from her computer, where she was working on the payroll.

"Is this a joke?"

Sebastian had the strange feeling that it had to be—one he wasn't in on.

"Have you ever heard of that?" he asked again.

She shook her head. "No, but I'm pretty new at this vampire thing."

He was relatively old, and he'd never heard of such a thing.

"Have you heard of a vampire having a cat?"

Jane pushed her chair back from her desk and regarded him with her vividly green eyes. "What's going on?"

"Have you met the new waitress?" he asked, sitting forward in his chair, resting his hands on the polished wood of her desk. "Wilhelmina?"

"No. Is she the reason you're so agitated?"

He wasn't agitated. Then he glanced down, realizing he was gripping the edge of the desk. He released the wood and slid back in his seat. He wasn't agitated. He was—confused. He had no idea what to make of Wilhelmina. He could sense emotions from her that didn't make sense. Anxiety, even a little fear—yet a very strong determination too. He had the feeling there was a lot going on in her head that she wasn't sharing.

"She's different," he said.

Jane nodded, a shrewd smile on her lips.

"Oh no. No, no," Sebastian said, waving a hand, knowing where her thought processes were going. "Different in a weird, and very unappealing way." Even as he said the words, he knew it wasn't true. He noticed appealing things about her, far more appealing than he'd expected. But she was not different in the way Jane was thinking.

Jane's eyes widened. "I've never heard you talk that way about a woman."

Sebastian frowned. Jane was right. He appreciated all women, and his words had sounded more than a little rude.

"What woman?" Sebastian's brother, Rhys, appeared in the office doorway. He leaned on the doorframe, arms crossed over his chest, sporting a look much like the one his wife had worn just moments earlier.

"Damn," Sebastian muttered, "I swear people in love are worse than drug pushers. You are always trying to get others, who are quite happily single, shackled to someone. It's damned annoying."

Rhys grinned at his brother, a gesture that still gave

Sebastian pause. After nearly two centuries of scowls and general brooding, the fact that Rhys now readily smiled managed to startle Sebastian almost every time.

Rhys stepped around the desk to Jane and reached for her hand. She slipped out of the chair and into his arms.

"You should really try it. You don't know what you are missing, baby bro."

Jane grinned and added in her best "pusher" voice, "Yes, try it. What? Are you scared?"

Sebastian rolled his eyes as his brother and sister-in-law grinned at each other and then kissed.

"Room. Find one. Now," he muttered.

Rhys pulled away from Jane, but his gaze didn't leave his wife's face. "My thoughts exactly."

Jane smiled impishly, the grin somehow naughtier on her innocent features.

They left the office hand in hand, leaving Sebastian in the office, forgotten.

"I'll be doing the same thing later tonight," he called after them. "And it will be just as good."

He leaned toward the door and added loudly, "Better even."

Jane's laughter was his only reply. A melodious, and altogether disbelieving, giggle.

Sebastian snorted, then rose to move to the other side of the desk. He settled down at the computer, minimized the payroll program that Jane had been working on, and opened the sales report. He started to peruse last month's numbers.

But quickly the columns of figures blurred as he thought about both Rhys and Jane's happy smiles. He did appreciate the love between his brother and Jane. Still, that didn't mean he wanted the same thing in his life.

Unbidden, a memory of Wilhelmina's small smile appeared in his mind, rather awkward and stiff, yet somehow endearing in its valiant attempt. He wondered what her real smile looked like. Would it be sweet? A little naughty? A bit of both.

He frowned at the computer. Why was he thinking about

this? He wasn't interested in the vampiress. She was weird with bad hair and glasses. What vampire wore glasses? And she owned a cat! Everyone knew cats didn't like vampires.

He determinedly refocused on the document on the computer screen. He had enough to think about without thinking about Wilhelmina.

She did have the softest skin he'd ever touched. He growled, pushing away from the desk. What was his fixation with this new waitress? Why did he find himself remembering the most unimportant details about her?

"Because you need exactly what your brother's getting," he stated aloud to the empty room. Well, not exactly what his brother was getting. He needed fun, dirty, *uncommitted* sex. Then he'd have control of his wayward thoughts.

The bass of the dance music in the club thumped in muffled repetition. A call to find his companion for the night. He punched off the monitor and stood just as Nadine appeared in the doorway. A frown pulled at her dark brows and created creases on either side of her wide lips.

"What's up?"

"Health inspectors are here," she said, seeming a little confused.

"Health inspectors? Why?"

"Apparently, they got a call stating we have a rat problem."

"What?" He strode out of the room, heading to see what this was all about.

Wilhelmina made her way through the crowd to where Sebastian stood talking to a man and a woman near the doorway that led to the employee lounge and back storerooms. Both the man and woman wore business suits, and didn't look remotely like regular patrons of the club. The woman reviewed a paper on the clipboard she held in her hand.

The health inspectors.

That hadn't taken long. Wilhelmina couldn't contain the smile that tugged at her lips as the woman wrote something on the paper. Probably the notice saying that the club would have to be closed down until the rat problem was resolved.

She stepped closer, trying to hear the conversation.

"We're sorry to have to take up your time like this," the man was saying in a raspy, almost breathless voice. His suit coat barely buttoned around his paunchy middle. The health inspector was hardly the image of good health himself.

Sebastian smiled at the man. "Well, you have to do your job."

Wilhelmina frowned. He was taking this too well. He had to be furious that his business would be closed indefinitely.

She edged a little closer.

"But it's unfortunate to waste your time, and ours, when there are obviously no health code violations here," the woman muttered and scribbled something else on her clipboard.

No violations! Wilhelmina stepped closer to the group. What was the woman talking about? There were a dozen rats roaming the backrooms. How could they have missed that?

"Can I do something for you?"

She startled at Sebastian's question.

He frowned at her. "Is there something you wanted to ask me?"

Hugging her empty drink tray to her chest, she shook her head. "No. Um, no." She hurried off to the bar, her mind still trying to wrap around the fact that the health inspectors had found nothing. Nothing. That couldn't be.

She stopped at the drink pick-up area at the far end of the bar, setting her tray down, still staring at the group. Sebastian spoke to them, another gracious smile on his full lips.

Wilhelmina shook her head, as if she could somehow shake away what she'd heard.

"Do you have an order for me?" Nadine asked, jarring Wilhelmina's attention from the trio.

"I—um. Yes." She rummaged in the pocket of her dress for her order pad. She tore off the top sheet and handed it to Nadine.

The bartender scanned the list, then nodded. She hurried away to fill the order.

Wilhelmina looked back over to see Sebastian walking the health inspectors toward the front entrance. She fought the urge to chase after them, to demand they check again, more closely. The rats were there. She knew.

But she couldn't do that. Not without giving herself away. And she wasn't prepared to out herself in front of Sebastian. Not even for the cause.

"Long Island Iced Tea, a Screwdriver, and two merlots." Nadine placed the cocktails on her tray.

"Thanks." Wilhelmina's gaze never left Sebastian, who still chatted with the two inspectors. Wilhelmina's eyes narrowed. She wanted to scream. Was Sebastian Young the most charmed vampire in existence?

"Wondering who the two suits are?" Nadine asked.

Wilhelmina nodded, not wanting to give her any reason to suspect why she was watching them so intently.

"Health inspectors," she whispered. "They got a call saying that Carfax Abbey was infested with rats. Crazy, huh?"

Wilhelmina nodded again, even though she didn't think it was crazy at all.

"We'd be the last damned place in New York to have a rat problem," Nadine murmured.

"Why?" Wilhelmina asked, surprised by the bartender's certainty.

Nadine leaned closer, so no one could hear. "Everyone knows that rats are terrified of preternaturals. And with the amount of preternaturals in this place, we are more effective than any exterminator. No vermin would come within a mile radius of this place. Not even a damned cockroach."

The tall woman straightened and grinned like the whole thing was the funniest joke ever.

And Wilhelmina supposed it would have been pretty funny, if she wasn't the butt of the joke—again.

Chapter 5

"Hey, this isn't my drink."

Wilhelmina stopped midstep and turned back to the table surrounded by a mixture of humans and what she suspected, if the men's sizes were any indication, alpha werewolves. The huge, heavily muscled man who'd spoken to her gestured to his drink. The cocktail on the table in front of him was pink with cherries and a purple umbrella. Definitely not the kind of drink a burly lycanthrope would order.

She quickly picked the glass up and placed it back on her full tray. She frowned at the drinks, guessing his was the pint of porter.

She carefully placed the dark beer before him and waited, hoping she'd guessed right. She had. He nodded and lifted the drink to his mouth, swallowing half the beer in one gulp.

She smiled stiffly and headed off to deliver more drinks, guessing at all of them, because her thoughts were not on her job but on the fact that she had again bungled her sabotage attempt. Why was she so clueless? Of course, if she understood herself and her kind better, she would have known about this.

If you do it right. Suddenly Lizzie's comment made sense. Lizzie had known how the rats would react. Wilhelmina obviously hadn't. But she should have guessed that the released rats would just run, leaving the nightclub altogether.

Equally as pathetic as her own ignorance was the fact that rodents had more sense than the humans she was trying to help. But the rats hadn't been told from birth that things that went bump in the night weren't real. They functioned solely on instinct. Not a bad thing.

She paused at her next table, trying to recall what the patrons here had ordered. Was it the wines or the beers?

Finally, after much debate, she just asked them. They told her the beers, which she placed before them and then moved along toward the next table.

"Can you believe that someone called the health department on the club?"

Wilhelmina stopped and turned to see Greta, one of her coworkers, standing beside her. Greta was all that a vampiress was supposed to be: beautiful, graceful, and seductive. Her Swedish splendor only enhanced by her undeath. But tonight, her ever-present, beguiling smile was missing.

"No," Wilhelmina finally said, trying to mimic Greta's amazed expression.

"Thank God they didn't find anything," the tall blonde said, hints of her Swedish origins lilting her words. "I can't afford to be without this job."

She leaned closer to Wilhelmina. "I need the money, and this is the only place I know of in the city where my secret is absolutely safe. It's not easy to be what we are and find a good job."

Greta sighed, then glided away to take a drink order from a table of mortals, the males and females alike watching her approach with appreciative fascination.

Wilhelmina stared at her for a second. Then her gaze moved to Crystal, another stunning vampiress who also waited tables. Then to Charlie, a lean handsome vampire who carried a huge tray high over his head. Constantine, a large Greek werewolf, held a post at the top of the upper level of the club, arms crossed over his broad chest, watching to be sure no violence erupted in the club below. David, or Dr. No as he called himself, a short thin human danced behind the large stereo system, a padded earphone pressed to one ear as he lined up the next song, which would begin as soon as the current dance song faded away.

There were at least twenty-five or more employees working tonight. All of them, with the exception of Dr. No, a preternatural of one kind or another. And Dr. No was so different, he didn't even seem quite human.

For the first time, she considered that these individuals, despite their preternatural fate, needed their jobs. They counted on them.

Disgust filled her that she'd never considered that fact when she was planning her attacks on the club. She should have. After all, she was no longer the sheltered, naive heiress, who didn't understand the ways of the real world. *That* was long gone. But she'd been so intent on stopping Sebastian that she'd lumped her coworkers together with him and his purpose for this club, when they were really just here for a job. Here to survive.

How had she overlooked that fact? Was she so focused on seeing this place closed and mortals saved that she was willing to hurt those of her own kind?

Not only that, she liked her coworkers. Even though she so obviously didn't fit into this place, they had accepted her. Perhaps it was because she was a vampire, but maybe it was something more. She didn't know. But she had intended to interrupt, and ultimately destroy, their source of livelihood.

"Hey," a man at the table a few feet away from her called. "Are those our drinks?"

She blinked down at the forgotten tray balanced in her hands, then nodded.

"Sorry," she said as she placed their drinks before them. This table was all vampires. Hungry vampires. Their need heavily scented the air, made it almost pulse.

She quickly stepped away from the table, their hunger making her skin crawl. The hairs at the nape of her neck stood up, and she shivered. Suddenly she remembered that kind of intense, frightening hunger focused on her. And the pain that followed.

She hurried on, not looking at them again.

They were the preternatural patrons that needed to be stopped, she realized, not Carfax Abbey's hardworking staff. But she didn't know how to do that.

She was still debating what could work, when she paused at her next table. All that was left on her tray were several froufrou pink cocktails with cherries and umbrellas like the one she'd tried to give the wolf. She cast a cursory glance at the booth, realizing it was occupied by young, giggly, and scantily clad mortals. These drinks *had* to be theirs.

She began to set the hourglass-shaped stemware on the table, when several of the ladies began to call, "Sebastian!"

Wilhelmina closed her eyes for a moment.

Great, he was coming this way. She hadn't seen him after the health inspectors had left and she hoped that he was gone for the night. No such luck.

"Good evening," he said as he reached the table, and Wilhelmina could have sworn he'd used just a hint of Transylvanian accent when he said it.

The women began to crowd together in the semicircular booth, making room for him to join them, which he did. The women's elation flooded around Wilhelmina, their desire like a heady, too sweet perfume. For a moment their emotions overwhelmed her, making her feel disoriented.

Then Sebastian turned his smile on her, and she could only focus on that lopsided curve of his pouty lips.

"Hi," Sebastian said to her. "Would you please bring these lovely ladies another round on me, and I'd like a scotch, straight up."

Wilhelmina watched as he turned his attention back to the mortals, flashing them that same sexy, lopsided grin. Although she noticed his intense eyes darkened as he admired them.

Then his hunger flared so powerfully, Wilhelmina had to step back. But unlike her reaction to the other vampires' hunger from earlier, something else mingled with her disgust. Something that made her knees tremble and skin feel hot.

Suddenly she realized all of them were staring at her, puzzled by the fact that she was still there, gaping. She forced herself to move back to the table and clear away the empty glasses and napkins that littered the glossy black tabletop.

"Betty, it's good to see you again," Sebastian said, returning his attention to the ladies.

The brunette next to him giggled. "It's Becky."

"Right, Becky," he said, and Wilhelmina wasn't overly shocked to see the woman readily forgive the mistake.

"And Gina." He grinned at the girl across from him. "I thought you were moving back to Boston."

The blonde laughed, which made her impressively large breasts jiggle and threaten to spill over the top of her tight beaded top.

"Nina," she corrected with no annoyance in her voice, even after he'd just confused her friend's name. "And I was planning to move back to Boise."

"Of course," he said with no embarrassment or remorse in his voice.

Wilhelmina had the feeling these mix-ups were a very common occurrence. After all, what did Sebastian really care about these women? They were nothing more than entertainment and dinner. And that was if they were lucky.

Although, she thought bitterly, most people could remember the name of their favorite meal.

Suddenly her irritation with his cavalier behavior was too much. For the first time since she'd met him, Wilhelmina did something clumsy that she fully intended. As she picked up another empty glass, she clanked the stem against Becky's full cocktail. The glass soared over and pink liquid splashed down the front of Sebastian's pale blue designer shirt.

Sebastian jumped up as what appeared to be a mai tai with extra cherries soaked into the material of his shirt and the crotch of his trousers.

The women in the booth handed him their drink napkins as he attempted to pat away the worst of the spill.

"Oh no," Wilhelmina said, "I'm so sorry."

Sebastian looked up from the wet splotches to see something akin to a smirk on Wilhelmina's lips. As soon as she realized he was looking, the smile faded into an expression of innocent dismay.

But Sebastian knew what he'd seen.

"Excuse me, ladies," he said and slipped out of the booth. Before Wilhelmina could step back from him, he caught her wrist and tugged her along with him.

He felt her struggling, and he also noticed a few patrons watching them, but that didn't slow him down, nor did it cause him to release her. Out of the corner of his eye, he even noticed Constantine, one of his bouncers, starting down the stairs toward them. But once the giant bouncer realized it was Sebastian, he stopped and returned to his post.

So he was making a scene. The truth was—he didn't care. He'd had enough of this klutzy, strange, and altogether distracting (in a bad way, he asserted to himself) vampiress.

Not to mention, this had already been a thoroughly unpleasant night. He'd had to deal with the health inspectors, which had been downright ludicrous. And dangerous. He worked hard not to give anyone a reason to question anything about this place. Now, twice in one week, the authorities had been called here.

One of his main concerns was always to keep Carfax Abbey on the right side of the law. That kept the law out of the club, which allowed the preternaturals who worked and patronized Carfax Abbey to remain safe.

He was equally religious about the security of his human patrons. Which was why he had so many bouncers and cameras stationed all around the club's bars, dancefloors, and exits. If an incident happened, which was rare, it was dealt with internally. But overall, he'd been lucky. The preternaturals that came here understood the rules and followed them. And keeping on the good side of the law and other officials had served him well and kept everyone safe.

The health inspectors had found nothing in the club to question and left feeling the caller's claims had been ridiculous. Just as the police had. But having two anonymous calls in a week to officials was too unusual to be a coincidence. That made him nervous.

And this clumsy waitress was the last straw of the evening.

He tugged her into the employee lounge. Valerie, one of his cocktail waitresses, stood in front of her opened locker, reapplying her ever-present deep red lipstick. When she saw Sebastian's expression, her eyes flashed between him and Wilhelmina. She swiftly tossed her lipstick back into her locker and shut the door, with a sharp, metallic clang.

She didn't speak as she passed, but Sebastian noticed she gave Wilhelmina a worried look as she left the room.

Sebastian frowned. He was hardly an ogre. Then he turned to look at the hand he had clamped around Wilhelmina's delicate wrist. She stared up at him, her eyes wide behind the lenses of her glasses. For the first time, he realized her eyes were blue, the deepest blue he'd ever seen, like a dark midnight sky.

And they were frightened. He now sensed that fear like a glacial chill snaking down his spine.

He dropped her wrist, suddenly feeling regretful of his abrupt behavior. As soon as she was released, she took several steps back from him, rubbing her wrist, those wary blue eyes watching him.

"I'm sorry," he said, feeling more guilt course through him. He wasn't usually an easily angered person. He'd made an art of being laid-back and carefree, but the events of the past few days had made him tense. Hell, forget cops and health inspectors, and anonymous callers, *she* made him tense.

He watched her, hoping she'd say something. She didn't. Instead she frowned down at her wrist. More guilt rushed through him.

"I shouldn't have grabbed you like that," he said.

"No, you shouldn't have," she agreed quietly. She still stared at her wrist.

"Listen," he said, stepping toward her. Her head snapped up at his approach, and she stumbled backward, keeping the same distance between them. Fear shot from her like warning flares, making the air snap with the emotion.

Sebastian frowned, but then stepped back himself. He didn't understand her extreme reaction, but he didn't want to scare her any more than he already had. His behavior had been bad and he was more than a little irritated with himself at his lack of control. But he didn't think it merited the kind of fear that surrounded them.

"Please forgive my rude behavior. I overreacted. It's been a rather stressful night, but I shouldn't take out my strain on you."

She didn't respond and continued to stare at her wrist. Her fingers played over the spot, caressing the place where his hand had touched her, as if to rub away pain. Suddenly he remembered the feeling of her skin against his. Its soft, velvety texture.

He pushed the memory away, trying instead to see if he'd hurt her. Despite his brusque behavior, he didn't think he'd grabbed her that roughly. Not to mention, vampires did not injure easily. He couldn't see any marks or redness marring the unusual paleness of her skin. Even the scratches he'd seen earlier were gone.

He paused, staring at the back of her hands.

"What's your cat's name?" he asked suddenly.

Wilhelmina's gaze snapped up to meet his. "What?"

"Your cat? What's its name?"

"Spot," she said without pause, but Sebastian could see more uneasiness in her eyes.

He couldn't tell if her uneasiness was over his question or just over him. Her expression certainly didn't reveal if his sudden suspicions were founded—that she was the one making the calls to law enforcement about his club.

Scratches weren't much of a lead. But then she had also set off the sprinkler, he knew that for a fact. Had that been another attempt to damage his business? Had she brought rats into the club?

He studied her, trying to see or sense something that would either validate or deny his thoughts. He found nothing. Just a small vampiress with the darkest blue eyes and palest skin he'd ever seen. And again, he was struck by the word Nadine used to describe her. Lost. At the moment, she seemed very lost.

Before he thought better of it, he touched her pale cheek. "Spot? Good name."

She remained perfectly still under his touch. Again, he felt a prickling of fear around her.

"Did I hurt you?" he asked softly, certain that he must have for her to be so scared of him. Even now.

She shook her head, causing his fingers to rub against her smooth skin. Wisps of her black hair, which had escaped one of the messy knots on the top of her head, tickled the back of his fingers.

Sebastian swallowed as overwhelming desire rocketed through him, sudden and intense and as unexpected as a landmine. He frowned, telling himself the need rippling over his skin and tightening his groin was just an inappropriate reaction to stress, just as dragging her through the crowded bar had been.

He told himself that several times, but he couldn't manage to stop touching her. Skin against skin, moving in gentle strokes. He wondered how her pale skin would feel against his body, and what her fingers would feel like touching him in return.

He dropped his hand from her cheek. Just moments before, he'd been seriously considering this woman might be the one who'd placed the anonymous calls. Now, he was thinking about. . . .

No, he wasn't going there again.

Instead he focused on his drink-splattered clothes. The pink liquid had turned the front of his blue shirt an unappealing puce-y color.

"Well, I've only known you for two days, and twice I've ended up soaking wet."

Her gaze moved from his face to his shirt. Then drifted slowly downward to the wet splotch darkening his trousers.

He felt himself react as her gaze lingered. He shifted, and her eyes snapped back up to his, the fear flaring again around them. But there was something else, barely perceptible under the sharp emotion.

"You aren't soaked," she said, her voice a little breathy.

His body reacted to the sexy sound, but he told himself to ignore it. "True, I'm not as soaked as I was with the sprinkler, but now I'm sticky."

Again her gaze dropped to his crotch. Damn. If she couldn't sense he was aroused, she could sure as hell see it. He shifted again, and her eyes returned to her wrist, her fingers touching that same spot.

Despite his better judgment, he reached for her again. She went rigid under his touch, but she didn't pull away. Neither did he. His fingers traced the curve of her jawline, his thumb brushing the corner of her red mouth. He tested the soft curve of her full bottom lip, wondered how her lips would feel against his. Would they be sweet like ripe berries?

More emotions crackled around them, but he couldn't read them. She didn't pull away, but she remained absolutely still, and he couldn't tell if she was enjoying his touch or not. Her emotions were too complicated, too jumbled to read.

She wasn't attempting to block them, but there were simply too many of them for any one to be clear. That bothered him. He wanted to know what she was thinking, feeling.

"I—" she said, her eyes meeting his, and he hoped she'd just tell him what was going on behind her inscrutable midnight eyes. Instead, she stepped back, moving out of his reach.

"I have to get back to work," she said her voice cool, distant as if she didn't feel any of the desire he was experiencing. That really bothered him. Nearly as much as the fact that he was feeling desire. Very intense desire.

"Unless I'm fired," she said after a few moments, when he still hadn't said anything.

Sebastian considered her. She'd given him an out. A way to be rid of her. If she was involved in the calls about the club, that would be taken care of. And even if she wasn't involved in the anonymous calls, she was a pretty bad waitress. He'd fired employees who were actually better. *And*, and at the moment this was the thought that was really troubling him, she would be out of his sight and no longer getting under his skin. Which she was, even though he couldn't figure out why.

If she weren't here, many of his problems would be gone. Just like that.

He opened his mouth to tell her that leaving might be for the best. Then his eyes met her dark blue ones, and he was struck by the pain he saw there. Then the emotion swirled away, disappearing into bottomless depths.

Instead of the "yes" his mind had been telling him to say, his mouth said, "No. No, Wi . . . Mina." Again his mouth seemed to function without consulting his brain. Somehow, she did remind him of Mina in *Dracula*. Dark hair, fair skin, innocent, yet determined. Lost yet searching.

"You're not fired."

But the idea of keeping this Mina in Carfax Abbey didn't make him feel particularly relieved.

Chapter 6

Wilhelmina unlocked her apartment door, stepping into the small living room. A lamp glowed dimly on the end table by the sofa, but the place was quiet. She paused, not sensing Lizzie.

She walked down the hallway, which branched off the far end of the living room, passing Lizzie's room. The door was open, the room dark. Lizzie was out. Wilhelmina knew she was likely at Dr. Fowler's Institute, where she was setting up her new lab.

A combination of relief and disappointment made her sigh. She didn't want to explain to a very perceptive wolf why she was so shaken. But she didn't relish being alone with her thoughts.

She entered her room. The tiny square space was pitch black. Without turning on the light, she stripped off the tight waitress uniform and pulled on her robe. She secured the belt around her waist as she walked back down the hall to the kitchen.

"Calm down," she muttered to herself as she walked toward the kitchen. She took in a deep breath and blew it out slowly, but the action did nothing to calm her. In truth, she had no idea how she'd managed to make it through the remainder of her shift at the club. Now that she was home, she felt more shaken than back there—where he was.

She walked directly to the refrigerator. On the top shelf, among two half-gallons of juice, two gallons of milk, and several liters of soda, she reached for her blue plastic pitcher. She took a tumbler down from the cupboard and poured herself a drink. A bit of the red, viscous liquid sloshed over the side of her cup, but she didn't reach for a paper towel to clean it up. Instead she took another deep breath and continued chanting to herself, "Calm down. Calm down."

She walked back into the living room and collapsed onto the sofa, pulling her legs up tight to her chest. Holding the glass with both hands, she brought it carefully to her lips.

As soon as the familiar tinny, salty, and bitter flavor filled her mouth, she felt herself relax just a little. She took another swallow and another until a calming warmth thawed the tension in her body, allowing her to relax, just a little. She rested her wrists on her knees, the glass still in her hand, and let her head fall back against the sofa cushions.

She didn't feed enough; that was why she was so agitated. But even as she told herself that, she knew it wasn't true. It wasn't the hunger that had her so overwrought that she couldn't stop the tremors making her limbs quiver like leaves rustled by a night breeze.

It was Sebastian.

She moaned, closing her eyes and trying to block out the memories, the feelings. She didn't want to think about what had happened tonight. But she could think of nothing else.

She'd believed she could handle this. When the Society had decided that Sebastian Young and Carfax Abbey should be placed among the top of their list of vampires who were dangerous to mortals, she'd volunteered to be the plant who would sabotage him. She felt strongly about the way he seduced and used mortals. And she knew she could handle his charms.

Now she wasn't sure of anything. Nothing had gone as she'd imagined or planned. Her sabotage attempts had failed. She never factored in that she would grow to like the employees of the club. And she didn't understand what had happened between her and Sebastian tonight, but she knew she wasn't unaffected.

She took another sip of her drink, then set it on the end table, because her hands were still shaking. Dropping her head onto her knees, curling herself into a tight ball, she tried to force away the sensations still tingling over her skin. She felt out of control and she hated to feel that way. Control was what she'd managed to gain over the years. And she'd never let go of it again.

But neither her mind or her body were listening tonight. Even now, she could feel Sebastian. Feel the sizzle of his touch on her wrist. On the back of her hand. Her cheek. Her lips.

You can't do this, she realized. She had to quit the club. The whole thing was more than she could handle. She hugged her knees tighter to herself and closed her eyes. She had to tell the members of the Society. She could imagine their looks. I-told-you-so looks. Because they hadn't believed she could stop Sebastian from the start. *She* should have known she couldn't.

Releasing her hold on her legs, she straightened. No. She wasn't going to think this way. Hadn't Dr. Fowler made her realize that she didn't need to cling to the shadows any longer? Made her realize that she could get her life back? She was a vampire now, but she still had her humanity. She had her soul. And she wasn't going to go back to being the scared, hopeless creature she'd been before Dr. Fowler found her. And now she had also the Society of Preternaturals. They were helping empower her too.

She could do it. She just needed a new plan. A plan that was focused solely on the real problem: Sebastian Young. He was the one setting the precedent at Carfax Abbey. He was by far the biggest user of mortals.

"He's the one who needs to be stopped," she said to herself, even as she felt her nerves stretching taut. Her fear building up again. But she ignored it. She had to do this. She had to prove to herself she could.

Sebastian Young's misuse of mortals had to be stopped. And she would be the one to find the way to stop him.

Sebastian poked his head into Mick's office. Mick, his head of security, sat behind his bank of computer screens, his booted feet crossed on the corner of the desk. To others, Mick might have looked too relaxed, too insolent to be a good employee, much less a successful head of security. But Sebastian knew he was the best.

"Have you found anything?"

Mick shook his head. "I've got someone working on the health department's computer system. He should be calling soon with a list of incoming calls on the twenty-fifth."

Sebastian nodded. "And the police?"

"Nothing there. But I haven't given up."

"Good," Sebastian said. "Let me know as soon as you hear anything."

Mick nodded, and turned back to the computer monitors, his features looking starker, more brutal in the bluish light.

Sebastian left the office and headed through the back entrance into the club. The place wasn't crowded yet, but he knew in a few hours the dance floor would be packed. He wondered if the anonymous caller would be there. If he or she was already there.

Even though the past couple of nights had been quiet, he still had the gut feeling that the person targeting his club wasn't finished. Maybe he was being overly cautious, but he'd learned in two hundred years that it was good to follow his instincts. And his instincts were on high alert.

He slipped into one of the booths on the upper level, scanning the main room below. His hunger was strong tonight. Very strong. A side effect of his instincts being on overdrive, that and things kept distracting him from his usual feedings. But given that he could do nothing except wait for Mick's report, he might as well rectify that last problem now.

Who would be his companion for the night? He cast a look around the upper level where he sat. As if by some colossal joke, Mina appeared at the small bar that lined the back wall.

He'd decided that his bizarre attraction to her had been a direct result of lack of feeding and lack of sex. That always made him a little off. Still he'd avoided her for the past two nights. And he got the impression she'd avoided him too.

Tonight, her hair was braided into two pigtails. The hairstyle should have made her look young and childish but combined with her snug black uniform, her pale skin, and her bowed, red lips, she looked more like a very naughty schoolgirl. His eyes roamed down her body. Her curves were gentle and lithe under the black brocade.

He gritted his teeth and forced his gaze to the dance floor. What was he thinking? Physically, she wasn't even close to his type. He liked flashy women with long hair, long legs, and abundant curves. Mina had an unremarkable figure, weird hair, and her legs were. . . .

Against his will, his gaze returned to her. From where she stood he couldn't see her legs. Although he knew from the sprinkler night, they had no flaws. Shapely and smooth and pale. His cock swelled against the denim of his jeans.

Bryce, the upstairs bartender, leaned forward, telling Mina something. From his angle, Sebastian could see only her profile, but he could tell one corner of her rosy lips turn up into a smile as Bryce talked. Sebastian realized he'd never seen Mina smile. A real smile anyway.

Bryce said something else, and Mina laughed. A brief, nearly nonexistent laugh, but Sebastian suddenly found himself leaning forward in an attempt to hear it. He pushed up from his table and strode to the bar, taking a stool next to where she stood.

"Good evening, Bryce," he said. "Mina."

Mina glanced at him, a quick flash of something that looked an awful lot like disdain flickered in her eyes, then she looked back to Brycc.

"Hey, Sebastian," Bryce greeted in his laid-back Southern drawl. The handsome werebear was every inch good ole Southern boy, and he always struck Sebastian as being out of place in the big city. Even though he'd been working here for nearly three years.

Sebastian glanced back to Mina. She looked out of place here too. But unlike Bryce, whose easygoing personality would allow him actually to fit in anywhere, Mina truly didn't belong here.

Again, his instincts niggled him. Again, he wondered why she was here. Could she somehow be involved in the calls to the club? He studied her as she waited for Bryce to make her drink orders. She had shifted down the bar away from him. Her sidling movements had been subtle, but he'd noticed the escape.

He tried to read her emotions, but as usual there were too many and she was too guarded for him to get a clear impression. He found it interesting that someone so reserved could be surrounded by such a whirl of emotions. He wondered what would happen if she loosened up and let them show. The idea excited him.

"Bryce, may I get a scotch?" he asked suddenly, needing a drink to calm his reaction to her. A little booze, a lot of blood, and he'd be thinking far more clearly. And not about Mina.

"Sure thing."

He chuckled at the bartender's words. "I need that too."

Bryce grinned. "Well, I reckon you won't have any problem finding one of those here tonight."

Sebastian sensed rather than saw Mina stiffen at their conversation. He glanced at her.

She looked down at her order pad, her brow furrowed, her

lips twisted slightly. He couldn't tell what her expression meant, whether it was disdain or maybe even jealousy.

Disdain, he figured. But either way, she was reacting, and for some perverse reason, Sebastian liked that he was getting some sort of response from her. It amused him to see her bow-shaped lips pucker as if she'd just sunk her fangs into a lemon. For a split second, he'd thought about what those lips would look like puckered for a different reason.

"There was a tall blonde here last night. I'm hoping she'll be back tonight. Legs that could make a grown man grovel," he said, watching Mina's face.

She concentrated on her order pad, and he wasn't even sure she was listening.

"And her ass." He couldn't help adding.

Mina flipped a page of the pad, maybe with more force than necessary, but otherwise she didn't acknowledge him.

Bryce, however, chuckled as he set a scotch in front of him. "Sounds good."

Sebastian studied Mina for a moment longer, wanting to see something other than her usual remoteness. But she continued to fiddle with her order pad.

Sebastian looked back to Bryce, only to find the bartender watching her too. A definite look of interest in the werebear's brown eyes.

A flash of something possessive squeezed Sebastian's chest. He frowned. What difference did it make to him if Mina and Bryce became Carfax Abbey's newest cupid's couple? Maybe a good lay from a wild werebear would loosen Mina up.

But even as he told himself that, his fangs distended, scraping the inside of his lips, agitating him.

What the hell was wrong with him? He'd never, never been interested in a woman, alive or undead, who wasn't interested back. Eternity was too long to work that hard when there were thousands of women in the world, in this city alone, who wanted a good time.

He glanced at Mina as Bryce placed a drink on her tray.

She smiled at the bartender. A small smile, definitely a reserved smile, but a smile nonetheless. A real smile. Something she'd never given Sebastian. Another wave of something that felt altogether too close to jealousy washed over him.

Without another word, Sebastian picked up his drink and left the bar, returning to his booth. He was obviously not getting enough female attention if he was feeling irritated by odd little Mina smiling at a coworker. After all, he might find her attractive in some weird way, but he didn't want her. And she didn't want him.

Wilhelmina watched Sebastian's abrupt departure with a mixture of confusion and relief. She'd spent the past two days keeping her distance from him. He unnerved her, and made it difficult to keep focused on her plan. Not that she had a plan. In fact, she'd come up with nothing that could stop his dissolute ways.

She'd considered starting rumors in the club. Things like he was in the mob or he was married, but she didn't think that would discourage women's interest in him. He was too charming, too sensual, and far too beautiful for rumors to stop him. She had her doubts that anything would deter mortal women from being with him.

As if to punctuate her point, a tall blonde, probably *the* tall blonde, sashayed up to his booth smiling broadly at him. Mina's gaze dropped quickly to her bottom. Yes, she was *the* woman.

Sebastian grinned up at the blonde, that lopsided smile of his making him look so charismatic, so charming, so harmless.

He gestured for the woman to join him, which she readily did, sliding her long legs under the round table as she scooted closer to him.

"Dang, that man is good," Bryce said from beside Wilhelmina. She turned to see the long-haired, goateed bartender shaking his head with admiration.

Wilhelmina frowned, ready to disagree. He was despicable. But Greta cut her off, setting her tray on the bar. "Who's good?"

Bryce jerked his head in Sebastian's direction. "Our boss."

Greta turned to look at him, a fond smile curving her full lips. "Oh. Why, yes, he is."

Wilhelmina gaped at the tall, stunning vampiress as the meaning of her words sank in. "You . . . with him?" She looked back at the booth where Sebastian chatted with the mortal.

A rich, throaty laugh escaped Greta.

"Don't be so shocked. It wasn't a big deal. We just ended up getting together one night." She fanned herself. "And what a night."

Bryce shook his head as he left to take a drink order at the end of the bar.

Wilhelmina stared at Greta, stunned. She knew that mortals couldn't defend themselves against Sebastian's preternatural charms, but she hadn't considered that other preternaturals would fall prey to him, too. Especially Greta, who was as dazzling as any vampiress she'd encountered.

"Why?" she finally managed to ask Greta.

Greta laughed at Wilhelmina's disbelieving look.

"You *have* looked at the man, haven't you?"

"Of course," Wilhelmina said.

"Then you can't deny that he's beautiful."

"No," Wilhelmina said, begrudgingly. "If you like that type."

It was Greta's turn to give her an incredulous look. "Who doesn't like that type?"

Wilhelmina started to say she didn't, until she made the mistake of glancing in his direction. The blond mortal talked animatedly to Sebastian. Sebastian stared past her at Wilhelmina. His intense topaz eyes locked with hers, sizzling with an emotion she didn't understand.

Wilhelmina's breath caught in her throat. They stared at each other for a moment, then the blonde touched Sebastian's hand, and the connection broke. Sebastian returned his attention to the woman beside him.

Wilhelmina pulled in another breath, trying to ignore the tingling in her limbs. Irritation filled her, irritation with herself, with Greta, with the stupid blonde who had no idea who or what she was flirting with.

"Doesn't it bother you that you were just one of the . . ." Even in her annoyance, Wilhelmina couldn't bring herself to finish her rude question.

But Greta laughed and finished it for her. "One of the many? No. Sebastian isn't the type to settle down, and I never expected it. We had fun, and we're friends. It's all good."

Greta picked up her drinks and glided away.

Wilhelmina watched her leave, an image of Greta and Sebastian flashing into her head, in full Technicolor. Their tall, lithe bodies intertwined. Golden skin to golden skin. Mouths and hands exploring . . .

The tingling, which had almost dissipated, sparked, searing over her skin. Even as nausea roiled in her stomach.

She let out a low growl, more anger filling her. How could Greta be so stupid as to be used by the likes of him? Mortals didn't know what he was. But Greta? The idea disturbed her. Upset her.

Was no one immune to him? Not even . . .

She glanced back at him. He talked with the mortal, charming. Alluring. Deceiving her with his feigned interest. When in truth he was only interested in one thing. Biting her. Hurting her.

She didn't know how to stop him, but she couldn't let another vampire hurt her. She frowned at her thoughts. No, not her. Humans. He couldn't hurt more humans. He wouldn't hurt this one.

Before she thought better of it, she strode to the booth.

Chapter 7

"How do you live with yourself?"

Sebastian looked up from the blonde, Lisa or Liza or something like that, to see Mina standing, hands on her hips, dark eyes flashing.

For a moment, he didn't respond. He was too stunned. Mina, who hadn't raised her voice much above a whisper since he'd met her. Mina, whose only perceivable emotion had been fear and agitation, stood next to his table, rage radiating from her like heat from a boiler.

"Excuse me?" he finally said.

"And why would you let him?" she asked the blonde beside him.

Lisa or Liza gave him a worried look. "Do you know this woman?"

Sebastian nodded, although at the moment he wasn't sure. He didn't know Mina well, but what he thought he knew was not this woman standing in front of him like a very small, pale and angry avenger.

"Mina? What's going on?"

An irritated laugh erupted from her. "See. He doesn't even know my name." She turned her flashing glare to the blonde. "I bet he doesn't know your name either."

Mina's eyes locked on him. "What's her name?"

Sebastian frowned. Okay, so he didn't know the blonde's

name. Well, he sort of knew it. What he didn't know, didn't understand in the least, was why Mina was so upset about that fact.

"Go ahead, tell me her name."

The blonde now turned back to Sebastian, also waiting for him to give her name.

Sebastian's frown deepened. "This is crazy."

Mina arched a smug, dark brow. "See."

The blonde gave Sebastian an assessing look, then said, "Isn't she one of your employees? Can't you do something about her?"

Mina's eyes widened. "About me? I'm trying to help you. I'm trying to keep you from being another in a long line of women this narcissistic, egocentric, depraved vam . . . and . . . and . . . vain . . . man uses for his pleasure and entertainment!"

Sebastian stared at Mina, too stunned by her opinion of him to react. For a moment. Then rage, sharp and biting, surged through him. She didn't even know him; how had she developed such a low opinion of him? Low opinion? That was too kind. She apparently thought he was just above scum. Below actually, since he didn't think scum really had any of the attributes Mina had just given him.

Her judgment infuriated him. Who was she, a strange, uninspiring, and plain vampiress, to cast that kind of judgment on him?

"Pardon me," he said to the blonde, gesturing that he wanted to get out of the booth. "I need to talk to my employee."

She rose, and to his surprise, without comment. He slid out from the booth and stood, staring at Mina. She stepped back from him, but, also to his surprise, she didn't flee. Her chin lifted and her eyes met his.

"I think we should discuss your opinion of me somewhere a little more private," he suggested.

Mina crossed her arms over her chest and glanced around. "Why? Everyone knows what you're like already."

Sebastian glared back at her, and before he thought better of it, he seized her arm and hauled her to the back entrance of the club. Without hesitation, he pulled her toward the narrow staircase at the end of the hall that led up to his apartment.

"No," she said, her voice breathy and panicked. "Let me go!"

She struggled, digging in her feet, tugging at his fingers that held her like a vise, but her attempts to break free barely even slowed his strides. Not until he'd started up the stairs and she tripped, falling to her knees on the steps, did he realize what he was doing.

He stared down at her, seeing the distress and panic in her eyes. What the hell was wrong with him? Why did he keep reacting like a damned Neanderthal around this woman?

Yes, he was pissed about what she'd just done. Yes, he wanted answers as to why she had such a terrible opinion of him. Especially given that he'd had two valid opportunities to fire her, and he hadn't. But that didn't give him the right to drag her around like some demented caveman.

He reached down, catching her elbow. She allowed the assistance, but as soon as she was on her feet, she shifted away from him. He allowed the slight escape, because he could feel her fear curling around them like wisps of smoke. He didn't want to scare her any more.

But he did want answers.

"Why do you have such a low opinion of me?"

She didn't answer or look at him, instead she moved down another step. He stepped onto the same one, their bodies forced to face each other in the narrow stairwell. But he made sure not to touch her.

"Tell me," he demanded with more force than he intended, mainly because she still stared down at the steps instead of at him, and her reluctance to even look at him irritated him.

This time he kept his voice calmer as he pointed out, "You've only worked at Carfax Abbey for a couple weeks.

What have I done in that time to give you this opinion of me?"

Still she didn't answer. More fear encircled them. Something about that fear bothered him. It was different, sharper, more desperate than any fear he'd felt before. Why?

"Better yet, why don't you tell me why you are so frightened of me?"

Her head snapped up, and she glared at him. "I'm not frightened of you."

He studied her for a minute, then sighed. "You know that's not true."

She straightened to her full height, which only brought her up to his chin, but her eyes focused on a point over his right shoulder.

"Mina—" he started, and her eyes snapped to his, narrowed and angry. Somehow he found that glare more bearable than the panic he'd seen there earlier.

"That's not my name," she stated.

He frowned, so they were back to this. "Your name is Wilhelmina, I know. But frankly, you don't look like a Wilhelmina to me. You look like a Mina. However, I'll gladly remember to call you by your full name if that will give you a higher opinion of me."

Her eyes searched his for a moment, then looked away again. "It won't."

He sighed. "No, I didn't think so."

They stood there for a moment, he watched her and she watched a point on the floor.

"Why are you so scared of me?" he asked softly.

She shifted away as if she planned to move down a step and then bolt. He couldn't let that happen, not before he understood what had brought on this outburst.

"Mi—Wilhelmina, talk to me." He placed a hand on the wall, blocking her escape down the stairs.

She glared at him with more anger and more of that uncomfortable fear.

"You can bully your mortal conquests," she said, her voice low. "But you can't bully me."

Sebastian sighed. "My earlier behavior to the contrary, I don't want to bully you. Or anyone."

"You can't seduce me, either," she informed him.

"I don't . . ." Seduce her? Was that what all this was about?

"Do you want me to seduce you?" he asked with a curious smile. Maybe that was the cause for her crazy outburst. She *was* jealous.

She laughed, the sound abrupt and harsh. "Hardly. I just told you that I *didn't* want you to seduce me."

"No," he said slowly. "You told me I *can't*. That sounds like a challenge."

Irritation flared from her, blotting out some of the fear. "Believe me, I'm *so* not interested."

He raised an eyebrow at her disdain. "Then why do you care about me being with that blonde?"

"That blonde?" she said. "Is hair color the way you identify all your women? It's got to be a confusing system, as so many of them are bound to have the same names."

He studied her for a minute, noting that just a faint flush colored her very pale cheeks

"Are you sure you don't want me to seduce you?" he asked again, because as far as he could tell, there was no other reason for her to care about the identification system for his women.

She growled in irritation, the sound raspy and appealing in a way it shouldn't have been.

Sebastian blinked. He needed to stay focused. This woman thought he was a jerk; that shouldn't be a draw for him.

"Why did you say those things?" he asked. "What have I done to make you think I'm so terrible?"

Her jaw set again, and her midnight eyes locked with his. "Are you going to deny that you're narcissistic?"

He frowned. "Yes. I'm confident maybe, but no, I'm not a narcissist."

She lifted a disbelieving eyebrow at that. "And you are going to deny egocentric too?"

"Well, since egocentric is pretty much the same as narcissistic, then yes, I'm going to deny it."

Her jaw set even more, and he suspected she was gritting her teeth, which for some reason made him want to smile. He really was driving her nuts. He liked that.

He was hurt that she had such a low opinion of him, but he did like the fact that he seemed to have gotten under her skin too.

"I think we can also rule out vain," he said, "because again that's pretty darn similar to narcissistic and egocentric." He smiled slightly.

Her eyes narrowed, and she still kept her lips pressed firmly together—their pretty bow shape compressed into a nearly straight line.

"So you see," he continued, "I think this whole awful opinion that you have formulated about me might just be a mix-up. What you thought was conceit, which is also another word for narcissism," he couldn't help adding, "was just self-confidence."

His smile broadened, and Wilhelmina fought the urge to scream. He was mocking her. Still the egotistical scoundrel. Even now, after she'd told him exactly what she thought of him. He was worse than what she'd called him. He was . . . unbelievable.

"What about depraved?" she asked. Surely that insult had made him realize what she thought.

"What about it?" he asked, raising an eyebrow, looking every inch the haughty, depraved vampire she'd labeled him.

"Are you going to deny that one, too?" she demanded.

He pretended to consider, then shook his head. "No, I won't deny that one. Although I'd consider myself more debauched than depraved. In a very nice way, however."

He grinned again, that sinfully sexy twist of his lips, and her gaze dropped to his lips. Full, pouting lips that most women would kill for. But on him, they didn't look the slightest bit feminine.

What was she thinking? Her eyes snapped back to his, but the smug light in his golden eyes stated that he'd already noticed where she'd been staring.

She gritted her teeth and focused on a point over his shoulder, trying not to notice how broad those shoulders were. Or how his closeness made her skin warm.

He shifted so he was even closer, his chest nearly brushing hers. His large body nearly surrounding her in the small stairwell. His closeness, the confines of his large body around hers, should have scared her, but she only felt . . . tingly.

"So, now that we've sorted that out," he said softly, "why don't we go back to my other question?"

She swallowed, trying to ignore the way his voice felt like a velvety caress on her skin. She didn't allow herself to look at him, scared to see those eyes like perfect topazes.

"Why are you frightened of me, Mina?"

Because she was too weak, she realized. Because, despite what she knew about him, despite the fact that she knew he was dangerous, she liked his smile, his lips, those golden eyes. Because she liked when he called her Mina.

Because she couldn't forget the feeling of his fingers on her skin.

She released a shaky breath. But she wouldn't tell him that. Her admission would just leave her more open, more vulnerable to him. She couldn't be vulnerable again.

Not to mention, she'd learned a long time ago that her fear and pain were all her own. She couldn't count on anyone else to protect her. Not really.

She started as his fingers brushed against her jaw, nudging her chin toward him, so her eyes met his. Golden topazes that glittered as if there were fire locked in their depths.

Once again she was reminded of the ill-fated moth drawn to an enticing flame. She swallowed, but she couldn't break their gaze.

"You don't have to be afraid of me," he assured her quietly.

Yes, she did. God, she did.

Before she realized his intent, his full lips brushed hers. Just a fleeting sweep, soft and silky and so sweet. And gone before she could respond.

He lifted his head, and she stared at him, never having closed her eyes. His gaze roamed her face as if he were reading her thoughts, or he wanted to. Then he dropped his mouth to hers again.

This time, his lips were more than just a whispering caress. They brushed against hers in a repeated friction until she couldn't help but react. Her eyes fluttered shut and her lips tentatively moved under his, caressing him back. Soft velvet skin stroking, molding together perfectly.

His tongue flicked against her bottom lip. Hot, roughened silk added to the warm velvet of his lips. She hesitated at the new sensation. Her body tensed as he pulled her fully against his hard chest. She'd never felt anything as wonderful, the pressure of her suddenly aching breasts flattened to him. The rippling of his muscles, powerful against her, under her hands.

"Mina," he murmured against her mouth, his voice heavy with need.

His need fired hers, making her body burn. She strained against him, her hand moving over his arms, his shoulders.

His mouth became more urgent, moving over hers in hungry kisses. His tongue tasting hers, his hands moving to her hips, walking her backward until she was between his hard chest and the wall. Pinned and trapped.

A flash of darkness, of cold and wetness whizzed through her mind.

She whimpered. Fear poured like ice water into her heated body, clearing her sensation-clouded brain. Her hands came up to his chest, pushing at his muscled strength, and Sebastian moved back, but didn't break the kiss. His lips gentled, once more light caresses, soothing her, coaxing her to respond. His hands moved to her face, stroking her, gentle soothing touches, and quickly the fire returned, heating the chill in her veins.

"Mina," he murmured, pressing kisses to her jawline. "I want you."

Helplessly, she moaned. Oh God, she wanted too. Her hands knotted into the front of his shirt, as his lips returned to hers. Again his tongue swept over the seam of her closed lips. She opened for him. His tongue tasted her in slow fiery sweeps. He groaned, the deep, rich sound rumbling in her mouth, against her chest.

She moaned in response, her body reacting to his touch, his need, his desire. She kissed as if she was starving, her need overwhelming her.

Then she felt them, pointy and razor sharp nicking the inside of her lower lips. Then a puncture, and shocking sweetness.

Terror choked her, and a strangled cry escaped her. She shoved at Sebastian, hard. Then she was running, scrambling down the stairs, seeing nothing but the hallway below.

Sebastian called to her, but she didn't look back. She didn't wait to see his expression. She didn't want to see him. She didn't want to ever see him again. At that moment, she just had to escape. Flee. Try to outrun what just happened.

She raced into the hallway, not even sure where she was going.

"Mina!" Sebastian called again, his voice echoing off the bare drywall, seeming to come from all directions at once.

A desperate, terrified cry wrung from her tightened throat, and made her feet move faster. Aimlessly running down the hall. Until somehow she found another set of stairs.

Nearly slipping on the narrow steps, she caught herself and barely slowed her pace.

The stairs led to another hallway, and at the end, she saw gray, metal double doors. They had to lead outside.

She reached them, fumbling with the many bolts and chains that secured the doors. She heard a noise behind her, but she was too frantic to sense who it was. Not that she didn't know. It had to be Sebastian.

She twisted the last lock and threw the heavy doors open, escaping out into a dark, damp alleyway. She heard the door slam behind her, then nothing. No footsteps, no familiar voices. Nothing except the constant roar of traffic on the street. Horns and the endless din of the city.

Still she sprinted to the street, racing past pedestrians. Bumping against some of them in her urgency. Their touch causing her more distress. Puddles of dirty water from an earlier shower splashed over her feet, her legs. She barely noticed.

She kept running until she was a block away from Carfax Abbey. Maybe two. She didn't know. She turned into a dank alley, pressing her back against the wet, dirty bricks of a building.

Her hands trembled as she pressed them to her mouth, trying to block out the taste, slightly salty and so sweet, in her mouth. Trying to forget the gentleness of Sebastian's lips. And the need still raging throughout her body.

She dropped her hands from her face, looking down at her trembling fingers. Faint traces of red marred her pale fingertips like spots of crimson paint or rouge. But the streaks weren't anything so harmless, so normal.

Blood. She tasted it on her lips.

Not her blood. Sebastian's.

Just as her fangs had pricked her own lips, they had also pierced Sebastian's. And she could taste him, feel him, even that small amount, inside her. His essence in her, real and warm and so thrilling.

And everything she'd never wanted to taste or experience again.

Chapter 8

Sebastian pushed away from the wall, trying to grasp what just happened. He called to Mina, but he could hear her racing away from him, the loud, hollow clacks of her shoes growing more distant.

He pulled in a deep breath, trying to calm the desire raging through him. Trying to clear his passion-hazed brain.

"Mina," he shouted again, but he knew she wouldn't stop. Her fear was all around him, almost as staggering as the lust in his veins.

He placed a hand on the wall and pulled in a deep breath. Roughness scraped his palm, and for the first time, he realized Mina's shove had actually damaged the wall. A hairline crack ran down the length of where his body had made impact, and the drywall was crushed inward.

Damn. He stared at the wall. One minute, they were kissing. A mind-blowing, totally erotic in its sweetness, kiss. Then he was hitting the wall with more force than a direct train hit. Okay, more like a direct hit from a mini. But either way, her response was completely unexpected. And not one he'd ever received from a woman he was kissing.

He pulled in another breath, then started down the stairs two at a time. What the hell had happened? Why had she freaked? Her opinion of him was clear, and he could see her being annoyed that he'd kissed her, but she'd been way more than annoyed. She'd been terrified.

The hallway was empty, but he could hear her at the back door fumbling with the locks. He hurried down to the next floor, only to see her disappear into the back alley. He started after her, then stopped as more rushes of emotions hit him. Fear, disgust, distress. With no hint of desire.

He stopped, still stunned by the rapid change of events. What the hell had just happened? How could things go from bad to damned awesome to amazingly bad in a matter of minutes?

Sebastian leaned on the wall, still staring at the closed doors, trying to decide if he should follow her or give her time to calm down. Could her violent reaction all be related to her opinion of him? Was she that disgusted by him?

He didn't think so. When they'd been discussing his personality traits, and her misunderstanding of them, he'd seen her eyes drift down to his lips. He'd felt wisps of desire whirling around them, budding into something stronger, something more certain.

The slight vibration had excited him far more than the outright crackle of longing that had been radiating from the blonde in the club. Before he'd thought better of it, he'd kissed Mina, wanting to see if what he'd felt was real.

If he'd thought Mina's barely-there desire had been exciting, he hadn't been prepared for the heady taste of her. And her tempting response. Intense, yet timid as if she'd never kissed a man before. Sweet and so thrilling Sebastian had had a difficult time keeping his own need under control. Especially when he'd felt the small prick of her fangs. He'd been ready to take her right then.

Then all hell had broken loose—and broken the stairwell wall, too. She might be small, but Mina packed a surprisingly strong wallop. Sebastian knew it had been her absolute terror that had given her the surge of strength.

He pushed away from the wall, suddenly needing to know what had Mina so scared. He had to know if her fear was of him, or something else. He just didn't understand.

He knew she would be reluctant to talk to him, but he had to try. An overwhelming sense of protectiveness tightened his chest, again making him pull in a deep, steadying breath.

He reached for the back door, when a gruff voice stopped him. "Sebastian."

He turned to see Mick, leaning on his office door, his tremendous bulk haloed by the blue of the computer screens behind him. His impassive features didn't reveal whether he'd just seen Mina panicking to escape the club. But of course, he had. Mick saw most things in the club. As an ancient faery, he had the uncanny ability to assimilate hundreds of things at once. Faeries' preternatural abilities to read their surroundings made vampires look like novices.

"Everything is okay," Sebastian assured him, certain Mina's panicked departure must be what had pulled him away from his computers.

"I don't think so," he said and held out several sheets of paper.

Sebastian hesitated, looking at the door, then approached him, taking the pages. Lists of phone numbers. Outgoing and incoming calls to the health department.

"I think you will be interested in the incoming call placed three days ago at 8:52 P.M."

Sebastian scanned the list until he found the number Mick had highlighted in bright yellow ink. A 917 area code. A New York cell phone number.

"Did you trace this—" Before Sebastian could finish, Mick held out another paper.

Sebastian took it. This one was from his own computer. A list of addresses and phone numbers for his employees.

He glanced back to Mick. "The caller was one of the staff?"

Mick nodded, then pointed to the sheet.

Sebastian didn't even have to look at the name, before a sinking feeling weighed heavily in his stomach. He knew exactly who the caller had been.

Sure enough. Wilhelmina Weiss was highlighted in more yellow ink.

He stared at the page, her name and address blurring in front of his eyes. He couldn't believe it. But hadn't he toyed with that very idea, too? He'd known something wasn't right about her behavior. And didn't that explain her opinion of him? No, not really. But it did verify just how much she disliked him.

The numbers matched. The date and time were right. She had made the call; there was no doubt. But why? What did she have against him and Carfax Abbey?

Wilhelmina wasn't sure how long she roamed the streets, lost in her own distressed thoughts. Not until the rain started falling again, making the sidewalks slick and her nerves on edge, did she realize she should go home.

As she entered her apartment building, she half-expected Sebastian to be waiting outside her door for her. But the hallway was empty.

Blessedly empty, she told herself, even as a strange feeling too much like disappointment caused her stomach to sink.

She unlocked the door to find the apartment dark. Lizzie was gone to the lab again. She walked directly to the bathroom, turning on the water in the shower. As the water heated, she stared at herself in the mirror. Not something she did often, because her translucent reflection only served to remind her of what she was. And while she'd learned to deal with her vampirism, she still couldn't handle such vivid and undeniable proof.

Her see-through likeness stared back at her, like her own ghost coming to haunt her. Just like her past was coming back to haunt her, too. A past she'd believed buried.

But ghosts always returned, didn't they? She stared at herself until the steam from the shower made her indistinct features disappear from the mirror completely. Then she turned to the shower, stripping off her clothes. The hot water burned her cold, undead skin. She shivered, even though temperature changes shouldn't affect her bloodless flesh. For some reason her body didn't seem to remember that fact.

Wrapping her arms around herself, she stood under the spray, willing the ice that snaked through her veins to disappear, just as she tried to make the memories disappear.

Sebastian's lips pressed to hers. The sizzle of her own desire. The taste of him on her tongue. Even now his sweetness filled her.

A strangled cry echoed off the tile walls, and it took her a moment to realize the sound came from her. She leaned back against the wall, closing her eyes.

Oh God, this wasn't supposed to happen. Couldn't happen. She didn't have feelings like this. Not once, since she'd been crossed over, had her body reacted to a man.

She was the perfect choice for this mission, she told herself, desperate for it to still be true. She wouldn't be attracted to a charming vampire. She couldn't react. Not like a vampire. Not like a woman.

But she had. God, she had.

She slowly sank down the wall, the water pounding down on her. She wrapped her arms around bent legs, pressing her cheek to her knee.

She'd failed. She'd failed in more than the mission. Nothing she'd believed about herself had been true. And now, she didn't know what to do. Where to start again.

She wanted to go back. Back to before she'd met Sebastian, and he'd made her doubt every truth she'd believed about herself. About who she was. About what she'd believed had changed in her. About the tight rein she kept on herself.

Clutching her legs tighter to her chest, she remained curled on the shower floor, willing away the feelings inside her. Feelings that terrified her. Feelings that had felt so wonderful, and reminded her that the kind of bliss she'd just experienced only led to excruciating pain.

Sebastian sat at the bar, staring at Mina's name printed in bold Times New Roman on the white page. Why had she done this? Why had she targeted him? She didn't even know him. Admittedly, he wasn't good with names, but he never forgot a face.

He never would have forgotten Wilhelmina Weiss.

So why him? Why his club?

The bar was nearly empty now, except for the remaining waitstaff, who were finishing their evening sidework.

Greta was moving the tables to vacuum. Bryce wiped glasses and placed them under the bar.

"How well do you know Mina?" Sebastian asked the werebear.

Bryce startled at the sudden question, probably surprised that Sebastian had spoken to him, given that he'd been sitting at the end of the bar, silent for most of the night.

"Mina?"

"Wilhelmina," Sebastian clarified.

"Not well. She's only been here a couple weeks, and she's pretty quiet."

That was the answer he'd expected, although Sebastian's muscles relaxed slightly. He told himself it was because he hated to think his employees knew more about the saboteur than he did. But he knew that wasn't the truth. He hated the idea that Bryce knew more about Wilhelmina, period. Given that she'd been trying to close down his club, he couldn't say why he cared. Just like he couldn't say why he was more disappointed than angry with her.

He looked back down at the paper, reading her address for the hundredth time. All night, he'd debated if he should go to her apartment and confront her. But he'd hesitated.

The likelihood was that, after what had happened between them, she wouldn't be back. She'd been too frightened, too distraught when she'd fled. He doubted she'd ever return. And if by some off-chance she did, he could have Nadine handle the situation and let her know her services were no longer required at the club. He never had to see the strange little vampiress again.

That idea didn't make him feel better.

Because he wouldn't have answers, he told himself. And he had *a lot* of questions.

So what held him back?

"Hey."

Sebastian looked up to see Rhys as he slid onto the bar stool next to him.

"Hey," Sebastian said, a little surprised to see Rhys in the club. Rhys was definitely the silent partner in Carfax Abbey. He'd never been that crazy about the place, and he never hung out there. But it *was* after hours.

Still he asked, "What are you doing here?"

"Nadine came up to talk to me. She said you've been sitting up here all night, nursing the same drink, and ignoring all the beautiful women who were trying to chat you up."

"So?" Sebastian said, confused as to why that would worry Nadine enough to go to Rhys.

"We all know that isn't normal behavior for you."

Sebastian frowned, irritation rising up in him. Did everyone have such a low opinion of him?

"What? Are you trying to say that I'm such a degenerate that I can't possibly just hang out here without hooking up with someone?"

Rhys gave him a worried look. "No. I don't think you are a degenerate. But I do know that you like your female company. Frankly, you, yourself have always made that quite clear."

Sebastian stared at his brother, then glanced away. That was absolutely true, and his own behavior had never bothered him before, so why should it now? Because of Mina's estimation of him? That was stupid. The woman was a saboteur and possibly a lunatic. Neither possibility made him feel better, however.

"What's going on, Sebastian?"

Sebastian looked at his brother. Then he slid the paper in front of Rhys. "This is going on."

Rhys frowned down at the paper, of course, not understanding what he was looking at.

"Wilhelmina Weiss, one of our employees, was the one who made the call to the health department and presumably the police."

Rhys eyes widened with understanding. Sebastian had mentioned the anonymous calls to him, and he'd agreed the timing between the two was a little too coincidental for them not to be connected.

"Really? So what did you do? Did you fire her?"

"Well." Sebastian sighed. "Not exactly."

Lifting an eyebrow, Rhys waited for him to continue.

Sebastian considered telling Rhys about the kiss, but instead he said, "We had an incident—not related to her sabotage attempts. And she's gone."

Rhys nodded. "Are you sure she won't be back?"

"Yes." Sebastian was sure, and he wondered why he didn't feel more relieved.

"I think you should report her to the authorities. Carfax Abbey is your baby. You need to make sure she doesn't do anything else to the club or the employees. She sounds like she must be crazy."

"You don't know Mina." Sebastian bristled. "She's got problems, but she's not crazy." Yet hadn't he just considered the very same thing? Why the hell was he defending her?

"Do you know her? Is she one of your past women, who's trying to hurt you to get back at you in some way?"

"No," Sebastian stated. Again with the women.

"Are you sure?"

Sebastian glared at him. "Why is it everyone thinks I can't keep track of my past women?"

"Because you can't."

Great. His brother thought the exact same thing about him that Mina did. Fucking great.

"I'm not narcissistic or depraved," Sebastian stated.

"I didn't say you were," Rhys said, frowning. "Listen, why are you getting so upset about this? I thought you prided yourself on all your women."

"I do," Sebastian said moodily. "But Mina is different."

Rhys raised an eyebrow, giving another of his irritatingly knowing looks.

"Not different like that. She's a damned saboteur, for Christ's sake."

Rhys nodded, still looking unconvinced. "So why aren't you off confronting her?"

That was the question of the night, wasn't it?

Chapter 9

Wilhelmina perched on a kitchen chair, her legs curled up to her chin, sipping from a plastic tumbler. Each drink of the glutinous, cold liquid tasted more bitter, more unappetizing than the last.

She forced herself to ignore the taste, telling herself the unpleasantness of the flavor was just in her imagination. The protein concoction had never bothered her before.

She forced down one more sip, then placed the cup on the table, pushing it away. She rested her cheek on her knees and looked out the kitchen window at the heavy rain falling, reflected in the streetlights below. She hated the rain.

After her shower, and her complete meltdown, she'd crawled into bed and waited for dawn to arrive. As she knew it would, the sun had forced her racing mind to slow, and sleep to overtake her. And for those blissful hours of daylight, she'd forgotten everything.

She'd awoken tonight feeling calmer, but no less miserable. With that one kiss, she felt like her world had been turned upside down, and she didn't know how to get back to the peace it had taken her nearly a dozen decades to find.

"Wil," Lizzie appeared in the doorway. "I was planning to head over to the lab. If you're okay?"

Wilhelmina forced a smile at her friend. Clad in leather

pants and a biker jacket, Lizzie hardly looked like the typical scientist.

"Yeah, I'm fine," Wilhelmina said. "Go on ahead. There's a Society meeting tonight and I want to go."

That was a lie. Wilhelmina didn't want to show her face to the Society. Not yet. Not with her failure so fresh. But she didn't want Lizzie to worry. And although Wilhelmina had assured her nothing had happened last night, she knew Lizzie was concerned.

Lizzie watched her with intense pale eyes. Eyes that somehow reminded her of another set of intense eyes—ones that were golden topazes rather than frosty blue.

"If you're sure? I'm really into something that I've been working on."

"Then go," Wilhelmina said, waving her away with an encouraging smile. "I'm good."

Lizzie hesitated, then nodded. She lifted her red motorcycle helmet in a gesture of good-bye. "I'll try not to be gone too late."

Wilhelmina smiled, knowing that once Lizzie got involved in her research she lost all track of time. "Good luck."

She listened to Lizzie leave the apartment, then turned back to watch the rain. Maybe Lizzie's way was the right one. To cure preternaturals, rather than to try to conform them.

She certainly hadn't been able to make a single change in the creatures of Carfax Abbey. In fact, she was the only one who'd come out of the experience changed. And not for the better.

She rubbed her cheek on her knee and tried to figure out how she could tell the others at the Society how badly she'd done in her attempt to stop Sebastian.

Sebastian. Even thinking his name made her remember things and feelings she didn't want to recall. She closed her eyes, hoping that would block out the memories, but it didn't. Instead she saw him, his beautiful features, his golden eyes.

The pouty softness of his lips. Even the mere memory of his heady taste erasing the earlier bitterness of her drink.

She uncurled from her chair and paced the tiny kitchen. She couldn't do this. She couldn't stay here alone, thinking about things that were best forgotten. She had to move on. She'd moved on before, she could again.

Despite her reluctance to admit her total defeat, she would go to the Society meeting. Talking to the others could be a way to cleanse her soul. To surround herself with the preternaturals who held the same ideals she did. A way to reaffirm what she knew was true. A place to feel safe and sure and . . . okay.

She had to go back, even if it was hard. Feeling better, she headed to her room to get dressed.

Sebastian finished buttoning his shirt, then looked for his shoes. Finding them where he'd kicked them off by his bed, he slipped his feet inside, telling himself he'd head down to the club and get back to his normal life. No strange waitresses. No anonymous calls. No sabotage attempts of any kind.

Just fun. Pleasure. No worries. That was what he wanted.

He strolled down the back hallway to the elevator. He stepped inside and pressed the button for the first floor. The lift jerked into motion, and he pulled in a deep breath.

Last night, he'd thought over Rhys's question in great detail. Why wasn't he confronting Mina? And he'd come to the conclusion that there was no reason to talk to her. She made her feelings abundantly clear. She disliked him enough to want to hurt his club. She fled his kiss. What was the point of talking to her again? She wasn't worth his energy.

The elevator shuddered to a stop and he flung open the metal gate. He strode into the club, crossing the empty dance floor to the bar.

Nadine stopped wiping down the polished oak countertop, the damp rag forgotten in her hand, as he approached.

"I heard about Wilhelmina," she said. "I'm sorry I was so wrong about her."

Sebastian shrugged. "Shit happens. At least nothing and no one was affected." Even as he said it, he knew that wasn't totally true. He felt very affected by Mina, but he planned to ignore the sensation until it disappeared.

Nadine nodded at him, but he could tell she wanted to say more. Instead she finished wiping down the bar and headed into the backroom.

Sebastian sat down, watching as the other employees went about their usual business. He shifted in his seat feeling edgy.

He'd feel fine once the patrons got here, and his nights went back to their normal pattern. He just needed to forget that Mina ever existed.

Nadine returned with a couple of packages of cardboard coasters. She dropped them on the bar.

"I just don't see how I could be so wrong about her," she said. "I really thought she was a vampiress who just needed a little help, a little direction."

"She needs help, all right," Sebastian muttered.

Nadine sighed. "Well, I'm sure she's gone for good. She disappeared last night in the middle of her shift. She must have realized you found out about her."

Sebastian nodded, not correcting her deduction. For some reason, he didn't want to share what had happened between himself and Mina in the stairwell. Not because he was embarrassed or even regretful. It was just private.

"I guess we never will know why she picked Carfax Abbey."

Sebastian nodded, and again the edginess filled him. He considered ordering a drink to calm himself, but he didn't think it would help.

When the patrons get here, he told himself again. He glanced at the door. A dark-haired woman walked in, and Sebastian straightened. Then he realized it was Valerie, late for work as usual. He leaned back again in his chair, trying not to question why he felt such sharp disappointment.

But his brain was rather insistent on telling him why. *She's going to bother you until you have answers. Until you understand*. This wasn't about attraction or desire. This was about getting the truth.

"I've got to go," he said to Nadine, sliding off the bar stool. He didn't wait for an answer as he exited the club into the drizzly night.

Flagging down a cab, he gave the driver Mina's address, not questioning why he'd managed to commit that to memory. Then he settled back against the seats feeling calmer than he had since the moment his lips had touched Mina's.

Sebastian knocked again, even though he knew the apartment was empty. He couldn't sense Mina.

He glanced around to make sure he was alone in the long hallway. When he was certain he was, he concentrated, his limbs slowly disappearing as he dissolved to shadow and slipped under the door.

On the other side, he reformed, his body appearing like a blurred negative slowly coming into focus. He glanced around.

Mina's apartment was small, typical for the city. The furniture was nice, but mismatched. Books and newspapers littered nearly every surface.

He could see Mina as a big reader. He supposed it could be because of the glasses she always wore. They looked scholarly, and were, of course, completely unnecessary. The glasses were just one of the many things he wanted to ask her about.

He strolled farther into the apartment, looking for any indication of where she might have gone. Although, if he didn't find one, he was prepared to stay and wait for her. Breaking and entering—or rather just entering—would probably tick her off, but he figured, what with her sabotage attempts, she wouldn't call the cops on him. Again.

He wandered down the hallway that he assumed led to her bedroom. He reached the first door and stopped outside the darkened room. Concentrating, he studied the feelings of the room, the scents, the residual emotions. It wasn't Mina's, although the room did belong to a female. A were. A wolf, he guessed.

He smiled. For reasons he chose not to ponder, he was pleased that Mina was living with a female.

His smile faded. Unless of course, Mina preferred females—which would explain her response to his kiss. Although her reaction seemed a little too over the top for that to be the case. Unless of course, she'd liked his kiss, which he believed she had, at least for awhile. But maybe that brief enjoyment had made her question her whole belief of her sexuality.

He considered that for a moment, then decided that was a dumb idea. She'd been far too responsive to him. Right up until the point she'd slammed him against the wall. He rotated his shoulder, just thinking about it.

He started away from the door, when something else stopped him. A scent, just barely there, drifted to him. Like a face where he couldn't recall the name, the fragrance taunted him. The reason the scent seemed familiar was right there on the tip of his tongue, but try as he might, he couldn't wrap his mind around what it was.

He concentrated a bit longer, then gave up, moving to the next door. The bathroom, small with a tub-and-shower combo. A toilet. A sink. The usual. Finally he reached Mina's room. He recognized her scent immediately. That subtle floral scent like lilies of the valley.

He breathed in deeply, then flipped on the light. Her bed was unmade, and her waitress uniform tossed over the footboard.

He picked up the dress, the material cold and damp like his own clothing. He lifted it to his nose, hoping to smell some traces of the desire he'd tasted on her lips still clinging to the silky material. But the brocade only smelled of sulfurous city rain and faint traces of lily.

He dropped the garment back to the bed, and quickly searched the room for any hints of where she might be. He found nothing but more books: *Pride and Prejudice*, *Sense and Sensibility,* and other classics. A stack of CDs—all classical—several news magazines. And one *Weekly World News.* He picked up the periodical. Apparently Bat Boy was on the loose again.

So Mina wasn't all seriousness and sabotage. That made him feel better.

He had a lot good insights into Mina, but nothing that would reveal where she'd go late at night. He flipped off the light and walked back to the living room. A search of that room revealed nothing either. The kitchen, however, was the jackpot.

On the tiny, café-style kitchen table was a note, written in messy, flouncy cursive.

Dear Lizzie,

I did go to the Society meeting. We are meeting in the back of a restaurant—Grindelia's, 21 W. 54th Street. If you get home in time, you're welcome to join us.

W.

Sebastian picked up the paper. The Society? What was that? He placed the note back on the table.

He didn't know if Lizzie would be able to make it, but he certainly planned on it.

Mina ducked around the corner of the restaurant and hurried down the narrow alley, skirting trash and other refuse. She reached the backdoor of the restaurant, just as the sky opened up and poured down on her. She knocked in a rapid sequence of timed raps. A large faery, who she thought was named Al, opened the door, allowing her entrance.

Because the preternaturals had yet to be accepted into the general populace, the Society considered it wise to keep their meetings secret. To join, you had to be invited. She wondered if her invitation would be revoked after she told them about the Carfax Abbey fiasco.

She entered the meeting room. The lights were low and the scent of baking bread and spicy red sauces permeated the brick walls. The smells no long appealed to her hunger, but Mina still enjoyed them. Funny how the aroma of food cooking, even foods she didn't eat, still made her feel warm and safe.

Vedette Grindelia, the owner of the restaurant and a very active member of the Society, greeted her with her usual warm hug. The woman was a werefox, a rather interesting irony, given her bosomy girth and grandmotherly looks.

"Glad to see you," she said with a welcoming smile. "How are you, cara?"

Mina nodded, and forced a stiff smile. She liked the older woman, but disliked her use of Italian endearments. Just hearing them made her skin crawl. "Good, and you?"

"Busy. Always busy." The werefox gestured to the chairs and the others, then bustled off to greet other arrivals.

Tonight, nearly fifty members mingled around the room. A large turnout. Of course. She would have a huge audience to hear about her sabotage catastrophe. She hesitated in the doorway, considering sneaking out before anyone saw her.

"Wilhelmina," a suave, slightly accented voice called to her.

Mina's heart sank. Jackson Hallowell. The Society's president.

He came forward, curling her hand in his much larger, much colder one. Tonight, the flamboyant vampire was dressed in a peacock blue suit with a black turtleneck and heeled and immaculately polished black boots. His usual flash attire. Everyone claimed that he was trying to hold onto his Regency roots—although she wasn't so sure about that.

"I'm pleased you are here," he smiled, his teeth perfect and blindingly white. "How is your work at Carfax Abbey going? Have you stopped that vile Sebastian Young?"

"Well," Mina began.

Another member called to Jackson, waving him over.

"Sorry, I must go," he said to Mina. "Perhaps you will give an update to the whole group tonight. Yes?"

"Umm," Mina hesitated.

"Excellent," he winked and strolled away to speak to a group near the podium at one end of the room.

Mina remained at the back, near one of the several brick supports throughout the room, hoping to hide as long as possible. But all too quickly, the meeting was called to order.

The Society's board members sat at a long table at the front of the room, and Jude Anthony, the vice-president, stood at the podium, waiting as the attendees hurried to find seats.

Jude was the opposite of Jackson. His appearance was that of a man in his early twenties, although he was actually much older than any of the preternaturals here. Or at least that was what Mina had heard; she wasn't sure of his actual age.

He was large and muscular with thick dark hair and piercing green eyes. The tall, suave vampire image created by Hollywood was blown by him. Jude looked like a tough and half-wild gladiator in a button-down shirt and faded jeans. Although Mina admired his work for the Society, he always made her nervous. He was going to make her really nervous tonight. Maybe it was a bad idea to come.

"Good evening," a smooth, almost oily voice said from beside her. Mina turned to see Daniel—she didn't know his last name. But she did know that if Jude made her nervous, Daniel made her downright jumpy.

Tall and thin, Daniel reminded her of the silent film vampires. A smile split his narrow face, making his slightly concave cheeks even more sunken. Definitely striking, but not necessarily in an appealing way. Yet, he was oddly mesmerizing.

"How are you tonight, sweet little Wilhelmina?"

Mina frowned at the strangely familiar greeting. But he always spoke to her that way, as if they were old friends rather than mere acquaintances, who only ever saw each other at these meetings and only spoke briefly.

As briefly as possible, she hoped.

"Have you been enjoying the warmer weather?" he asked, and again she felt as if ordinary small talk about the weather was referring to something she should but didn't understand.

"Yes, although I'm glad I didn't have to go out into the downpours earlier," she said, just to say something.

"I like the rain," he said with an enigmatic smile as if he was letting her in on a secret. Again, one that she didn't understand.

"It reminds me of the summers I used to spend on the coast," he said, a smile splitting his face again. "We had the most marvelous storms there. Very violent."

Mina stared at him, her breath catching in her throat. Suddenly she felt very threatened, but she couldn't say why.

"Welcome," Jude greeted the crowd and Mina released her pent-up breath, thankful that the meeting was beginning.

Daniel gave her one more inscrutable smile, then moved to sit up front.

Mina took a seat at the back, glad to be rid of him. She pulled in a calming breath, telling herself everything was fine.

That was until Jude said, "I'd like to get right to what our members have been doing since the last meeting."

Mina's stomach sank again.

Jackson pushed up from the table to join Jude, waiting, none too patiently, to speak. Jude gave the other vampire a sharp look, but he stepped back from the podium allowing the more flamboyant president to take the stage.

Jackson grinned at the crowd, a winsome flash of his perfect teeth.

"But before we get to the updates from the members on their assignments, I believe I see several new faces here tonight. So I would like to go over the Society of Preternaturals' mission."

Mina relaxed against the back of her metal folding chair. This would take awhile. Jackson was notoriously longwinded. Even though she'd heard the Society's philosophies and goals many times, she welcomed hearing them again. That was why she came tonight, to remember what she was working toward.

"We are a group of preternatural beings who believe that we can be accepted into mortal society. Although we are different from human beings, we have all made a solemn pact to live as closely as human as we can. That means we do not feed, hunt, or use humans for any type of preternatural sport.

"The Society has worked very hard to change the perception of our kinds. We are not monsters," he paused dramatically, "nor are humans our food source. We have a creed we all live by, which is . . ."

Again he stopped, to give his next words more impact.

"'Humans are super and natural, too.'"

Mina paused. Even though she'd heard that motto many times before, she even had a mug with the phrase on it which she purchased at a fund-raiser, it suddenly struck her as a little silly.

She straightened in her chair. *But* the organization did have a wonderful goal. She had to remember that.

Sebastian coughed, fighting back a laugh.

Humans are super and natural, too. Catchy.

He shifted closer to the brick column he leaned on, hoping he hadn't drawn attention to himself. But as the room was suitably dim and gloomy, he imagined he had gone unnoticed.

Sebastian shook his head. Good Lord, these preternaturals were nuts.

"We also feel that it is our sworn duty to stop any injustices we see other preternaturals enacting on humans. Integration is not a possibility if we are feared by mortals. We cannot allow ourselves to be seen as fiends."

Sebastian frowned. Seen as fiends? He was pretty sure none of his mortal patrons saw his preternatural clientele as fiends. Okay, maybe as sex fiends, but he knew that was half the draw of Carfax Abbey. Great hookups.

And in truth, none of the humans at his bar saw the preternaturals as anything *but* human. After all, that's how vampires and shapeshifters had survived for thousands of years. What the hell were these wackos talking about? They were integrated. Or as integrated as they would ever get.

After watching the speaker, who looked like an undead Liberace, for a moment longer, he considered leaving. He couldn't stand listening to this nonsense any longer. Then two messy, knotted ponytails on the other side of the room caught his attention. Mina. And fortunately she was in the back row.

Carefully, he approached her, not wanting to draw the attention of the nutcase at the podium, or the large faery guarding the entrance.

He'd lucked out getting into the place by straggling in with another group, when he realized he had to know some sort of silly secret knock. The faery hadn't even glanced at him, but he didn't think it would take much to make the members here realize he wasn't one of them.

As the vampire at the podium droned on about the injustices perpetrated daily on humans, Sebastian crouched down near Mina's chair, touching her arm.

She turned, her eyes growing impossibly large behind her glasses. She opened her mouth as if she was going to scream. But before he could clap a hand to her mouth, her bowed lips snapped closed as if she didn't want to draw any attention to herself, either.

"Come with me," he whispered.

She hesitated, and he thought she was going to refuse, but instead she gave him a slight nod. Then she glanced around as if to be sure no one saw him, which they didn't. Everyone was focused on the speaker, who was saying something about vampires being just like humans, except for their fangs, their liquid diets, their inability to go into the sunlight, their shapeshifting abilities, their unnatural looks, and their immortality.

Sebastian rolled his eyes. *Yes, we're practically humans.*

Mina carefully stood up and tugged on his sleeve. She gestured to the door, and he could tell she was anxious. Obviously she wanted out of this place as much as he did.

Then he noticed her looking around again, worrying her bottom lip with her teeth. No, she didn't want to leave, she just wanted to be sure *he* left before anyone saw him.

The idea pissed him off. She was embarrassed by him. When she was hanging out with these weirdos?

But he didn't react; he just turned and headed toward the door. They both slipped outside without incident.

Once they were around the corner from the door and in the dark, wet, smelly alley, Sebastian spun to face her.

"So is this group of loons the reason you were trying to sabotage my club?"

Chapter 10

Wilhelmina gaped at Sebastian. When she'd turned to find him at the Society meeting, her first thought was she had to get him out of there. Since he was one of the Society's enemies, she didn't think he was safe. She didn't question why her first thought had been to protect him, but it had.

Now that she knew he was here about the sabotage, maybe she should have remained inside and let him fend for himself with the Society. Although she had to admit he appeared surprisingly calm.

"Did they convince you to do it?" he asked.

She considered playing stupid and denying everything, but she got the feeling he wouldn't buy it.

"No, I offered," she told him.

Sebastian's golden eyes flashed with surprise. "Why?"

"Because you use humans. You treat them like sport, existing solely for your entertainment. Because you are immoral and . . ." She struggled for an appropriately insulting word.

"Narcissistic?" he supplied.

"No! Well, yes. But that's not—"

"Depraved, then?" he suggested, and she realized that he was again making light of her insults. This man had a colossal ego.

She groaned, frustrated.

He leaned toward her, a sudden and beguiling smile curving his lips. "I love it when you do that."

She started to groan again, but caught herself. She'd be damned if she was going to do anything this egotist enjoyed. As weird as those things might be.

When he realized she wasn't going to speak, he shifted away from her and asked, "But why me? I know we've never met, so how did you choose me?"

"Are you sure we've never met?" she couldn't help asking. Given his memory, they could have met half a dozen times and he'd never recall.

She was surprised, when he shook his head with absolute certainty. "No. We've never met."

"Like you'd remember," she muttered.

He reached out and toyed with a piece of her hair sticking out of her twisted ponytails on the top of her head. "Believe me, I'd remember you, Mina."

Her knees grew weak as she felt the slight tug of her hair where his fingers continued to stroke the escaped strand. She told herself to move away from him. To put distance between herself and the out-of-control feelings he caused inside her. He was dangerous, but her legs wouldn't move, except to continue trembling.

"So why me?" His voice again a brush of warm velvet.

She swallowed, trying to ignore the fingers still playing with her hair. Then she made the mistake of looking in his eyes. Golden fire. Her knees wobbled.

"Because you were on the list," she told him. "That's all." Maybe if she just told him the truth, he'd leave her alone. Stop making her feel like her skin was sizzling.

"What list?"

"The Society of Preternaturals Against the Mistreatment of Mortals has created a list of the most dangerous preternatural beings."

Sebastian's eyes widened, and he stopped touching her

hair. She closed her eyes briefly; the truth was working. She managed a shaky step back from him.

"*I'm* on that list?"

She nodded. "Number three."

"Number three! That's crazy. I'm not dangerous."

Mina frowned, slightly taken aback by his offended reaction. He seemed more upset by this news than by the fact that she'd been targeting his nightclub.

"Are you going to deny that you feed from mortals?" she asked. "You use them for the blood and the pleasure you get from them?"

"No," he said readily. "But I am a vampire. That's sort of what we're supposed to do."

She frowned at him, disgusted by his cavalier attitude.

"Come on, Mina, don't tell me that you don't love a nice . . . long," he stepped closer to her, his body nearly touching hers, his mouth practically brushing her ear, "slow . . . bite."

She shivered, tempted to lean against him. Instead she stepped back. "No."

"I don't believe that."

"Believe it," she said, meeting his eyes.

"So you are going to tell me that you don't bite, ever."

"Not just ever—never."

"You know that's not true. You bit me. Well, a nibble anyway."

She gritted her teeth. Of course he'd bring that up. "That—that was an accident. A reaction to being caught off-guard."

"Uh-huh." He looked thoroughly unconvinced.

"It's true. I don't bite. I don't . . . enjoy it."

"That's just wrong," he stated.

"Well, I think what you do is wrong."

"No," he said slowly. "What I do is normal. It's super *and* natural, if you will." He smiled, pleased with his joke.

She ground her molars, even as her body reacted to that beautiful smile. He really was impossible. She needed to get away from him. Even his lame jokes were making her insides do odd little flips.

"So you have the truth," she said. "I assume we're done."

Sebastian's smug smile disappeared. "I don't think so."

Her breath caught, apprehension filling her. Did he intend to punish her in some way for her attempts on the club? She stepped back from him, her bottom hitting a metal trash can. The lid slid off, clattering loudly in the narrow passage.

She jumped, and Sebastian reached out and caught her wrist.

"I really wish you would believe there is no reason to be scared of me," he said, his thumb rubbing the back of her hand in what he meant to be a soothing gesture. But the touch did anything but soothe her. Her skin felt electrified where he stroked her.

Oh, there were so many reasons to be scared of him.

"I'm assuming the Society is not pleased with the fact that you didn't stop me or my club in our dastardly deeds."

He waited for her to confirm.

"They don't know. I haven't told them yet."

"Well," he said, contemplating her, "I'll give you the out you need with them."

She frowned. Why would he do that? But she didn't ask; she waited for him to continue.

"I'll agree not to bite any humans for . . ." He thought for a moment. "For a month."

"And what do I have to do?" she asked, regarding him suspiciously.

He smiled, his lopsided, charming smile. A smile that made her very nervous.

"All you have to do is let me show you how much fun it is to be a vampire."

She frowned. Why on earth would he want to do that? And why would she consider agreeing?

She regarded him closely. He watched her with those intent eyes, no smug curve to his lips, no mocking light in his eyes. He was serious. And it appeared as if her answer was very important to him.

"I won't have to bite anyone?" she heard herself ask as if someone else was in control of her mouth.

"Not unless you want to."

"And I won't have to exploit mortals in anyway."

"Absolutely not," he assured her.

She considered him. Why was she even giving this crazy proposal any contemplation?

Because it would ultimately achieve what she wanted. Sebastian would bite no humans for a month. For thirty days, mortals would be safe from him. Not to mention, it would keep her from having to announce her hideous failure to the Society. *And* he was offering to show her how to be a vampire.

She did need help with that, she realized. She'd been so intent on being as "human" as she could that she hadn't seen how a better understanding of her vampire abilities could have helped her in her sabotage attempts. Like with the rat fiasco, for example. Learning more about her undead skills could be very useful the next time she went on a mission.

She smiled slightly. She could use his teachings against him. Oow, she liked that. But what was in it for him?

"Why would you want to show me the pluses of being a vampire?"

"Because I'm surrounded by vampires who don't understand how great it is to be undead. My brothers, to name two. They just don't get it. How thrilling it is. How empowering. Granted, their experiences as vampires haven't always been wonderful. Sometimes they have been downright terrible, but they are past that now. They have love and happiness and still they don't get it."

Mina stared at him, surprised by his candor. Surprised that the Sebastian Young she'd heard about was using words like love and happiness—and not sneering at the concepts.

"They are all into this Dr. Fowler guy," he paused, then

glanced back toward the entrance of the meetingplace. "Is this that Fowler guy's idea?"

She shook her head. "No. Most of the members of the Society also follow Dr. Fowler's beliefs, but they feel that the doctor is too—passive in his ways of integrating into human society. Dr. Fowler promotes getting humans to understand that the differences between our species are all physiological. He's very keen on research and study. The Society endorses more proactive and assertive actions."

"Like sabotage," Sebastian said, looking a tad incredulous.

She supposed it did sound a little overzealous, but she knew that the Society's goals were good, although she didn't think she could convince Sebastian of that. Especially since he was one of their targets.

She considered that, then asked, "I really wouldn't have to hurt any mortals?"

"Not a single one."

Maybe she was looking at an even bigger coup than sabotaging Sebastian's club. If she could get him to see the importance of the Society's work, if she could convert him, wouldn't that be far more impressive? He did say again that she wouldn't have to harm anyone. And it would also give her a month in his company to sway him. This could work. And if it didn't, she'd be better prepared to take on the next immoral vampire. Maybe.

"Okay," she said, although her agreement wasn't as confident as she'd hoped.

He grinned and tugged her hand, leading her down the alley toward the road. "Good, let's go."

"Where are we going?" she asked, her voice even more uncertain, although she did fall in step with him.

"Away from here. If you are constantly hanging out in garbage-filled, stinky alleys, it's little wonder you don't enjoy being a vampire."

* * *

Sebastian reached the street and turned left, trying not to think about why he was so pleased that Mina had agreed to his deal. After all, he'd agreed to not bite for a month. That wasn't fun. And he was willingly hanging out with a woman who'd tried to close down his club. He should be very wary of her. He should be livid.

Yet, he wasn't. He was . . . pleased. Very pleased.

Weird.

For a moment, he wondered why she had agreed so easily, but he cast the thought aside. He was just glad she had. And of course, his pleasure was clearly derived from the opportunity to corrupt one of Dr. Fowler's followers. Bring her over to the dark side. No, to show her what she considered the dark side wasn't dark at all. And he planned to show her he wasn't dangerous. Which brought him back to this crazy Society. He definitely wanted to know more about them.

Even with the lateness of the hour and the rain, a few people hurried along the sidewalk. Sebastian made another turn, heading toward Central Park.

Since she had agreed, for whatever reason, he planned to start his work right away. He paused at the crosswalk directly across from the park. More people crowded around them, waiting for the WALK sign. He didn't release her hand, still thinking she might dart. She'd agreed too easily; he didn't trust her not to change her mind. And she did seem agitated, casting glances at the people around her.

The WALK sign lit, and the pedestrians moved in a herd off the sidewalk. He headed toward an entrance to the park. But as soon as Mina realized where he was going, she stopped. He did too, turning to look at her.

Sparks of fear flashed in the air between them. She tugged her hand from his hold. She was scared again, and he didn't know why. She hadn't been frightened in the alley with him, not like this, just her normal wariness. And that was when she discovered he knew about her sabotage. Certainly a more appropriate time to be scared than now. On the street, with people milling by.

"What's wrong?"

She looked at him, then glanced at the walkway that disappeared like a gray ribbon into the grass and trees of the park.

"Why are we going there?"

"I wanted to show you something." He'd wanted her to experience the grass and the trees and the rain with her vampire senses—something he had the feeling she'd never done. Too uptight for that. Plus he wanted to have her alone, but he didn't question that desire too much.

She shook her head. "It's late. Can't we start this experiment tomorrow night?"

He frowned, wanting to ask her why Central Park would cause her fear. Or maybe he was causing her fear. Maybe, unlike him, she had no desire to be alone. In fact, he'd bet money on that reason. But he also got the feeling that if he asked which of the above it was, she wouldn't tell him. He was going to have to go slow with her to get the answers he wanted.

"Sure, we can start tomorrow," he said, and immediately her fear waned.

Again he took her hand, feeling her stiffen for just a moment, but then she allowed him to link his fingers through hers. They started back down the street, avoiding other pedestrians and puddles. Neither spoke, and Sebastian could sense the uncertainty still encompassing her. He wondered what Mina was like when she wasn't so guarded. He'd experienced just a glimpse of it when they'd kissed. But he wanted to experience more.

He glanced at her, his eyes fastening on her red lips, moist from the misting rain. His body reacted immediately, his cock hardening against the length of his zipper.

He definitely wanted to experience a lot more with Mina. This agreement was going to be more fun than he'd had in ages.

"How did you know where I was?" she asked suddenly.

He didn't break stride as he considered what to tell her. Finally he decided there wasn't much point in not telling the truth.

"I went into your apartment and found your note."

She stopped, turning to him. "You went into my apartment? Was Lizzie there?"

"Sorry, no. I just sort of invited myself in."

He saw anger, real anger like he'd seen when she'd informed him of her high opinion of him. Her midnight blue eyes glittered, her jaw set. Oh yeah, she was pissed.

"You can't go into someone's home uninvited," she stated.

Sebastian smiled. "Are you referring to that old myth about having to be invited into a place? Because we both know it isn't houses that one refers to."

Mina frowned at him, and for a moment he thought she actually didn't know what he was talking about. Maybe she didn't. Her kiss had been surprisingly innocent, and the legend that vampires had to be invited in did actually refer to sex. Maybe she didn't know that.

Her eyes narrowed, making her nose wrinkle quite cutely. "It's illegal."

Sebastian smiled at that. "I'm pretty sure what you did at my club is illegal, too."

She glared at him a moment longer, then broke their stare.

Rain started to fall harder, large drops spattering loudly on the concrete sidewalk.

She blinked up at the sky, raindrops running down her pale skin, making her features look as if they were created by perfect, wet brushstrokes. He stared at her, his fingers curling with the need to touch that smooth, creamy skin.

Her gaze met his again. "Then since you know exactly where I live, you know that we have a long walk ahead. Maybe we should get a cab."

He shook his head. He didn't want to leave this moment. Not yet. Even when she was irritated, he enjoyed her, liked being with her. He didn't question why. He also couldn't help noticing he liked the way her plain cotton shirt clung to her damp skin. Her skirt hugging the shape of her legs. He wanted to hold her, to kiss her irritation away. But he knew she'd run again.

"No cab." He reached for both her hands. He positioned himself a few inches from her, their linked hands between them.

"What—what are you doing?" she asked, her eyes wide, unsure.

"This is your first lesson in appreciating what you are. So just trust me, and do what I say."

She tilted her head, her eyes dubious behind her glasses.

"Come on, trust me. I'm only the third most dangerous vampire in the city. Or is that the state?"

When she didn't answer, except with a roll of her eyes, he added hopefully, "The world?"

"Leave it to you to see that as a compliment."

He smiled, then carefully reached forward for her glasses. She flinched away.

"You don't need them for this," he explained. "Of course, you don't need them anyway, do you?"

She grimaced at him, but she once more surprised him by slipping them off. Her eyes looked a more vivid, deeper blue, and he could see the delicate angle of her cheekbones.

"Okay, now hold my hands and do what you just did a moment ago."

She gave him a muddled look. "What did I do?"

"Lift your face up to the sky."

She stared at him as if she truly thought he'd gone mad, but to his surprise, she did what he asked.

"Good," he said, watching her. "Now focus on the rain on your skin."

Her brow creased slightly as if she were studying his request for a pop quiz later.

"Okay, let me amend that. *Feel* the rain on your skin."

Her brow was still furrowed, her stance stiff, but very slowly her features relaxed as she did as he asked. Her eyelids fluttered with each drop, her black lashes wet and spiky against her cheeks.

She pulled in a deep breath, the action making her chest rise and fall. He watched as beads of water rolled slowly over the milky skin of her throat, her collarbone, her chest. The pale blue material of her shirt molding to the curved outline of her breasts, her nipples beading underneath the fabric like the rain on her bare skin.

Sebastian pulled in a deep breath of his own, his cock pressing against his jeans. His fingers squeezed hers in his attempt to temper his needs. She squeezed his fingers back, and then licked the wetness of her lips. A slight smile curved her lips, softening her features, taking his breath away.

Before he thought better of it, he pulled her to him and kissed her.

Mina never liked rain. At least not since that night. . . .

She forced that memory away and did what Sebastian asked. She just *felt* the rain rather than the memories it conjured.

She realized the droplets on her face felt like dozens of tiny caresses. But more than that, she could feel the texture of the water, the way the molecules bonded, the exact grouping and regrouping as they rolled in cool, silky paths on her flesh. The water was cold, but her skin didn't sense it as a chill, but rather a pure, refreshing tingle. Even the scent of the rain, a strange combination of freshness and city, was more than she recalled ever experiencing.

At first she hadn't understood what Sebastian wanted her to do. All she could focus on was his hands holding hers, his strong fingers against the backs of her hands, his thumb pressing into her upturned palms. But then she let herself go. Let herself feel.

She smiled at the wonder of such a simple thing, amazed

that she'd never really felt the rain before—not like this. It was incredible, fantastic, exhilarating.

Then her world shifted, and she found herself pulled against Sebastian. Her chest flattened against his broader, muscular one. Their damp clothes clinging, a wet friction between them, making her breasts tingle with each brush. Before she could even begin to become accustomed to those sensations, his soft, persuasive lips molded to hers, licking the rain from her. Tasting the moist heat beyond.

Desire snapped over her already oversensitized body like electricity over a bare powercord. Her fingers dug into his shoulders, trying to find something solid, something concrete to ground her, before her body just went up in sizzling smoke. But the feeling of his hard muscles, the undulations of them under her palms did nothing to lessen the crackling need, making her weak and overwhelmed. And all the while, his lips, strong and soft all at once, molded and remolded to hers like the rain had done on her skin. Except Sebastian's kiss was a hundred—a thousand—times more thrilling.

His large hands on her back pulled her tighter against him, and she found the strange urge to rub against him. She wanted more—much more—of something she didn't even understand. She whimpered against his lips, overwhelmed, desperate.

He used the slight parting of her lips to slip his tongue inside her mouth. The rasp of his tongue, the taste of him. Then his mouth left her lips, licking the rain on her cheeks, clinging to her jawline.

"God, I want you," he whispered against her ear.

She wanted him too. She did. She had to at least admit that truth to herself. And her need scared and excited her all at once. But like with the rain, she just wanted to feel him.

She groaned, shocking herself by turning her head and kissing him fully, her tongue slipping into the moist heat beyond his sculpted lips. Her arms locked around his neck and she rubbed against him, feeling. Only feeling. No thoughts. Just sensation.

His tongue traced the curve of her bottom lip. She licked him back, the rain adding to the tang of his mouth.

"You taste so good," he murmured against her lips, the words low and velvety—and as sobering as if the rain falling on them had suddenly turned to sleet.

She pulled away, blinking at him. What was she doing?

He stared back at her, his golden eyes hooded, dazed. He started to reach for her again, but she stumbled backward, her heel catching on a grate in the sidewalk. Sebastian caught her, but dropped his hand as soon as she was steadied.

"I should go home," she said, surprised her voice sounded so calm.

Sebastian stared at her for a moment. Then he nodded. He glanced up at the sky. The rain fell in big fat drops, splattering loudly on the concrete. He gestured to a storefront with a large striped awning.

"Wait under there until I find a cab."

She nodded numbly, automatically doing as he asked. She watched as he strode to the curb, waiting for a cab to pass. Even though she was shaken, she couldn't help noticing how beautiful he was, standing in the rain, his clothes clinging to his tall, muscular body, his hair wet and tangled.

Her body ached, but she forced herself to focus on the rain, the passing cars, the buildings surrounding them. Anything but that man and her desire.

Finally, he flagged down a taxi and gestured for her to join him. She did, still feeling like her body wasn't her own. Once in the car, she slid to the other door, putting as much space between herself and Sebastian's big body. Sebastian didn't close the space, staying against his door. They were both silent.

"I'll walk you up," Sebastian offered once they reached her apartment, but Mina shook her head, opening the cab door.

"No. I'm fine," she managed to say, surprised how calm her voice sounded. She was anything but fine, her legs were trembling, her hands . . . She was a mess.

She started to step out onto the curb, when his fingers

caught her wrist, the contact making her breath catch. She looked at him, knowing her eyes were wide, anxious. But that simply wasn't something she could disguise. She was far too overwhelmed by him.

He smiled in a way that he meant to be comforting, but it just made her all the more aware of how beautiful he was.

"Mina," he said softly. "I'll come here to get you tomorrow night."

She nodded, unable to speak. His quietly stated intent wasn't said to sound ominous, but it sent another chill through her.

"Night," he said, releasing her. She nodded again, and half-scrambled, half-fell out of the taxi. She didn't look back to see if he was chuckling over her gracelessness. Her only thought was to get into her apartment to where she could think.

Once locked inside her empty home, she collapsed on the sofa, dropping her head into her trembling hands.

What the hell had she been doing? She couldn't feel this way about him. She had agreed to the bargain he'd proposed, but only to learn how to better stop vampires like him. To avoid telling the Society she had failed. And to maybe go back and tell them that Sebastian Young had been converted to one of them.

Not to fall into his arms.

She thought of that kiss. She couldn't let that happen again. He was still the enemy, although it was getting harder and harder for her to remember that fact.

She had to remember that the Society had picked Sebastian as a dangerous vampire for good reason.

"It was the rain," she stated to herself. That had to be the reason she'd reacted to him so completely. He'd helped her overcome something that she'd thought would always haunt her. She'd just . . . reacted. Well, her body had.

But her body had misled her before. She had to remember that. And she also had to remember she wasn't that same young girl she'd been. She could handle this situation with Sebastian. She could keep control. She could.

Chapter 11

When Sebastian arrived at Mina's apartment the next night, he half-expected her to be gone. But as he walked down the characterless hallway with its beige walls and dark carpet that might have been blue at one time but was now a murky gray, he sensed her. The scent of lily of the valley and something inherently Mina reached him, and suddenly the antiseptic surroundings seemed far more interesting.

Last night, he'd been stunned by the intensity of his need for her. He knew he'd wanted her, but he was shocked how quickly his desire had spun out of control. He wanted her more than any woman he could recall for a long, long time.

At first, he'd found his loss of control unnerving. He just didn't lose control like that. Then he decided it wasn't totally unexpected. Mina presented a challenge, and he loved a challenge. That was really all there was to it. That simple.

He was looking forward to tonight.

He knocked on the door, and it opened immediately as if she'd been waiting for him. Although her narrowed eyes behind her ever-present glasses and her bow-shaped lips drawn tight didn't exactly state she was pleased to see him.

Okay, maybe she wasn't waiting in excited anticipation.

"Hello," he said and couldn't help adding. "Couldn't wait for me to get here, could you?"

She gave him a wry look of her own, but moved back for

him to enter the small apartment. He noticed right away that her black hair was in braids, and his eyes strayed down her body to see if she was wearing a naughty little Catholic schoolgirl outfit. No such luck. A simple pale pink shirt and faded jeans.

"Come on in," she said, "since you've been here already, I guess I don't need to show you around."

Sebastian smiled at her as he passed. "Someone is cranky tonight."

She followed him into the living room and waited for him to sit, before she said, "Not cranky. Serious."

Sebastian groaned. "That's almost worse than cranky. Mina, has anyone ever told you that you are altogether too serious?"

"Well, someone has to be," she said, although she sounded a little insulted at his observation. That had to be a good sign. There was a naughty schoolgirl in there somewhere. Although he'd be happy with a real smile tonight. Or a laugh. But best not to get his hopes up.

"Sebastian," she started, and he smiled.

"What?" she demanded, when she saw his pleased expression.

"That's the first time you've said my name."

She gave him a look that stated that she thought he was a lunatic.

"Go on," he said, relaxing against the sofa cushions.

She stared at him for a moment, but her eyes were unreadable. Although that could just be the damned glare of the lamplight off the lenses of her glasses.

"Sebastian," she started again.

"Why do you wear those glasses? I've never heard of a vampire with myopia."

She paused, her frown returning. "What?"

"Your glasses. You don't need them."

"No," she agreed. "I like them." She took a breath and

started again on the important thing that Sebastian could tell she was geared up to tell him.

"I want you to know that—"

"Do you have to wear the glasses tonight?"

Her mouth snapped shut, then she said flatly. "Yes. I do."

"Okay," he agreed. "But you can't know unless you ask, right?"

She frowned at him as if she was trying to decide if he really wanted an answer. Obviously deciding he didn't, she started her announcement again. "I want you to know that I fully intend to—"

"I like your hair tonight," he said. "I like the weird, messy ponytail things too."

She stopped again, giving him a look that said she thought he was mad. "Has anyone ever told you that you are rather annoying?"

"You know, you'd be surprised how often I've heard that."

"No," she stated, "I don't think I would. Are you done now? Can I speak?"

He nodded, trying to look properly contrite. Although he was thoroughly enjoying himself. He loved how easily he could get to her—it sort of made up for how easily she aroused him. He straightened against the sofa cushion as if he planned to be a good boy and listen.

She watched him for a few moments, then when he was settled, she asked, "Are you ready now?"

He nodded.

"Okay, I fully intend to keep the deal with you, but I think we need a few ground rules."

Rules. Okay, now she really did have his attention and not in a good way. He didn't like rules. In fact, all his plans for her were about breaking rules. Did no one understand that was what vampires were supposed to do? Break rules. Exist outside normal conventions.

But he didn't speak. He wanted to hear the rest of this nonsense.

"My first rule is no flirting."

Oh no. These rules were so not going to work for him.

"Also no touching. No holding hands. No . . . well, no contact, period."

Sebastian stood up at that request, his action smooth and sudden. Mina immediately moved back, even though he wasn't near her. Fear instantly permeated the air.

Sebastian frowned, but kept his tone calm. "Why not?"

She stared at him for a moment, then stated coolly, "Because I don't like it."

Sebastian nearly laughed. She was lying, and they both knew it. "You didn't like my kiss last night?"

For a fraction of a second, her gaze dropped to his mouth, then she met his eyes. "No. I didn't."

He knew she wasn't telling the truth; he'd felt her desire for him, tasted it on her lips. Even now, tiny flares of her need mingled with her nervousness. She wanted him, and he wanted her. It was that clear and simple. But her denial bothered him far, far more than it should have. Her distant expression bothered him, too.

"Are you making up these silly rules because you don't like me? Or because you are afraid you might like me too much? After all, it wouldn't do to actually like the Society's Number One enemy."

He stepped toward her, and again she backed up a step. More fear pulsed in the room, but somehow this alarm felt different. He wondered if he'd come close to the truth.

But instead of denying or confirming his suspicions, her gaze fell to the floor. "You aren't the Number One enemy."

Sebastian slowly approached her, but stopped a few inches away. "Mina, I'm not your enemy, period."

She looked up at him, and for just a moment, her expression was torn somewhere between hope and uncertainty. Her dark eyes, heartbreaking. But then the emotions disappeared, her pale features unreadable, doll-like.

He hated that empty look. He wanted the woman who'd

allowed herself to enjoy the rain. The woman who looked aroused and dazed by his kiss. Even the woman who gritted her teeth and glared at him.

He started to reach for her, but caught himself. She said she didn't want his touch, and he would abide by that. But he had a rule of his own.

"Okay, I'll agree to your rules."

Her eyes brightened.

"But I have one of my own."

She hesitated. "What is it?"

"I can ask to touch you. You can say no, and I won't. But I can ask."

Mina frowned, surprised by his compromise, wondering if she could really trust him to keep to his word. Of course, he hadn't done anything aggressive to her yet. Actually given what she'd tried to do to him, he'd been surprisingly kind. Even the times he'd lost his temper with her, he'd not stayed mad more than a few moments. Even when she publicly insulted his personality. Even when he'd discovered her attempts to harm his club.

She studied his features, trying to see any deception there. His golden eyes regarded her back, waiting for her agreement.

"Okay," she said, and he smiled, those sinfully full lips turning up, one corner a tad higher than the other. Lord, he was beautiful.

She forced her gaze away, studying a loose bit of yarn in the worn carpet.

"Want to shake on it?" he asked, holding his hand out. She hesitated, her first instinct to tell him no, but that seemed silly. A handshake truly was harmless.

She slipped her hand against his, noting the slightly rough texture of his palm, and his long fingers curled around her smaller ones. His touch was gentle, and she found herself reminded of his lips that had tasted hers so gently, only to grow more urgent.

She pulled her hand away, and he released her readily. Okay, nothing was harmless when it came to this man.

She expected to see a smug smirk on his lips, as he was probably well aware of her body's reaction to the brief touch, but instead he just nodded.

"Good, we are agreed. Now let's go to a toy store."

Mina was still confused as she followed Sebastian down her apartment stairs and out to the street. He turned right, walking briskly over the cracked concrete.

"A toy store?" she asked, jogging every few steps to keep up with his pace.

When he realized she was having a little difficulty keeping up with him, he slowed his strides. "Yes. Have you ever been to a toy store?"

"Of course, I've been to a toy store."

He gave her a sidelong look. "Since you crossed over?"

She started to say, of course again, then paused. No, she hadn't. Of course, she hadn't. Why would she need to go to a toy store? She didn't know any children. She hadn't for centuries. The idea saddened her slightly, but instead of dwelling on the strange sense of loss, she focused back on Sebastian.

"What about you? Have you been to a toy store?"

"Sure. I love toy stores."

"Even now?" she asked.

He laughed at her incredulous expression, the sound lush and warm. "Yes. Even now."

"Why?"

He glanced at her. "I like the kids."

She stopped, her abrupt halt causing two teenage girls, who were talking animatedly in half-sentences, nearly to bump into her. The girls glared at her, then she was forgotten as they spotted Sebastian. They did a double take, then leaned into each other giggling about him as they continued down the street.

Mina frowned at the girls, then turned her attention back to Sebastian.

"You like the kids?"

He shook his head and smiled, tolerantly. "Yes, I like the kids. But *not* in the 'nice-little-appetizers' way you are thinking."

"I wasn't—"

He cut her off. "Yes, you were."

He started walking again, and this time she fell in step with him easily.

"So why do you like toy stores and kids?"

"You'll see."

He turned down another street but Mina's steps slowed as the crowd began to grow denser. Soon they were weaving through the masses, her shoulder bumping against Sebastian at her side and the other shoulder being brushed by passers-by. With each unintentional contact, she felt more confused.

By the time they reached Times Square, she felt like she was neck-deep in a sea of sensory overload. Tourists talking in fast, loud voices. The honks of cars, the roar of engines, more voices. Bright lights burned and flashed in sharp colors at odds with the hazy scent of the city. The scent of exhaust and trash. The scent of body odor and strong perfumes and under all that the sweet, clean scent of blood.

That alone would have been enough for her to feel overwhelmed. But she was also bombarded by the emotions of those brushing past her, walking in front of her, walking close behind her. So many emotions swirling around her, excitement, exhaustion, irritation, even attraction.

She found it hard to focus on any one thing, everything twirling like a kaleidoscope with no place for her to focus.

She closed her eyes for a moment, trying to get her bearings, but her foot caught on the uneven sidewalk. Her eyes snapped open as she tried to catch herself, but instead she overcompensated, and began to fall.

A strong arm came out to catch her around the waist, and she found herself pulled tight to Sebastian's side. Suddenly all the swirl of human emotions and scents and sounds faded. All she could feel was that strong arm like a life preserver tossed to her in a stormy sea. He made her feel safe, protected, and while she knew she should find that fact alarming, at this moment, all she could do was appreciate it.

Quickly, he whisked her out of the main rush and into a small alcove of a doorway. He released her immediately, frowning down at her, and she wanted his arm back, making her feel centered. And oddly calm.

"Are you okay?" he asked, leaning down and looking closely at her face.

"Yes," she assured him. "I just tripped."

"Are you sure?"

She nodded. "I'm not used to so many people, so close to me. I can't seem to concentrate."

He frowned. "You look pale, even for you."

She shifted at that comment. She knew she was very pale, but something about his pointing out the fact made her self-conscious. Was that bad?

"Yes. I just couldn't seem to get myself or my mind focused. Everything was swirling."

"Is it now?"

She paused, realizing that people still rushed passed them, although they weren't touching her. They weren't in her space. She could still sense all the smells. All the sounds and lights, but she could distance herself from it all. She could focus on one thing at a time, like the repeated honk of a cab. The loud voice of a woman yelling to her husband. And Sebastian, close to her in the small doorway, his rich, spicy scent. His strength in the air.

"Did this happen at the club?"

"No, not really. Once in awhile I got overwhelmed, but not often, not like this. But usually no one touched me there." No one but you, she amended to herself—and he'd been just as overwhelming, but in a whole different way.

"Well, the preternaturals probably sort of diluted the

human emotions," he guessed. "That would be my guess. So it's just large groups of humans that affect you?"

She nodded.

Sebastian frowned at her, certain what he was thinking couldn't possibly be true. But it was the only thing that made sense. Somehow, she didn't know how to do something as simple as block mortal reverberation, the "noise" of their emotions, which could be very overpowering. How had she survived in New York City, where there were thousands of mortals per square mile? How had she survived period?

"When were you crossed over?"

She frowned as if she couldn't imagine why he'd ask such a question. He supposed age was a rather personal question, even for vampires.

"In 1903."

She was a relatively young vampire, but she had lived over a hundred years. That was a long time to not know how to control the vibrations of humans. Humans were very powerful in their own right, so how had she done it? Survived without losing control?

Hell, she'd managed to go beyond not losing control; she repressed most of her vampire nature. She was clumsy, she was self-conscious and apprehensive. She was plain.

He amended that. She gave off the impression of being plain, but she wasn't. His gaze roamed the features of her face, her beautiful cheekbones, the line of her nose, her bow-shaped lips, and those deep, bottomless blue eyes. No, she was far from plain. But she still wasn't like any vampire he'd ever encountered.

"Your initiator must have been a real ass. That is one of the first things you should have learned when you were crossed over. How to block emotions. The vampiress who crossed me and my brothers over was crazy and damned evil to boot, and even she taught us about our new selves."

When he saw the troubled look in her eyes, he caught himself, regretting his words. He shouldn't have assumed her initiator was a jerk—although he could find no other explanation for her unawareness of herself and the basics of being a vampire.

Again he wondered how she'd survived over a hundred years without learning this. Sebastian remembered all the books and magazines scattered all over her apartment. She reminded him of Rhys. His brother spent centuries hiding from the world of mortals. Surrounding himself with books and music and not much else. Until Jane—then they had learned to live together. It had taken an unorthodox way for it to happen, but Rhys had found peace.

Mina needed that too—to learn to live as a vampire. He'd been absolutely right when he'd made this bargain. She needed to awaken herself to all the amazing senses and abilities she had. And even if she still thought the Society was a good thing when the month was over, at least she'd be more aware of herself. And maybe more aware that vampires, who actually liked being vampires, weren't all evil.

But Times Square wasn't the best place to start. It was too much for her first outing.

"Maybe we should do something else tonight. I don't want you to be too overwhelmed here."

He'd assumed she would jump at the chance to leave, but she surprised him by shaking her head.

"I'd like to go to the toy store."

"Okay," he agreed slowly. "But you do need to learn how to handle all the emotions around you. I don't want you freaking out when a kid comes up behind you and tugs on your shirt because he's mistaken you for his mother."

She gave him a funny look as if she didn't really understand that example. Then her dark eyes grew hopeful.

"You could do that? Make crowds not so overwhelming?"

He hadn't ever done it before, since he'd never crossed a mortal over, but he imagined he could. "Sure."

"How?"

He considered how he'd learned to block all the reverberations. Now he wasn't even consciously aware he was doing it, so it was hard to remember how he learned. But he wasn't going to let Mina know that; she had such an expectant look on her face.

"I focus on something outside of myself," he said. "Like a distant point outside of the crowd, outside of the emotion."

Mina frowned, obviously not understanding what he was saying.

"What did you focus on this time to get you centered and calm?"

Her cheeks colored slightly, only making her skin a tad less pale—but he could definitely see a blush. She looked away from him.

"Okay," he said, realizing she wasn't going to tell him, although he was very intrigued. "You don't have to tell me, but could you keep focusing on that?"

She nodded her head, still not meeting his eyes. Her cheeks were almost pink now.

He smiled at her bowed head, getting the distinct feeling he might have been what she'd focused on. That idea pleased him.

As if to test his theory, he said, "Maybe it would be best if we held hands through this crowd. You know, to keep you close, in case you panic."

Mina stared at his outstretched hand, then she took it, her small, delicate fingers curling around his. "That would be good," she admitted.

"Okay," he said, turning back to the busy street. "Ready to try this again?"

She glanced at their linked hands, then nodded resolutely. "Yes."

As they stepped back into the masses of pedestrians, Sebastian knew he was right. She was using him as her focal point, as her center. The realization created an odd tightening in his chest, a tightening that felt good and strangely right.

Chapter 12

For the rest of the walk to the toy store, Mina seemed to remain calm. A couple of times, her fingers squeezed his as if she was struggling with her focus, but given that she was shoulder-to-shoulder in an ocean of humans, she was managing very well.

The crowd didn't lessen as they reached the doorways of the huge store, but Sebastian hoped that it would be a little more manageable inside.

He approached one of the glass doors, but Mina stopped.

He turned, expecting her to say she couldn't do it, she couldn't handle any more, but instead she stared up at the giant screens across the top of the building, a bemused half-smile on her lips.

He gazed up with her as the images changed. Toys and kids and a giant cartoon giraffe.

"I knew this was all here," she finally said. "But I've never really been able to . . . enjoy it."

He smiled at her. "Well, that's what I'm here for. To show you a good time."

She looked away from the screens, studying him. Then she nodded.

"Ready to go inside?"

She nodded again.

They stepped through the doors.

"Welcome to my favorite tapas bar."

She paused, then grimaced at him.

"Just kidding." He smiled.

But even before he finished his assurance, Mina's attention was turned to the store. A vast children's wonderland. Toys and dolls and stuffed animals everywhere. Children and adults alike wandered around with looks of amazement on their faces. And in the center of the store was a ferris wheel—three stories tall.

Mina's fingers squeezed his as she gaped around her.

"Are you okay?" he asked.

"Yes," she murmured, her eyes flitting from one thing to another, finally stopping on the ferris wheel. Sebastian watched her expression as she watched the large metal ring spin slowly around and around.

She released his hand and walked over to the railing to get a closer look. He followed her, leaning on the rail next to her. He smiled at her awed expression. She looked like one of the children, her mouth a small "o," her eyes widened, shining.

She was so lovely.

She tore her gaze away from the large, metal-strutted wheel to him. "Are we going to go on that?"

"Absolutely," he said.

She smiled, small to be sure, but the first real smile that she'd given him. The gesture was like a sucker punch to his stomach. Damn, she wasn't just lovely, she was beautiful.

And he had to touch her.

"But I want to show you something first."

She glanced back at the ferris wheel longingly, but then nodded.

He moved so she was positioned between himself and the railing, his chest a couple of inches from her back. She stiffened at the position, but didn't say anything. After all, he wasn't breaking her rules. His body wasn't quite touching hers.

"Is this okay?" he asked anyway. It wasn't his intention to

intimidate her. When he did touch her, he wanted her to want it every bit as badly as he did.

She nodded, shifting closer to the railing. He allowed her the tiny space, but placed his hands on the top rail, boxing her in, still not touching her. Her posture straightened, but again she didn't balk at the position.

"Okay," he said softly. "Close your eyes."

She glanced over her shoulder at him. "Close my eyes? Why?"

He smiled at her, noticing again that her nose crinkled cutely when she frowned. "Just do it. I swear, you'll really like it."

She narrowed her eyes as if she wasn't quite sure she should trust him. But then she did as he asked.

He studied her face, amazed that he hadn't noticed right away how long her black eyelashes were. How perfectly smooth her skin was.

He forced his gaze away from her, and out at the busy store.

"Okay. Can you feel the emotions in the air?"

"Yes," she murmured in her breathy way, and for a moment, he really wished she was saying that yes to something else. Like coming back to his apartment and spending the whole night in his bed.

He closed his eyes too, realizing he was the one who needed to get his focus centered.

"What do you feel?" he asked.

"Excitement. Joy." She paused. "Longing."

Sebastian knew she was picking up the vibe of the kids. Their excitement and their joy. And their longing, for a new doll, a new teddy bear, but he couldn't help wondering if she was reading some of his longing too. Even though he was trying his damnedest to mask his feelings.

"Do these feelings seem different from the other times you've sensed them?" he asked.

"Yes," she murmured, and again he found her breathy voice altogether too arousing.

He pulled in a steadying breath. "How are they different?"

She was quiet for a moment, then she said, "They feel more vivid, more fresh. Not tainted by anything else. Just pure excitement. Pure joy. Pure . . . longing."

Sebastian gritted his back teeth at the way she said the last with such yearning of her own. He started to release the railing. He needed to put more space between them. He couldn't stand this close to her and not touch her.

Then she surprised him by touching him, leaning back until her back was lightly against his chest. He froze, afraid that she might startle if he moved.

"Why do the emotions feel so different?" she whispered.

He leaned forward, just a little, so he could see her face. Her eyes were still closed, her red lips parted. She looked the picture of pure bliss, and he wished the hell they weren't in the middle of the biggest toy store in the world.

"The emotions of children are less tarnished," he explained, trying to keep his voice even, his body stationary. As much as he wanted to feel the friction of their bodies rubbing together, he didn't want to risk her breaking the contact, not when she'd offered it to him.

"Children haven't learned to temper their emotions. They just feel."

She nodded, then she was still. A deep sigh escaped her parted lips. Her back rubbed his chest, a minute shift of her body against his, but he nearly groaned.

Before he thought better of it, he moved forward until her body was sandwiched between him and the railing. Her back tight to his chest, her bottom nestled snug against the juncture of his legs. He nuzzled his cheek to hers, breathing in her scent. Feeling her longing and his.

Damn, he'd never wanted a woman like he wanted Mina. Here and now.

Mina swallowed, the delightful emotions of the children

fading away as Sebastian fully enveloped her, his body solid and warm at her back.

She'd been aware that she'd leaned into him, because the intense emotions in the air were making her feel a little disoriented. And as out on the sidewalk, Sebastian's touch seemed to give her focus and a surprising sense of calm.

But calm was the last thing she was feeling now. Sebastian nuzzled her cheek, the brush of his skin, the tickle of his unruly hair, making her body burn. His hands remained on the steel bar of the top railing, but she could feel every movement of his muscles along her back, over her bottom as if he was stroking her.

She told herself to tell him to stop. But she couldn't find her voice. All she could do was feel him, all around her. His strength, his heat, so thrilling she was helpless to do anything but revel in the sensations.

Suddenly, he was gone, and she had to grasp the railing to keep from toppling backward. His hand pressed to the small of her back to steady her, but as soon as she had her balance, he dropped his hand to his side.

The coloring along his cheekbones seemed a little darker, but otherwise, he didn't appear affected by their contact. She did notice his usually ready smile was gone, and his eyes burned a darker gold.

"Want to ride the ferris wheel now?"

She agreed, even though she wasn't quite sure she was ready to release the railing and walk. Between the delightful innocence of the children's emotions and the sinfully exciting feeling of Sebastian, she was drained. Her senses almost ravaged.

But she followed him down to the lower level where a queue was forming to get on the ride. They were both quiet as they waited with the others. Mina noticed that Sebastian, while he didn't attempt to touch her, tried to keep himself situated between her and the others in the line. Trying to keep her from getting overwhelmed.

Warmth filled her at the realization. She couldn't remember a time when anyone looked out for her. Not like that, not to anticipate her needs.

"Yes!" he suddenly exclaimed, and she followed his gaze to the ferris wheel.

"What?" she asked, not seeing anything that should have him so excited.

"We're going to get the Mystery Machine."

"Huh?" She had no idea what he was talking about, although that often seemed to happen with him.

He gave her an incredulous look. "The Mystery Machine? Scooby-Doo?"

She shook her head, still not following.

"You've got to be kidding?" he said, obviously very disheartened at her lack of knowledge. "I do not know how you have survived all these years."

She didn't know either. It hadn't been easy, and not until Dr. Fowler found her, and then she'd found the Society, had she had any sense of understanding and purpose.

A pang of guilt tightened her chest. The Society had helped her so much, and here she was enjoying the company of one of the vampires they considered a serious threat.

She looked at Sebastian. His eyes sparkled with the anticipation of the Mystery Machine, whatever that was. He grinned at her, his smile sincere, guileless. Her breath caught at the sight of it.

Maybe the Society was wrong, she thought for a second. Maybe they misjudged Sebastian. Then she remembered all the women she'd seen on the receiving end of that smile at the nightclub.

No, Sebastian was charming. He was fun. He even was quite sweet. But he still used humans. She had to remember that, no matter how much she found herself liking him.

"Yes!" he cheered again as they got to the head of the line, and a gondola in the shape of a blue van with psychedelic flowers and swirls pulled to a stop. A brown dog with black spots was perched on the front.

"This is the Mystery Machine." He grinned at her and waved his hand with a flourish for her to enter. "And you should be darn happy we didn't get the Cabbage Patch Kid car."

He shivered with mock horror.

She shook her head, still having no idea what he was talking about, although she was amused by his animated antics. And she had to admit it, at least to herself, she did like Sebastian.

But once they were seated, and the ferris wheel began to move, Mina's attention was only on the ride. She sat forward on the small plastic seat, watching as they spun round and round. Up, up to the very top, swinging there high above the ground, then down, down until the gondola nearly scraped the ground.

She smiled at Sebastian as they reached the highest point again, then started their descent.

"A carnival came near our house once in Newport," she heard herself saying, "when I was twelve or thirteen. They had a ferris wheel, and I thought it was the most amazing thing I'd ever seen. But my father wouldn't allow us to go. Even though it was a new invention and they'd even had one at the World's Fair a few years before, he considered it too lowly for his family. But I remember watching it from my bedroom window, spinning and spinning in the distance. And I dreamed about how it would feel, to go up and down through the air."

Sebastian's grin faded slightly as he leaned forward. "How does it feel?"

She gazed at him, the warm glitter of his eyes, the poutiness of his lips. His long legs taking up much of the room in the small car, his knees occasionally bumping against hers. The innocent brush of denim against denim.

"It feels even better than I imagined," she admitted.

They looked at each other, his face her focus while the world moved in her peripheral vision. Again, even with her body so aware of his, her attraction a palpable thing between them, she also felt more peace than she could remember in a very, very long time.

Suddenly, a man, maybe in his early twenties, was unlatching the gondola door, waiting for them to exit. She hadn't even noticed that they had stopped spinning.

Gathering herself, she scrambled out of the seat, aware her movements were awkward and jerky as the car swayed slightly with her attempt to step down to solid ground.

As throughout the night, Sebastian's hand came up to steady her, offering her a center, even as that same touch made her dizzy with so many emotions, desire, yearning, uncertainty, and even a little shame.

When they were off the ride and back into the store proper, she turned to him, deciding she needed to tell him that, while she'd had a wonderful time, perhaps the best time of her life, she needed to go home. She needed to be away from him, where she could think more clearly.

But Sebastian wasn't looking at her. In fact, he stood stock-still, his brow furrowed, his eyes distant, as if he was concentrating intently on something.

"Do you hear that?" he asked.

She started to shake her head, when he caught her hand and dragged her toward a set of escalators.

"Where—where are we going?" she asked as she trailed after him, nearly stumbling as they stepped onto the moving treads. His hand tightened on her, again offering her balance.

"I think she's up here," he said, cocking his head as if to home in on a faint sound.

She? Mina paused, her first thought that he must be sensing one of his women. The idea doused her pleasure at the ferris wheel ride like a splash of icy water on a newly lit flame. But she didn't pull away from him. Maybe she needed to see this reunion to remind herself why she should fear him.

He led her past the Empire State building created out of interlocked small plastic blocks. Then toward a pink façade that looked like a dollhouse. He kept going until he reached an aisle lined with different dolls, all with hourglass figures and catlike eyes.

Mina glanced around, expecting a live woman who matched these dolls to turn the corner and exclaim, "Sebastian!"

But instead she heard a small noise. A soft sniffling.

Sebastian dropped her hand and walked toward the end of the aisle. Curious, she followed.

In among the boxes with pink and purple castles pictured on the fronts, a small girl huddled, clutching a ratty-looking stuffed animal, her chubby cheeks blotchy from crying.

Sebastian approached the girl, slowly. Then he crouched so that he was eye level with her.

"Hi there," he said softly. "Are you lost?"

The little girl clutched her animal tighter, refusing to look at him.

"It's okay," Sebastian assured her. "We'll help you find your mommy."

At the word mommy, the little girl's face crumpled and more tears rolled down her face.

"Shh," Sebastian soothed, then held out a hand. "Come on, Mina and I will help you find her."

The little girl still hesitated, but finally she blinked up at Sebastian, and Mina saw large cornflower blue eyes. The child couldn't be any more than three or four.

When the girl saw Sebastian, she blinked again. Then she slipped her hand into his, her chubby baby fingers looking impossibly tiny against his broad palm.

Sebastian rose and helped the girl stand. When he turned and saw Mina's stricken look, he offered her an encouraging smile. "Don't worry. We'll find your mother."

Mina knew that reassurance was for her as much as for the child.

They walked down the aisle, back toward the open space at the entrance of the dollhouse façade.

"What's your mommy's name?" Sebastian asked the girl.

"Mommy," she said, in a soft, quavering voice.

Sebastian smiled at Mina. "Of course. Silly me."

Mina watched as Sebastian knelt again. "What's your name?"

"Ananda."

Sebastian paused. "Amanda?"

The girl nodded. Mina noticed that the girl was now watching Sebastian with wide, awed eyes as if she was looking at a fairy godfather or an angel.

"Hi, Amanda. I'm Sebastian, and this is Mina. Can you tell me what your mommy looks like?"

"Like me," she said, "only big."

Sebastian laughed at that. "Okay, so we'll just look for the second prettiest girl in the store."

Mina smiled as the girl stared at him, not sure what he meant, but then she smiled shyly. It seemed no one was immune to his charm.

Sebastian rose, and they headed toward the escalator. "Let's go see if they can page your mother."

But before they even reached the escalators, a blond woman with an older boy in tow came bustling toward them.

"Amanda!"

The little girl squealed, "Mommy," and pulled her hand out of Sebastian's, running to the woman. The woman scooped up her child, her relief reaching Mina, making her take a sigh of relief too.

Amanda explained to her mother who Sebastian was, not even remembering Mina. But then Sebastian had been her hero. The mother thanked them, and Mina noticed that mother, like daughter, seemed enchanted by Sebastian.

But, as much as she didn't want to admit it, so was Mina.

On the walk back to her apartment, both Mina and Sebastian were quiet. Occasionally, Sebastian would comment about something, the weather, something in a shop window, but then he'd fall silent again.

"Are you all right?" he finally asked, when they reached the outside stoop, which led up to the green front door of her apartment building.

She nodded, but then she admitted, "I don't know."

"What don't you know?" He tilted his head, trying to catch her gaze, but she continued to stare at a wad of chewing gum flattened onto the pavement.

"You confused me," she admitted, still not meeting his gaze.

"Me?" he said, sounding surprised. "Hell, I'm easy to figure out."

"No, you're not," she said, looking up at him.

"Well, what's confusing you?"

"Why you helped that little girl."

He laughed. "That's easy. She was lost and scared and needed help."

Mina bit her lip, considering whether she should ask her next question. Finally she decided she had to ask. "You didn't do it to impress me? You know—to make me think you are nice?"

Sebastian's smile faded, and his golden eyes grew cool, the fire in them extinguishing.

"To make you think I'm nice," he murmured. "I guess that would be the only possible reason, wouldn't it?"

He didn't say another word. He simply turned and walked down the street away from her. Even though she wanted to call him back, she just let him go. Maybe it was for the best if he left and never saw her again. Before she decided to think he was one of the nicest guys she'd ever met.

Chapter 13

Sebastian stormed into Rhys and Jane's apartment, barely acknowledging his brother, who leaned on the kitchen counter, as he strode to the refrigerator, whipping the door open.

Out of the corner of his eyes, he did see Rhys raise an eyebrow and set down the mug he was holding.

"Good morning."

Sebastian grunted, staring into the white interior of the fridge.

"Can I help you find something?" Rhys asked, his tone blasé, even though Sebastian knew he must be curious about his abrupt behavior.

"I'm looking for some of that crap that you and Jane drink."

Rhys moved to peer into the fridge over Sebastian's shoulder. The only items on the shelves were several clear bags filled with blood. And an old bottle of mustard—still hanging around from Jane's mortal days.

"Hmm," Rhys said, pretending to ponder Sebastian's gruff request. "Well, good luck finding that."

Sebastian fought back a sneer as he snatched one of the bags and brushed past Rhys to get to the counter. He opened the cupboard and pulled out a mug. He started to open that bag, then paused, turning to his brother.

"Do you think I'm nice?"

Rhys frowned. "Excuse me?"

"Nice. You know. Do you think I am?"

"At this moment? Or in general? Because at the moment, you're coming across more deranged than nice."

Sebastian glared at his brother. Okay, he did know that he had just barged into his place. He knew that the shirt he'd thrown on was wrinkled—he glanced down—and misbuttoned. He knew that his hair was sticking out in a fair impression of Einstein's, but he was thoroughly incensed. He'd been livid when he got home last night, and he hadn't risen feeling any better.

"Did you know that I'm on the list of the most dangerous vampires in New York City?" Sebastian pointed at himself. "I am the third most dangerous vampire in this whole city."

Rhys raised an eyebrow again, although he didn't look like he knew whether to be impressed or shocked. "Really?"

"Yes," Sebastian said, turning back to the bag of dark red liquid, popping the stopper with more force than necessary. "Apparently some group called the Society of Preternaturals Against the Mistreatment of Mortals—do you know this group?" He turned a suspicious eye to Rhys. "Are you a part of it?"

Rhys gave him an exaggeratedly wounded look. "Sebastian, dear brother, don't you think if I was affiliated with the Society, I'd have made sure you were the Number One most dangerous vampire in the city?"

"Ha-ha," Sebastian said, scowling down at the mug as he poured himself a full cup of the cold blood.

"I do know of the Society," Rhys said, all humor gone from his voice. "They are an extremist group, who branched off from Dr. Fowler's teachings."

"Yes, I know that." Sebastian took a drink of cold liquid. He made a disgusted noise and set the mug aside.

"They're pretty out there," Rhys added.

"I know that too."

"So how did you learn all this? I wouldn't expect you to even pay attention to this sort of stuff." Then realization lit Rhys's eyes. "That vampiress who tried to sabotage the club was a member of the Society."

Sebastian nodded, picking up the cup again, taking another sip. "Yep."

"Shit."

"Yep."

Both brothers were silent, lost in their own thoughts about the whole thing, when Rhys asked, "What does this have to do with being nice, though?"

Sebastian stared at his brother. "I went to confront Mina."

"Mina?"

"Wilhelmina. The saboteur."

Rhys nodded, waiting for Sebastian to continue. When he didn't, Rhys said, his voice more than a little confused, "And she said you weren't nice?"

"Well, not so straightforwardly. But yes."

Rhys stared at him for a moment. "And her opinion bothers you why?"

"Exactly!" Sebastian exclaimed, banging his mug onto the counter.

Rhys's eyes flashed to the mug, probably expecting it to be broken, then back to Sebastian. "I'm really, really not following this."

How could he not follow?

"I went to confront Mina, and I made a deal with her that I'd not bite any humans for a month, but in exchange, she would have to allow me to show her how great it is to be a vampire. Because frankly, I'm so sick and tired of being surrounded by self-pitying undeads. No offense."

Rhys shrugged. "None taken."

"So last night, we went out. I thought it was going pretty well. She seemed to be enjoying her vampire nature. Hell, she even smiled. And then . . ." Sebastian found, as he had with their first kiss, he didn't really want to share the details with

Rhys. Strange, since he was usually prone to sharing more about his women than Rhys would ever want to know.

"Well, let's just say it didn't end like I thought it would."

"Okay," Rhys said, still looking perplexed. "So it didn't work. How can you be that surprised? She's a follower of the Society. She was willing to try and ruin your club. Why should you care about her opinion?"

"It—it doesn't matter. Forget about Mina." He straightened and tucked his shirt into his jeans. He smoothed down the wrinkles and ran a hand through his unruly hair. "I'm going down to my club and I'm biting seven—no, eight—women and each one will be even more beautiful than the last. And then, I'm going to bite one more, even sexier woman. Just because I can, dammit."

Sebastian picked up the mug and polished off the rest of the blood.

"That sounds good," Rhys said after he was done. "I just have one question for you?"

"What?"

"If the bargain is off, then why are you still drinking cold blood, which you absolutely hate?"

Sebastian stared at his brother, then set the cup on the marble counter, shoving it away from himself. He left the apartment without speaking to Rhys, slamming the door behind him.

Jane entered the kitchen, her hair damp from her shower. "I thought I heard Sebastian?"

Rhys stared at the door where his brother had just exited. "You did."

Jane frowned at her husband, who looked a tad bemused.

"What's wrong?" she asked, moving to wrap her arms around his waist, rubbing her hand over the hard muscles of his abdomen.

Rhys looked down at her, his amber eyes still a little dazed, but he smiled. "I think my little brother has finally met his match."

* * *

Mina curled her legs up onto the sofa and tried to concentrate on the book she was reading. *Persuasion* by Jane Austen. She read one page at least half a dozen times, but the words didn't seem to make any sense to her, or they simply blurred as her mind drifted.

Giving up, she dropped the dog-eared paperback onto the cushion beside her and wandered to the kitchen. She considered pouring herself a glass of her protein drink, but she decided against it. She'd drunk three glasses already. Apparently, vampires ate when they were bored too.

She wasn't bored, exactly, she told herself. She was restless and twitchy and . . . lonely.

She paused at the thought. She was never lonely. She preferred her solitude. After all, that was easier than being around others and seeing over and over that she was nothing like them. Nothing like humans. And not like vampires. She'd had years to become accustomed to being alone. And alone, she was just Mina.

Mina? When had she come to think of herself by that silly name? Mina. She wasn't Mina. She was . . .

Mina. She thought about the way the name sounded when said in Sebastian's deep, rich voice. A voice like the brush of dark, warm silk on her skin.

She shivered. Stop it, Mi—Wilhelmina. Stop. Sebastian was gone, for good, and it was for the best.

She walked back to the sofa, flopping down on the soft cushions. What was he doing right now? She closed her eyes, not really wanting to think about it.

He was probably surrounded by a gaggle of beautiful women, each vying for one of his charming smiles. For the touch of his hand. His lips.

Her eyes popped open. She couldn't keep thinking about him. Okay, she did like him. She did have fun with him. She did sort of . . . miss him, which was stupid since she barely knew him, really. But she needed to stop this nonsense now!

A sharp rap rattled the door. Her head shot up, a rush of excitement making her stomach swoop. Sebastian! But as she rushed to the door, she told herself she was being an absolute ninny. He wouldn't be back. And even if it were him, which it wasn't, what did she expect to happen. Friendship? Some torrid fling? Love?

Her hand hesitated on the doorknob, and a startled laugh escaped her. Love? She really was going mad. Love? Really.

To prove to herself that her overactive mind was just getting out of control, she called, "Lizzie? Did you lose your key again?"

She swung the door open to find Sebastian. He stood there, looking very disheveled and absolutely dazzling.

"It's not Lizzie," he said coolly. "And I think we both know that losing the key wouldn't keep me out."

Mina stepped back, stunned by the angry sparks flashing in his eyes. She knew he'd been mad last night, but there was more rage on his face now than she'd ever seen.

She considered closing the door, her flight impulse telling her that was the wisest course of action. But he had just said he didn't need a key to enter her apartment, so she couldn't keep him out if he was intent on getting inside.

And there was also another part of her, a small, tenuous part of her that was beginning to believe, despite his apparent anger, Sebastian would never hurt her. He'd never threatened her since they met, even after everything she'd done to him.

So she took a deep, calming breath and pushed her fear aside.

"Please, come in."

He strode into the apartment, stopping in the middle of the living room and then turning to look at her.

Mina calmly closed the door. She hesitated, but then took a couple of cautious steps toward him.

"Let's get this straight, right off the bat," he said, his tone hard, no hint of his usual smooth, silky resonance. "I didn't help that little girl for any other reasons than the ones I told you."

Mina opened her mouth to speak, but Sebastian continued on. "I realize that you have been brainwashed or whatever by the Society, but I refuse to allow myself to be vilified by a group of crazy preternaturals who actually thought that an organization with the anagram SPAMM was a good idea."

Mina frowned. She'd never noticed that before.

"And," Sebastian said, "I agreed to this bargain with you, and I'll be damned if I'm backing out of it. Because that is exactly what you expect me to do. You don't believe I can go a month without biting a human. And I intend to prove you wrong. But if I'm keeping my end of this damned bargain, so are you."

She nodded, but he didn't notice.

"And I'm also not going along with your stupid rules. I flirt, that's what I do. And as far as I know that isn't a crime against humanity."

"No, it's not," she agreed, but he didn't seem to hear.

"And this rule about touching is ludicrous. If I touch you and it bothers you, then just tell me. I can certainly stop, it's not like I'm some uncontrollable monster who's going to ravish you against your consent . . ."

The rest of Sebastian's words faded away as his face was replaced by another. Dark hair, dark eyes, and a wide smile that suddenly twisted and distorted.

Mina made a tiny noise in the back of her throat, then blinked, her eyes refocusing on Sebastian. Tall, lean Sebastian with his unruly golden hair, his golden eyes, and lopsided smile.

Not that Mina could see the last attribute at the moment, because he continued to rail on, his golden eyes darker in his anger.

Suddenly Mina could feel laughter bubbling in her belly. He was mad. As mad as she'd ever seen him, and really she wasn't scared.

She was scared of the things he made her feel. She was scared to open up to someone like him. But that was her own problem. Her own issue to overcome. She believed him when he said he'd never do anything against her consent. That didn't make her own fears any easier to overcome, but it did mean that she owed him an apology. Maybe for a lot of things.

She walked toward him.

"I've never forced a woman, and I sure as hell wouldn't start—"

"I'm sorry," she said, touching his arm. "I shouldn't have asked that question last night. Not after the wonderful things you showed me."

He stared down at her, his eyes roaming her face. Then slowly that smile she'd been imagining returned, lopsided and lovely.

"You're forgiven."

She blinked at the sudden shift in his mood, not sure what to say. He'd been very angry, and though she honestly had no experience with the moods of men outside of her father and her brother and they'd been gone from her life for nearly a hundred years, she hadn't expected him to forgive her so easily.

"Great," he said. "Now go get dressed. Not that I don't really like those."

She looked down at the pale turquoise silk pajamas that she'd forgotten she was wearing until he pointed to them. The pajamas were cut in a baggy men's style, but suddenly she was very aware that she was naked underneath the smooth, fluttery material.

She nodded and hurried down the hall to get away from the hungry glow in Sebastian's eyes. And she knew the small jolt of fear inside her was not due to his look, but the fact that she liked it.

Sebastian watched her dash toward her bedroom.

Well, that had gone better than he'd expected. He'd expected her to either shut down or run away as she had during their other confrontations. But she hadn't. She'd reached out to him. Touching him, apologizing. Huge, huge steps. And he'd sensed very little fear in her. That realization made him ridiculously happy.

He sighed, relieved that his angry outburst hadn't frightened her. He hated to lose his temper. Anger was emotionally draining, not particularly fun, and usually unproductive. And frankly, he'd lost his cool more in the time he'd known Mina than in most of his undead existence. And with Mina, getting angry could have been the end of any possible trust. She wanted to believe the worst about him, yet she hadn't.

He had to be making headway with her. She couldn't truly believe he was an ogre and agree to continue the bargain. All progress. Maybe she was starting to trust him. Again happiness zipped though him, and he smiled.

Then he thought about the way she'd looked in those silky pajamas, the way the material clung to her breasts, casting them in a mellow glow. The V of the collar revealing a modest little glimpse of milky skin.

He collapsed into a chair, shaking his head slightly at his body's immediate reaction to the mere memory. The women at the club often wore the equivalent of skimpy lingerie, and he'd never found any of those outfits as exciting as Mina's modest pajamas.

He wanted her. He wanted to follow her into her bedroom, throw her down on the bed and make love to her for hours. But he also knew he couldn't rush Mina. He knew she wasn't ready for too much from him, too fast.

He'd never been a patient man, but he'd be patient for Mina. Right now, he was just pleased that she was sticking with their deal.

A few moments later, Mina rejoined him. Tonight she wore a blue tailored shirt a few shades lighter than her eyes, and a black skirt with blue flowers the exact color of her shirt. She looked prim and proper and Sebastian thought his cock would burst through the seams of his jeans at the sight of her.

Patience, buddy.

His cock leapt in response, the organ as insubordinate as ever. Sebastian ignored it as he stood and ran his palms over the front of his jeans, hoping the action would pull the snug denim away from the rather prominent bulge. He didn't look down to see if his tactic worked, afraid she'd follow his gaze.

Instead he smiled at her and held out his hand. "Are you ready?"

She nibbled her bottom lip, then nodded. She slipped her small, cool hand into his, and his chest tightened as though he'd made the biggest conquest of his life.

Chapter 14

"Where are we going?" Mina asked as they slid into the backseat of a taxi.

"To LaGuardia," Sebastian leaned forward to tell the driver.

Mina frowned at him. "The airport?"

He nodded, a mischievous smile on his lips.

"Why?" she asked.

"I really think you should just learn to trust me." His smile remained roguish as he settled back against the vinyl seat.

Trust him. He kept saying that to her as if it was the easiest thing in the world to do. She supposed for some people it was. But trust hadn't been a part of her makeup for so long, she didn't know if she even could. Absolute trust—without any doubts.

Still, she felt herself lean back into the seat. She glanced at Sebastian. He was watching her, and she immediately turned her attention to the window, although she didn't see the city going by. She was still debating trust—and why of all the beings in the world, she wished she could trust this one.

Mina waited on the curb as Sebastian paid the fare. At this time of night, the airport wasn't bustling like it must have been during the day, but there were still plenty of people milling about. Some struggled with heavy suitcases. Others rifled through their bags for tickets and IDs and other misplaced items; and there were those who walked resolutely, eager to be already at their final destination, wheeling small bags with long handles behind them.

"Okay," Sebastian said, appearing at her side. "Ready?"

He held out his hand. She looked at it for just a moment, then slipped her hand into his. Holding hands with this man was becoming almost second nature to her. Almost.

"You're still not going to tell me what we're doing here, are you?"

"Nope."

She walked through the sliding glass doors, to see roped-off sections creating queues in front of the airline desks. People waited there, more luggage and harried expressions. The air seemed to crackle with tension. Excitement, nervousness, irritation.

"It's just as intense, but it feels totally different than the toy store, doesn't it?"

Mina blinked up at him, surprised he was so aware of what she was thinking. "Yes. Not nearly as nice, really."

"Wait," he assured her. They walked down the wide corridor until they reached a bank of hard-looking, molded plastic chairs. Sebastian led her to them and gestured for her to sit.

She frowned, but did. He sat too, his long leg pressed against the side of hers. She glanced down at where their bodies met, surprised at how much she reacted to the innocuous touch. She could feel the contact in every nerve ending, every cell of her body.

Was *this* what he wanted them to do here?

She moved her gaze from their legs to his face. He didn't seem to notice the touch, his attention turned to the travelers.

Mina smiled slightly to herself. He wouldn't notice something as tame as their legs touching. After all, the first time she'd ever seen him, he'd been running his hands all over a woman on the dance floor. His hands all over her body. She wondered what that would feel like if just the pressure of his leg sent her body into sensory overload.

She glanced at his hands, resting relaxed on his legs. He

even had beautiful hands, broad palms, the knuckles slightly pronounced and long, masculine fingers.

He sighed, and her gaze snapped back to his face.

"We might have to wait a little while."

"For what?" she managed to collect her thoughts to ask, but before he could respond, she answered for him. "I know, I know, I'll see."

He laughed, his wonderful laugh tingling over her. Did nothing this man did not affect her?

"You're catching on," he said.

"I don't think I've had a choice."

He laughed again. "Oh, you always have a choice. But I think you like the mystery."

Mina looked at him askance, but had to admit she did rather like the mystery. She never would have guessed that about herself. And the spontaneity. Sebastian was a person who just did what he wanted, because he wanted to. That was exciting, even if it was also a little scary too.

"If you could go anywhere in the world, where would it be?"

Mina blinked at the sudden question. Even the man's conversational skills were spontaneous.

"I—I don't know," she admitted. She'd never really thought about traveling, at least not since she crossed over. She couldn't very well get on a crowded plane or train. Between the people and the twelve hours or more of pesky sunlight, travel just hadn't seemed a possibility.

"Do you travel?" she asked.

"Sure. I was just in West Virginia visiting my brother, Christian, when I got called back because of . . ." He paused. "Well, you know why."

Mina nodded, not quite able to meet his eyes.

"But," he continued, "I've been to just about every country."

"Really? How?"

"It is a little tricky," he admitted. "Night flights, and you have to pray for no delays or layovers. Sometimes I just travel in my coffin in the cargo holds of ships surrounded by crates of soil from my homeland."

Mina gaped at him.

"A joke. You know, Dracula."

She nodded, looking away so he wouldn't see she actually appreciated his dumb humor.

"Is that why you call me Mina? Because of Dracula?" she asked suddenly.

Sebastian nodded. "In part."

She considered pressing him further, but she wasn't sure she wanted to hear that it was some sort of joke or something. Instead she asked, "Isn't it dangerous—traveling?"

"Sure. But that's part of the fun."

She gave him a dubious look, and he laughed.

"Really. It is."

"I'll take your word for it."

Sebastian shifted in his seat. Mina could seem to feel the ripple of muscles through the denim of his jeans.

"If you did feel like you could travel, where would you want to go?"

He leaned toward her, and she realized he had the amazing ability to make a person feel like their responses were very important. She felt warm for a moment, then she remembered she'd been conned by a similar behavior once before—and the high cost of that con.

"Come on tell me," he encouraged, his gaze still intent.

What would it hurt to answer him? She was wiser now, and this was just harmless conversation. She thought about his question, for the first time in a long time allowing herself to think about the dreams of her childhood.

"Well," she gave him a cautious look, wondering if he'd find her choices rather predictable and dull. "I'd love to go to London and Paris."

Sebastian studied her for a moment, then reached out to cup her cheek, running his thumb along her cheekbone just beneath her glasses' frame.

"Why would you be embarrassed by that?"

Mina's lips parted, finding it hard to concentrate on his question when he was touching her so gently. "Because they aren't as exotic and mysterious as other places."

"Well, you've never seen Soho after dark. Very exotic. Of course, the mystery aspect comes from whether the women on the streets are in fact women or men."

Mina frowned, not quite following what he was saying. But she was growing rather accustomed to that.

"So you've been to London?" she asked.

Sebastian laughed at that. "I'm British. Was British, I guess. I'm not sure how that works if you haven't lived there for over a hundred years."

Mina smiled. "Well, your accent is gone."

"Is it now, mum?" he said, slipping into an exaggerated English accent. "Blimey, I do believe you are right."

He sounded like a bad impression of the Artful Dodger.

Mina laughed, and Sebastian's smile faded.

"You have a lovely laugh." His thumb traced the curve of her smile. "You should do it more often."

Mina's smile faded too, and her gaze dropped to Sebastian's lips.

He leaned forward again, that same intensity in his expression. As though she was very important to him.

As if having a will of their own, her lips parted in expectation. But just as his lips would press to hers, he pulled back, dropping his hand from her cheek.

"Umm." He frowned as if he was trying to remember something he'd forgotten. "So yeah, I grew up in England, mostly on our estate in Derbyshire. But we'd go to London for the season. We had a townhouse there. Still do actually. Not the same one, though."

Mina suppressed the strange unsatisfied feeling swirling low in her belly, intrigued by what he was saying. "You must be old."

He grinned at her question. "Why? Do I look aged?"

A flush heated her normally cool skin, and she looked down to smooth her skirt. "You know you don't."

His grin widened more, and she knew he was pleased with her flustered embarrassment and almost-compliment—after all he was a vampire. She glanced quickly at him. Although he did look better than any vampire she'd ever seen. Of course, he knew that.

"I'm two hundred and ten years old. Born in 1796."

Her eyes widened. "You lived during the Regency in England," she murmured.

She knew many vampires in the Society who were older, much older, but she found it fascinating to meet a person who actually lived through the time period she loved so much.

"Your favorite." He smiled, and she started to ask him how he knew, but then she remembered he'd looked around her apartment. She had so many books from and about that era, and he must have seen them. The idea unnerved her. It was like he'd gotten this deeply personal insight into her, and she had none of him.

"I met Jane Austen once. At a house party in Cheltenham."

Mina gaped at him, the uneasiness instantly forgotten. "Really? What was it like?"

His perfect brow furrowed as he tried to remember. How could he forget something so monumental?

"As I recall, the house party was quite dull. Bad punch."

Before she realized what she was going to do, she smacked his leg. "Not the house party. Jane Austen!"

He laughed, and she realized he'd known what she meant all along. "She was interesting—she was older than I. In her late thirties. A lot more interesting than many of the other women there. Very perceptive and funny. And she did a mean quadrille."

Mina stared at him. She imagined him in a crowded ballroom, twirling *the* Jane Austen around in his arms, talking and laughing.

Suddenly, she felt envious, and she wasn't sure if it was because he'd met and talked to Jane, or that Jane had gotten to see him in his Regency finery, got to dance with him and enjoy his appreciation.

She looked away from him and studied her skirt again. Had he done more with Jane than dance and talk? Even with the propriety of the time and the differences in their ages, would Jane have been capable of saying no to him? Had she thought she'd met the embodiment of her Mr. Darcy? No, no, her Mr. Wickham—lovely and flirtatious but also dangerous.

"So tell me about you. You're just a baby by our standards."

She frowned. She supposed she was, although she often felt ancient.

"Have you always lived in New York?"

She nodded. "Yes, for the majority of my—life. My father was the founder of Weiss Steel."

Sebastian's golden eyes widened. "Wow—one of the Gilded Age's industrial moguls."

She nodded. The Gilded Age. She always found that rather amusing. Gilded cage maybe. Of course, she should have stayed in her cage, shouldn't she? There were much worse cages than gilded ones. Far, far worse.

"You must have hobnobbed with the rich and famous of your time then."

She shrugged. "No one as interesting as Ms. Austen."

"So how is it that a woman who had to be heir to one of the largest fortunes in the United States is living in a tiny apartment on the East End? Surely you were able to do something to ensure you got some of that money?"

Mina fiddled with her skirt. She didn't want to talk about her family—or why she now lived on a modest sum that she'd inherited when she'd turned twenty-one and managed to maintain through investments. Well, modest when compared to the billions her father's company had earned.

"I'm sorry," he said as soon as he realized she didn't plan to do anything but intently trace the pattern of her skirt. "Maybe we should get back to why we're here."

She nodded, still unsure of why they were here. But anything had to be better than talking about the family who'd betrayed her.

Sebastian cast a gaze around the room and stopped on an older couple, standing not far from them.

He subtly gestured to the couple. "Concentrate on them."

Mina did, focusing on their emotions, feeling excitement, happiness, a little nervousness.

"Can you feel them?"

She nodded. A few travelers passed the older couple and their emotions jumbled, making it hard to focus on anything. In a much smaller scale then in Times Square, but still confusing.

"Focus," Sebastian said with his uncanny ability to sense what she was thinking.

"It's getting confusing," she admitted as a large group spurred on by anxiety and tension rushed past.

"Use your focal point. Center on something else until you can get control again."

She pressed her leg tighter to Sebastian, concentrating on the feeling of him next to her. The jumbled emotions like several necklaces knotted together began to untangle until each emotion was one delicate and fragile chain.

She laughed, a small surprised sound. "It worked."

"Good job," Sebastian said, sounding truly pleased with her. "Now, can you get distinct emotions? Each one separate from the other?"

"Yes," she said, amazed, feeling every emotion crystal clear, strong and distinct from each other. Human emotion always had hit her like too much noise, no sound distinct from another. Even last night, the emotions had been lovely and manageable, but it was like listening to a symphony. Now it was like hearing the violin and then the flute.

"The man is more," she focused, "apprehensive than the woman."

Sebastian gave her a pleased look. "Yeah."

"And the woman is—really excited."

"Yes." Sebastian waited for her to continue.

Mina grinned at him. "How am I doing that?"

Sebastian stared at her, that gorgeous grin as disorienting to him as the emotions had been to Mina. Just the simple curve of a mouth, but truly the most awe-inspiring thing he could recall ever seeing.

"You are learning to control naturally your ability to block emotions, and just focus on one thing at a time. Eventually you will be able to tune them out completely if you want."

Mina looked back to the older couple, then she laughed. One of her small, barely there laughs. "Now that I'm not overwhelmed, I find I don't want to block them."

"It can be fun," he agreed, focusing on her. Her happiness. Her pride.

"It is a bit like eavesdropping though, isn't it?" she said, feeling a twinge of guilt.

Sebastian shrugged. "Maybe a little, but we can't really read minds—despite what Hollywood would lead the masses to believe."

Mina turned to find Sebastian. She wondered about that. He seemed to read her mind, and she wished she could read his right at the moment. She couldn't even read his emotions.

"Why can't I read your emotions?" she asked, realizing she'd never been able to perceive any of his feelings, except via the normal methods. His expression, his tone of voice.

"I can mask mine. You will be able to do that too, as you practice."

She nodded, wanting to ask him why he felt the need to mask his, but then she wasn't sure she wanted the answer.

"Okay. Try him." Sebastian gestured to a man in a gray business suit, carrying a briefcase and with a cell phone at his ear.

Mina concentrated, then she frowned. "Anger. Impatience. Frustration."

Sebastian whistled lowly. "He's like my brother before he met Jane."

She frowned at Sebastian. "Your brother was like that?"

"Add some self-derision and general angst, and that was Rhys. Until Jane. Thank God for the miracles of true love."

Mina studied Sebastian, who still watched the passersby. Again, she was surprised at his easy acceptance of an idea like true love. The vampire who had a different woman for every night of the week. It just seemed strange to her.

She joined him watching the travelers. A young man, maybe in his early twenties, strode toward them—his tall figure covered in worn fatigues, his expression very serious, almost grim. Mina nearly skipped over him, searching for more of the happy travelers. Then a woman, also in her twenties, came running toward him, and suddenly the corridor seemed to explode with vivid, breath-stealing emotion. Elation, relief, and love.

Mina couldn't look away. She watched, rapt, as the man dropped his bag and caught the woman as she launched herself at him. They hugged, laughing. Then they were kissing. Their mouths trying to devour each other.

Mina nearly gasped as desire, intense and urgent, hit her. A living, breathing thing pulsating in the air around them. Their mouths molded together, their hands moving over each other. Desperation in their touch. A desperation that was satisfying just in its existence. The wonderful freedom to want.

She wanted to experience that, Mina realized. Her body ached for that kind of openness, for that lack of restraint. She glanced at Sebastian, expecting him to be watching them too. They were impossible to ignore.

He wasn't. He was watching her. Their eyes met, his eyes darker, the color of ancient amber.

Suddenly the desire swirling around them wasn't the soldier's and his girl's. It was Mina's desire, hot and achy and desperate for Sebastian. Her gaze fell to his lips, and she realized she wanted that kind of passion, that lack of restraint, for herself, not as an eavesdropper.

Chapter 15

Sebastian saw the dazed yearning in Mina's eyes. He felt her longing pulsing around him. He breathed in shallowly, her desire an intense pulsation on his skin. What would it be like to feel her body pulsating around him? His cock buried deep inside her.

No, he warned himself. Her reaction was being affected by the reunited couple. He had to keep his head, and go slow. His gut told him Mina wasn't ready. After all, not even three days ago she thought he was evil incarnate.

Although she did seem to be over that opinion. She was looking at him with pure desire burning in her dark blue eyes. But beyond that desire, buried deep in her need was a hint of wariness. He could feel it, even if he couldn't see it.

Go slow.

"Sebastian," she murmured, her voice breathy. "I—I want . . ."

His body reacted instantly to her unsure words. His cock straining against his jeans, his muscles coiling with the need to touch her.

She doesn't even know how to ask you for what she wants, his mind warned him.

"Mina," he tried to keep his voice steady, his thoughts clear and rational, "I don't think—"

Her small hand came out and caressed him, tracing the shape of his jaw, her fingertips brushing over his lips.

A growl escaped him at the deliciousness of her shy exploration. Before his mind could even register what his body intended to do, he caught the hand touching him and pulled her up from the bench. He started down the corridor, not sure what he planned, just knowing that he needed to get Mina to a private place. Even a semiprivate place. Hell, who was he kidding? He was ready to set her on the belt to the X-ray machine and take her right there.

Fortunately, he spotted bathrooms before he was forced to take that option.

He tugged her toward the one marked "Family." He prayed as he turned the handle that it was unoccupied and that it was a single bathroom. He lucked out on both counts. The room was empty with one toilet, a plastic changing table mounted to the wall and a sink with a large counter.

Not the perfect place for seduction, but he'd gladly spend hours seducing her later. Right now, he just had to touch her, taste her.

As soon as the door was shut and locked, he pulled Mina against him, walking her backward until she was pinned between him and the wall.

She stiffened, staring up at him with wide eyes. Desire still burned there, but that glimmer of wariness that he'd felt earlier now showed in her eyes. A faint flash, gone as soon as he relaxed his hold and met her gaze.

Calm, he told himself, calm. Don't be so demanding, so impatient. Just touching her, he felt like an overeager schoolboy. Finesse, buddy. Finesse.

Her hands came up to touch his face, her palms pressed to his jaw. Her fingers brushing the hair at his temples. The simple, almost innocent, touch sent fire roaring through him. The hands that rested on the gentle swell of her hips flexed, desperate to press her roughly against the wall and bury himself to the hilt in her pale flesh.

Finesse, he reminded himself.

Then she rose up on her tiptoes and pressed her lips to his, tentative and a little awkward—and utterly perfect. And all rational thought fled. He was lost in sensation. The velvety softness of her lips, the sweet taste.

The hands touching his face, moving over the shape of his jawline as if she was trying to memorize his features.

He groaned, deepening the kiss. She opened for him, her lush lips parting to allow him to brush the texture of her mouth. The smoothness of the inside of her lips like raw silk. The sharp contrast of her tongue like roughened suede. The hardness of her teeth.

She whimpered, the small sound desperate.

He groaned in response, the hands on her hips moving up her sides, feeling the delicateness of her body, the narrowing of her waist, the rise and fall of her ribs, the weighted softness of the underside of her breasts.

A growl rumbled deep in his chest at the slight contact, his knuckles brushing the tempting fullness.

Damn, it was insane how much he wanted this woman.

Even as he told himself again to go slowly, he pinned her fully to the wall, trapping her with his body, feeling the softness of her curves crushed against him. Her breasts against his chest. His erection hard against the gentle swell of her belly.

She whimpered again, wriggling against him. Her fingers tightened on his face, and he tilted his head, kissing her as if he intended to devour her whole.

She squirmed, the movement rubbing his erection. His cock throbbed, a granite intensity in his pants.

Her fingers gripped his cheek, her fingertips curling into the vulnerable skin underneath his jaw. Even that pressure seemed to spur on his need. He slid a hand back down her side, finding the bottom of her shirt and slipping his fingers underneath. The skin of her waist and her stomach was as smooth as he imagined, cool and downy. His hand moved farther upward toward her breasts.

Another whimper escaped her, a slight vibration against his lips, and she moved her head back. He followed her, capturing her lips fully again, nipping her bottom lip. And still his hand moved upward.

She gasped as his hand cupped her breast through the cotton of her bra. Her nipple prodded his palm, taut and eager. He wanted to taste, feeling it rigid against his tongue. He released her mouth and moved to kiss the corner of her lips, her jaw, the spot just below her earlobe.

She stiffened. Her reaction registered in the back of his mind, but he didn't understand it. His lips pressed to her neck, his fingers gently squeezing her nipple. His only thought to kiss her breasts. He nipped the soft skin of her neck, imagining how smooth her breasts would be.

"No!" she cried, jerking from him, the hands on his face shoving so hard his head snapped back with dazing force.

Before he could recover from the sudden reaction, she'd darted away, across to the other side of the small bathroom.

He blinked, trying to focus. The jerk of his head hadn't been enough to really hurt him, but it had been disorienting. The whole thing was disorienting. One minute he was feeling tremendous need, the next he was receiving a shove that would have probably snapped a mortal's neck.

What the hell had just happened? He blinked again, and then he realized that the room was filled with fear, the air saturated with the emotion. Mina was terrified. Had his own desire been so strong that he'd missed that?

He turned to her. She waited in a corner of the room, watching him with wide, petrified eyes, although he noticed that she didn't seem to be seeing him. Her blue eyes were distant and dazed like she was looking straight through him.

"Mina," he said softly, afraid of what she might do if he startled her. He rotated his head just imagining.

She blinked, the faraway look disappearing as she met his eyes.

"I—" She shook her head as if she didn't know what to say.

"Did I hurt you?"

She shook her head, but her gaze dropped to the floor.

"What's going on, Mina?"

Mina closed her eyes, trying desperately to squelch the sick feeling inside her. The nausea and overwhelming fear that had blotted out and destroyed the wonderful sensations Sebastian had been creating inside her. And made her react like a crazy person. Not a feeling she wanted to feel, not now. Not with Sebastian.

Now that she was distanced from him, now that she was looking at his face, so beautiful—not cold or cruel, the fear was subsiding. But in its place was frustration and embarrassment.

She stared at him. He watched her with confusion and concern clear in his beautiful eyes.

"Why do you keep doing this?" she asked, not realizing she'd actually said the words out loud until they echoed off the tiled walls.

"Doing what?"

"Being so nice to me."

Sebastian gave her a sad little smile and shook his head. "You should really just accept that I am nice."

She studied him, his mussed hair, his lips reddened from their kisses, his sexy sleepy eyes. He didn't look nice. He looked sinfully beautiful, he looked dangerous. But she wasn't scared. Not of him.

"Come on, Mina," he said quietly, "talk to me."

She wanted to talk to him. To tell him what scared her. That she'd been sure he was going to bite her. That she was terrified of being bitten. She really did want to tell him.

Never had she wanted to share her past with anyone. Never. But she wanted to now. With this man. This vampire. The third most dangerous vampire in New York City. It was crazy. There was that word again.

But she couldn't make herself say the words. She'd learned long ago letting anyone inside gave them the power to hurt her. She couldn't do it. She wanted to, but she couldn't.

"I—I think I should go home."

She started toward the door, but Sebastian blocked her path. Blocked the door.

Immediately more panic rose in her. She looked around realizing she was trapped. If Sebastian decided he wanted her to stay in here, she couldn't stop him. He could do . . . anything.

"Sebastian. Please."

He shook his head. "You've got to tell me why you are so scared. Why you get scared every time I get too close."

She eyed the door, not able to think of anything but getting out of that small room.

"Mina."

She forced herself to meet his eyes. She saw concern there. Not malice.

"Sebastian," she managed to say, her voice sounding reedy to her. "I need you to let me out of here."

He looked confused.

"Please."

He frowned at her as if he wanted to object, or at least to say something else. But instead he nodded.

He unlocked the door and stepped back so she could exit, not attempting to touch her as she passed.

He never intended to hurt her, she realized as she looked around the airport corridor. He wasn't going to hurt her.

She glanced at him as they walked down the hall. He wasn't looking at her, but she could tell he was confused by her behavior. And she could hardly blame him. But she couldn't tell him. Not yet. Maybe never. She just didn't know.

They exited out into the warm night air. She pulled in another breath, and waited as Sebastian got them another cab. Soon they were speeding back to the city. Back to her safe little apartment, back to her books and her insulated little world.

Streets and lights and buildings flew past as they got into the city. Soon they were pulling up to her apartment building.

"Will you come tomorrow night?" she asked suddenly realizing she was afraid her strange behavior had driven him away forever. Afraid that he was thinking she was a lost cause.

He looked at her, his eyes vivid gold even in the dim light. "The deal's still on, right?"

She nodded.

"Then I told you, I'll be damned if I'm going to be the one to back out of it." He smiled, tempering his words.

She looked at him, and then smiled too.

"But I won't be able to meet you until after midnight or so," he said.

Because he was meeting someone else, she wanted to ask, but caught herself. What difference did that make? She had no say about his personal life. What they were doing was more like field trips. Educational outings.

She thought of their kiss and her bizarre reaction. This field trip had been a little more educational than either of them had expected. She felt like she'd somehow failed. Failed him. But more than that failed herself.

Sebastian strolled into the club, barely registering the greetings of patrons and employees as he approached the bar. He'd hated to leave Mina tonight. He wanted to understand what the hell had happened in the bathroom. He knew she would require him to go slowly. To give her time to trust him and realize he wasn't everything the Society had painted him to be. But now he thought her fear wasn't just related to the things the Society had told her. She had wanted him, he knew that. And then, in a flash, she'd been frightened. It wasn't just mere wariness. Mina had been absolutely terrified. Why?

"There you are," Nadine greeted him, yelling over a particularly bass-driven song.

"What's up?" he asked. Had something happened in the club that needed his attention?

"I could ask you the same thing. Where have you been?"

Sebastian frowned at her. "What do you mean? You know where I've been. Here."

"You haven't been *here*. And that's causing quite a stir."

Sebastian's frown deepened. "What do you mean? Why would that cause a stir?"

"Because none of us can remember a time when you haven't come by the club for three nights in a row unless you were out of town, of course. Where have you been?"

He stared at his bartender. Was she kidding? Why would anyone be talking about his not being at the club? He didn't go to the club every night. He sometimes . . . Well, he . . .

"I do other things besides hang out here," he stated. Just because he couldn't think of them at the moment, didn't mean he didn't.

"Mmm-hmm," she said, shaking her head. "Never. You never miss more than a night here and there."

Sebastian shrugged. "Well, I've just been busy."

"Who is she?" Nadine grinned.

"It's not like that."

"It's not a woman?"

Sebastian considered lying outright, but couldn't do it. "She's just a friend."

Nadine laughed, a husky, rich sound—and utterly grating. She nodded. "Yeah, sure."

"Why is that so hard to believe?"

"Because you don't spend several nights with a woman just to talk. We all know that."

"That's not true."

Nadine gave him a disbelieving look. "Okay, name a female that you just talk to."

"You."

She laughed. "Okay, outside of me."

He thought. He knew there had to be someone. He started to say Greta, but he'd slept with her. And frankly, he didn't really like talking to her that much. She wasn't the sharpest tool in the shed.

"Jane," he said, giving Nadine a smug look.

"Well, I should hope she's just a friend," Nadine stated. "You *are* a player, but I hope you aren't enough of a player to try and scam on your brother's woman."

She did have a point about that one too. He frowned as he tried to think of women who came to the bar that he just talked with—nothing physical.

"Okay, you keep thinking about that, and I'll get back to you." She pushed away from the bar and left to take a drink order.

Sebastian stared after her. He'd had female friends. Women with whom he enjoyed just conversing without anything physical. Mina wasn't his first.

Of course, he didn't want to just talk to her either. Although he did enjoy her company. A lot. And he wanted her to talk more than she did. She was different. He wanted—everything from her.

That realization made him pause, but he quickly pushed aside the directions of his thoughts. She was different, because he was essentially teaching her how to be a vampire. He hadn't crossed her over, but he was taking the role of initiator. And that was bound to make him feel differently about her. He was like her . . . father.

He grimaced. Okay, bad, *bad* analogy. He didn't want to be anything close to a father to her. He wanted . . .

He was done with this line of thought. Nadine was making more of his time away from the club than it merited. He didn't need to justify or even consider his actions. He was doing what he wanted to—just like he always did. See, further proof he wasn't acting any different.

But he decided he'd better leave before she grilled him more. He turned, but before he could even take a step toward the back exit of the club, a tall, very curvy redhead rushed up to him.

"Sebastian!"

Sebastian stared at the woman, trying to remember her name. He couldn't even come up with a "sounds like," so he just offered her a forced smile. "How are you?"

The redhead stopped just inches from him, and for the first time Sebastian could remember, he had the urge to step back from a gorgeous woman.

"I was sure you'd be here last night," the redhead told him, batting lashes thick with mascara. "I've never been here on a Friday night when you haven't been here."

Good Lord, was everyone making note of his whereabouts?

"Well, I've been rather busy lately."

"Really?" More batting of the lashes. Then she came closer to catch his arm, cuddling against him. Her ample breasts pressed to his upper arm. "With what?"

"Or with whom," Nadine said from behind him, and he nearly groaned. Great, she was back.

Sebastian shot a glare over his shoulder at the bartender.

"Seems Sebastian here has a steady woman in his life," Nadine informed the redhead.

The redhead gasped in disbelief.

Okay, apparently it wasn't believable he could have a female friend *or* a girlfriend. What did that mean? He could only have sex with women. He paused, realizing that was what everyone thought. Even the women he slept with. This was great.

Not to mention that three dates with Mina made her his steady. Everyone was a lunatic.

"You have a girlfriend?" More disbelief in the redhead's voice.

"Will you excuse me?" he asked, not waiting to hear the answer. He'd had enough of this conversation. And he didn't speculate on why, while his libido had been left very unsatisfied tonight, he hadn't told the willing redhead that Nadine was nuts. And that he was very available.

Chapter 16

"Wil, stop that."

Mina stopped midstep and looked at Lizzie. She didn't even need her roommate to clarify what *that* was. She'd been pacing for the last five minutes.

Lizzie didn't look up from the notes she was making on her research, but her brow was furrowed, more with concern than annoyance.

"Sorry," Mina murmured. She walked quietly over to the sofa, sitting down and picking up her book. She opened to the bookmark, sighed and started to read.

What was Sebastian doing? Was he at the club meeting with one of his many lovely mortals?

She sighed again.

No, she wasn't going to think like that. She had no reason to care. She and Sebastian had a deal, not a relationship.

Although they had kissed. Three times.

She sighed again, this time feeling weak at the memory of his lips to hers.

Three kisses. That didn't mean anything to a guy like Sebastian. And they only meant something to her because he was the only man she'd wanted to kiss in a hundred years—even though she was still scared.

She sighed again.

"Okay," Lizzie said, flipping her notebook closed. "What's wrong?"

Mina gave her friend a startled look. "Nothing. Just—antsy."

"I can tell. So what's bothering you?"

Mina could hardly tell her friend that she was fixating on whether Sebastian, aka Super-Fang, was with a mortal—and not because she was worried about the poor mortal, but because she was . . .

Jealous? She considered the sensation tightening her chest and making her feel like she couldn't bear to sit still. It sure felt like jealousy.

"I guess I'm just tired of sitting around," she said, deciding she couldn't tell her friend the truth. After all, she'd spent more than a few nights telling Lizzie that vampires like Sebastian had to be stopped. Lizzie had even plotted sabotages with her. She couldn't admit now that she was having doubts.

"Want to go to a movie? They are having a film festival in Soho. Old monster movies." Lizzie gave her an expectant look, and for a moment, Mina was reminded so much of Sebastian.

She shook her head slightly. Everything made her think of the man.

"Frankenstein, The Wolfman," Lizzie said. "And Dracula. Something for everybody."

Mina smiled. Sebastian would love those movies.

She paused. When had she started to think about her life in the context of what Sebastian would like?

"I think I'll pass," she said. "The Society is meeting in an hour or so. I think I'll go."

She needed to keep one foot in reality, she realized. She was getting too caught up in Sebastian's world. Even seeing monster movies without him seemed too much like Sebastian's world.

She also didn't want to admit this, but she could make the

Society meeting before she was supposed to meet Sebastian. Not that she was planning her life around him.

Sebastian fought the urge to tilt his head to look at the wristwatch of the woman sitting across from him. She was spreading out more plan ideas on the table. Different options for tables and chairs and how they could be arranged. Color schemes. Flooring options.

"So you could do something like this." Eve—or maybe it was Julie—he forgot now, even though he'd spoken to the woman several times in the past couple of months, pointed to a blueprint of the club.

Sebastian stared at the print, not even remotely following what . . . Julie? Yeah, it was Julie. Well, whoever she was, he wasn't following anything she was suggesting.

"You know," he said suddenly. "This is a lot of information. I think I could use a little break to digest everything. Would you like a drink?"

Julie smiled. She had a nice smile and very dark eyes. Dark brown, not dark blue.

"I'd love a club soda," she said.

Sebastian nodded, sliding out of the booth. He headed to the bar. It was Sunday night. Not a big evening for the club. Some diehard (no pun intended) patrons sat at the bar and milled around, but otherwise it was relatively quiet. Even David kept the music more sedate tonight. But the calm atmosphere was doing nothing to help the agitation inside himself. What was making him so restless tonight?

Nadine leaned on the bar. An uncommon occurrence. Rarely did Nadine and Ferdinand ever get a break.

"How's it going?" Nadine asked as he approached.

"Good," Sebastian said automatically, hoping she wasn't going to return to her topic of conversation the other night. He didn't want to discuss Mina with her.

Nadine gave him a searching look. "You don't seem very

enthused. I thought this woman was one of the best designers in New York?"

"The United States actually." He knew that, but he couldn't remember her name. He was a mess.

He'd waited a few months to get this appointment with the renowned designer. Julie Winchester, that was her name, had a very busy schedule and a waiting list. Not to mention that, being a vampire, he did have to ask her to come here at unusual times. Of course, enough money could get you any time appointment you wanted.

Sebastian had been willing to wait, though, which was rare for him. But she was the best. And he wanted the best for Carfax Abbey. And now, he wasn't even listening to her ideas. What was wrong with him?

He couldn't stop thinking about Mina. Their kiss. Why she pulled away, so frightened. What was she doing right now? Why hadn't he flat-out denied that she was his steady girl? He would have if Nadine had ever suggested that with his other women. Without hesitation.

This was absolutely nuts. Totally. He was going to see her in awhile. And Carfax Abbey was his love. He wouldn't have had any trouble admitting that too.

"I need a club soda and a double scotch on the rocks."

Nadine raised an eyebrow. "When do you drink while discussing business?"

"How do you know the scotch is for me?"

Nadine gave him a look that stated she wasn't a fool, but she grabbed a glass and turned to the back wall of liquors.

Sebastian leaned on the bar, surveying the club. He did love this place. He'd started it over ten years ago now. He loved the dark rich colors, deep red walls, red velvet upholstery, and ornate woodwork. Chandeliers, glittery and opulent. The large club looked like a goth bordello—a contrast he loved with the image of a true abbey. He liked the feel.

Maybe he didn't want to change the place. Maybe that was why he wasn't listening to the designer. There was nothing wrong with the club. It was more popular than ever. It wasn't showing any signs of its age. The place offered patrons a haven to have a good time in. Why mess with a good thing?

Nadine returned with the drinks. He nodded his thanks and headed back to the table where Julie sat, looking around the club with an artistic eye. Sebastian could see the excitement on her face as she thought about the changes she would make.

"This place is really great," she said as she accepted the soda water. "It has this great feel to it. I don't think I'd do that much to change it."

Sebastian was surprised by her comments, so much like his own thoughts.

She glanced around again. "I just think I'd add some more privacy to the booths. Maybe nice thick draperies, sectioning off between them. And I think the tables should be changed to a heavier wood. A nice solid feel. And the lighting now is dramatic, but I think it could be more subtle and make just as much of an impression. I'd like to give the club more sophistication and less flash."

Sebastian followed her gaze around the room. He supposed it did look a little . . . over the top.

Maybe he did need to change. Or rather the club needed a change.

The Society meeting was crowded again tonight. Mina slipped in just as Jackson Hallowell called the meeting to order. She took a seat toward the back of the room as she usually did, and waited for the president to announce the topics of the meeting.

"Tonight, I would like to hear from the 'Society's Saviors,' the new name for our missionaries as voted on by our board during last night's board meeting."

The Society's Saviors? Mina glanced around to see if anyone else found the title a little absurd. Only Jude reacted. He frowned, but then his face returned to its usual stoic expression, so Mina wasn't sure whether that was a reaction to the name or not. Everyone else just listened intently.

Mina turned her attention back to Jackson. Maybe she was being too critical. Maybe she was letting Sebastian's beliefs of the Society affect her feelings. Even though he'd said very little about them. Although the SPAMM thing was sort of funny.

"The Society's Saviors go out to the frontlines and try to stop the preternaturals before more mortals are hurt. Without these brave volunteers, we will never hope to be integrated into society. First, I'd like to ask Daniel to come up here."

Mina watched as the tall, thin vampire walked to the podium. As always, the vampire made her uneasy. Something about him just set off warning bells—and a strange sense that she should know why. But she didn't.

"Daniel, here," Jackson clapped the vampire on the back. Daniel's lip twitched slightly at the touch, but otherwise he remained unemotional. "Daniel has been brave and dedicated enough to the Society to take on the mission of stopping Franny Millhouse, the vampire whom we have deemed the most dangerous in New York."

Mina felt a smile tug at her mouth. She'd forgotten the most dangerous vampire was named Franny Millhouse. Not a very menacing name. Sebastian would be so upset that a "Franny" beat him for that Number One spot.

She paused, realizing that she was finding humor in something that could be very dangerous. Just because the vampire was named Franny didn't mean she couldn't be hurting humans.

"So Daniel, please tell us about your mission so far."

Daniel stepped up to the podium, not offering a smile to the group as he started.

"As you may recall, Franny Millhouse was chosen as the most dangerous vampire because she runs an escort service in which humans hire preternaturals."

Mina frowned. That sounded more like humans using preternaturals, not the other way around. Of course, they didn't know exactly what they were getting when they hired an escort. That could be very dangerous.

"I infiltrated her business as one of her employees."

Mina studied the thin, pale man. Did women actually hire him? She paused. That was unkind of her. She focused on his words rather than his looks.

"Once there, I found out how she handles situations like sexual contact between escorts and clients. As we suspected, sexual contact is not discouraged." His eyes glittered, and Mina got the impression the idea excited him.

The group began to murmur, obviously distressed by Daniel's announcement. She frowned. Maybe she was missing something here, but they didn't seem to be talking about biting. Wasn't biting the issue they were concerned about? Biting, using humans as food sources, hurting them. Biting and drinking their blood, those were the things that made them appear as monsters. Not sex. Humans had sex. Sex wouldn't stop them from being integrated.

Mina rose from her chair. "Excuse me."

The whole room seemed to turn in unison to look at her, and for a second she considered just sitting back down. But she knew she couldn't. She needed answers about this

"I . . ." She cleared her throat. "I thought that we were more concerned with whether she was using the escort service as essentially a take-out restaurant for her employees. Not about—other relations between humans and preternaturals."

Daniel's eyes narrowed then his eerie gaze slid down her body. She fought the urge to wrap her arms protectively around herself. A spine-chilling smile curled his thin lips. "Dearest Wilhelmina, you do know that those acts generally go hand in hand, don't you?"

Mina frowned. What was he implying? She shivered, her skin feeling like it was crawling to get away from his dark, disturbing stare.

"I agree," someone else said. "As preternatural creatures we all know those two acts are often hard to separate."

Mina looked at the speaker, a female vampire dressed a bit like a fortune-teller. Was that what Daniel had meant? That they all should know the dangers? Somehow, Mina felt he was implying that she'd have no basis to know that. But he couldn't know that.

"But do we know that's what's going on there?" Mina asked, directing the question to Jackson and Jude. "Have there been any reports of violence?"

"Indeed there have," Daniel answered instead, and again Mina felt there was a hint of glee in his announcement.

"Although," Jude added, "we haven't been able to verify if that was actually linked with the escort service. It was one of Ms. Millhouse's customers, but it was the night after she'd hired an escort."

Mina noticed Daniel shot Jude a disgusted look.

"Does Ms. Millhouse have any rules that her employees have to follow? Such as—intimate acts are okay, if initiated by humans. And is biting off-limits or is that encouraged too?" Mina asked.

Daniel raised his chin and didn't meet her gaze. "I don't know about that."

"You work for her, yet you don't know her rules?" Mina shook her head. "That doesn't sound right."

Daniel's gaze met hers. Sinister eyes. Unease pooled in her belly.

"Mina," Vedette, who sat several rows away from her, stood. "Why are you questioning this? We know she's a dangerous vampire. Anyone running a business such as hers must be."

Mina looked at Vedette, who frowned at her as if she was a wayward child who was speaking out of turn among the "adults." It was a look she remembered well from her own parents. And this time, she refused to cow to that scolding look.

"I just want to know that we are pursuing real threats."

"Maybe you'd like to tell us how your mission is going?" Daniel suggested.

Mina met his gaze, unwilling to let this vampire intimidate her.

"I've gotten Sebastian Young to agree to stop biting for a month," she announced.

She noticed that Vedette and Jackson looked impressed. Jude's handsome face showed no emotion, and Daniel looked angry.

"And what did you offer him in return?" Daniel asked. "Sex? Is that something you readily offer these days?"

Mina gaped at him, shocked that he'd said such a thing. First he'd implied she knew nothing about preternatural sex, now he was insinuating that she was having sex with Sebastian. And what did he mean *these days*?

Jude rose. "Daniel, I think you should watch yourself."

Daniel offered Jude a sycophantic smile. "I only mean to say that since Wilhelmina doesn't seem bothered by Franny Millhouse selling sex, maybe she'd be willing to bargain with it too."

Mina gritted her teeth. "No. That wasn't part of the deal."

"Well, I think your accomplishment is wonderful," Jackson said, offering her one of his ultra-bright smiles. "By whatever means you did it. Humans are safer. Good work, Wilhelmina."

Mina nodded at his acknowledgment and sat back down. A week ago that praise would have made her feel so proud, would have verified to her that she was doing the Society's work and it was good work. But now she only felt slight regret, and more confident that humans didn't need protection from Sebastian Young.

She glanced back up at Daniel. He still watched her with narrowed, resentful eyes. But they might need protection from some of the preternaturals here.

Mina pulled in a deep breath as she slipped out of the meeting. The overly warm night air was less stifling than the meeting room had been. She hurried down the alley, wanting to get away before any of the other members left. Especially Daniel. But she didn't want to talk to any of them. And not about Sebastian.

By the end of the meeting, Mina was more convinced that the Society wasn't what she'd believed. Other members had reported about their missions with their "dangerous" preternaturals. A werewolf who ran a home for runaway teens—and even though there was no evidence that he'd hurt any of them, he was deemed a threat and should be stopped. Another told about a vampire who drove a cab—again, he was a legitimate employee of Yellow Taxi, and there were no substantiated reports that he drove his fares to secluded places and savagely bit them. But they bumped him up to Number Seven on the most dangerous list.

Mina shook her head as she strode down the street. They were more interested in casting judgment than helping humans. She wasn't sure any of them were doing this to help humans, period. It seemed more like some form of vigilante justice against preternaturals whose lifestyles they didn't agree with.

Of course, she'd been guilty of that too, hadn't she? She'd never seen or even heard any accounts of Sebastian hurting mortals. In fact, from the way women flocked to him, he was doing anything but hurting them.

Again, she wondered if women were flocking around Sebastian right now. Tightness tugged at her chest and this time she didn't bother to ponder its meaning. She knew this emotion well—jealousy.

Instead of turning toward her apartment, she strode in the direction of Carfax Abbey. She wanted to see Sebastian now. She wasn't going to lie to herself or justify anymore. He'd shown her more in three days than she'd learned in a hundred years. He'd made her feel more alive than she ever had. Even when she was alive. She wanted to be with him.

Chapter 17

Outside Carfax Abbey, Mina hesitated. If she went inside, she was going to have to face all the people she'd worked with—the people who had accepted her so readily. And who she'd cast unfair judgments on.

Maybe they didn't know. But that seemed unlikely. She'd experienced club life, at least for a little while. Everyone knew everyone else's business. And they must have asked someone. After all, she'd just stopped coming to work.

Maybe it would be wiser to head back to her apartment and wait for Sebastian there.

No, she straightened her shoulders. She needed to do this. She needed to tell them she was sorry. She needed to see Sebastian too. She needed to tell him that she'd been wrong about him, too.

Oh, he'd be smug about it, and he'd never let her forget that she'd misjudged him. But she could take that. Being teased by him was as enjoyable as everything else the man did.

"Hi, Constantine," she said quietly as she came up the club's large granite steps.

The tall Greek werewolf stood like an ancient sentry in the doorway. His arms were crossed over his broad, black t-shirt clad chest. His leather encased legs were spread slightly like he was ready to block her entrance. Instead he smiled, his smoldering dark eyes holding not even the slightest hint of dislike. In fact, his gaze roamed down her body.

"Hey, Wilhelmina. Lookin' good."

She was surprised by his reaction, then she remembered what she'd chosen to wear tonight. A dark red, satiny sundress that she barely wore. She'd dress up for the Society meeting? No, she realized. She'd put on this dress with the intention of coming here—to Sebastian.

"Thanks, Constantine."

"Where you been lately?" he asked, and for a moment Mina didn't know what to say. Apparently he hadn't heard she was the one who'd tried to shut down the club and end his job.

She knew she should tell him the truth. She'd been fired, but instead she said, "I've been off for a few days."

"Nice," he said, then turned to take the ID of a lovely brunette waiting to enter the club.

The brunette smiled interestedly at Constantine, and Mina knew the werewolf's attention was otherwise engaged.

She headed into the club. It was the slowest she'd ever seen the place, but it was Sunday night. And she suspected that Carfax Abbey was still busier than most bars on a Sunday. She scanned the large room, looking for Sebastian. She couldn't find him, but she noticed that Greta had spotted her.

"Wilhelmina! I'm so glad you stopped by. Nadine told us that you were taking some time off."

Mina was again shocked. Greta hadn't heard either. Mina glanced at where Nadine stood behind the bar. Nadine saw her too, but rather than gesturing for Constantine to come and throw her out, she just nodded.

Mina waved, not sure what else to do.

"So why are you taking time off?" Greta asked. "It can't be because you're sick." She laughed.

No, vampires didn't get colds, did they? "I just needed a few days to . . ." She didn't know what to say. "Is Sebastian here?"

Greta looked around. Thankfully, the blonde was easily distracted. “He was here. Oh, I think I saw him head into the back with some woman.”

Mina’s heart sank. He was with a woman. She shouldn’t be surprised. After all, she’d guessed he would be, and they didn’t really have anything between them. Other than their field trips and a kiss or two. Or three.

“Want me to get him?” Greta offered.

Mina shook her head. “No, that won’t be . . .”

Sebastian came out of the back hallway talking animatedly with the woman at his side. She was of an average height, maybe 5’5” or 5’6” with glossy brown hair pulled back into a stylish twist. She wore a tweed business suit. The green of the material, somewhere between a lime and an olive color, saved the outfit from looking too severe. And she had pretty dark eyes that sparkled as she talked to Sebastian.

Mina had told herself the whole way over to the club that Sebastian was likely with another woman. But telling herself and seeing the evidence with her own eyes were two very different things. Watching him chatting and laughing with the lovely woman was like a sucker punch straight to the gut. Over and over.

She couldn’t handle this. Her feelings about Sebastian were too new to her, too bewildering. She couldn’t handle this.

No, she said, annoyed with herself. She shouldn’t feel like she wanted to run away. Sebastian certainly hadn’t said that they were exclusive—or that they were even dating for that matter, but they had kissed. And that meant something to her. But she knew that it probably meant very little to him. She knew that. And she could be as nonchalant as he was.

She looked down at herself. She suddenly wished she was wearing something more sophisticated. She touched her hair, knotted in the usual messy style. One thing she had changed was her glasses. She hadn’t worn them, but now she wished she had. She wanted something to hide behind, since she couldn't just sink into the ground.

Okay, who was she kidding? She couldn't play it cool. All these feelings inside her were too new, too scary. And she just wanted to run.

"There he is," Greta said, in an almost amusingly "after-the-fact" sort of way. Almost amusingly.

"You know, I think I need to go," Mina said. She couldn't talk to him now. Here, in front of the whole bar. Or if she was smart, ever.

She couldn't handle someone like Sebastian. She didn't believe he was the threat that she'd once thought, but he was still too dangerous for her. Or rather, he *could* be dangerous to her.

"But you just got . . ." Greta started.

Mina didn't stay to listen. She spun and walked quickly toward the door, her only thought to get out of the club before Sebastian saw her. What if he introduced her to that woman?

Mina, meet my first date of the night. First date, this is Mina, my second date. Or rather my special project. Because she is a total mess, who really, really needs my help.

"Mina?"

She closed her eyes as she heard Sebastian's deep, velvety voice. That was a mistake. She took one step with her eyes closed and her ankle twisted in the stupid sandals that she rarely wore. For this very reason.

Her eyes snapped open just in time to see Sebastian jogging toward her and the tile floor rising up to meet her. She landed in a huddle, her skirt hiked up, one of her already messy ponytails unknotting and falling into her face.

"Mina," Sebastian crouched down beside her, touching her bare knee.

She jerked away, her body reacting too sharply to his touch. How could her darned, wayward body react, when she was sprawled in a pile, looking like an idiot in front of everyone. Especially Sebastian and that woman.

"Don't," she said, pushing back away from him. "Don't do this."

Sebastian gave her a confused look. "Don't help you up?"

"No," she gritted, keeping her voice low. "Don't come into my life and mess up everything. I've worked damned hard to make my life okay, and you are just . . . You're just—messing it all up!"

She knew she'd repeated herself, but she didn't care. She just wanted to go back to before this man was suddenly so important to her. And could hurt her worse than some old vampire bite.

Sebastian stared at Mina, not sure what she was talking about, but he could see she was near tears. He knew she didn't want his help, but he caught her hand anyway and pulled her to her feet.

"Wait, right here," he stated. "I mean it."

She didn't give him a reaction of any sort; instead focusing on smoothing her skirt.

He frowned at her for a moment, then rushed back to Julie. He didn't want to leave Mina, but it was a little too rude even for him to leave a business associate without saying a word.

"Julie, I'm sorry, but I'm going to have to cut this a little short."

Julie smiled. "Girl troubles?"

"Apparently."

Julie laughed at his perplexed expression. "Then you better go. I've got enough information here to get a proposal written. I'll drop it by sometime next week."

"Great. Thank you." He quickly shook her hand and then strode back to Mina, feeling Nadine, Ferdinand, and Greta's eyes on him as he passed the bar. He didn't acknowledge them, he was more concerned with getting back to Mina. To his surprise, she was still standing in the same spot, her arms curled tightly around herself as if she were cold. Her gaze directed at the floor.

He caught one of her hands. "Okay, let's talk."

"Are you sure you're done?" she asked, her voice sharp with sarcasm.

"Actually I wasn't, and I had to wait a damned long time to get her, but that's okay."

Mina jerked her hand out of his hold, and he turned to see her glaring at him. She spun and started back toward the door.

"Oh no," he stated, catching her hand again. "You are not leaving until we talk."

She lifted her chin as if she planned to argue, but then she let him pull her toward the back hallway.

Once they were in the elevator with the gate closed, he released her hand and faced her.

"What's going on?" he asked.

Mina stared at him for a moment, then looked down at the elevator's corrugated metal floor.

"I want to end the deal," she said flatly.

No. No way. But he didn't say that. "Why?"

She looked up at him, misery clear in her blue eyes. He was the one making her this unhappy. The idea killed him.

"Baby," he murmured, touching her cheek. "Tell me what's going on, please."

She closed her eyes, then straightened her spine against his soft, rich voice. Then she met his gaze directly. "If you are meeting women, mortal women, then how do I know you aren't biting them? There's no way for me to know. You could have bitten women every night since we made the deal. I'd be none the wiser. And—I just can't . . . I just can't do," she gestured to them, "this. The deal is done."

Sebastian digested her words. "You're jealous, aren't you?"

She didn't answer, but she was sure her miserable expression said enough.

Despite her obvious angst, the idea made him feel like giving a triumphant whoop.

"Why are you smiling?"

He tried to be sober, but couldn't.

"It's cruel to enjoy someone else's distress," she informed him primly.

"Oh baby," he said sincerely, "I'm only enjoying it because this is a major breakthrough."

She eyed him as if she thought perhaps he was mad.

"If you are jealous, then you must like me a little bit."

"Yes," she admitted, with a begrudging roll of her eyes.

"I'm really glad about that. Because I have to admit, I like you a little bit too."

Her eyes narrowed. "You definitely have a weird way of showing it."

"That woman. Her name was Julie Winchester, she's an interior designer who came to look at the club and give me some suggestions."

Mina stared at him and then blinked as if she wasn't quite sure if she'd heard him right. And if she had heard him right, whether or not she should believe him.

"A designer?"

He nodded. "That's it. I haven't bitten a woman, slept with a woman—or barely spoken to another woman since we started this deal."

Mina knew that she should have been relieved by what he was saying. He hadn't been with another woman. Not the way she'd thought anyway. But his explanation only made Mina realize that he wasn't with a woman *this* time. But he would be eventually.

He wasn't the type to settle down, isn't that what Greta had said? He wasn't a one-woman man, and she simply couldn't expect it. If Greta had no hopes of keeping him, then Mina's chances were nil. And Mina didn't think she could handle that.

But she wanted to. She wanted more time with him, even though the idea scared her senseless. But such a different fear from that which she'd lived with for years. The fear of losing, instead of being trapped.

Her gaze roamed his face. The sharp angle of his jawline was such a contrast to the lush fullness of his beautiful lips. His straight nose and the splash of eyebrows a shade or two darker than his unruly hair. And those golden eyes filled with concern and kindness and desire. All for her, she realized, and she didn't know what to do with that.

"Come here," he said, crooking a finger at her, giving her that lopsided smile that she loved so much.

Even with all the doubts still whirling in her mind, she was helpless to deny him. She stepped closer and he pulled her against him. Gently his lips pressed against hers, soft and strong all at once—with hunger and possession lurking just beneath his gentleness. A heady combination. A thrilling promise of more to come.

He continued to kiss her like that for several minutes not forcing more reaction from her than she was willing to give. And because of his lack of demand, she gave him more. Opening her mouth for him. Her tongue brushing his.

She pressed her body to his lean strength, her fingers tangled in his silky hair. She moaned as he broke off the kiss, not ready for his wonderful mouth to leave hers.

"Come with me to my apartment." The invitation, offered in his low, velvety voice, was as tempting and delicious as his kisses.

She nibbled her bottom lip, still tingly and sensitive. She didn't know if she could do this. She wanted to. Lord, she did. She wanted to feel normal and whole. She wanted only him to make her feel that way. No one else. Ever. And that scared her, because she knew that wasn't what he was offering. He would live forever, but he wouldn't love forever. She knew that.

She stared at him again, his beautiful face, his mesmerizing eyes, and she nodded. She had to take this chance. She hadn't felt this way in over a hundred years, and she couldn't give up a single moment with him.

He smiled reassuringly and then lifted the gate to the elevator. A loud, metallic clatter echoed down the hallway, and Mina couldn't help hoping it was the sound of her prison finally being opened. Maybe she'd finally be free—free of her awful past. Free to feel again.

Linking his fingers with hers, he led her down the hallway. Her hopeful feelings diminished slightly as she stepped inside Sebastian's beautiful apartment. The place, despite its warm, homey atmosphere, was still where he brought all his women. His love nest.

"Would you like to have a seat?"

She nodded and perched on the edge of the plush gray sofa. He glanced around as if he didn't know quite what to do. His uncertainty made her feel a little better, for some reason.

"Would you like something to drink? Wine?"

She nodded again. She needed some other focus than Sebastian.

He nodded in return and then crossed the room to a small sideboard arranged with several bottles and glasses. He started to pick up one of the bottles and then paused, glancing over his shoulder.

"White or red?"

"White," she said automatically. For once in over a hundred years, she wanted to drink something that wasn't red. The beginning, maybe, of a different life.

He turned back to the drinks, and she studied his back. His broad shoulders and the way the muscles rippled with each of his movements under his black shirt. She couldn't remember ever looking at a man's back and wanting him. Not even . . .

Sebastian finished pouring the drinks and carried them over to the sofa. He sat down beside her, leaving a little space between them as he handed her the wine goblet.

"Mina, we still have more that we need to talk about."

"Like what?" She looked down at her glass, pretending

she didn't know what he meant. But she did. He wanted answers to her behavior in the airport restroom.

Sebastian reached out, hooking a finger under her chin, gently forcing her to meet his gaze.

"I don't know," he said, his expression searching. "That's what I want you tell me."

"I'm not sure what . . ."

"I want to know why when we kiss it usually ends with you attempting to do me bodily harm?"

That wasn't true, was it? She knew she'd panicked, but she hadn't hurt him, had she?

She opened her mouth to deny that, but he continued, "And why you don't know anything about being a vampire. And why you are so scared."

She looked back down at the goblet that she now gripped in both hands.

"Mina, please. Tell me."

She gazed into the pale gold liquid in her glass, watching the way the light shimmered in its depths. So sparkling and fresh. She wanted to go back to when she'd been that way. Sparkling, fresh, able to believe in the goodness of others, unafraid.

"I've only drunk wine once before," she said suddenly. Maybe it was the memories brought on by the wine. Or maybe it was going to the Society meeting and realizing they weren't what she'd believed. Or it was just Sebastian himself, but she suddenly needed to talk. She needed to tell someone—no, not just someone. She needed to tell *him* about her past. Even though she was ashamed of it.

"Really? Only once?" he said. His voice was falsely interested in that way that people responded when they weren't sure where the conversation was going.

"Yes. My twenty-second birthday. Rather old, I guess. But my father was very strict. He had to be."

"Why?"

"Well, all his daughters were heiresses, of course. We had to make good impressions, and we couldn't make any bad choices. My father was a firm believer that alcohol led to many bad decisions."

"I'd have to agree with that one," Sebastian said, even as he took a sip of his own drink. Hard liquor of some sort, golden like his eyes.

She sipped hers too, amazed she could still remember the tangy sharpness of the flavor, even after all these decades. It was amazing what could stay buried in the recesses of the mind. Sharp and clear and unforgotten.

"Both you and my father were right," she said. "I only drank one night and that night I made the worst choice of my life."

Chapter 18

Sebastian watched Mina as she took another sip of her wine, grimacing just slightly at the taste.

He waited. He wanted to understand her, to know how she'd become a vampire. He needed to know how she'd come to be as old as she was and still have no idea how to use the powers that she'd been given. But most important, he wanted to know why she was scared of him.

"It was the evening of my twenty-second birthday. I remember him walking into the ballroom. And I remember thinking he couldn't be real—that men weren't really that beautiful." She laughed slightly, the sound eerily hollow.

Sebastian started to reach for her, wanting to soothe away the distant, haunted look in her dark eyes, but he was afraid the touch might startle her. Might stop her. And he had the feeling she needed to tell him this as much as he wanted to hear it.

"He came to one of the house parties we held every summer at our estate in Newport. It was a week-long event. The Rockefellers, the Carnegies, all the rich and famous attended. But from the moment Donatello strolled into my parents' home, I couldn't see anyone else."

Sebastian shifted, his chest contracting at her words. Disgust, he told himself, because he knew what this Donatello was. Not because Mina had once longed so intensely for another man.

"He was different from all the other men in the room. Tall, dark, breathtakingly beautiful. Mysterious too."

Another sharp squeeze. Oh yeah, he hated this guy.

Sebastian watched Mina take a drink of her wine.

"My eldest sister, Lorelei, was the lovely one. She was tall and elegant and—" Mina sighed. "Well, she always captured notice. She couldn't have stopped it if she wanted to, which she didn't. My second sister, Ava, was also beautiful and intelligent and bold. She drove my parents mad with her antics, but they also adored her. Then there was my baby brother. The son that a father always wants. Daddy doted on Bertram. And between the second daughter and the favored son was me. Another girl. Plain and bookish and socially inept—at best."

"Mina," Sebastian said, no longer able not to touch her. He reached for the hand that rested on her knee, but she moved it out of his reach.

"I'm not telling you this to make you feel bad for me." She shot him a look that dared him to pity her.

"I know," he assured her. "I just want to hold you."

She hesitated, staring at the hand he extended. Finally she slipped her hand into his, her fingers slender and cold. Protectiveness filled him at her delicateness.

She took another sip of her wine, then she continued, "When Donatello arrived at the house party, my sisters noticed him right away. But he didn't seem aware of them. He centered all his attention on me. That should have been my first warning sign."

"Mina—"

"Let me just keep going. Please."

Sebastian nodded.

"But I'd drunk that wine, and I felt bold. So I talked with him. And danced. As I said, the party was a week-long affair, and every night Donatello was there at my side, attentive and charming. He listened to my interests. Telling me all the things I longed to hear. Oh, I wasn't so naïve that I didn't suspect he was after my fortune. Of course, he had to be—or so I thought as well."

Sebastian frowned at the offhanded certainty. Didn't she have any idea how lovely she was? How sweet and funny and perfect?

He squeezed her fingers, but didn't interrupt to tell her his opinion, because he knew she wouldn't want to hear it.

She didn't acknowledge his touch.

"My parents didn't approve of him. They knew, too, that he had to be after my inheritance and they didn't hesitate to tell me so. They told me if the man was truly interested in a love match, then he would have chosen Lorelei or Ava. But if he wanted only money, then I was the obvious choice."

"Why?"

"Because I was quiet and meek and wouldn't give him any trouble when he decided to spend my money freely and to find satisfaction elsewhere."

Sebastian couldn't keep his thoughts to himself any longer. "Forgive me, but your parents sound like assholes."

Mina blinked at him, and he expected her to be furious. After all, they were her parents. And he knew no one should insult someone else's family. Hell, he'd even defended Christian a time or two, and he'd been pure evil at the time.

Instead, she just shrugged.

"My parents were nothing if not practical."

Sebastian gritted his back teeth. There was nothing practical about their behavior. It was cruelty. How could parents hurt a child like that? How could they openly favor certain children over another? His parents had never shown preference to one of their children. He and his brothers had all treated their sister, Elizabeth, like a pet. But she was the baby and the only girl. And never had their parents favored her.

"Even though I knew my parents were probably right, I ignored their warnings. I sneaked around, finding ways to meet Donatello." She stared straight ahead, her expression faraway as if she was recalling each of their clandestine meetings.

Sebastian didn't want her remembering those meetings, moments locked in another man's embrace. Suddenly he realized he was more worried that she was recalling pleasant memories rather than bad ones. Selfish of him but true.

"I never saw him in the daytime," she said suddenly as if just realizing that fact for the first time. She laughed slightly, the sound hollow. "But I guess it wouldn't have made any difference if I had noted that fact. Thinking someone is a vampire isn't one's first suspicion, is it?"

Sebastian shook his head. Not until after the fact, no.

"As the end of the week neared, Donatello became more insistent that I needed to meet him away from my home. He told me he wanted to be alone, where no one could find us."

"And you went."

She nodded, still staring out at the room.

"Where did he take you?"

"We agreed to meet in the woods on my parents' estate. It was private, and I knew my parents would never go there, but it was still close enough if I had second thoughts and wanted to leave, then I could." She took a deep breath, and if possible, her complexion grew even paler. "Or so I thought."

Sebastian squeezed her fingers. They were freezing and stiff like icicles against his palm.

"Once in the woods, Donatello started acting so strange. Not at all like the man who'd charmed me for the week before. He was aggressive and . . ." she took a breath, and Sebastian could see she was starting to panic at the memory.

"Mina, baby, don't. If it hurts too much, you don't have to talk about this."

She turned to him, and for the first time since she started the story she really seemed to register him beside her. Unshed tears made her eyes sparkle like sapphires. The pain there nearly made Sebastian gnash his teeth. He wanted to kill this Donatello. Rip him to shreds.

"I—I need to tell this," she whispered.

He nodded.

"It started to rain. Pouring rain." She shivered as if she could feel the rain now. "I told him that we should go back. Wait for another night. He laughed at me and told me that a little rain wasn't going to stop his plans. He'd waited as long as he was going to for me. He pushed me up against a tree, holding me there. I screamed, even though I knew no one would hear. I fought, but he was very strong. Of course, I didn't know how strong and that I didn't stand even the slightest chance of escape."

She took another gulping breath, talking quickly as if she had to get the story out as fast as she possibly could.

"His touches were brutal and degrading. I thought he planned to rape me, but that wasn't the plan. That wasn't his interest."

Sebastian felt his muscles relax just a little at her words. He knew what had happened to her had been violent, and had ultimately taken her human life. But he couldn't bear to think of this monster violating her that way, too.

"We'd brought a lamp with us, and I remember him grabbing it and holding it up to his face. His beautiful features were gone, replaced by a hideous, distorted mask, pointed, razor-sharp teeth, glowing eyes."

Sebastian paused at her description. Glowing eyes? Vampires didn't have glowing eyes. When a vampire got ready to bite, their features did change and their pupils dilated until the eyes looked totally black. They only glowed in the movies. She must have distorted that memory, the attacker becoming something of fiction.

"I remember thinking that this couldn't be happening and that I was going to die." Mina's voice broke, and Sebastian forgot about the strange description of his cruel vampire.

"Mina." Sebastian couldn't stop himself; he caught her

around the waist, lifting her easily onto his lap. She was stiff against him, but she didn't struggle to get away.

If she had, he would have released her. He didn't want to be anything like this asshole she was describing. He never wanted her to think she was being forced to do anything against her will again. Never.

"He told me that he was going to kill me." She took another breath. "But then he pretended to ponder the idea. He told me that he did rather like me, and he'd let me go. All I had to do was agree to let him cross me over. I had no idea what he was talking about, but I would have agreed to anything. Anything to get away from him, to go home. I just wanted to go home."

Sebastian hugged her to his chest like a child, wishing he'd been there. That he could have protected her.

"I remember screaming yes, he could cross me over, then I don't remember much after that. Just pain. Extreme pain. Then blackness. When I came to, I was lying in the mud and he was gone. It was early morning, overcast, pouring down rain. I remember the smell of the ocean being so overwhelming that I nearly vomited. Of course, I didn't realize that was because I'd changed. That I was now undead, and every sensation was overwhelmingly intense."

The vampire had just left her. Suddenly, her lack of understanding about herself made some sense. Although he still had no idea how she hadn't learned anything in the past hundred years. And why would a vampire cross over a mortal and just leave them? It made no sense. Why hadn't the vampire just killed her?

"Somehow, I managed to get home," she continued. "I remember stumbling into my house, yelling for my parents. But they didn't come for me. They couldn't leave their guests. They couldn't reveal what happened to the world's elite. The servants hurried me away to my room. My parents didn't even come see me until the next day. Once all the guests had left.

Sebastian heard her voice crack, and he pulled her tight against him, rubbing his cheek against the top of her head, wanting desperately to take away her pain, even as he seethed over her parents' cruelty. In their own way, in a worse way, they had been as vicious as the vampire.

She fell silent then. Not until he felt her tiny trembles did he realize she was crying.

"Mina," he murmured against her hair. "I'm so sorry."

She didn't answer; she just nestled against him as if she wanted to burrow into his skin. He held her, whispering to her, not even sure what he was saying, just knowing he wanted to take away her pain. He wanted to protect her.

He'd suspected her fear had been based around sex, since she had panicked whenever they'd gotten intimate, but that wasn't it. Was she simply scared of him because he was a vampire? Did the act of kissing and making love remind her of the moments leading up to her attack? He still wasn't sure.

And he still didn't understand how she could have survived. Left alone with no understanding why or how she'd changed. He didn't think her parents would have been too accepting of what she'd become. Had they even known? Had they believed?

"Mina, I know you're upset, but I have to ask this."

She nodded, not lifting her head from his chest.

"How did you survive? What happened after that night?"

She was silent for a moment, then she pulled in a breath that seemed to shudder her whole body. "I—I had no idea what was happening. All I knew was I couldn't stand the light. It hurt and felt heavy on my skin. I was starving, but I couldn't keep food down. I remember feeling crazed like a caged animal."

Sebastian nodded. That crazed feeling was what happened without blood. It did make a vampire almost insane.

"My parents assumed I'd gone mad, believing I'd been sexually assaulted. I told them over and over what happened, but, of course, they didn't believe me. They brought in doctors, who also didn't understand what was wrong with me. They understood what their tests were saying—my temperature far below normal, no heartbeat. And they certainly couldn't name my ailment. And I just grew more and more insane. Finally, one day . . ."

She stopped—hiding her face against his shirt as if she couldn't bear to recall the memory, much less talk about it.

Sebastian rocked her. "It's okay."

"I was alone with one of the servants, a young girl, only about sixteen or so." She shuddered again, and Sebastian knew where this conversation was going. Had Mina killed the girl?

"I didn't kill her," she answered as if she'd heard his silent question. "But I did attack her. Bit her."

She took another deep, almost gulping breath as though the memory sickened her.

"That very night my parents had me institutionalized."

Sebastian closed his eyes, horror-struck at the idea of her in an asylum. Alone. Scared. He didn't know how she survived. Many couldn't have, without the added fact that she couldn't possibly understand what she'd become. Not fully.

"I was there for years. I don't know how long. Occasionally I'd be moved to another institution. This went on for . . ." She shrugged. "I don't know."

He hugged her tighter, remembering her terror when he'd blocked the bathroom door in the airport. She was afraid of being confined, unable to escape. Of course, being a vampire, she would have been able to escape, but since she didn't know how to use her powers, she couldn't. She'd stayed in those hellholes. God, she was strong, stronger than she knew.

"Until finally, Dr. Fowler, having heard reports of the crazed woman who believed she was a vampire, came to see me. He was the first visitor I'd had in—two decades, three maybe."

Sebastian closed his eyes, cursing her parents. They'd been as evil as the vampire. Leaving Mina there. Forgotten.

"Dr. Fowler believed me, and he managed to get me discharged. He helped me find a place, I guess you'd call it a halfway house for preternaturals, and taught me how to manage what I was, as best he could. But being a werewolf himself, he couldn't tell me how to use my powers. And at that time, I didn't want to. I just wanted to be—normal. As normal as I could be."

For once, Sebastian actually appreciated Dr. Fowler. Maybe he wasn't quite the loon that he'd always believed.

"And I've been just going on since then."

"You never saw your family again."

She shook her head. "The Weisses are not insane. No, my parents told the world I died. Which I did."

He caught her face, cupping her tear-streaked cheeks tenderly. She looked like a porcelain doll that had been left out in the rain, and he realized that analogy wasn't far off.

More rage filled him.

"You aren't dead," he told her firmly. "And you are not responsible for what happened to you. You are amazing, don't you understand that?"

She stared at him, her gaze roaming his face. Then she touched him. Her fingers stroking his jawline, his cheek, the shape of his lips. He remained perfectly still, letting her touch him as she wanted.

Her trembling fingers remained against his cheek as she leaned forward, pressing her mouth to his, her lips tremulous, unsure and heartbreakingly sweet.

He responded, but didn't take control of the kiss, letting her do what she wanted. She brushed her soft lips over his mouth, then to his cheek. As her lips nibbled his jaw and then returned back to his mouth, his cock blatantly ignored his command to remain calm. He shifted, not wanting her to feel the rock-hard erection against her bottom.

"Baby," he murmured, "maybe we should slow down."

She lifted her head, regarding him with those heartbreakingly solemn eyes of hers. "I like kissing you."

He swallowed as her hand moved to his chest, caressing him through the cotton of his shirt. "Mina, I like kissing you too, but you're upset and not thinking clearly. I'm not sure you would decide this is what you want under normal circumstances."

She nodded, nibbling the redness of her bottom lip.

God, even that was turning him on.

"I'm going to admit something to you," she said. "And this is even harder than telling you about my past."

"Okay." He couldn't imagine anything more difficult than that story. It had been hard for him to listen to—and he could only imagine how hard it had been for her to tell. For her to live through.

"I—I really want you." She made a funny face as if she were almost sorry. "I do. More than anything."

Why would she be apologetic about that? He wanted her too, more than he could recall wanting anyone or anything. Then he realized her dilemma.

"But you don't want to want a vampire, do you?"

She stared at him. "Sebastian . . ."

He nodded with dawning understanding. She was going to tell him that he was the last vampire she could ever want. The Society had convinced her that he was pure evil. The last man, undead or otherwise, that she should be attracted to. A vampire like the one who'd destroyed her world, and left her to rot.

But she was attracted to him, dammit. And he wasn't that vampire.

"Mina, you can't let that damned crazy Society tell you—"

She pressed her fingers over his lips to silence him. But he wasn't going to be silenced about this. Not about something as important as them being together.

"Mina," he trapped her fingers in his, moving them from his lips, "I know I mentioned this before but you are believing an organization named after processed meat and unsolicited email."

"Shh," she insisted, placing her fingers back over his mouth, then she smiled. Why was she smiling?

"Sebastian, let me say this. Please. Because I'm only saying it once."

He nodded, his lips still pressed to her fingers.

"I don't know anything about processed meat or email for that matter, but I do think you might be right about the Society." She gave him a stern look, warning him with her eyes not to interrupt. "And I don't think you are the third most dangerous vampire in New York. In fact, I don't think you are dangerous at all."

At that he couldn't resist nipping her fingers, then he said, "Oh, I'm dangerous all right. Just not in the way ole SPAMM thinks."

He expected her to at least smile, but instead she regarded, him soberly, and for a moment he worried that his teasing remark had frightened her, although he didn't feel fear radiating from her.

"Sebastian, I want you," she said softly. "Well, you know I do. But—"

He didn't want buts. He wanted her, she wanted him. It was simple really. And right. He could feel that.

He caught her face and pulled her against him, kissing her gently, coaxingly. She moaned and tilted her head so he could deepen the kiss. Her hands touched his face, his hair, his shoulder, the touches desperate and hungry. His own need flared, quickly, wildly out of control like it always became whenever he touched her.

Without breaking the kiss, he stood, easily lifting her with him. She made a small noise at the sudden shift and wrapped her arms around his neck.

"Wh—where are we going?"

"I don't intend to make love to you on the floor. Not your first time anyway."

His words stunned him too. Was he going to be her first? A

strong wave of satisfaction and possessiveness washed through his veins at the idea.

She looked at him with large, wary eyes.

"This is the first time, right?" he asked.

Her nod was almost imperceptible, but it was there. Another wave of satisfaction tumbled through him, followed by a smaller ripple of misgiving. He needed this to be damned good for her. She'd waited over a hundred years. That was pressure.

He gazed down at her face. Her beautiful pale features, those blue eyes that he wanted to drown in, those ruby lips that he wanted to kiss all night.

He was up to the challenge.

He strode to his bedroom, using his foot to nudge the door open. Instead of setting her on the mattress, he gently slid her down his body until her feet touched the thick gray carpeting.

Sebastian cupped her upturned face in his hands. He leaned forward and kissed her, tasting those red lips. No rushing, no demands, just infinitely tender caresses. So thrilling. So breathtaking.

She made a small noise, and for a second, he worried she was nervous. Instead she wrapped her arms around his neck, arcing her body to his. He smiled against her lips and kissed her more possessively.

She whimpered, the sound sending a chill through him, a jarring contradiction to the fire also burning in his limbs.

"Are you okay?" he murmured.

This time, he felt the curl of her smile. "Yes."

"So should we keep kissing?"

"Yes, please."

He made a noise somewhere between a chuckle and a groan as his mouth caught hers again.

Go slow, he told himself and managed to maintain gentle, brushing kisses. Velvet against velvet. He continued his tender onslaught until the need inside him swelled to the point that he had to touch more of her.

She groaned as if she was reading his mind and moved closer to him.

"Are you okay?" Sebastian asked, his lips not fully leaving hers, even though he didn't sense fear.

"I want . . . more."

"I want to give you more." He kissed her again, this time more possessively. His lips molded to hers, wanting to devour her. He slipped his arms around her and brought her flush to his body. She gasped as their bodies rubbed together. He paused slightly, but then couldn't stop his hands from stroking down her narrow back to the soft swell of her backside. He walked her backward until she was against his bedroom door, his cock pulsing against her belly.

His lips left hers with a small, teasing nip and moved to the corner of her mouth. He pressed kisses along her jawline, fluttery kisses designed to get himself in check.

Then he moved to her neck. She stiffened slightly, and he kissed her gently, soothingly, licking the smooth skin just beneath her jawline. Sweet, silky skin. The softest he'd ever touched. The scent of lily of the valley surrounded him.

He kissed her again, then nibbled.

Suddenly, a strangled cry escaped her lips and her hands were at his chest shoving him, sending him backward.

"Stop!" Mina cried. "Stop."

Chapter 19

Mina had told herself to stay calm. When he'd pressed her against the door, she'd told herself it was okay. This was Sebastian. She trusted him. She wanted him. Calm. Stay calm.

Then she'd felt his teeth. Just a gentle nip at her neck. Not painful. Not frightening. But her words couldn't seem to penetrate the images in her brain. Being held against that tree. Unable to escape. Then his bite. Violent. Painful. Terrifying.

She opened her mouth to tell Sebastian to stop, but her throat felt like it was constricted closed. No words could escape, only a small whimper.

Then she'd been shoving him, her only thought to protect herself. She couldn't be bitten again. Never again.

Sebastian now stared at her, his hand on the bedpost, which he'd grabbed for balance.

She gaped at him for a moment, then dropped her head into her hands. Why couldn't she let the damned past go? Why?

"Mina," he said quietly. "What did I do? Did I hurt you?"

She shook her head, not looking at him. He hadn't hurt her. He hadn't hurt her at all. She touched her neck, then her shoulders slumped.

"I don't think I can do this."

He stepped back to her, not quite touching her.

"What scared you?"

"I—I thought you were going to bite me."

"Baby, I wouldn't bite you without you saying it was okay."

She lifted her head.

His look was heartbreakingly kind. He brushed a curl from her cheek.

"No biting. None," he promised. "Nothing that you don't want."

She stared at him, so disappointed in herself. So angry at the vampire who'd made her the mess she was now. He'd taken her life. He wasn't going to take this. He wasn't going to ruin this moment.

She nodded, and before she thought about it anymore, she reached forward, tugging at Sebastian's shirt. Even though she could see he was confused, he allowed her to pull it over his head.

She stood back admiring the muscles of his chest and stomach. Then she noticed two marks on the golden skin. Two small red imprints, the size of hands. Her hands.

He'd mentioned that in her other moments of panic she'd hurt him. And she had again. And he'd never reacted except to make sure she was all right.

He wouldn't hurt her, ever. She had to believe that. She did believe it. She moved forward, pressing her mouth tenderly to the redness, marring his perfect skin.

Gently, he caught her. "Mina. You are running way too hot and cold for me. What is going on?"

"Please just give me one more chance. Please."

He studied her, then nodded. "Okay. Of course."

She leaned up and kissed him with all the desire she had for him, and all the fear too. Sebastian responded, his arms coming up around her.

She waited for the fear to fill her again, but it didn't. This was Sebastian; she wanted him to touch her like this. She ached for him.

She gripped his shoulders, feeling his smooth skin and rock-hard muscles under her hands. Her fingers wandered over his arms. Sebastian's arms. Then his chest, more sinew, more perfection.

He groaned low in his throat, then he stepped back from her.

"What—what's wrong?" she asked, unsure why he pulled away.

"We need to go a little slower," he said.

She smiled slightly. "That's my line."

He smiled back, then his smiled faded. He touched her mouth with his fingertips. "God, I love your smile."

Her chest swelled at his words. Her gaze dropped to his lips. She loved his smile too. He was the most beautiful thing she'd ever seen. She closed the small space between them, capturing his mouth, mimicking the possessiveness of the kiss he'd given her earlier.

His arms came around her back and she was pulled tightly to him. Her chest crushed to his, her dress the only thing keeping her chest from melding with his—becoming one.

Again, she waited for fear, but she couldn't feel anything but longing.

He stepped back, pulling in a deep, steadying breath.

"I want to please you," he said.

"You are," she assured him, leaning back in to kiss him.

He stopped her, placing his hands on her bare shoulders.

"No," he clarified, "I want you to tell me exactly what you like and what you don't. This is about you. I want to touch and kiss you."

His gaze slid down her body, and she felt the look like a slow, sizzling caress.

She swallowed at the yearning crackling in her veins. "Isn't that what we were doing?"

He smiled, the curve of his lips indulgent. "I want this to be only about you. About your pleasure. I want you to know what it should feel like to have a man love you."

Her breath caught at his words. *To have a man love you.* She imagined being the focus of his love. The idea made her light-headed. Giddy. She knew it wasn't love, not really, but she still wanted what he was offering her, here, tonight. Even if it was only for tonight.

She wanted Sebastian to be the one to erase the horrible memories of the past. She wanted him to replace it with him. Only memories of him.

She took a deep breath, steadying her quivering body.

"I want that too."

He smiled as if she had granted him the greatest gift. His hands slid unhurriedly down her arms. She pulled in a quick breath at the sizzling need left in the wake of that slow caress. She had no idea that such a simple touch could be so arousing.

"I like this dress," he said, his gaze slowly gliding down her body. "Very pretty."

She gasped as his hands left her arms and moved to her waist. His eyes snapped back up to her face, reading her reaction, making sure she wasn't scared. His concern was almost as much of a turn-on as his touch. Almost.

She smiled at him to reassure him that she was fine.

His large hands splayed over her, running a path up her ribcage, his thumbs brushing over her belly, stopping just under the curve of her breasts. His hands burned her, even through the silky material of her dress.

He pulled in a breath, the sound uneven and shaky. "Mina, I want to touch your skin."

She met his eyes. They glittered golden and hot.

She nodded.

"You have the most beautiful skin I've ever seen," he told her, brushing his fingers over the beadwork at the neckline of her dress, then they moved to the tiny buttons that ran the length of her dress.

"Too pale," she whispered, watching as his strong fingers worked open the button at the neckline.

"No. Perfect like pearls."

She looked up at him, for a moment thinking he must be teasing her. But there was no mocking in his eyes, only desire as he slowly unfastened one button, then the next. He bent his head to press a kiss to her chest, the valley between her breasts, the spot just below the center of her bra. Soon he knelt at her feet, and she stood before him, her dress undone and parted.

"Will you take it off?" he asked.

Unable to do otherwise, she nodded. She pushed the dress down her arms, letting it pool around her feet, leaving her bare except for her white panties and bra and sandals. She'd never been one to wear anything lacy, but she suddenly wished her plain underwear had even just a little lace, although Sebastian didn't seem to notice the lack of ornamentation.

He rose up on his knees and pressed his mouth to her stomach, just below her belly button. She jerked at the sudden rush of need that crackled through her body. Her breasts ached, as did her sex. All the feelings were so new to her, so overwhelming.

"Are you okay?"

She shook her head. "No. My skin feels like it's on fire." And that was just the beginning of what she was feeling, but she was too embarrassed to tell him what other parts of her were blazing with need, too.

He kissed her belly again, then rose to his feet. "I think I can help with that."

He kissed her lips again. Then he lifted her in his arms, his mouth never leaving hers, and he placed her on the bed. She sank down into the mattress. Instead of following her down, he sat beside her.

Lightly he ran his fingers over her, over her shoulders, down her arms, across her stomach. His fingers grazed down her thighs, over the curve of her knee to her feet. Deftly, he untied the sandals, even his hands on her ankles making her body feel like it was about to engulf in flame.

"Very sexy shoes," he said with that sinful smile of his. He tossed them to the floor. Then he leaned back up to kiss her lips lingering, thoroughly. His mouth left hers to press small kisses across her chest, over her breasts where they swelled slightly over the top of her bra.

"Can I take this off?" he asked, then he flicked his tongue over the protrusion of her nipple as if to demonstrate what he wanted to do without the barrier of plain cotton.

She nodded and struggled upright to unfasten the hooks, but her body felt weak and rubbery. Sebastian caught her hands, stilling them, then he unhooked the bra, sliding the straps down her arms. He gently nudged her back against the pillows.

His eyes moved to her breasts, studying her until she nearly covered herself in embarrassment. Then his hand came out to cup one of the aching swells.

"Beautiful," he murmured, his voice low and reverent. Desire tore through her at his expression and at his worshipping touch.

He leaned forward and captured one of the swollen nipples, sucking and licking, until she was caught somewhere between ecstasy and hints of glorious pain. Pain. She had no idea pain could make her yearn, make her need. He squeezed the other nipple between his thumb and forefinger, more of that exquisite, exciting pain shot through her.

She writhed, gasping at the need swelling inside her.

He lifted his head. "Are you okay?"

She responded by hooking a hand around the back of his head and forcing his lips back to her throbbing nipple. He chuckled, the vibration of the laugh against her skin snaking downward to between her thighs.

She wriggled again, wanting his touch everywhere. Her breasts, her skin, inside her. She startled at the idea, then realized that was what she wanted more than anything. To feel his power, his strength, his passion inside her. Making her whole.

"Sebastian," she pleaded, not sure how to ask for what she wanted. She pushed upright, wanting to touch him too. But he stopped her, kissing her until she fell back against the mattress.

"I need you," she whispered, when he lifted his head to gaze down at her.

"You'll have me," he assured her, his hand stroking down her body, molding over her breasts, skimming over the swell of her stomach, stopping at the top of her panties. He toyed with the elastic at the waistband as he leaned over her, raining fluttery, barely-there kisses over her. Moving downward, slowly, slowly. All the while, his fingers playing with her panties, until she was squirming, panting, barely able to contain her need.

His mouth stopped its leisurely wandering at the waistband. He licked along the edge of it, his tongue searing hot, thrilling.

"You taste so good." He licked her again.

She gasped, her hips rising off the bed. His words should have frightened her. Being tasted was the last thing she wanted. She only knew that phrase as a lead-up to pain. But not here. Not now. Those words from Sebastian's lips only made her ache to be tasted more—by him—only him. She wanted more of his hot tongue on her skin.

Her fingers tangled in his hair as he hooked his thumbs under the waistband and peeled the panties down, tossing them to the floor. Mina realized that she lay absolutely naked in front of him. This beautiful, perfect man. She waited for embarrassment to fill her. It didn't.

All she could think about was the fact that she wanted him to keep touching her. Keep looking at her with those smoldering, golden eyes.

He shifted then, the mattress rising and falling as he situated himself between her legs. She rose up slightly on her elbows, startled by this new position. A position that left her spread wide for him to peruse. She started to tell him maybe she wasn't so comfortable with what they were doing. Then he touched her.

His finger brushed the dark curls at the apex of her thighs, another of his barely-there touches that left her gasping for air and her body tensing with powerful yearning.

"Are you okay?" he asked, watching her intently.

Okay? No, that wasn't the word for what she was. She was dying and this time it was in pure desire, pure ecstasy.

She nodded. Then he parted her, his finger flicking over the small point at the top of her sex that ached for his touch.

Her hips shot upward, instinctively demanding a firmer touch. Sebastian grinned and gave her what she wanted. The pad of his finger stroked her, swirling, teasing. Each brush lifting her toward something that she didn't truly understand, but she knew she wanted.

She closed her eyes, panting, her hands knotted in the covers of the bed.

Suddenly, his hand was gone, and she whimpered at the loss. But before she could beg for him to keep touching her, *please* keep touching her, pure fire shot through her body.

She cried out, and Sebastian froze, his tongue pressed to the ultrasensitive nub of her sex. He seemed to brace himself, as her hands flew to his head. But she only pulled him closer to her, pushing that needy little nub against his tongue.

"Oh, Sebastian," she pleaded. "Don't stop. Please don't stop."

She felt his smile against her. Against her sex, the gesture overwhelmingly, thrillingly personal. More need zoomed through her.

Then he lapped her. His tongue scorching, raspy, heaven. He swirled, then sucked gently with his pouty, wonderful lips to the point, just like with her nipples, it was almost painful, marvelously painful. Then as if he knew just when she was about to shatter, he'd again tease her with more fleeting whirls of his tongue. Her fangs extended as her passion grew and for the first time she could recall, she didn't care. All she cared about was Sebastian and what he was doing to her.

He continued his lovely torture until she was panting, squirming, calling his name over and over in dazed repetition. She cried out as he slowly sank one of his fingers into her damp heat. Then he eased in another. When she felt stretched and full, he suckled her clitoris hard, this time not pulling back as she neared the point of explosion. And with one final flick of his tongue, the whole world splintered around her.

Chapter 20

Sebastian moved up against the pillows, studying Mina. Her eyes were closed, her thick lashes inky against her cheeks, her red lips swollen, parted. Her pale, pale skin was actually flushed.

And never had he felt so rewarded by a woman's orgasm.

His first thought was he wanted to do it again. Make her scream his name over and over. But he remained by her side holding her. This was a huge step for Mina. And he didn't want to ruin her tenuous trust by being overzealous.

Oh, he wanted to bury himself deep inside her tight little body, but he could wait. He could wait as long as she needed, until she totally believed he didn't want to do anything but share pleasure with her. He wanted her trust as much as he wanted her passion. He wanted her to feel safe with him.

Mina pulled in a deep breath that made her creamy rose-tipped breasts rise, then fall. His fingers twitched, wanting to touch those perfect nipples, but he kept his hand at her narrow waist. Patience. He'd never had it, but he would with her.

Mina opened her eyes, turning to look at him. Her midnight gaze was bemused as if she still didn't know what to think of what just happened.

"Wow," she finally murmured, then smiled. He couldn't help kissing that adorable, pleased grin.

"Good?" he asked against her lips.

She nodded. "I had no idea."

"Baby, our existence is not supposed to be about pain."

Her eyes locked with his, and he saw hope there. God, he never wanted this woman to know another moment of pain. He wanted to protect her. He wanted to . . . He just wanted her, here, with him.

She snuggled against him, her hands shaping over his arms, then moving to his back. Her caresses made it difficult to maintain his decision to go slowly. The insistent organ shoving against the unforgiving material of his jeans wasn't helping either.

"Do you do—that to all the women you bring up here?" she asked suddenly.

He lifted his head, surprised by the question.

"I don't want to talk about other women," he said. He didn't want to think about anyone but Mina.

"Me neither," she agreed readily.

He smiled and leaned in to kiss her leisurely.

"But you—you know—do other stuff with them, don't you?" she asked before his lips made contact.

"Other stuff?" He frowned.

She shrugged, her cheeks actually coloring a little more. "You know. Intercourse."

Sebastian gaped at her, then laughed. "Here I thought I was doing a good deed by going slow and you're feeling shortchanged."

Mina blushed more. "No. No, that's not it." She looked away from him.

He laughed. "Oh, baby, come here." He pulled her against him and rolled until she was on top of him. She peered down at him, watching him with unsure eyes.

"I'll happily give you anything you want. We can make love all night. I just don't want to overwhelm you."

She wiggled on top of him, situating herself more securely on his chest, her movements rubbing her lush breasts against his chest. Her eyes left his, instead focusing on the pillow behind his head. Or maybe his left ear, he wasn't sure.

"Can you do that? Make love all night."

He couldn't help laughing at her shyly intrigued question. "Uh-oh, I've created a nymphomaniac with one orgasm."

Mina actually blushed a true pink and buried her face in the crook of his neck.

He ran his hands down her back, savoring the satiny texture of her skin, the delicateness of her bones and muscles, the softness of her bottom. He stroked her there, loving the gentle curve of her hips, the cushion of that perfect little rear end.

Her hands touched him too. His arms, his shoulders. Her lips brushed his shoulder, his collarbone. They touched each other like that, until she was wriggling against him, her legs splayed on either side of his denim-covered hips.

"Baby, I can't do this much longer," he muttered in her ear, careful not to get his lips too close to her neck. "Pretty soon my penis is going to have a permanent imprint from my zipper."

She gave him a concerned look, although he didn't think she really understood what he was talking about. Taking her with him, he sat up, then gently slid her off him onto the mattress. He jumped up and unfastened his jeans. He pushed them down, his granite-hard cock immensely happy to be freed.

When he looked up, he found Mina staring in rapt fascination at his erection. The hardened length pulsed against his stomach; her look was insanely erotic.

"Mina, if you keep looking at me like that . . ." he gave a slightly stunned laugh, shaken that her gaze could make him feel as if he could come right then, without even a single touch.

"Sorry," she said, her gaze moving to his face. But moments later, her eyes were back on his penis.

He groaned and crawled on the bed. He pulled her to him,

kissing her hungrily. Then he fell back against the mattress again pulling her with him, until she was straddling him.

He fought the urge to rub his erection against the silkiness of her damped curls. Mina had no such qualms. She tilted her hips, grinding herself against him.

He caught her, holding her still. "Baby, you can't do that unless you want me to bury myself in you right this minute."

She gave him a startled look at his roughly muttered words, then she slipped off him. For a moment, he was afraid he'd scared her. Instead she sat facing him and reached out trembling fingers to touch his swollen length. She started as his penis leapt at her slight touch.

"Does it hurt you?" she asked, staring at the organ with amazement.

"Not *hurt* precisely."

She nodded as if she totally understood that. Her midnight eyes moved up to lock with his, and his chest swelled with the yearning he saw there.

"You are so beautiful," she said, shaking her head as if she couldn't quite believe her reaction to him. He understood, looking at her kneeling beside him. Her black hair, tumbled from its ponytails, brushing her pale shoulders, her rounded, upturned breasts, her lovely bowed lips, her heartbreaking eyes.

He couldn't recall ever aching like this for a woman.

Again, she touched him, grazing her fingers over the sensitive underside of him. Again, he pulsed against her hand. She smiled.

"I didn't think a . . ."

"Penis," he provided for her.

She nodded. "I didn't think it would be pretty."

"Hmm, a pretty penis," he said with a strained smile, because her fingers were shaping the rounded head of the pretty object in question. "I'm not sure that's what a man likes to hear about his dick."

She frowned. "Why not?"

"Not very manly."

"Oh," she said with a nod as if she was filing that information away for another time, for another lover. He dug his fingers into the bedding, this time with irritation, rather than arousal. He didn't like thinking about Mina with another man.

Sebastian's attention was snapped back to Mina as she curled her fingers around his girth. His hips lifted slightly at the increased pressure.

"Okay, enough touching," he gritted, catching her wrist.

"Did I hurt you?" Her eyes widened, and she released him.

"No. But I'm at great risk of looking like the inexperienced one here."

Again, she frowned as if she didn't understand, and frankly that was just as well with him.

He shifted quickly, his barely contained desire and impatience making his movement swift and a little rough. She froze as soon as she was pinned under him, and he immediately cursed himself for his abrupt action. He rolled again, so she wasn't trapped under him, but straddling against his hips.

She blinked at the rapid sequence of motions, and he gave her a reassuring smile. "I don't want anything to remind you of that night."

She stared at him, her eyes suddenly glittering with tears. He didn't fully understand her reaction, but he sat up, pulling her to him. Her chest flattened to his, her bottom to his crotch, her legs curled around his waist. He cradled her in his arms, wanting to take all those memories away. Wanting to shield her from them.

She wrapped her arms around his neck and then they were kissing, their lips clinging to each other, desperate, hungry, and a little frantic.

Mina knew she was doing it again, giving Sebastian mixed signals, but his concern when she'd been pinned under him made her feel . . . She didn't dare to give the emotion swirling in her chest a name. But she knew it was intense and real and she wanted nothing more than to be one with this man.

She ached again, and she rubbed against him, loving the way her sex was opened against him. Loving the rasp of her nipples against his chest.

"Please Sebastian, I want . . ." She had to say it. His other women would just say it. "I want you inside me. Please."

He groaned deep in his throat and shifted, one of his hands leaving her back to slip between them. She thought he was going to position himself to enter her, but instead he touched her splayed sex. With his thumb, he stroked her clitoris.

"Sebastian," she pleaded, loving his touch but wanting all of him this time.

"Shh," he whispered against her lips. "Let me make sure it's good."

She closed her eyes, opening her mouth to him, his tongue brushing against hers as he continued to stroke her. When she was again feeling like she couldn't take any more, his hand left her and positioned his erection. The large head pressed against the entrance of her sex.

He braced his hands on her hips, poising her against him, guiding her.

"Easy," he gritted, controlling her awkward grind against his hard length. She nodded, moving cautiously, more worried about hurting him than herself.

"I do have a precedent of causing you injury, don't I?" she breathed as the head inched in.

He released a shaky laugh, his fingers gripping her tightly without hurting her. "Baby, I'm way more worried about you right now."

His concern was again the ultimate aphrodisiac for her, and she couldn't hold back, she bucked her hips forward, his huge, hard length filling her to the womb, stretching her. She gasped at the staggering sensation. Foreign, yet so absolutely right.

His large hands planted to her back, holding her firmly

against him, allowing her to adjust to the feeling of him inside her.

"Are you all right?" he asked, his voice tight and a little rough.

She nodded, lost in his gaze, hot and beautiful, as his body curled around hers. Then he began to move, his powerful arms holding her on the outside, his body caressing her own on the inside. Slowly, steadily. Bodies straining, stroking. Their eyes locked. One.

His gaze stayed on her until their lips met, then they were wild. Their mouths devouring each other. Their bodies moving faster, more urgently, until she was sure she would explode in his arms.

He lifted her against him, thrusting deep, filling her, hot, slick and amazing. Over and over until she cried out, unable to take any more. Her fangs extended, and she managed to control them, not willing to hurt him. Even though her body told her that biting him would give her the release she wanted.

Instead Sebastian splayed a hand across her lower back, driving her fully onto him, impaling her with his body. And instantly, release rocketed through her. She screamed his name, arcing under the intensity of her orgasm.

She registered Sebastian growling low in his throat, then she felt him pulse wildly against the walls of her sex. Straining against each other a moment longer, they finally collapsed into a drained heap. She only barely registered Sebastian covering them with the comforter before she fell into an exhausted sleep.

Sebastian lay beside Mina, watching her, but not touching her, as if she was something he was afraid of breaking. Or maybe that might somehow injure him.

He sat up, rubbing a hand over his face and through his hair. He tried not to wonder why his hand was trembling. But it was pointless. He couldn't think about anything but the fact that he was truly shaken. Absolutely stunned.

Sebastian had had sex, he couldn't even begin to count the number of times, and while it had always been good and fun and worth a repeat performance, it had never been like this. This was . . .

He rose out of bed, trying to be as careful as possible not to disturb Mina. Not just for her sake, but because he couldn't face her at this moment. He walked out into the living room, pacing back and forth silently over the plush carpeting.

What the hell just happened? He tunneled his hand through his hair, telling the damned appendage to stop shaking. What was wrong with him? He'd had a great orgasm, an amazing, stupendous, and absolutely unbelievable orgasm. But it had just been an orgasm. There was no reason to be freaking out like he was. He was just overwhelmed by the pressure of making sure Mina's first time was good.

Yeah, right. He'd never, never had an orgasm that earth-shattering that hadn't been aided by a bite. Hell, their straight sex had been more powerful than any bite had ever been, even the one that had crossed him over.

He stopped pacing and stared back at his bedroom. From his angle in the living room, he could see Mina's pale face. A perfect face, beautiful and doll-like, as she slept. As was becoming the norm, Sebastian felt an intense wave of possessiveness flood him.

He shook his head slightly as if he could just shake the emotion off. But when he looked at her again, the feeling was still there. Just as strong. A feeling that no matter what else happened in his long eternity, Mina had to be his. He had to have her—forever.

Eternity was a very long time, which was why he'd never seen himself with just one woman. Hell, a human life lived in fidelity would be a stretch for him. He looked at her, snuggled in his bed. She could give him an eternity, just like tonight. But that was a long time for her too. And to have only one man, him. The idea filled him with more possessiveness, and an odd pride. But he wasn't offering her forever, and it was unreasonable to expect him to be her only man.

He gritted his back teeth. Another man touching Mina; that made his insides feel as though they were being wrenched and twisted.

He paced again. Then he stopped. Was this what Rhys and Christian felt about their women? He looked back to Mina, his fallen angel, asleep in his bed. Was she his soulmate?

Chapter 21

"How do you know your soulmate?" Sebastian asked as he strolled into Rhys and Jane's library.

"Do you ever knock?" Rhys looked up from the book he was reading.

"No," Sebastian answered, flopping down into one of the overstuffed chairs. He put his feet up on the coffee table, noticing two glasses of scotch, for a minute wondering if Rhys somehow knew he was coming. But he disregarded the idea and waited for Rhys to answer. He didn't.

"Jane and I could have been in a position that requires privacy."

"Whatever. Like that's bothered you two before. Why do you think I moved out?" Sebastian leaned forward in his chair. "So answer the question. Soulmate?"

"Do you know it's nearly dawn?" Rhys looked pointedly at the lightening night sky out the large arched windows that made up one wall of the room.

"So answer quickly."

Rhys frowned, then he looked past Sebastian's chair toward the door. Sebastian sensed someone behind him.

"Good. Jane will answer me. Hey, Jane, how do you know your . . ." Sebastian turned toward the doorway, expecting to see Jane's petite form. His gaze was met by a tall, muscular male. His other brother, Christian, leaned in the doorway.

". . . soulmate?" Sebastian groaned, sinking back into the chair. "Great. Now I'm going to get the whole family's opinion on the topic."

Christian strolled into the room. "You'd trust Jane's opinion over mine. Thanks, bro."

"Women do know more about these things," Rhys agreed. "Maybe we should get Jane and Jolee in here too." He opened his mouth to call for his and Christian's mates, but Sebastian waved his hands.

"No! No. I can't handle that kind of interrogation right now."

Rhys regarded Sebastian, then nodded. "Okay."

"So? How can you tell?"

Rhys and Christian looked at each other. Then back to Sebastian.

"You just know," Christian said with a shrug.

"Well, what does it feel like?" Sebastian asked. "It's got to feel like something."

"How do you feel?" Rhys asked.

Sebastian considered for a second, then said, "Freaked out. Sort of weird—and umm, a little ill."

Both brothers gave him dubious looks.

"I don't know . . ." Christian said, shaking his head slowly.

Sebastian straightened in his chair. "So you think it's just—something else."

Rhys nodded. "Yeah. It sounds like it to me." He looked over at Christian, who nodded his agreement.

Sebastian smiled then and blew out a long breath. "Okay. Good."

He rose and headed to the door. "Hey, Christian, it's good to see you. Why are you here? Did Jolee kick you out?"

"Not yet," Christian said. "We just decided to come for a little visit."

Sebastian nodded. "Well, then I'll see you tomorrow. I

have to go . . ." He gestured vaguely down toward his apartment. "You know, to bed."

"Okay, see you late," Christian said agreeably.

Sebastian nodded and disappeared out of the room.

Both brothers stared at the empty doorway for a moment.

"I'm so glad you called me," Christian said.

"Oh, I knew you'd want to see this." Rhys grinned.

Christian shook his head, a huge grin curving his lips. "He is *so* fang-whipped."

"I told you."

Both brothers reached for their glasses of scotch on the coffee table, raised them to each other, then took long, satisfied drinks.

"Oh, *so* fang-whipped." Christian chuckled.

Mina woke with the strangest disoriented feeling. Then she recalled why. She rose on her elbows, looking around the only vaguely familiar room. She'd been a little too busy with Sebastian the previous night to take much notice of his room.

It had a cozy feel like the rest of his apartment, with slate gray walls, large antique furniture, and another fireplace against the far wall. She looked at the other side of the bed, only to discover rumpled bedding and an indentation on the pillow where Sebastian's head had been. Reaching out to touch his pillow, she listened. The apartment was quiet.

She threw back the covers, actually surprised to discover she was nude. Of course she was nude. She'd made love with Sebastian, her toes curling at the memory, and then she'd promptly fallen unconscious.

"Hey," Sebastian greeted her from the doorway. She squeaked in surprise and quickly pulled the covers back over her.

He raised an eyebrow at her reaction, then strode to the bed. He carried two large mugs. He sat on the bed and handed one to her.

She peered at the red, viscous liquid.

"Since we are both on the wagon, I took the liberty of stealing us some breakfast from my brother. Go on, it's B-negative, my personal favorite."

Mina tried, as she didn't want to appear rude, but couldn't quite suppress her grimace.

"What?" He peered into the mug too as if he expected a fly to be floating in it. "Not a fan of B-negative?"

"I don't drink human blood."

Sebastian stared at her as if she'd just admitted that she couldn't walk and chew gum. Which, given her clumsiness, she might not be able to do.

Then he frowned. "Is it because of attacking the servant?"

She nodded. That was part of it. The memory of that still made her feel ill. But she didn't say so. Instead she pointed out the main reason. "I wasn't given human blood when I was institutionalized."

"Did they give you blood at all?"

"Yes. A combination of bovine and porcine blood."

Sebastian actually looked as if he might be ill. "Cow and pig blood." He did shiver. "You can't live on that."

"I have," she stated.

"Always? That's not possible."

"It is," she said, knowing she sounded defensive. "I've done it."

Sebastian stared at her, and for the moment, she worried that her diet somehow made her unattractive to him. Then she straightened. If it did, then he was shallow and unworthy of her interest. Although the idea did hurt her.

"That's why you are so pale," he said suddenly, touching her bare shoulder. "And it probably affects you other ways too. That's probably why you fall down."

She suddenly felt self-conscious, aware of him studying her pasty skin. Of him remembering her several clumsy moments. She shoved her mug at him and started to slide across to the other side of the bed.

He quickly set the mugs on the nightstand, and caught her before she could escape from the large bed.

"Where are you going?"

"I'm—" She didn't know what to say that didn't sound sulky and childish. "I like what I drink."

That wasn't it.

"I don't care what you drink, baby."

She narrowed her eyes at him, trying to decide if he was making fun of her.

"I don't," he assured her. "I just don't know how you survived on that."

He slid farther over onto the mattress. "You know this isn't how I pictured this evening going."

"How did you picture this evening going?" she couldn't help asking as his body moved closer to hers.

"Like this." He pulled her against him, kissing her.

Despite the awkwardness of their conversation, she didn't even hesitate to melt against him. She liked this beginning to the evening much better too. One arm remained around her body as his other hand slipped underneath the covers exploring her naked skin. Her side, her waist, over her belly up to cup her breast. She didn't even think to stop him. His touch was simply too wonderful.

"God, you feel good," he murmured, breaking their kiss to look at where his hand touched her breast. He plucked the nipple, watching intently as it beaded tightly under his touch, then he dropped a lingering, suckling kiss to it. She moaned, arcing back against his arm, offering him better access.

He groaned too, but straightened away from her. "We can't do this now." He eyed her breasts regretfully.

"Why?" she asked, a little dazed even from his brief ministrations.

"I have plans for us."

"Do they involve . . ." She looked significantly at him, then the bed.

Sebastian grinned, shaking his bed. "I think I've created a monster."

She blushed, feeling like maybe he was right. All she could think about was him, taking off his clothes, crawling into bed, and making love to her. All night.

That was so not—her. Or maybe this was her. Finally. Mina the sex fiend. She had to say, she kind of liked the title. It sure beat Wilhelmina the weirdo, which was who she'd been until she met Sebastian.

"Drink up," he said, holding out one of the mugs.

She shook her head. "I can't."

"Because it's human blood?"

She nodded.

"Come on," he coaxed. "It's blood-bank blood. Willingly donated. It's like free-range blood, if you think about it. And knowing Rhys and Jane, it's probably expired stuff the bank was going to toss anyway."

Mina hesitated, then accepted the mug. She sniffed the liquid, then took a small sip. It was sweet, very sweet and the flavor more powerful than her usual mixture. She took another swallow, and then had to set it aside. Her stomach roiled slightly, but she wasn't sure whether that was because she was disgusted or because she had enjoyed it too much.

Sebastian looked as if he was going to try to persuade her to drink more, but instead he nodded at her, and then polished off his own.

"Okay, let's get you in some clothes before I change my mind about going out tonight."

She considered trying to persuade him to stay in, right here in bed. But she chickened out. She wasn't quite brave enough to try to seduce him. Because she was afraid it would be too easy for him to reject her. She couldn't handle that. Not with the way she wanted him.

Plus, if she went out with him, she still got to be with him. And there was no way she wanted to risk that.

* * *

"Where are we going?" Mina asked again as Sebastian led her down another side street.

"You'll see," Sebastian said. He loved being mysterious with her. It drove her crazy. She was as impatient as he was. One of the many ways that she was like him, which he found surprising. He would have said they were nothing alike. But they found the same things funny—well, when she actually understood what he was talking about. They liked the same books. And music—well, classical composers anyway. And most important, he reminded himself, now that he'd gotten her into his bed she was as intense and as demanding as he was. He hardened just remembering.

It had been damned hard to turn down the invitation in her eyes when he'd kissed her this evening. The hardest thing he had ever done. He'd very much wanted to just push her down onto his mattress and explore every inch of her body.

But he'd wanted to take her to this place, too. A damned hard decision. But he knew it was so important for her to discover her vampire self. And in a strange way, it was important to him to know he could resist her. That while he liked her, she was no different from many other women in his life.

And he fully planned to take her back to his place afterward and make love to her until the sun rose. He could wait for his pleasure, especially if he was helping her feel more comfortable with herself.

He turned down another street and walked up to a set of dirty concrete steps, which led to the entrance of a run-down bar.

Mina frowned, looking up at the shabby-looking place, then she gave him a dubious look. "This is where you had to bring me?"

"You are going to love it."

She raised an eyebrow, but followed as he pulled her up the stairs. The bouncer at the door just nodded at Sebastian as he entered the smoky, dark room.

"Do you come here often?"

"Once in a while."

"The bouncer seemed to know you."

"Baby, I make an impression." He winked at her. But she knew that while he thought he was only making a joke, he had stated the absolute truth. Sebastian Young did make an impression, and he would be impossible to forget. While she wanted those memories of him to block out the the bad ones of the past, she realized memories of Sebastian, once he'd moved on to another woman, would be a new form of torment.

She decided she couldn't worry about that now. She still had him and she wanted to enjoy him. Although she wasn't sure she wanted to enjoy him here.

The room they entered was dark, smoky, and crowded. Not very pleasant, really.

"Couldn't we have just gone to your bar?" Mina asked.

"Not the same," he assured her, then he zigzagged toward the far side of the room.

Mina glanced around again. No, Carfax Abbey definitely wasn't the same. The people here, predominately human, were a far rougher crowd than those who patronized Sebastian's club. Even rougher than the alpha weres, and that was saying something.

Mina cast a wary look up at a giant bald man in a studded leather jacket and torn jeans. She glanced down at her outfit, the same dress she'd worn last night, although Sebastian had suggested that she wear one of his shirts tied over the top. She hadn't understood why until now. Of course, it made her more aware that she wore no panties under her skirt, because Sebastian hadn't given her a chance to go home to get clean clothes. Of course, Sebastian was the only one who knew that she was going without.

The large man eyed her up and down, then licked his lips. She suddenly wished she had on a lot more clothes.

"I—I don't think I like it here," Mina said, leaning against him.

"Don't worry. I'm right here with you."

She glanced once more at the huge biker, then followed Sebastian through the crowd away from the creepy man.

"Okay." He stopped in among the crowd, positioned Mina in front of him. He wrapped his arms around her waist, bringing her back tight against his chest. "Now, we just wait."

Mina tried to focus on the room, on what she was supposed to be waiting for, but all she could seem to center on was the strength of Sebastian's arms holding her and the splay of his hands on her belly.

"What are we waiting for?" she finally asked over her shoulder.

"Patience," he said, giving her one of his maddening smiles.

His fingers gently stroked the curve of her stomach, slipping under his shirt, knotted around her waist. The thumb of his other hand toyed with the button of her dress, just between her breasts. Was this the lesson of tonight? Patience while he tortured her with his thrilling touch?

Each brush of those fingers drove her mad. She closed her eyes and let her head fall back against his chest, basking in each caress—as maddening as they were. But Sebastian seemed to have other plans.

"Oh no, you don't." He physically lifted her away from him, so she nearly brushed up against the man in front of her. The man didn't seem to notice.

"Why not?" she asked, knowing her tone sounded petulant. But really, he couldn't touch her like that and not expect her to respond.

"Sorry," he said against her ear. "I have to behave myself. It's very hard, knowing you're naked under that skirt."

She didn't comment, because she couldn't. Her body was too busy aching for him to allow for actually coherent thought. His hands returned to her waist, but he kept his fingers still this time.

More people crowded in around them, bumping against her in their attempts to get closer to the . . . For the first time, she realized they were standing in makeshift rows, and over the sea of heads and shoulders, she realized they faced a stage.

"We're here for a band?" She frowned back at him. He'd rather be in a run-down bar listening to a band than in bed with her? She couldn't help feeling a little offended.

"For the band, among other things."

Her breath caught at the mention of "other things," but his hands remained still at her waist. She frowned, casting another look around at the patrons surrounding them. More leather. Lots of makeup. Lots of aggressive vibes. These humans were here for a good time, but they were a tough crowd, the men and the women alike. She waited for their aggressive emotions to bombard her.

A woman to her right lurched against her as she tried to light a cigarette, and Mina waited for the contact in conjunction with the rest of the crowd to overwhelm her.

But it didn't.

"Sorry," the woman said, then exhaled a long stream of smoke.

Surprised by her lack of distress at the woman's touch, Mina only managed a nod in response.

The woman looked her up and down with a frown. She obviously found Mina's silky, feminine dress and the white cotton shirt tied over the top rather out of place. The woman then glanced at Sebastian, her eyes widening slightly. She looked him up and down too. She smiled. Obviously Sebastian's black t-shirt and faded jeans passed the woman's inspection.

Mina rolled her eyes. Of course, Sebastian could have been wearing a pink tuxedo and the woman wouldn't have been put off.

She noticed the woman stepped closer to him.

"I don't think this is my kind of place," Mina muttered to Sebastian.

He chuckled and pulled her closer to him. She had the feeling he knew the other woman's interest bothered her. Oh well. It did.

"A little too wild for you, huh?" he asked, his lips brushing her ear. "My goody-two-shoes." She felt him smile.

"'You don't bite. Don't shift. What do you do?'"

She didn't recognize the tune to which he sang his comments. And she tried hard to ignore that fact that his singing voice was as rich and sexy as when he spoke, because she got the definite feeling he was making fun of her.

She started to turn in his arms, to tell him she didn't appreciate his teasing, when the crowd swelled up around them in a loud cheer.

She watched as the band, which was composed of rather haggard-looking older men, took the stage. Some of the band members had long hair, others didn't. All had traces of gray.

"Who is this band?" she asked.

"The Grateful Dead," he said, then laughed at some joke only he got. "No, not really. They are just a cover band that I really like. They play some good rock."

"I like classical music," she said primly.

"I know."

And again, for a split second, she wondered how he knew. Oh right, from his uninvited visit to her apartment. For some reason, that didn't bother her as much as it once had.

"This is classic rock. You'll like it, too," he assured her with a little squeeze. Then the band started to play.

They sang about some boys being back in town. Then they were getting no sugar tonight in their coffee. Or apparently their tea either. And currently they were just going to let it ride. She didn't really understand the lyrics, but she had to admit she did like the beat and the lead singer had a nice voice. Of course, she suspected the solid feeling of Sebastian pressed against her back, holding her, swaying to the music helped her opinion. And she loved the low timbre of his voice as he sang a verse here and there. Much better than the lead singer's, really.

"Like it?" he asked her when the song ended.

She smiled at him over her shoulder. "If I admit I do, will you be smug about it?"

"Absolutely." He leaned forward and stole a quick kiss.

"Okay," he said, his lips again by her ear so she could hear him over the guitar intro to the next song. "An appreciation for classic rock. One objective down. Now, for the real reason we are here. What do you feel around you?"

She shot him a wry glance as a woman in front of her tossed her hair, the long lock nearly hitting Mina in the face.

"People. Lots of people."

Sebastian raised his eyebrows expectantly as if he waited for her to add something else.

She shrugged.

"What don't you feel?" He rested his chin on her shoulder, waiting, as she again cast a look around the mobbed room.

She didn't feel the humans' emotions, she realized. She looked at the woman, who'd been admiring Sebastian earlier, and focused. She could feel the woman's attraction to Sebastian. She could feel her enjoyment of the band, and a little bit of loneliness. But until she'd thought about it, Mina hadn't noticed any of those things.

"I'm blocking the emotions," Mina said excitedly.

Sebastian smiled back at her. "See, once you learn to look outside of the emotions, it just starts to happen naturally until you have to focus to feel the emotions. Not the other way around."

She couldn't stop smiling as she looked around the room, focusing first on one person, then another. She felt each person's emotions separately, and when she moved on, they weren't there any more bombarding her.

"That's wonderful," she said, with a sigh. She felt almost normal, she realized.

He leaned forward, catching her chin, turning her head so he could kiss her fully, slowly. Then she didn't feel normal at all, she felt like her skin was sizzling, desire snapping through every nerve ending in her body.

Sebastian continued to kiss her a moment longer, his tongue brushing against hers. Then he broke the kiss as they watched the band again, who now, quite appropriately, sang about feeling like making love.

Sebastian's hands moved on her waist, one sliding under the loose cotton shirt. Nimbly, his fingers plucked open the buttons of her dress, until his fingers could slip inside to touch her bare skin. Throughout the remainder of the song, his hand caressed her stomach, the underside of her breast. She could feel the moisture gathering between her thighs, her arousal somehow more keen with the lack of underwear.

"Is the lesson done?" she asked her voice breathy when the song ended.

He growled low in his throat, the sound thrilling. "Yes, very soon. Because I need to get you alone. And naked."

She nodded, leaning heavily against him, feeling his erection prodding her bottom. She pressed against it, wiggling her hips, feeling him pulse even through their clothes.

"Then let's go now." She wriggled against him again.

He growled again, a low rumble against her ear. She felt his chest expand as he took a deep breath.

"Okay, one more lesson, then we go."

She took a deep breath too. "Okay."

"I'm going to go to the bar and get us drinks," he said, dropping his hands from her body.

She turned and frowned at him. "I don't want a drink. I want you."

He smiled indulgently. "*And* you are going to see if you can handle the crowd with your focal point gone."

He nodded as if to tell her to get to it and then he headed toward the bar on the other side of the room.

She gaped at him, unable to believe he could behave so calmly. She felt like she was going to implode. She pulled in a calming breath and tried to do as he asked. Handle the crowd without her focal point.

It wasn't until the crowd shifted back around her, nearly

blocking Sebastian from her view, that she realized exactly what he'd said. *With your focal point gone.*

He'd known all along that she'd been using him as her center.

She shook her head. That overconfident—

"Hey."

Mina's thoughts stopped as she looked back from where Sebastian had disappeared to stare directly into a barrel chest clad in white t-shirt and black leather. Her gaze moved upward until she saw that the mountain beside her was the huge, bald man she'd first seen when she entered the bar.

"You looked like you were having fun." His gaze dropped pointedly to where Sebastian had been touching her. Her dress was still unbuttoned, though the man couldn't know that since it was hidden under Sebastian's shirt.

"I can show you a good time too, darlin'."

He grinned at her, and even without her focal point, she realized she could center easily on his emotions. They were loud and clear.

Lust. Lust and violence.

Chapter 22

Sebastian was impressed with Mina. She learned how to handle human vibration very quickly. Far more quickly than he would have thought possible given the fact she'd been a vampire for so long and had never been able to control it before. He'd thought it would be harder for her. But she was a quick study.

Then he thought about the way she had just so provocatively rubbed against him. Mina was a quick learner in many areas.

Once he reached the bar, he glanced at the other patrons who waited for drinks. He guessed it would be a good ten minute wait. And frankly, Sebastian wasn't that thirsty. He definitely had other things he'd rather do than stand here.

The lesson was a success. He knew she was handling the reverberation just fine without him. He forced himself to finish this lesson, because he wanted Mina to be comfortable with herself and with the world around her. That was important to him. But now that the lesson was done and a success, he wanted to teach her things that were far more fun—and involved far fewer clothes.

He weaved through the throng back toward where he'd left her, but he didn't see her. He scanned the crowd. Then he sensed it, a prickling of fear, Mina's fear, an emotion of hers he knew too well. But still he couldn't see her.

Then a humongous man, at least 6'5", in a studded leather jacket, moved, and Sebastian realized the hulk was looming over Mina. Mina stared warily at the man, but what made Sebastian more nervous than her expression was that fear, thick in the air like a giant fogbank swirling all around her.

Sebastian strode toward the man, restraining himself from shoving the giant away from her.

"Excuse me," he said instead.

The hulk turned slowly, eyeing Sebastian with an unimpressed scowl. Despite the man's size, Sebastian was equally unimpressed.

"What do you want, buddy?"

"Leave my woman alone," Sebastian stated.

The man crossed his tree-trunk arms over his massive chest. "I don't see anything on her that says she's yours."

What a damned Neanderthal. Sebastian wanted to just punch the idiot and be done with the situation. But then he looked at Mina's wide, frightened eyes and decided against it, afraid violence would be too much for her.

"Well, despite the fact that I have indeed neglected to scrawl my name all over her, she is mine," he said with a small polite smile. "So I'd advise you to leave now."

The man raised an eyebrow, then reached out and snagged Mina's wrist. She gasped, and Sebastian felt her fear spike.

"If I go, I'm taking her with me." The giant eyed him as if to say that there was no way in hell a man an inch or two shorter and a good seventy-five pounds lighter was going to stop him.

Mina made a small noise, and Sebastian acted purely on instinct, lunging at the guy. He easily knocked the giant away from Mina and landed a punch before the jerk even saw the blow coming.

Sebastian couldn't help smiling with satisfaction as the giant's hand flew up to his nose, pressing his fingers to the flow of blood that ran from both nostrils.

Broken, Sebastian thought smugly. Definitely broken.

Unfortunately, Sebastian's satisfaction was short-lived. Distracted both by his smugness and Mina, he didn't sense the other humans behind him until they had grabbed his arms. The hulk, surprisingly fast for his huge size—and broken nose—punched Sebastian square in the face. The blow didn't hurt, but Sebastian did hear a crunch.

His nose. Figures.

Highly irritated by his lack of awareness, Sebastian threw off the two men restraining him with a little more strength than necessary. Both men flew through the air, smashing against the wall over ten feet away. They crumpled to the ground, dazed and with the wind knocked out of them. Sebastian spun back toward the Neanderthal.

The man's expression was no longer indifferent. Now it was almost comically alarmed as he gaped from Sebastian to his fallen friends and back to Sebastian, unable to believe what he'd just seen.

Well, it would have been comical if Sebastian's actions hadn't drawn the attention of most of the bar. A crowd had formed around them, and Sebastian could tell from the other patrons' expressions that they too had found Sebastian's fighting skills to be more than a little unusual.

Damn. It was never wise to draw that kind of attention. But he hadn't been thinking about appearing normal. He'd only been thinking to protect Mina.

Surprisingly, however, it was Mina who seemed to gather her wits first. She hurried to his side, tugging at him.

"Let's just go."

He looked down at the two men, still huddled on the ground. They would be okay. They'd be hurting for a while, but they'd survive.

Sebastian glared at the hulk. He was the only one Sebastian had really wanted to injure. Mina tugged Sebastian's hand again, and he allowed her to pull him away from the growing crowd of onlookers. But Sebastian couldn't resist taking a step toward the huge man as he passed. The giant jumped back like Sebastian was a poisonous snake about to strike.

Sebastian snorted. Ha, that ass would think twice before he touched someone else's woman. Sebastian grinned to himself, which quickly turned to a grimace as he tasted the blood trickling from his nose. He wiped the droplets away with the back of his hand, and then let Mina lead him outside.

Mina didn't release him, as she hurriedly tugged him away from the bar, not looking at him, just hell-bent on getting them away from the place.

"Mina, stop." Sebastian dug in his heels.

She stumbled to a stop, but she didn't look at him.

"What's wrong?" he asked, leaning forward, trying to see her face.

Finally she looked up at him and he could see tears in her eyes, making them glitter like polished sapphires.

"You were right," Mina said, barely able to look at his battered face.

"Well, I often am," he said with a slight smile. "But I'm not actually sure what I'm right about at the moment."

Somehow he managed to look cocky, even with a broken nose. The realization didn't make her feel any better, however.

"I panicked and you got hurt," she told him.

He frowned at her. "You think that was your fault back there?"

"I shouldn't have panicked," she said miserably. "I should have handled it."

"You could have," he agreed. "You are a vampire and that makes you physically strong enough to deal with a jerk like that."

He stepped closer to her, touching her cheek, brushing a wisp of her black hair back from her face. She fought the urge to nuzzle her cheek against his large palm.

"But you didn't have to," he said quietly. "I wanted to protect you. That guy was a damned Neanderthal."

His words made her insides turn to quivering jelly. He wanted to protect her. She couldn't remember anyone wanting to do that for her. She waited for it to not be real—that somehow Sebastian would be a fantasy. The embodiment of all her childhood dreams.

She gazed up at him, and he tucked another loose strand of her hair behind her ear, his fingers strong and yet so gentle against her skin.

"I hate that look," he told her. "You look like you want so badly to trust me, but you don't. Not quite."

She blinked, stunned that all those feelings were there in her eyes. The exact feelings that were in her heart.

"Does it hurt?" she asked gesturing to his nose, not wanting to discuss her insecurities any longer.

"Not bad. Is it still bleeding?"

She shook her head. Then she smiled slightly and gave him a pained cringe. "It's very—crooked, though."

Sebastian fingered the bump there.

"I knew that bastard broke it," he said, disgruntled.

She moved closer to inspect the injury, her body brushing against his. His hands caught her waist as she rose up and gently pressed a kiss to the bridge of his nose. Then to his cheek, then to his mouth. She wanted to care for him the way he had her.

But she was only allowed a couple more gentle ministrations, then he tugged her tightly to him, deepening the kiss, and all her tender thoughts fled. She just wanted him. This man who'd protected her. This man who made her feel alive. And safe. And lo—

She pushed the word away, putting all the emotions inside her into her kiss. They stayed like that, locked in each other's arms, their lips clinging together as if they would die if they had to part.

Then a group of loud young humans passed them, cheering and hooting at their behavior. Only then did they seem to realize where they were. On the sidewalk in a dubious part of the city.

Sebastian stared down at her, a stunned look in his golden eyes.

"How do you do this to me?" he murmured almost as if he was talking to himself.

She didn't know what she did, but if it was anything even remotely like what he did to her, she was humbled.

"Should we go?" she asked, her voice breathy, her eyes heavy-lidded, dazed.

He nodded.

They walked only a block, when Sebastian suddenly veered into a dark alleyway. He continued deeper into its litter-strewn depths until they were concealed in the shadows of a rickety fire escape.

"What are we doing?" she asked, confused.

"I have to touch you," he said, his voice low, desperate. "Just a little."

She didn't consider telling him no. She had to touch him too. The need crackled in the air between them.

Sebastian sucked in a breath as her hands moved to his sides, sliding over the sinew of his torso. She stepped closer to him, her face turned up to his, and he didn't hesitate to take her invitation.

His mouth fell on hers, his touch not tempered with any restraint or gentleness. She moaned, reveling in his hunger, his urgency. The same need raged through her.

One of his hands moved to cradle the back of her neck, the angle opening her mouth to him. His tongue swept over hers, hot and insistent, each brush stoking the hungry desperation inside her.

She made a small noise in the back of her throat as his fingers tugged at the knot at her waist. He managed to yank the material free, and he found the already opened front of her dress. His hand slid inside, stroking her, finding the swell of her breast, kneading the aching flesh.

Her hands massaged over him. The broadness of his shoulders, the hard, perfect muscles of his back, covered in a layer of thin cotton. Her fingers strayed under the material, wanting to feel his bare skin. Velvet over rippling steel.

"Mina," he growled against her lips. He started to pull back as if he realized how quickly their passion was spiraling out of control. She sank her fingers into his muscled back, anchoring him to her.

"No," she said against his lips. She didn't want to stop. Not yet.

He hesitated, but then growled again. His lips molded to hers, opening her, tasting her. Her arms came around his neck as she strained to get closer to him. Wanting all of him.

She barely registered as he shifted them, only vaguely aware of coarse hardness against her back. The relentless tease of his hand at her breast, grazing over and over her hard nipple was far more distracting. Breath-stealing. Wonderful.

Humid air clung to her skin as he loosened the rest of her dress, exposing her throbbing breasts. He gazed at them for a moment, before dropping his lips to kiss one of the taut peaks. Having first one, then moving to the other painfully pebbled nipple.

Her head fell back against the hardness at her back as he licked and suckled first one nipple, then when she thought she would scream out from sheer need, he turned to the other, repeating the process.

"Sebastian," she cried as he worked the hardened nub between his amazing lips.

She felt his smile as he pressed a kiss to the side of her breast, then she felt his hands going to her skirt, gathering the material upward. More humid, heavy air brushed her bare legs and grazed the tight curls of her sex.

She gasped, raising her head to watch Sebastian sink down in front of her. Her fingers tangled in his hair as he brushed his full lips against her thigh.

She whimpered as his breath stirred the curls. He nudged her legs apart, then just as gently, he parted her. Then his tongue touched her, intense, incredible fire licking between her thighs.

She cried out, her head falling back. Her arms came out to her side, her palms pressing into the rough wall behind her. Her fingers dug into the coarse bricks as she arced her hips forward, demanding more pressure from Sebastian's amazing mouth. He gave her what she wanted, his tongue relentlessly flicking over and around her throbbing clitoris.

She called out his name, her head still raised toward the sky. At first she didn't recognize the wetness on her face, on her bared breasts. The warm roll of moisture was just more torture on her already sensitized skin. All she understood was Sebastian's touch. His fingers holding her open, his tongue delved into her. Her own urgent need.

Then Sebastian was gone.

She stared down at him, disoriented by the sudden loss of his touch. He looked up at her, his eyes golden in the dim light. Intense, searching.

"Sebastian, what is it?"

He glanced up at the sky, and for the first time, she realized the moisture on her skin was rain. It was pouring. She hadn't even known.

She laughed, the sound sudden, surprised.

Sebastian frowned at her as if maybe she was going mad. Maybe she was. She tugged at his shoulders until he rose. Her fingers went to the button of his jeans, fumbling with the damp material. He caught her hands, stopping her.

"Mina, I don't want anything we do to ever remind you of that night."

She gazed into Sebastian's golden eyes. Warm eyes. Beautiful eyes. Nothing about this man would ever remind her of that night. Not again.

"I want this," she said, pressing her mouth lingeringly to his. Rain clung to his lips. To her lips.

Her fingers began to fumble with his jeans again. He stopped her clumsy fingers, but this time to unfasten them himself.

She watched as he released himself, his penis jutting proudly from his parted zipper. She touched him, the rain making the smooth skin slick. A glistening idol in the dim light, dusky and dazzling.

"Are you sure?" he asked, his voice strained. He didn't want to stop, but she knew he would if she said she'd changed her mind. That alone was enough to make her absolutely sure.

She nodded, then kissed him, nipping the lush softness of his bottom lip.

Sebastian groaned and shifted so she was pinned between the wall and his hard, hot body. Instead of feeling fear at the trapped position, she reveled in the weight of him. His hard muscles, his powerful strength.

His lips found hers, and she could taste the uncertainty on his lips. Concern for her. She linked her arms around his neck, her mouth plundering his, showing him the intensity of her need.

He responded with a groan as his hands came up to cup her bottom, lifting her until his hips were wedged between her legs, his erection tight against the wet flesh of her sex.

He held her that way, kissing her, his hips grinding against her, his penis stroking her swollen clitoris until she was writhing between him and the wall.

"Sebastian, I need you inside me," she breathed against his ear.

Easily he levered himself away from her, still holding her aloft. He positioned himself, inching into her with a glorious deliberate glide until he was buried deep inside her. Stretched and full and complete.

"Baby, you feel too good," he gritted, staying perfectly still inside her.

"Is there such a thing as too good?" Mina asked, squirming, needing him to move. Needing him to end this ceaseless yearning inside her.

"With you? I think maybe." Something flashed in his eyes, an emotion she didn't quite understand. But she didn't get a chance to question him, because he began to move, his erection pulling out of her until only the swell of the head remained inside her. Then thrusting back in filling her totally, completely. Each thrust a maddening friction, over and over until he was driving into her with violent force.

She arced against him accepting every thrust readily. Reveling in it. Until her desire ripped through her, every nerve, every cell disintegrated into pure ecstasy.

"Sebastian," she shouted and she felt him tense against her, his own release overwhelming him.

She lifted her face toward the sky, the rain washing over them. Pounding against her tingling skin, as relentless as Sebastian. As perfect.

"I love you," she murmured against his wet skin.

Sebastian stiffened against her, and Mina wanted the words back, but she realized that would be like getting the rain back into the clouds.

Chapter 23

Sebastian watched Mina as she struggled to straighten her clothes. Her fingers trembled as she fumbled with the rain-slicked button of his shirt that she wore.

He was as shaken as she was, but he gently nudged her hands away and began to work them closed. She stared down at his fingers rather than meeting his gaze. He knew exactly what he could say to end this awkwardness between them, but instead he finished pushing the last button through its hole and said, "There."

"Thank you," she mumbled, still not looking at him. Instead she focused her gaze on the streetlight visible at the end of the alleyway.

He stared at her for a moment, knowing he should say something. Anything. But he didn't. He just reached for her hand. He was surprised when she didn't yank it out of his hold. She simply fell into step beside him as they headed back out to the sidewalk.

The rain had begun to let up, just a steady drizzle. Not that it mattered. They were already soaked, he thought, trying to think about anything other than the three words she'd just said to him, back in that alley.

"Mina," he said slowly. He had to say something to ease the awful tension.

"Please, don't," she said. "I was, you know, just caught up in the moment. It's really not worth talking about."

He studied her for a moment, then watched the sidewalk ahead of them. He should accept her excuse; he didn't want her love. It wasn't what he was offering her. But now that he'd gotten the words, it bothered him that she was denying them. Which made no sense to him. He had heard them before, and they always meant things wound up ending uncomfortably.

It was always best to keep things simple. Uncomplicated.

He focused on her, trying to read her emotions, but he couldn't get anything from her. No emotion at all.

She'd learned to block them, he realized with begrudging pride. Right at this moment when he wanted more than ever to know what she was thinking.

That had to be irony.

"I mean, I like you well enough," she said suddenly. She glanced at him. "I mean, I wouldn't do what we just did with someone I didn't like. You know?"

"Right," he agreed. "Nor would I."

She pursed her lips slightly, then nodded. They both watched the sidewalk again.

Sebastian stopped, pulling her to face him. Suddenly, he needed to say something. To let her know that while this might not be love, it was special to him.

"Mina, I like you. More than just well enough."

Her midnight blue eyes roamed his face, then she nodded with a slight smile. "Yeah. I like you more than just well enough, too."

He kissed her, then they started walking again, hands still linked. He had no idea what the hell that conversation really meant. And he still couldn't read her real feelings, but at least the air seemed less tense between them.

When they reached Carfax Abbey, he started to lead her toward the back entrance, but Mina hesitated.

"Why aren't we going in through the club?"

He shrugged. "I figured this would avoid a lot of unwanted questions."

"Because you don't want everyone in the club asking about me? And why we're together—again?" Hurt made her chest tighten at the possibility that was why, but she tried to keep her expression indifferent.

"No," he said slowly. "Because I look pretty rough."

He gestured to his still battered face, which already looked a little better, but was still quite noticeable. Then she also saw the knees of his jeans were caked with filth from where he'd knelt in front of her in the alley. His clothes were soaked and askew, his hair a mess, and his lips pinker from their kisses.

"And while you probably look much better than I do," he said as he watched her perusal of him, "you still look like a woman who's been pretty thoroughly ravaged against a brick wall."

She let her gaze drop to the ground, feeling ridiculous and petty. He wasn't trying to hide her from the employees at Carfax Abbey, he was trying to save her from being embarrassed in front of them. He might not love her, but he wasn't ashamed of her. But then, she suspected that Sebastian was rarely embarrassed about anything.

"I'm sorry," she said quietly. "I shouldn't have said that."

He shrugged and gave her a brief smile, then he started toward the side alley, but this time Constantine stopped him.

"Sebastian," the large wolf yelled from his post at the front door. "There you are. Everyone's been trying to find you."

Not releasing Mina's hand, Sebastian started up the steps. She waited for Constantine to frown or make some surprised expression about their contact. But he didn't seem to notice.

"Why? What's up?" Sebastian asked once they reached the bouncer.

"Some guy . . ." Constantine frowned at Sebastian. "Is your nose broken?" His dark eyes moved to Mina, his gaze drifted over her disheveled appearance. "What happened to you two?"

"We got mugged," Sebastian said automatically, then asked. "So what did this guy do?"

"Oh, yeah right. He attacked a woman. In the back alley."

"Shit," Sebastian muttered. "Was he—you know?"

Constantine glanced at the people waiting behind them to enter the club. Three humans. A man and two women.

"Yes, he was different," Constantine said.

"Shit," Sebastian said again.

"Your brothers are with the girl. They are waiting for the police."

Sebastian nodded again to the bouncer and hurried into the club.

As soon as Nadine saw them, she pointed to the backroom. Sebastian nodded again and strode in that direction, never releasing Mina's hand.

They entered the employee lounge to find two tall, very handsome vampires standing near the door. Right away, Mina could tell they had to be Sebastian's brothers. Two female vampires sat on the lounge's worn sofa with a human woman between them. The human had her head down and she was crying quietly.

As soon as the male vampires saw Sebastian, they gestured for him to go back out of the room. Again, Sebastian didn't let go of Mina as he followed them into the hall.

"What the hell happened?" Sebastian asked as soon as they were away from the distressed mortal.

"Apparently, one of the vampire patrons convinced her to leave with him and he attacked her. In the alley," said the taller of the two men. Then his eyes, the same color as Sebastian's, narrowed as he surveyed Sebastian.

"What the hell happened to you?"

"Mugged," Sebastian said.

"Wow, that sucks," said the other brother. He was the same height as Sebastian, but instead of golden brown eyes, his were the palest blue Mina had ever seen.

No, that wasn't true, she realized. Lizzie had nearly the same color eyes.

The blue-eyed brother held out his hand to her. "Hi. I'm

Christian, Sebastian's brother. Sorry to meet you under circumstances like this."

"Hi," she nodded, accepting his hand. "I'm Mina."

"Rhys," the taller brother said. She shook his hand too.

"Did he bite her?" Sebastian asked, barely registering the introduction. Mina could see he was very upset by what had happened.

"Yes, but Mick interrupted him before he could really hurt her. She's badly shaken, but she will be okay. I don't even think she'll need a doctor," Rhys said. "The bite is already fading."

Mina noticed that while Sebastian seemed relieved about that news, he still looked worried. "The police are going to have a lot of questions. Especially when she tells *how* the guy attacked her."

"I don't think so," Rhys said. "They'll think she's a very upset woman, who isn't recalling things accurately."

Mina stiffened. She knew how it was to be that woman. Sebastian must have sensed her tension, because he squeezed her fingers.

For a minute, she considered that Sebastian was only worried about the club. Protecting it from inquiry and other bad press.

"Shit," he muttered, running a hand through his hair. "The patrons here know the rules. They know that any violence won't be tolerated. This is the first problem in over eighteen months, since that wacko weredingo got a little too frisky with one of the ladies. And he didn't actually hurt her, just got a little too overexcited."

"Weredingos are crazy anyway," Christian said.

"Exactly," Sebastian agreed. "But this attack sounded premeditated, and he has to be found. I bet he won't stop at this girl."

Mina suddenly felt terrible for thinking he was only concerned with Carfax Abbey. He wasn't. He was upset because a mortal had been hurt. And others might be too.

He turned to her. "Do you mind waiting here with my

brothers and their wives? I want to talk to Mick before the police get here?"

"No, go ahead."

He nodded, then strode down the hallway toward Mick's office.

"Were you really mugged?" Christian asked as soon as Sebastian disappeared.

"No," Mina admitted.

"Did you break his nose?" he asked.

Mina's eyes widened at the question. "No!"

"We wouldn't blame you if you did," Rhys said. "He can be a real pain in the ass."

Mina frowned at Sebastian's brothers, until she saw the affection in their expressions.

"He can be," she admitted.

They chuckled, then ushered her into the room.

Mina was quietly introduced to Rhys's wife, Jane, a petite, almost elfin-looking woman with huge green eyes and a sweet smile. Jolee, Christian's wife, was taller and willowy with gorgeous dark red hair and wide, sultry lips.

Both women were stunningly lovely, Mina thought, shifting awkwardly, realizing how she must look to them. A drowned rat. A plain, pasty drowned rat. They had to be wondering what on earth Sebastian was doing with her.

Mina focused on the human, instead of her own awkwardness. The woman looked very young, maybe just twenty-one. Dark hair, lovely skin, sky blue eyes. She looked wholesome rather than gorgeous.

Mina's heart went out to the poor girl. She'd stopped crying now, only sniffing a bit, and she looked like she just wanted to leave. Occasionally she'd glance at Rhys and Christian, and Mina suspected the big men were making her nervous. They were rather nerve-wracking.

"Can I get you a drink, Annie?" Jane asked the mortal, her voice was as sweet as her face. "A soda or something?"

The young woman nodded, seeming to relax just a little. "That would be nice. Thank you."

Annie's voice contained a lazy twang. She wasn't from here, Mina realized, and she wondered if she had any family nearby. Then she wondered if her family would be supportive of her. Or would they blame her for the attack? Blame her for being in a nightclub. For letting a guy convince her to leave with him.

She hoped not.

Jane left the room to go get the drink, and Mina moved closer to the woman.

"Do you have anyone you'd like to call? Your parents?" Mina asked, perching on the sofa beside her.

Annie shook her head. "I'm here for college. My parents didn't want me to come to New York in the first place. They'll make me go home if they find out."

"You're going to have to tell them something," Mina said.

Annie shook her head again. "I'll be okay." She offered Mina a tremulous smile. "I have my roommates and other friends."

Mina nodded. At least she had them. Mina hadn't even had that. She wondered how different she'd be now if she had had someone.

Mina looked up as she heard footsteps entering the room, hoping it was Sebastian. She suddenly felt the need to see him. To be near him. But it was Jane, returning with a glass of soda.

The room fell silent as everyone waited for the police to arrive. Soon they did, followed by Sebastian and Mick, a large, bald, goateed preternatural. A faery if Mina was reading him right. For a moment, Mina thought of that huge biker back at the other bar—Mick did look similar to that man. But the physical resemblance was where the similarities ended. Mick didn't give off any of the violent vibes the biker had. Mick protected the helpless, like Annie, not preyed on them. Then Mina looked at Sebastian's poor battered face. He may not love her, but he had protected her.

She glanced at Annie. Sebastian would see that this woman was protected too.

"Okay," Rhys said to the mortal. "I guess we should clear out so that you can talk to the police. Good luck, Annie."

Annie nodded, giving both of Sebastian's brothers her thanks. Jane hugged her. And Jolee smiled at her reassuringly, telling her to take care of herself. Mina also started to rise, but Annie touched her arm.

"Please stay," she asked and Mina nodded, wanting to stay, because she did understand this woman's fear, and Annie seemed to sense that too. Mina looked to Sebastian, then she sat back beside the woman. Mina took Annie's hand as the two officers began to ask the young woman questions.

"So he attacked you in the alley between Carfax Abbey and the parking garage?" one officer asked.

Annie nodded.

"Did he have a weapon?"

She shook her head. "No, but he was very strong. I tried to fight him, but he was just . . ." She shook her head as if she couldn't explain, which she couldn't. Mina knew preternatural strength was hard to put into words. Mina gently squeezed her cold fingers to give her comfort.

"He was just very strong," Annie said with a helpless shrug.

"What did he look like?"

Annie took a breath. "He was about six feet tall. In his mid-twenties. Curly brown hair. Dark brown eyes."

Mina shifted, an uncomfortable feeling coming over her. She looked at Sebastian, who watched her rather than Annie. She offered him a reassuring smile. This woman was describing a thousand men. There was no reason to think this person could possibly be—

"He had a dimple in his left cheek. And an Italian accent."

Mina swallowed, her stomach roiling. Sebastian saw her discomfort and took a step closer.

"Did he give you a name?" the officer asked.

Annie nodded. "Yes, Donatello."

Mina would have bet that vampires couldn't faint. She proved herself wrong.

Chapter 24

He was back. Oh God, he was back. She had to escape. Terror flooded Mina as she pushed upright. She struggled to catch her breath, then she cried out.

"Baby, I'm right here," Sebastian said softly, his arms coming up around her, a safe haven in the dark. Only then did she realize she wasn't back in that wet, black forest. She was in Sebastian's bedroom. In his bed. Safe.

She wrapped her arms around his neck, letting his steady warmth replace the fear chilling her skin. His large hands massaged her back as he told her over and over she was fine. He was there. He was there.

Gradually she became aware of the fire crackling in the fireplace. The thick quilt that he'd wrapped around her. The ways he'd tried to make her feel warm and secure.

"I passed out," she said as if he didn't know that.

But instead of giving her one of his half smiles, he only nodded, looking very serious.

"I bet that confused the police," she tried to say lightly, wanting one of his smiles to reassure her everything was fine.

"The police and the girl were fine. It was—fine." He touched her hair almost as if he needed to be sure she was fine too.

"It was really him, wasn't it?" she finally asked.

His eyes locked with hers. "We don't know that for sure. It could just be a coincidence."

"Do you really believe that?"

Sebastian shrugged. "Even if it was him. He's gone again. He won't come back here. And I don't believe he was looking for you."

She nodded. If he'd wanted to find her again, he certainly had the time to do it. A hundred years worth of time.

"I will admit it is a weird coincidence, but I really believe a coincidence, nonetheless."

She nodded again, wanting to believe him.

"Mina." He brushed her mussed hair from her cheek. "I won't let anything happen to you. You know that."

She met his eyes, seeing the concern clouding their golden depths. She did know that. She caught the hand still stroking her hair and pressed a kiss into his palm, the skin against her lips warm and slightly calloused. She kissed there again, her tongue flicking out to test the roughness.

He groaned, his hand moving away from her mouth to curl into her hair. His other hand came up to hold the other side of her head. Then he gently, tenderly brushed kisses to her forehead, across her fluttering eyelids, to her nose and finally to her lips. His mouth remained soft, soothing as it molded over and over against hers.

His lips never leaving her, he eased her back against the pillows. She felt his fingers move to her clothes, unhurriedly working the buttons loose. Then he pressed fluttering, open-mouthed kisses to each inch of skin that he exposed until her dress was open, her body bared to him. With hands that Mina could have sworn trembled, or maybe it was only a trick of the firelight, he stroked her naked skin. A leisurely exploration of her body that was staggeringly arousing because of his almost innocent touches. Her belly. The sensitive spot behind her knee. The arch of her foot.

By the time his hand slipped between her thighs, she was burning for him, as hot as the flames in the fireplace.

"Sebastian," she whispered, awed by the adoration of his touch, the reverence in his eyes. She understood that he didn't return her feelings in the same way, but she felt unable to contain the emotions inside her. Maybe she was a fool, but she didn't care. She had to tell him.

"I do love you."

Sebastian's breath caught at her whispered words. Words that shook him as if she'd bellowed them from the highest mountaintop. Words that he desperately wanted to hear, even as he told himself again that he didn't. Words that terrified him just as much as they excited him.

He watched her face as he caressed her, the damp curls of her sex tickling his fingers. The pulse of her tiny clitoris against the pad of his thumb. He studied the rapid rise and fall of her beautiful breasts. The redness of her bottom lip as the soft skin pillowed around her white teeth. The little whimpers she made as she strained against his hand.

No woman had ever fascinated him as she did. No other woman had been this important to him. This essential to him. His hand paused at his own thoughts, then he pushed them aside, falling back on the mattress so he could strip off his shirt and jeans.

He returned to her, their mouths melding, their bodies fitting perfectly together. He took her gasp into his mouth as she accepted him inside her. His full length deep into her body. He pulled back, gazing down at her. Her perfect pale skin, her beautiful eyes, so dark, so blue he wanted to drown in them. His eyes remained locked with hers as he began to move in a slow easy rhythm. Gliding nearly out, only to slide back in to the hilt, filling her completely again and again.

Her lips parted, a ragged breath escaping her with each stroke. He kept that leisurely pace, fascinated with watching her, painfully aroused by the desire in her eyes. Then she began to squirm under him, her hands growing frantic as they stroked his shoulders, his back.

"What do you want, baby?" he murmured against her lips.

"You," she answered automatically.

"Like this?" He plunged deeper.

She cried out, her head bobbing. "Yes. Oh, yes."

He filled her again, deep, hard. Building the pace until she was thrashing under him, the muscles around his cock clutching him in the same way her arms clasped his body.

"Come for me, Mina," he said, as he moved his hand down to where their bodies joined, finding the tiny bud in the curls of her sex.

He just touched her when she screamed, her body convulsing around him. His fangs distended, but he easily ignored them, lost in the strong quiver of her body. He pumped once more, hard and deep, then his own orgasm rocked his body. He collapsed on top of her, weak, trembling.

As he fell into a state of satisfied unconsciousness, he tried to recall how his orgasms had felt before Mina. Had they been as mind-blowing, as awe-inspiring?

Oddly, he couldn't seem to recall.

Sebastian stretched, a smile of tremendous satisfaction on his face. "Damn I'm good."

Mina rolled her eyes. "You would be proud of that," she said, attempting to roll across the bed away from him, but he easily snagged her around the waist and pulled her back.

"Damned right. Five orgasms in . . ." He lifted his head from the pillow to look at the digital clock on his nightstand. "In forty-seven minutes. That's got to be a record."

She grunted, pretending not to be impressed. But as she was the one who'd received the five orgasms, she was actually quite impressed and very, very satisfied. Her whole body felt heavy and boneless.

"Man, you're a tough lady," he said with a weary sigh. "Okay, I'll go for two more."

He started to slide back down under the comforter, but she groaned and caught her arm. "Okay, you win. I don't think my body can take any more."

He slid back beside her, his irritatingly smug grin back in place. But even as she told herself he really was far too self-satisfied, she snuggled against him with a contented sigh.

They remained that way, Sebastian leisurely stroking her back, she basking in the exhausting afterglow of his love-making.

"Do you still think I'm narcissistic and depraved?" he asked suddenly.

She lifted her head, seeing that his brow was furrowed, his golden eyes serious.

"No. You are definitely confident. And definitely very wicked." She rubbed a leg up his as she said the last, to let him know she very much liked his brand of wicked. "But I'm starting to like those qualities in you."

His eyes roamed her face for a moment, then he cupped one of his big hands around the back of her head and pulled her in for a kiss, slow and sweet. When they parted, she sank against his chest, rubbing her cheek against his smooth skin.

They were silent again, until Sebastian moved.

"Okay," he said sounding far more awake and together than she was. "We need to get dressed. I've got plans."

She groaned, falling back against the pillows as he rose from the bed. "Can't we just stay in?"

"Nope."

Mina watched him as he strode across the room to his dresser, admiring all his golden skin and taut muscles. Narcissistic, confident, depraved—the man deserved to be whatever he wanted. He was breathtaking.

With great disappointment, she watched as he shrugged on a green shirt and a pair of jeans. Then he padded barefoot back to the bed, the shirt unbuttoned and a line of muscled chest and stomach still peeking out at her, teasingly. He sat on the edge of the bed and she couldn't resist slipping her hand over his belly. Tight muscles, a shallow navel surrounded by coarse hair that dipped down into his jeans.

He smiled at her as her fingertips snaked under the waistband toying with the curls below his belly button.

"And I'm the third most dangerous vampire in New York? Woman, you are going to kill me."

She smiled, but didn't stop touching him, not until he caught her hand.

"I want to touch you," she told him. "You've done all the touching since you woke me up."

And what a way to be woken up, she thought, her toes curling.

He glanced at the bed, and she could tell he was tempted. But instead, he removed her hand from him and rose. "Later. Definitely later. But we have another lesson."

She groaned. Sebastian's lessons to help her understand her vampire self were the last thing she wanted to do.

"Plus, you want time to stop by your place, don't you? For clean clothes?"

Now that was a temptation she couldn't resist. She couldn't bear to wear that damp, dirty dress any longer. Especially when Sebastian looked all fresh and clean.

"Okay," she agreed. "But I get to touch you as much as I want later."

Sebastian grinned at her. "You say that like you think I might say no. You should know me better than that. Later, I'm all yours."

Mina smiled back until he left the room. Not quite all of him was hers. She crawled out of bed and reached for her crumpled dress. But she'd be happy with what she did have.

"I like your apartment," Sebastian called to Mina from her living room. Mina straightened from looking in her fridge, a blue, plastic pitcher in her hand.

"A bit smaller than what you're used to," she said as she went to the cupboard and pulled down two mugs.

"It's cozy," he said, appearing in the doorway.

She smiled over her shoulder, then returned her attention to pouring thick red liquid into the mugs. She didn't realize he was right behind her until he pressed a kiss to the back of her neck. She noticed he kept the touch very brief, always aware of the fact that his lips at her neck might scare her. It didn't, not anymore. She couldn't imagine Sebastian hurting her. Not physically anyway.

She turned, their bodies touching, but he made no further attempt to kiss her. In fact, after a few moments, he stepped back. She knew he was trying to behave. To keep on track of the night's plans. Plans he, as usual, hadn't filled her in on.

She reached for the mugs, offering him one. He accepted it, sniffing the concoction doubtfully.

"The pig-and-cow mix?" he asked.

She nodded, lifting the mug in a toast.

He grimaced, but raised his too.

She took a sip, fighting back her own grimace. The mixture was unappealing, she knew. And grew more so of late. Sebastian actually sputtered, but managed to get the drink down.

"Good Lord, you lived on this?"

She nodded, trying not to reveal that now she was nearly as stunned by the idea as he was. She didn't know how she'd managed. Except that she'd had to and then it had become her norm.

"Well, it is a little stale," she said, although she knew being fresher wouldn't make it any more appealing to him.

He made another disgusted face and set the mug back on the table. "I think I'll wait until I get back to my place for some of Rhys's blood-bank stuff." He glanced again at the mug, then shuddered. "And I thought his stuff was awful."

She tried not to laugh at his extreme reaction and forced herself to finish hers.

She placed both mugs in the sink. "Okay. I need to get a quick shower and clean clothes."

Sebastian followed her as she headed to her bedroom. He wandered around the room, touching this, inspecting that as she tried to figure out what to wear.

He just set down a book about day-to-day life in Regency England, when he asked, "Your roommate? What's she like?"

Mina looked up from her underwear drawer, where she was lamenting her lack of pretty undergarments. "Lizzie? What about her?"

"Lizzie." For a second, he looked as if he was considering something.

"How long have you been roommates?"

"Only about three months. She just moved to New York. She was living in Colorado or Montana. Somewhere like that. She's a scientist. She came here to work with Dr. Fowler. She's a werewolf."

Sebastian nodded, then he noticed the pale blue panties she held, forgotten, in her hand.

He walked toward her, but stopped before he touched her. Pulling in a deep breath, he smiled. "You'd better get that shower."

He didn't have to add, before they ended up back in bed. Her bed, this time. She glanced longingly at the simple white wrought-iron bed with its pale lavender comforter.

She grabbed a bra and her jeans and shirt—and the blue panties and squeezed past him. She did need a shower—a cold one. Although she didn't think cold showers worked quite the same on vampires.

Once in the bathroom, she kept her attention on starting the shower, getting out of her rumpled dress, anything but the idea of Sebastian gazing around her apartment. There was something very exciting about his being here, in her world.

She tested the water before stepping into the tub. She

closed her eyes, letting the hot water sluice down her body. Then she opened them, not really seeing, her mind on all the things Sebastian had done to her when they'd awoken together. Her toes curled against the slick porcelain of the tub. He was amazing. And she now understood how a person could become fixated on making love. Although she knew for her, her fixation was more about Sebastian. She knew she couldn't enjoy sexual intimacy like that with anyone else. It was all about Sebastian and what she felt for him.

She closed her eyes for a moment, sighing deeply. She knew she'd have to move on from him eventually. It was inevitable. But she didn't want to think about that now. About a time without Sebastian.

She opened her eyes, her skin tingling. She looked down at herself. Steam swirled around her, like mist just before a strong storm. She continued to watch as her nipples puckered, forming tight little beads. Her skin grew more sensitive, more aware of the water and the continual brush of that damp steam on her skin. Her breasts grew heavier, achy. And between her thighs, she felt more throbbing need.

A small whimper escaped her as she closed her eyes and moved her legs apart. The water and the mist lapped between her thighs, making her wet and desperate.

Could just thinking about Sebastian make her ache this way? She opened her eyes, telling herself she was out of control. She needed to get a handle on her need for the man. And still the mist swirled like a mini-twister around her body.

She whimpered again, her hand moving to her breasts, cupping her aroused skin. Skimming her palms, her fingers over her nipples. Imagining it was Sebastian touching her that way.

In the mist she could see him, his damp features, the curl of his wet hair, the glistening of water on his skin. She really was far too obsessed. Then her misty, fantasy image spoke.

"I like watching you touch yourself."

She made a startled noise, her hand pausing on her breast.

"Don't stop." Sebastian stepped forward and Mina realized he wasn't a fantasy. He was real and solid—her eyes drifted down his naked body. Very, very solid.

"How did you do that?" she asked, even as she knew the answer. Vampires could change form. She knew that intellectually, although she'd never been able to do it herself. And she didn't know that in their other forms they could still touch another.

"You were doing that," she murmured. "Swirling around me. Touching me."

He nodded. "But it's not a substantial touch. More just a faint, stimulating stir of the air. Nothing more than mist. Or shadow."

She nodded, then she realized her hands still cupped her breasts. She started to drop them, but Sebastian shook his head. "No, keep touching yourself."

"Sebastian." She blushed. They had done so much together. But somehow standing before him, pleasing herself, made her too aware of herself. Too aware of him.

"Please," he said with his sexy grin.

She mustered her courage, then rubbed her hand over her water-slicked breast. He watched her, the heat in his golden eyes encouraging her. She caressed the other breast, her fingers toying with the tightened nipple.

Sebastian's gaze remained fascinated on her. His attention excited her. She squeezed one breast, wringing a low moan from herself. When she opened her eyes, Sebastian was gone.

"Sebastian?"

Then she felt him, the mist again eddying around her. She gasped, the touch of him in that form just as he said, faint, barely there, yet so exciting, so, so arousing.

Helpless to stop herself, one of her hands left her breast, gliding down her stomach to the curls at the juncture of her thighs. She parted herself, finding her clitoris. Desperately she began to stroke herself. The mist also stroked her, spinning and churning around her, driving her mad. She pressed her fingers hard to herself, feeling herself being twirled toward her release.

Just as she started to cry out, Sebastian was there, hard and real at her back, his hand joining hers between her spread thighs. She screamed, her orgasm flooding her like a storm amid rolling fog.

Sebastian held her tightly as she trembled with the power of her release. His own desire was only barely held in check, but he managed to control it.

He had no idea using his shifting abilities could be so much fun, so damned sexy. That had been . . .

"Wow," Mina finally murmured, still boneless against him.

"This wasn't exactly how I planned this lesson to go," he said, kissing her ear.

"Mmm," she rubbed back against him, from satisfaction rather than arousal. His cock pulsed anyway.

"How was the lesson supposed to go?"

"I was going to take you to the botanical gardens. They have a lovely herb and perennial garden that reminds me very much of the gardens we had outside of our estate in Derbyshire, back before I crossed over. I planned to teach you how to shift, then we could sneak in to see it, since it's after closing hours."

She turned in his arms, a small, dreamy smile curling her rosy lips. "That does sound lovely. But this was lovely too. Very lovely."

Sebastian gritted his teeth, trying to stay focused on their conversation rather than the slick rub of her breasts against his chest.

"But you didn't learn anything new about your vampirism."

Her eyes widened and she laughed. "Didn't I? I think I learned something very new. And I want to learn more, right here in this shower."

"Like what?" he asked, liking the naughty gleam in her blue eyes.

"Like how to please a vampire."

He laughed this time, a startled laugh. "Oh baby, you already know exactly how to do that. No lessons needed."

She smiled again. "Oh, I think I do."

She ran her hand down his sides and over his hips as she slid her body down his front until she was kneeling before him.

He watched as her hands came out to touch his penis jutting forward, steely hard, pulsating. She stroked him, studying every detail of his reaction to her fingers, the curl of them around him. The pumping strokes.

He swallowed, trying to stay calm as one of her hands cupped his testicles, the other still pumped his cock. Then she leaned forward and kissed the swollen head.

His hands sank into her hair, not controlling her movements, just giving him an anchor.

She kissed him again, her tongue flicking across the very top. "Do you like that?"

"God, baby," his voice was ragged, "you have no idea."

She licked him again. Then again. Tasting the head, the sensitive length of the underside. The head again.

His hips arced forward, his head fell back against the tile wall. When her lips formed a perfect "o" and pulled him into her hot, wet mouth, his whole body jerked and he nearly came right that instant.

Instead he forced himself to calm, to just absorb that amazing, amazing feeling of her lips, her tongue, her mouth.

"Isn't . . . this a better . . . lesson . . . for tonight," she said between lick and sucks.

"So, so much better," he muttered roughly.

And damn, he thought, his head falling back against the shower wall as she took him fully into her mouth again. She really was such a fast learner.

Chapter 25

Mina sat at one of the booths in the nightclub, watching the dancers on the floor below. Then she glanced around, feeling like she was being watched in return. She was. Two women sat at the bar staring at her, whispering. When they realized Mina was looking, they had the good grace to look away. Most didn't.

Mina had found herself to be the novelty of Carfax Abbey. Sebastian Young's steady woman. Apparently the first, if all the buzz was any indication.

"Hey, Mina." Greta appeared at the table. "Can I get you a drink?" Her friend smiled at her.

Mina had been very surprised by Greta's reaction to the fact that Sebastian and Mina had been at the club together for the past several nights. She'd been surprised by all the employees' reactions. They'd taken it in stride. Of course, they still didn't know she was the one who'd tried to sabotage the club. Only Nadine knew, and she didn't show any signs of holding it against Mina.

"Shit happens," the tall, gorgeous werewolf had said with a philosophical air. "You needed to see who Sebastian really was. And he has helped you, right?"

Mina had nodded with no hesitation. Yes, Sebastian had helped her more than anyone, including Sebastian, could know.

"And you've helped him, too," Nadine said. "So it's all good to me."

Mina didn't know about that. But she hoped, in some small way, she'd made Sebastian happier or something.

"I swear, girl, you are the most lovesick person I have ever seen," Greta said laughingly.

Mina blinked, realizing she hadn't answered her question.

"I think Sebastian is getting our drinks. Thanks, though."

Greta looked to see Sebastian at the bar. Sebastian spoke to Bryce, then turned and started toward them. His eyes sought out Mina's. He smiled, his full lips curling more at one corner than the other.

Would that wonderful, lazily sexy smile always make her heart do flips? She knew for certain it would. Forever.

"I take that back," Greta said with another laugh. "I think you two are equally lovesick."

Mina looked away from Sebastian, surprised by her friend's words. Greta watched his approach too.

"No," Mina said with a laugh of her own. "He's just a consummate charmer."

Greta shook her head. "No. He's crazy about you. Everyone knows it. It was bound to happen someday. I'm just glad it's someone who will be good to him."

Mina couldn't believe Greta's words. "But you yourself said that Sebastian would never settle down."

Greta shrugged, her beautiful blond hair cascading over her shoulders. "Yes, I did think that. I certainly knew he wasn't going to settle down with me. But you . . ."

She gave Mina a pleased smile.

"Hi, Greta," Sebastian said as he reached the table, sliding into the booth, close to Mina.

"Hi, Sebastian. How are you?"

Sebastian glanced hotly at Mina, then said, "Great."

Greta gave Mina an I-told-you-so look and waved her good-bye.

Mina watched her sashay across the room, more than a little dazed by Greta's words. Sebastian wasn't interested in settling down. Mina knew that. Yes, everything had been amazing between them. She'd stayed at his apartment since the night of the altered shapeshifting lessons. He'd even been the one to suggest that she pack enough clothes to stay for awhile.

But he'd been quite sensible about the plan.

"I don't think Donatello will be back," he'd said, "but I feel better knowing you're safe."

Not the vow of love she'd wanted. But he did make her feel safe, and she loved being with him.

Sebastian had also decided he needed to stay close to Carfax Abbey. He wanted to be sure this Donatello, whether he was *the* Donatello or another one, didn't hurt anyone else. So they spent part of their nights at the club, and part just alone together.

She hadn't expected to enjoy the club. After all, the club was overwhelming with its loud music and rowdy people. And there were the women, who flocked to Sebastian. But Sebastian had dismissed all of them with polite smiles and a few amiable words, which had surprised her. She didn't think he could have kept himself from flirting. But he hadn't. That definitely hadn't spared Mina from the angry glares, but it had spared her from having to share him. This was her time, and as long as it lasted, she wanted him to herself.

"What were you and Greta talking about?"

Mina gave him a vague smile. "Nothing." Then she added, "I feel strange having my old coworkers trying to wait on me. After all, I was one of them not too long ago."

Sebastian raised an eyebrow at that. "Mina, you were never one of them. Believe me."

She turned in the booth to face him. "What do you mean?"

"Mina, my love," he said with a sheepish smile, "you were probably one of the worst waitresses I've ever seen."

Mina would have been offended, except she was too distracted by the fact that he'd just called her *my love*.

"But," he added quickly, "because I happened to like you so much, I'd consider hiring you again. If you want."

Because I like you so much. That sort of deflated the elation she felt at being called his love. She had to remember that while he did like her—and she did believe a lot—he wasn't the type to fall head over heels. Despite what Greta said. What did Greta know?

"So what do you say? Are you ready to wait table again? I think I have a uniform in the backroom that would fit you."

She frowned at him, tempted to say yes.

But seeing the deliberation in her eyes, he shook his head. "On second thought, I don't think so. I'm not letting all the men here ogle my woman as she slings drinks."

She rolled her eyes at that—certain he was really teasing now.

Bryce appeared with a bottle of wine and two glasses. Mina noticed that Sebastian stiffened slightly when the friendly werebear smiled at Mina and chatted for a few moments.

"And," he pulled her tight to him after Bryce left, picking up with his conversation as if the bartender had never been there. "I don't think you will have time to serve drinks. You'll be far too busy with me."

She tried to look disappointed, but couldn't. She sank against him, lifting her face to receive his kiss.

"Are we interrupting?"

They parted to see Rhys, Jane, Christian, and Jolee.

"No," Mina said quickly, feeling her cheeks flush. She'd met Sebastian's family a few times since the night of the attack, but still she felt awkward around them. Even though they were all nice, she knew they had to be wondering about her and Sebastian's relationship. And they had to be surprised that he was having whatever their relationship was with her.

And she couldn't help noticing that Sebastian always acted a little strange too. Uncomfortable.

"We decided to join you, since Christian and I are heading back home tomorrow," Jolee said, offering one of her wide smiles.

Mina slid over to offer them more room, her movement bringing her flush against Sebastian. He slid an arm around her, the action rather surprising her.

"So you're heading back to the wilds of West Virginia, eh?" Sebastian said, grinning.

Christian gave him a wry look.

Sebastian had told Mina about how Christian had fallen for Jolee. And while Sebastian was happy for his brother, the idea still struck him as amusing. From what Sebastian had told her, Mina could see the humor of his brother, who'd been snobby, rude, and at one point downright evil, falling for a big-hearted, down-to-earth human and—Sebastian's favorite part of the story—karaoke bar owner. Well, he was torn between the karaoke bar and the fact that they lived in rural West Virginia. Although they'd apparently moved out of the trailer park where they'd met to a sprawling farmhouse. Which Sebastian still found amusing.

"Christian didn't even like our estate in Derbyshire," Sebastian had laughed as he told her about the trailer park. "And we'd had at least twenty-five servants and all the amenities of the time."

Mina watched as Christian tucked Jolee against him, giving her a smoldering look that showed every bit of the love he felt for the gorgeous redhead. Jolee gave him an adoring look of her own, then touched his jaw and pressed a quick kiss to his lips.

"He loves West Virginia," Jolee said after they parted. "Even if he won't admit it."

"No, you love West Virginia," Christian said. "And I love you, so I live there."

Jolee rolled her eyes and shook her head.

"He loves it," she mouthed.

Mina laughed at the two of them.

"So has the club been quiet?" Rhys asked.

Sebastian nodded. "Not even so much as bickering among the clientele."

"That's good," Jane said. "I really hope Annie is okay. She was badly shaken, and understandably so."

Mina had thought about Annie often, hoping she was okay, too. She knew how hard it was to shake off an experience like that. Although, thankfully, hers had turned out better than Mina's.

Sebastian seemed to sense her train of thought, because he pulled her closer to him and pressed a kiss to her hair. Again, the gesture, in front of his family, surprised her.

Then the conversation turned to other things: how someone named Jed, who apparently lived behind Jolee and Christian's bar, was; when was Jane going to play them one of her always-promised but yet to be heard funeral songs on the piano in her and Rhys's apartment.

"Would you want to hear that?" Jane asked Mina, shaking her head, although she smiled at their teasing.

"You're the one who boasted you can play a mean funeral dirge," Sebastian pointed out.

Mina laughed with everyone. It was sort of funny that Rhys had ended up marrying a mortician's daughter.

"It's true," Rhys agreed with his brother. "You do keep promising."

"The undead sitting around listening to funeral hymns. You are all sick," Jolee teased.

"That's what I say," Jane agreed.

"It's bad enough that Sebastian insists on singing "I Died in Your Arms Tonight" every time he's at the karaoke bar." Jolee laughed.

Christian groaned. "That one, and 'Only the Good Die Young.'"

"Hey, those are fine songs," Sebastian defended himself. He started to sing the Billy Joel song, until Jane clapped a hand over his mouth.

"Thank God," Rhys said.

Mina laughed at their antics. She looked around the table at each of them, amazed at the sense of family she felt. Here they were, vampires, the undead, monsters, and she felt more of their loving and caring for each other than she'd ever felt in her supposedly perfect family.

Mina looked at Sebastian who laughed at something Christian said. God, she never wanted this to end. Never.

"You know," Sebastian said, "I was thinking we should all go to England this year. You know, go see the old estate. I'd love to see how the place looks now."

Mina glanced at the others. Christian and Jolee both seemed to think the trip would be a good idea. Jane did too, although she gave Rhys a worried look. Rhys frowned, not appearing as keen about the suggestion as the others.

"Rhys," Sebastian said quietly. "I know the trip would be hard. But I think it would be good too."

Rhys nodded, still sober.

Jane touched him, tucking a lock of his long hair behind his ear. "Elizabeth would want you to go back."

Rhys nodded. Jane pressed a kiss to his jaw, then he caught her, kissing her passionately.

Mina felt strange watching their embrace, but it was hard not to. Sebastian had told Mina about their little sister, Elizabeth. And about how Rhys still felt guilt over her death, even though the vampiress who'd crossed all the Young brothers over had been the one to kill her. Still, it was amazing to see that even as shaken as Rhys was by Sebastian's idea, he found such solace, such strength in Jane. Mina knew she found both in Sebastian, but what did Sebastian get from her?

After they parted, Rhys agreed that a visit might be nice. Again the conversation returned to lighter things, but Mina kept thinking about that trip to England. She'd love to go with Sebastian, with his family. But she didn't believe she'd be around by the time they went. She wondered who would go in her place. Maybe no one, but Sebastian wouldn't lack for female companionship. He'd meet plenty of women while there, Mina was sure.

"Hey," Sebastian suddenly whispered, his lips near her ear. "What's got you so serious?"

She forced a smile at him. "Nothing."

"Is all this family time overwhelming you?" he whispered.

"No," she said readily, honestly. She liked it—far too much.

"Well, it is for me. I want to hold you. Let's dance."

"Oh," she shook her head, casting a wary glance to the crowded dance floor. "I don't know."

"Come on," he coaxed. "The crowd won't bother you now." He caught her hand, and asked Jane and Rhys if they'd let them out of the booth.

They did.

As Sebastian led Mina down the curved staircase, Mina tried to stop him again. "Sebastian. I'm not—" She hated to talk about her shortcomings, especially in this club of amazing beauty.

"You're not what?"

"I can't dance," she admitted. "I trip over my own feet. You know that."

Sebastian gave her an indulgent look. "Don't worry."

He led her out into the center of the undulating mob, then he pulled her into his arms.

Very quickly, Mina realized that dancing with Sebastian was not at all like the dancing she'd been thinking about. It was like making love. Their bodies tight together, rubbing, grinding, only to the beat of a song, rather than the pace they set themselves.

"See." He grinned down at her, but she couldn't grin back. She was far too aware of the friction of their bodies. He saw the desire on her face and he leaned in closer, his lips to her ear.

"Did I tell you how much I love your dress tonight?"

He had, earlier. It was a simple black dress with spaghetti straps and a slightly flared shirt. She'd bought it on impulse, nearly a year ago, and she'd been certain she'd never wear it. Until Sebastian.

He kissed her bare shoulder. The music mimicked the pulse of need in her veins. She pressed tighter to him, her breasts pressed to his chest, her nipples prodding his hard muscles.

"Mina, I just can't seem to get enough of you," he said, his hands roaming over her back, cupping her bottom to pull her fully to his arousal.

They were surrounded by people, yet she didn't care. She reveled in his touch, remembering the first time she'd seen him, how he'd been dancing with that mortal. She'd never believed she'd be doing the same thing with him. Maybe she should feel badly to be one of his many women. Maybe she should feel used in some way, but she didn't. She just knew she wanted him as long as she could have him.

His hands continued to stroke over her, until he groaned and suddenly released her. Before she'd even adjusted to his being gone, he grabbed her hand and led her off the dance floor toward the back. There in an alcove somewhat hidden from the rest of the club, he pinned her to the wall and kissed her as if he was going to die if his lips couldn't be against hers. She kissed him back with the same hunger.

"Mina," he breathed, his forehead pressed to hers. "I don't know what you are doing to me."

She gave him a shaky smile. "Whatever it is, I want to keep doing it to you."

He stared at her for a moment, then kissed her again, the embrace full of hunger and passion. He nipped her bottom lip, then her jaw, then her earlobe. She turned her head to the side wanting to feel that nip against the fragile skin of her neck. That realization gave her a moment's pause, but then she understood the need. She'd given herself to him in every way she knew how, except that one.

"I'm going to go up and tell them that we are leaving," he said, pulling away from her before his lips, his teeth, touched her neck.

She blinked, at first confused by who he was referring to. Then she realized he meant his family.

"I don't want them to come looking for us," he explained. "Not during what I have planned for you."

Her toes curled at the hot promise in his eyes. She nodded.

"Wait here," he said.

She nodded again, then as he started away from her, she caught his wrist. He turned back to her, a questioning look in his golden eyes.

"I want you to bite me."

He stared at her as if he couldn't have heard her right. She moved closer to him, pressing her own lips to his neck. Then she whispered in his ear. "I want you to bite me. And I want to bite you in return." She nipped him.

She pulled back, and he gaped at her for several seconds.

Then he shook his head slightly as if he couldn't wrap his mind about what she'd just said. He stared at her a moment longer, then he held up a hand, motioning for her to wait there.

"I'll be right back. Don't move." He strode quickly into the dancing crowd.

Mina watched him go, leaning heavily on the wall, her body too overwhelmed to support itself.

"My, wasn't that a touching scene," a voice said from right beside her.

Chapter 26

She froze as she saw the tall, cadaverlike figure next to her. "Daniel." All the wonderful desire and anticipation that had been flowing through her veins disappeared. "What are you doing here?"

"Jackson sent me here. The Society heard about the attack here the other night, and they decided someone should come see exactly what's happening here. With you." He stepped closer. "They will be quite surprised, won't they?"

"There's nothing happening here that involves the Society," Mina stated.

"Isn't there?" Daniel cocked his head to the side. "When a member, who claims to be one of the group's missionaries, starts fraternizing with the enemy—" his eerie dark eyes wandered down her body—"in a very intimate way, then I think the Society needs to know."

Mina swallowed, refusing to be intimidated by this vampire. There was something different about him tonight. He still made her very nervous. Nervous in a way that told her she needed to run. That he was dangerous. But there was something else there. Just beyond her grasp. Something pushing at her brain, telling her she should know more about this vampire.

But she wouldn't be intimidated. She faced him squarely, lifting her chin. She needed to hold her ground, not only for herself, but for Sebastian. She couldn't let this creepy vampire go back and tell them she'd gone over to Sebastian's side. Not because she cared about their opinion of her; she was afraid of how the Society might retaliate. She couldn't let Sebastian or the club be hurt. She would protect him as he'd protected her.

"Daniel, I've done exactly what I promised to do. I've stopped Sebastian."

Sebastian's steps slowed as he got away from Mina. She'd just told him she wanted him to bite her. Biting—for Mina the ultimate act of trust. Or surrender. To him.

Instead of feeling elated, he felt scared to death. He wanted Mina. That he didn't doubt. He cared about her more than anyone, outside of his family. Hell, he wanted to be with her every moment. And when he wasn't with her, he was thinking about her. But he hadn't been able to tell her he loved her. Saying those words seemed like giving up all control. It was like losing himself.

He stopped on the other side of the dance floor, casting a look back to where he'd left her. He couldn't see her past all the dancers.

He took a deep breath, and tunneled a hand through his hair. "What am I doing? She's offering you everything. Take it."

"Hi, Sebastian." A svelte brunette, who he vaguely recognized, stopped by his side. "You look lost. Can I help?"

Sebastian stared at the woman. She was tall with a perfect figure, sultry bedroom eyes, full lips, and Sebastian felt—nothing. Nada. Zip. This woman was a knockout, and all Sebastian could think about was Mina.

He wanted Mina forever, and it was that simple. The realization didn't scare him any less, but he knew it was what he wanted. He wanted to take this final step between them. He wanted to make her his in every way he could.

"Umm," he frowned at the woman beside him, "yeah, I

have to go." He didn't wait for her answer as he weaved back through the mob of gyrating bodies.

This was right, he told himself. Mina meant so much to him. He loved making love with her—more than loved it. But he also adored talking to her. He loved hearing her opinions. He loved her laughter. Her frowns. He loved watching her read. He loved lying in her arms and holding her in return. He loved everything she did. It was insane. But true.

And he still felt like he might hyperventilate.

But then he saw her, and suddenly everything seemed right. Just as it did every time he saw her. The world just seemed better and to make sense.

He picked up his pace, needing to tell her just that. But as he got closer, he frowned, his steps slowing. He could feel her emotions sharply in the air. Not the desire he'd felt when he left her. This was—agitation. He picked up his steps. He was definitely sensing her agitation. Not fear exactly, but rather nervousness. And maybe fear, although she was working hard to block that emotion, he realized.

He reached the alcove where he'd left her, for the first time seeing the tall, thin vampire standing near her. Sebastian started to interrupt them, but Mina's firmly stated words stopped him.

"Daniel, I've done exactly what I promised to do. I've stopped Sebastian."

"Stopped him, how?" the tall vampire asked, his voice smooth, oily rather than appealing.

"He isn't biting."

"Which you've stopped by," the vampire's dark eyes roamed down her body, "allowing him to—mate with you?"

"My strategy isn't your business," Mina stated, her small chin rising.

"My, won't you go that extra mile for the cause."

"Yes, I will. So there is no reason to go to the Society. I've got him under control."

Sebastian gritted his teeth at her words. She had him under

control. Fang-whipped, as he liked to say about his brothers. Was he that easily manipulated?

"What of the attack here? Are you denying there was one?"

"There was, but it wasn't Sebastian. I was with him."

The tall vampire laughed, the sound cold, rusty. "I'm sure you were. But as I see it, if the club is still functioning, then you haven't really fulfilled your mission. Perhaps the Society needs to be more aware of that."

Mina paused at the vampire's statement, seeming to flounder a minute for what to say. "Daniel, that will take more time. But—but the more I have Sebastian under control, the more I can get him to do."

Daniel laughed again, the sound grating over Sebastian's skin. His fangs distended in rage.

"So, you plan to seduce him into closing the club."

"Yes," Mina said with no hesitation.

"You really think you can do that. That he is so charmed by you?"

"Yes," she said again, no doubt in her voice.

More rage filled Sebastian. Here he'd thought she was a rather endearingly bumbling saboteur, but she'd known exactly what she was doing the whole time.

"We'll see," Daniel said, although he didn't sound remotely convinced. Then the vampire disappeared. Not to shadow, not to mist, or even into a bat. He simply disappeared, which Sebastian had never seen a vampire do. Sebastian paused over that, but only for a fraction of a second. Like he gave a shit about the SPAMM freak's shifting abilities. All he cared about was what he'd heard come straight from Mina's mouth.

He stepped out from the shadows, and Mina jumped.

"Sebastian," she said, her voice full of relief. She took a step toward him. But Sebastian's expression must have stopped her.

"Sebastian?"

"Who was your friend?"

She frowned at him, and he knew she intended to deny the other vampire's existence. More rage filled him.

"I have to agree with your friend. You really are willing to go the extra mile for the Society, aren't you?"

Lightning fast he was against her, pinning her to the wall.

Mina made a small squeak at his speed, at his roughness, but she remained still in his hold.

"Sebastian, please, you have to listen to me. I can explain." Mina's voice was pleading and he could feel her fear. This time the fear didn't affect him. Maybe that was an emotion she could turn on and off at will. Another way she'd controlled him.

"I heard enough, Mina," he ground out. And not once had he heard her defend him. She hadn't said that Sebastian wasn't a threat. That the club wasn't used to hurt humans. Not once had she told that freak vampire to go back to the Society and tell them that she was now on Sebastian's side.

"You know," he said, "I remember wondering why you agreed to that bargain I made so easily. Perhaps I am narcissistic after all, because I just decided it was because you liked me. You know, deep down." He said the last two words in a way that sounded almost dirty. Mina shifted against him.

"But you were very clever, weren't you? You saw an opportunity and jumped on it. Literally. And through a way you knew would work. I'm never one to turn down a willing woman."

"Sebastian, please. Stop," she said, trying to break away from his grip, but he held her easily, her wrists over her head against the wall. The position held chest to chest, his face only inches from hers.

"Please, what? Please screw you?" He moved so his knee was between her legs, parting them. "Please bite you? What other trick do you plan to offer to maintain your control over me? To make me not bite humans? To make me shut down my club?"

"Sebastian, I just told him that so he wouldn't go to the Society. So the Society wouldn't send someone else to hurt you." Her blue eyes pleaded with him to believe her.

He didn't. "Why would I believe that, Mina? After all, you were willing to do anything to see this place closed earlier. Fire. Police. How do I know *you* didn't stage the attack the other night?"

She gaped at him. "Why would I do that?"

"To get the patrons scared. To make them think twice about coming here."

"You know I didn't do that!"

Sebastian shook his head, looking down at the first woman he could recall allowing himself to care about. He heard the adamancy in her words as she'd talked to Daniel. Was that an adamancy to protect Sebastian? Or was it panic not to destroy her hard work?

"I don't know anything anymore," he admitted.

"Yes, you do. You know that I trusted you to make love to me. You know you were my first. You know about my past. You are the only one who knows that whole story. I never told it to anyone but you."

He glared at her. "Hell, people light themselves on fire for their causes. They run suicide missions. Losing your virginity for your cause was hardly a hardship, baby. And as far as your past, who the hell knows if that was even true. You could have told me anything, right?"

Mina shook her head, her eyes still pleading with him, even through the hurt he saw there.

"But I told you I love you."

He snorted, even though her words ripped at his insides. Oh yes, she had said that. And he'd believed her.

"Like I said, you could say anything, couldn't you?"

"Sebastian, I didn't just say that. I do love you."

He growled deep in his throat. He didn't want to hear this. He couldn't.

He pressed her wrists tighter to the wall. His body pinning

hers. "If you love me, then let's have that little bite you offered earlier. Were you really going to do that for the cause too?"

He smiled, showing his full fangage.

She stared at his fangs, a strangled noise coming from her throat. "Sebastian, please, you are scaring me." Her voice crackled, and tears began to roll down her pale cheeks, her eyes huge with fear.

He made a strangled noise of his own and pushed roughly away from her. He turned unable to look at her. To look at her wounded eyes.

"Sebastian, please." He felt her hand on his back, and he whipped around. He didn't want to feel her touch again. Ever again.

"Leave now, Mina, or I swear to God I won't be held accountable for what I do."

She stared at him for a moment, then nodded. He watched as she fled through the club. And even though he'd told her to go, somehow her leaving solidified what he believed. She'd played him for a complete and utter fool.

Mina didn't remember leaving the club. She didn't remember how she reached her apartment building. She only recalled sinking down on the concrete steps, crying.

She'd told Daniel those things to protect Sebastian. To stop Daniel from going to the Society and convincing them that Sebastian was a bigger threat. Her only thoughts had been to protect Sebastian.

Sebastian hadn't even listened to her. He'd been convinced she'd been doing everything for the Society. How, how could he believe that after what they'd shared? Hadn't he known, felt, everything she'd felt for him was real? She wasn't doing any of this for the damned Society. She didn't care about the Society. She only cared about Sebastian.

Anger started to replace her heartbreak. Hadn't he made the "no biting" bargain to begin with? Hadn't she tried to deny her attraction to him? How could he believe those things to be her manipulations? She felt like since she'd met Sebastian he'd been controlling her. She hadn't minded that control, because she had learned to trust him—to love him. And he didn't trust her one tiny bit.

He certainly doesn't love you, she realized. He couldn't think the absolute worst and love her.

She pushed up from the steps and headed into her apartment. The place was empty as usual. Tonight she wished Lizzie was home. She needed a shoulder to cry on. And she no longer had Sebastian's.

She raised her chin. She needed to start this minute forgetting about him. If he couldn't trust her, then they'd had no future anyway. Which she'd known all along. The end had just come sooner and with much more anger than she'd imagined.

She wandered into the kitchen. Lizzie had left her a note on the table that said she was going to the lab, if Mina should happen to come home. She also had her cell phone with her should Mina need anything. Lizzie also hoped everything was okay.

"No, everything is not okay," Mina announced to the empty room.

She considered calling Lizzie's cell, but thought better of the idea. What would she say? She hadn't told Lizzie what was going on, purely because she hadn't physically seen Lizzie since things had gotten more involved between her and Sebastian, and it had all seemed a little too strange to explain over the phone. The story was even weirder now, and too much to tell in a phone conversation.

As if taking offense at that decision, the telephone mounted to the kitchen wall rang, the sound loud and jarring. Mina moved to answer it before another grating ring echoed through the apartment.

"Hello?" she said.

"Wilhelmina? It's Daniel."

She paused, her first thought to hang up the phone. But then more anger filled her. "What do you want, Daniel?"

"I've been asked to call you. To let you know that the Society has organized an emergency meeting. Tonight. To deal with the issue of Carfax Abbey and Sebastian Young. And you, too."

Mina frowned at the clock on the microwave. The time glowed in blue digital numbers: 2:42 A.M.

"It's rather late for a meeting, isn't it?" she said.

"Well, once I spoke to Jackson, he realized this was of immediate interest to the group. All the board members will be there. And I recommend you be there too."

Mina shook her head at how fast that little snitch had gone back to the board. But she intended to be there. She was going to tell them the truth. That she was no longer involved with Sebastian Young, and that Carfax Abbey and its owner were in no way a threat to humans or anyone.

She brusquely asked Daniel where the Society was to meet, then hung up the phone.

She hurried to her bedroom to change. She was going to tell the Society exactly what she thought of their list of the most dangerous vampires. And she was going to tell them exactly what she thought of Daniel.

Chapter 27

"So, I was standing there with one pair of Hypes and one pair of Enzo Angiolinis. And I just couldn't make up my mind."

"Yeah, that's tough," Sebastian said vaguely, having no idea what the woman was talking about. He shifted against the booth seat, the nap of the velvet seeming like nettles through the fine lawn of his shirt. He moved again, then took a swallow of his scotch, hoping the liquor would calm the anger and the agitation inside him. Not that the four before this one had done much good.

"In the end, I didn't get either pair, because they didn't have either of them in orange, which is my signature color this season." The blonde gestured to the orange-and-white retro dress she wore.

"Very nice," Sebastian said automatically, then took another longer gulp of his drink. He'd decided to talk to this woman when she'd mentioned she was a model. A mode—he glanced at the woman. A tall, stunningly gorgeous model. The surefire thing to get Mina and her deception right out of his mind. Okay, he'd been played the fool, but losing himself in this gorgeous woman's body would help soothe his wounded heart.

Pride, he corrected. Wounded pride.

". . . Isn't that the funniest thing you ever heard?" The

blonde laughed, leaning toward him, giving him an eyeful of tanned cleavage.

"Yes," he said with conviction, though he was pretty sure that even if he had heard what she'd said, it wouldn't have been the funniest thing he'd ever heard. But she didn't need to be funny to fulfill the needs he had tonight.

She giggled some more, the sound as nettling as the velvet against his back. He polished off the remainder of his drink, then set the glass away from him with a sharp bang.

"What do you say we head up to my place?"

The blonde seemed a little startled by his sudden request, but she nodded with a blinding grin. "Sure."

He smiled back, rising from the booth. He gestured for her to go ahead of him, then he followed her toward the back of the club. Just as they would have slipped through the back-door, Rhys appeared.

"Where's Mina?"

Sebastian scowled at his brother. "Who?"

"Mina. Your girlfriend. The one you've been with for every moment for days, weeks."

Sebastian glared at him. Weeks. He made it sound like so much more than it was. Weeks. Right. Sebastian glanced at the woman beside him, offering her an indulgent smile.

"Rhys, as you can see, I'm a little busy at the moment," Sebastian said tolerantly, politely.

"You were busy with Mina earlier. What happened?"

Sebastian shot the woman next to him another glance, then forced a polite smile and said to her, "Would you excuse me for a moment? I need to chat with my brother."

The blonde nodded, clearly bewildered. Not that that was unusual for the poor woman.

Sebastian followed Rhys back toward the booth where Christian still sat. Thankfully, Jane and Jolee were gone or he'd have really gotten an earful.

"What the hell are you doing?" Rhys demanded as soon as Sebastian sat down in the booth with them.

"What do you mean?" Sebastian said casually. "I'm doing what I always do."

"What about Mina?"

Sebastian's chest tightened at her name, but he managed to keep his voice cool. "What about her?"

Both Rhys and Christian gave him disbelieving looks.

"Umm," Christian said as if he clearly thought Sebastian had lost his mind. "You are in love with her."

The tightening in Sebastian's chest threatened to strangle him. But he managed a look that matched Christian's. "Where did you get that idea?" He forced a brief laugh. "Me love Mina. That's quite funny."

Christian gaped at him. Rhys just looked thoroughly unconvinced.

"You two know me," Sebastian said. "I'm not the type to settle down. I like my freedom." He turned and waved to the blonde, who actually looked confused by the gesture, but she did wave back.

"I like my women."

"Yeah, and you love Mina," Rhys stated. "So what is all this about?" He jerked his head toward the other woman. *The other woman*—that made it sound like he was cheating on Mina, which he wasn't. How could he cheat on a relationship that hadn't been real to begin with?

Sebastian crossed his arms over his chest, wondering why he didn't just get up, tell his nosy brothers to mind their own damned business, and head up to his place with the redhead.

He glanced over his shoulder. The blonde. The blonde. Mina would have a field day if she knew that he was now not only forgetting their names, but their hair color, too. The tightening in his chest suddenly became hideously painful. Mina. She'd been playing him the whole time.

"Sebastian, what's going on?"

Sebastian stared at Rhys, the words right there. The truth of what Mina had done, but he couldn't bring himself to say them aloud. To reveal what a total sucker he'd been.

"You know you were the one who urged me not to let Jane go. And you were right," Rhys said. "Why are you blowing your chances with Mina? When you have a chance at the same happiness?"

Blowing his chances? Sebastian hadn't been the one to blow anything. He'd started to believe he could be with Mina forever—that maybe she was his Jane. His Jolee.

Yeah, the idea had scared him. How could he let a person have that much control over him? What if she hurt him? But he'd been right there, ready to take those chances.

Then all his *what if's* happened. Mina had hurt him. God damn it.

"You really don't know shit about this," Sebastian gritted, irritated that his brothers assumed he was the one who'd ruined things. Had he? Had he been wrong to make her leave while she was begging for him to believe her? Trust her?

"Then tell us what happened." Christian said.

Sebastian hesitated, but then he couldn't seem to stop himself. He had to have his brothers see the truth, and come to the same conclusion. He needed them to verify he hadn't just mistakenly sent away the only woman he could ever love.

Mina frowned as she peered at the warehouse. She checked the address. It was the one Daniel had given her, but the place looked abandoned. Still the Society did meet at some strange places, and they often changed meeting venues because they didn't want to draw too much attention. Again making her wonder if the Society was the one who believed they were oppressed, not humans.

She glanced over her shoulder, debating if she should leave. Something didn't feel right here. But she took a deep breath and pushed open the large metal door. She couldn't risk Daniel's being the only one heard tonight. She didn't want to think of what they might decide to do to Sebastian and Carfax Abbey.

She remembered Lizzie's suggestion that Mina just burn

the place to the ground. Mina knew others in the Society wouldn't have the same hesitations she'd had. And she couldn't let something awful happen.

She stepped inside. The place was dark and definitely deserted. A noise of something scurrying away from her scratched on the concrete floors. But she saw a light in a distant room.

She walked slowly in that direction.

"Hello?" she called as she reached the doorway. The room was small and appeared empty, but there were chairs set up in neat rows. Maybe she was early. She stepped into the room, looking around.

"Hello?" she yelled again.

This time her call was answered by the loud slam of a door behind her. She spun to find Daniel leaning on the doorframe through which she'd just entered the small room.

"Daniel," she breathed, her gaze moving warily to the closed door at his back. "Where is everyone?"

"Hmm," he said as if he was considering the question. "They couldn't make it."

Her fear immediately flared, although she tried hard to block it from him. "Are they going to meet another time?"

He nodded. "I'm sure they will. The Society does love their meetings, don't they?"

Daniel stepped away from the door, but rather than moving toward her, he walked a slow circle around the room. She glanced at the door, taking a small step toward it.

Daniel stopped, spinning to look at her with his eerie dark eyes. "Don't bother. I'm much faster than you."

She paused, trying to calm herself. Trying to pretend she didn't know what he meant. "What do you mean?"

"I mean that you and I need to have a little chat."

"W—why?"

"Because you have made things difficult for me."

"H-how?" She forced herself to meet his eyes, even though

something there terrified her. Something so familiar, even though she didn't know what it was.

"Surely what I'm doing with Sebastian Young should have no effect on you," she managed to say.

"No, not really," he agreed. He began walking again, his hands clasped behind his back, his eyes focused on the floor just in front of his precise footsteps. "But you have ruined a good thing for me."

"What? How?"

He stopped again. "You really don't remember me, do you? I was so certain you did."

She frowned, staring at him. His profile, then his back as he continued his circle.

"Daniel, I have no idea what you are talking about."

He turned back to her, a smile splitting his face, as creepy as his eyes. Again she did feel she should know him, but she couldn't quite place from where.

"No, you don't, do you?" He smiled smugly.

Suddenly, whether it was something in that smile, or it was the fact that she could now sense him in a way she hadn't been able to before—not until Sebastian had helped her focus her vampire senses—she knew why this vampire made her so uneasy. So scared. Yet, what she was realizing couldn't be possible.

His smile slowly faded as he became aware of the change in Mina. She tried to block her emotions, her thoughts, using the techniques Sebastian had showed her. Focusing outside of herself. On Sebastian.

"But it will be great fun getting reacquainted," he said and began walking again, his back to her once more.

She took another backward step toward the closed door. And another, but she stopped as he spoke again.

"Let me refresh your memory, cara mia."

Daniel turned back toward her, but this time it wasn't that cadaverlike face that greeted her. It was a wide, charming smile. Dimples. Dark eyes and curly hair.

Mina stumbled back, fear seizing her, strangling her.

"Oh my God," she cried, scrambling backward not even aware of where the door was, where she was. She just needed to get away.

He slowly walked toward her.

"Now is that any way to greet your first love?"

Chapter 28

"Earlier I discovered Mina with one of the members of the Society," Sebastian admitted to his brothers. "She was telling him that the sabotage was working. She had me under control, and it was only a matter of time before she convinced me to close this place."

Both Rhys and Christian looked surprised by his words. Not nearly as surprised as Sebastian had been to hear them.

"Mina said that?" Rhys said.

Sebastian nodded. "She told this guy that she was doing whatever she had to do to control me."

Again Sebastian thought of her offer to let him bite her. An offer that he'd seen as the moment when they'd truly be committed to each other. Sure, he'd bitten many women, but this was going to be the first time he'd bitten, not solely for sustenance, not solely for pleasure, but to make them one. He'd believed that was what she was offering.

What a fool.

"Did you confront her?" Christian asked.

"Yes."

"What did she say?" Rhys asked.

"She denied it all. She claimed that she'd said those things to protect me."

Both brothers stared at him for a moment.

"And why didn't you believe that?" Rhys finally asked.

"I don't need protecting from those idiots."

"But maybe Mina didn't believe that. Maybe she thinks they are a bigger threat than you do. And she should know. She was a member, after all," Rhys said reasonably.

"Apparently she's still a member," Sebastian said bitterly. "A very active member."

"Sebastian, why is it so impossible that she was honestly just trying to protect you?" Rhys asked.

"I don't need her protection," he said again. "I'm very capable of protecting myself. She should have defended me. She should have told that guy that she knew I wasn't a threat to anyone. And that Carfax Abbey wasn't a threat. And that she was in love with me. Period."

Understanding lit both his brothers' eyes, and Sebastian wished he'd just remained silent.

"Sebastian, you are a friggin' bonehead, you know that," Christian said with a shake of his head. "That's exactly what she was saying by trying to protect you."

Sebastian opened his mouth to argue, but he saw his brothers' expressions. They believed Mina. And his brothers were not quick to believe in anyone. Lilah, the evil vampiress who'd crossed them over, had seen to that. Yet, they trusted Mina.

Suddenly, Sebastian knew they were right. Mina had been trying to protect him. But he'd refused to listen. He'd been too worried that she was going to hurt him. That he'd finally fallen in love, and she'd just been pretending. But that wasn't Mina. And he should have known that. He should have trusted her, as she'd trusted him.

Rhys clapped Sebastian on the back. "Don't worry about it. The Young Brothers are notoriously slow on the uptake when it comes to love. Just go find her and apologize."

Sebastian nodded, praying that his mistrust and, he cringed, his threatening behavior hadn't ruined his chance with her, with the woman he did want to spend eternity with.

He waited for that idea to scare him senseless, but now he was far more scared that she wouldn't want him back.

He started to slide from the booth, when he suddenly heard Mina in his head. Her voice clear—and terrified. He fell back against the seat, overwhelmed by the intensity of the echo in his head.

"Sebastian?"

He could hear Rhys, although it sounded as if Rhys was far, far away. Sebastian blinked, trying to clear his mind, to calm her voice in his head.

He turned to his brothers, trying to tell them what was happening, but before he could speak, he heard her again. Scared, desperate. And this time he could see an image. A room. A face. A face he didn't know, but that had been described to him.

"It's Mina," he managed to tell them. "She's in danger."

He was barely aware of Rhys and Christian helping him from the booth and leading him to the club's exit. All he could do was center on Mina, calling to him.

"D—Donatello," Mina heard herself say as if her voice was very far away from her.

"In the flesh." He smiled, strolling toward her.

She backed away, bumping into one of the lined-up chairs, stumbling.

"Really, Wilhelmina, you were ungainly when you were alive, didn't undeath help at all?"

She didn't answer, she just kept moving away. Terror making her movements jerky.

"Have you been following me all this time?"

He laughed at that, his dark eyes dancing. "Hardly."

"But—but you disguised yourself as Daniel. Went to the Society meetings. Always spoke to me."

"Actually," he stopped stalking her, "this is my disguise. Much more effective with the ladies, as you can attest to. As for seeing you again at the Society meeting, that was sheer coincidence. But I did enjoy speaking to you, making you uncomfortable even though you didn't understand why. Until now. Sadly for you."

"Why did you ask me here tonight?" Mina asked. She glanced at the door, realizing that in her fear she'd backed away from it, rather than toward it.

Donatello, or rather Daniel, followed her gaze, then smiled complacently. "Well to finally finish you off, of course. After all, I left you to die the first time, but somehow you didn't."

Her fear threatened to overwhelm her, render her unconscious, but she knew she couldn't allow that to happen. If she did, she was as good as dead. Truly dead.

"Why now? Why after all this time?" she managed to ask.

"Because you have ruined a very good thing for me. I was using the Society as my cover, you see. It was perfect. I'd kill lowly humans and see that those deaths were blamed on the Society's most dangerous preternaturals. It allowed me easy access to humans, such as Franny Millhouse's escort service, and the perfect scapegoat when I was done."

Mina frowned. "But you don't need a scapegoat since you can change your looks, no one would know it was you to begin with. You'd never get caught."

"True," he agreed. "But it's not nearly as much fun. I like killing a human, and then walking into a Society meeting and being heralded as—what is that silly name again? Oh yes, a Society's Savior. It's deliciously ironic, isn't it?"

Mina stared at this monster that could hide behind the mask of an archangel. He was like a serial killer who liked to stay at the crime scene, watching the police struggle for clues. Pure evil.

"How—how did I ruin things for you? I didn't know any of this."

"No," he agreed. "But you did start to ask questions. Enough questions that Jude began to watch me. Jackson Hallowell, of course, never would have put it together, but Jude, he has a dark soul. And your questions about the escort service got him thinking. Of course, he doesn't realize yet that I'm on to him. But I know it's only a matter of time now before I'm added to the most dangerous list. But of course, unlike the case of your lover, I *am* very dangerous."

"Why did you attack that woman outside of Sebastian's club?" Mina asked at the mention of Sebastian.

Daniel shrugged. "For fun. To scare you. To make sure Sebastian stays firmly planted on that most dangerous list until he and his club are destroyed." He smiled sweetly. "Just to be mean."

"Is that why you chose to attack me from the beginning? To be mean?"

"Oh no," he said sincerely. "I needed you."

"Why?"

"You were a virgin, and I need virgin blood to survive. That's what sustains a creature like me."

"What are you?" she asked.

"I am a vampire, but I'm a variant of the undead. An incubus—far more powerful than an average vampire. But to maintain that power, I must survive on the blood of virgins."

She stared at him, even surrounded by all the preternaturals that she was, this seemed almost unreal.

"But why did you cross me over if you intended me to die?" she asked.

"Because the blood is so much sweeter if I cross the victim over. And until you, I don't believe any of my other victims did survive. I left them, just like you, and they burned in the sun. Or starved. Or were killed because they'd become little more than raving lunatics."

Mina stared at him, realizing she could have easily suffered any of those fates. She'd been lucky—an odd thought given the horror she had survived.

"But why me? Why not my sisters?" She always wondered that. Since he hadn't wanted her money? Or her sexual favors?

He laughed. "Well, that is simple. They weren't virgins."

Then he sobered. "Enough talk. It's time to do what I came here for. To finish what I started so long ago."

Mina watched as the handsome mask of Donatello melted away, replaced by the hideous creature who'd haunted her for so long. Jagged, razor-sharp teeth, skeletal features, glowing red eyes.

Panic filled Mina, but she tried to stay calm. As he started to stroll toward her, she darted for the door. She made it, her hand on the handle, when he caught her by the back of the neck, hurling her into the center of the room. She landed amid the chairs, fallen, breathless. She scrambled along the floor as she heard him approaching, but he easily caught her, picking her up by the throat. She gasped as he lifted her off the ground, her feet dangling several inches from the floor.

She clawed at the finger digging into her throat, but she couldn't begin to break his crushing hold. Spots started to appear before her eyes, and she struggled to stay conscious. She couldn't die. She couldn't.

Suddenly, she heard a voice that she never believed she would hear again. "Let her go, or I'll kill you."

Sebastian watched as the vampire holding Mina released her, her body crumpling to the floor. Relief flooded Sebastian as she pushed herself upright, her frightened eyes locking with his. He offered a slight smile, which she didn't return. She appeared in shock.

His eyes left her, returning to the other vampire, now seeing his handsome features, wavy hair, and charming smile.

"So you are Donatello?" Sebastian said, managing to keep his cool. "Mina, what were you thinking? He's not nearly as attractive as you said he was."

Donatello laughed, the sound loud and hoarse. Evil.

"And aren't you the heroic lover?" Donatello said with a smile. "Charging to your lady's rescue." He glanced from Sebastian to his brothers. "And bringing reinforcements, too. Isn't there a phrase that goes something like 'the more the merrier'? I would say that applies to this occasion."

"Just get away from her," Sebastian stated.

"Well, I could do that," Donatello agreed. "Or you could just come get her?"

"Don't do it," Mina cried. "He's not a normal vampire. He's an incubus."

"Oh, Wilhelmina, giving away all my secrets," Donatello lamented.

Sebastian paused at Mina's words. An incubus. How the hell did they fight that? He glanced to Rhys, who just glared at the vampire-demon. Sebastian then looked to Christian, realizing if anyone would know about something this evil it was Christian.

Christian gave Sebastian a look that didn't reassure him.

"You got nothing for me?" Sebastian asked Christian.

Christian shook his head. "Not really."

Donatello laughed again, and Sebastian decided they were just going to have to go for it. Three against one had to be some sort of odds.

Sebastian charged the vampire, both Rhys and Christian right there too. But Donatello easily threw them off, sending them flying. Sebastian hit the wall, fighting back a groan at the force of the impact, but he was on his feet again instantly. Rhys slammed into the metal door, denting it. He seemed slightly dazed, but he managed to pull himself up to his feet. Christian landed on the wooden chairs, several breaking under his weight, but like his brothers he quickly got back to his feet.

This time the brothers circled Donatello.

Donatello watched them, looking unimpressed. Sebastian wasn't heartened by that look.

"This thing is friggin' strong," Sebastian murmured to Rhys.

"And fast," Rhys agreed, not sounding any more pleased about their odds.

Sebastian sneaked a glance back to Mina. She still remained on the floor, although he noticed she seemed to have scooted back among the scattering of broken chairs.

"I tell you what," Donatello said, drawing Sebastian's attention back to him. "Let me have Wilhelmina, and I'll let you boys go."

Sebastian shook his head. "No deal."

Donatello shot Mina a disparaging look. "I really think it's quite a deal."

"No deal," Rhys said this time for Sebastian.

"No deal," Christian agreed.

The brothers geared up for another attack and just as they would have lunged at Donatello again, Mina shouted, "Sebastian."

He turned toward her just as she threw the broken leg of one of the chairs like a spear. But in true Mina fashion, her aim was off. The leg flew toward Christian, who ducked just as it would have struck him in the head. The makeshift stake hit Sebastian, grazing his shoulder, then deflected from him, flying off sideways.

Mina cringed, and Sebastian spun back to Donatello, afraid the vampire would use the distraction to attack them. Instead Donatello remained where he was, staring down at himself. It took Sebastian a moment to realize what the monster was staring at—the chair leg protruded from his chest, just under his left collarbone. Then the incubus's eyes found Mina where she still sat on the floor, giving her an almost surprised look.

He let out an enraged shriek that seemed to shake the entire building. His face began to contort, his features changing from one mask to another, only his sharp fangs and glowing red eyes remaining the same.

She'd been right about the eyes, Sebastian realized. But he didn't consider the monster's features any longer, as he saw that Donatello's long, taloned fingers were curled around the chair leg, trying to remove it. Sebastian charged forward, driving the stake farther into Donatello's chest with a satisfying crunch.

Slowly the incubus's features changed again, and Sebastian saw the tall, thin vampire who Mina had been talking to at Carfax Abbey. Then in a violent rush of air that seemed to suck the oxygen from the room, the monster imploded. Ash rained down in the spot where he'd been.

"Shit," Christian said flatly.

Rhys just stared at the ash, a rather dazed look in his amber eyes. And Sebastian spun toward Mina.

She stared at him, and he stared back, neither able to speak. Overwhelmed by what had just happened.

Then he was hurrying toward her, pushing chairs aside to get to her. He crouched down, yanking her against his chest, kissing her face, her hair.

"You're trembling," she finally managed to say between frantic kisses.

"Mina Weiss, you are going to be the death of me."

A broken cry escaped her and she kissed him, her hands frantic on his face, his shoulders, his arms

"How did you find me?" she asked once they parted.

"I could hear you and see you. I just knew where to come."

Mina stared him. "How?"

"Soulmates," Rhys and Christian said in unison.

Sebastian and Mina looked at them, then Sebastian gave them a warning glance.

"Can I have a moment alone with her?" he asked them.

"We risk our immortality getting him the girl, and this is the thanks we get," Christian muttered.

"Typical," Rhys agreed. But they gave Mina a smile, then left the room.

"Mina," Sebastian said as soon as they were gone, but she interrupted.

"Your shoulder." She touched the spot where the chair leg

had hit him. There was a tear in his shirt and a small amount of blood. "Did I really hurt you?"

He smiled at that. "No more than usual. Now, *shhh*. And listen." He caught her face in his hands. "I'm so sorry I didn't trust what you were telling me. That I believed the worst."

Mina shook her head. "That's okay."

"No, it's not," he told her, gently brushing her hair back from her cheek. "I wasn't kidding, you've been scaring me to death, woman."

Mina gave him a disbelieving look. "Me?"

"Yeah, you. You've shaken up my whole existence since the moment we met. And I haven't had a clue how to handle that. I've always considered myself the wild Young brother, the one who loves being a vampire. The playboy."

"Well, that's all true."

"Yes, but I had let myself use that identity as a way to always be in control. A way to keep myself—safe. I always imagined love would feel out of control."

Mina gave him a hesitant look. "It does."

"I know," he told her.

She stared at him as if she didn't know what to make of his response.

"Mina, I've known since the first time we made love—hell, probably since before that—that you are my soulmate. I tried to ignore it. Deny it. But it was the truth. And tonight, I really thought I'd lost you. And that was the most out of control I've ever felt. Far scarier than anything I was feeling before. Then I saw that thing attacking you, and I was terrified I'd never get the chance to tell you."

"Tell me what?" she asked in that breathy way he loved.

"Mina, I am hopelessly, head-over-heels in love with you. And I want to spend eternity driving you crazy with my narcissistic, egocentric, and depraved ways."

She laughed, throwing her arms around his neck. She kissed him.

"That sounds wonderful to me." She grinned at him and they kissed again.

"God, I love you," he said shaking his head, unable to believe the intensity of what he was feeling.

"I love you, too," she told him, then her smiled widened.

"What?" he asked, tucking her hair back from her face.

"I can feel your emotions. They aren't blocked."

He laughed. "No, somehow I don't think anything will be blocked from you again." Another loss of control, and he realized that idea didn't scare him in the least.

She grinned even wider.

He smiled back, then he scooped her up against his chest and strode to the door.

"Where are we going?" she asked.

"I'm taking you out for a bite." He shot a glance to her pale neck. "That is, if the offering is still on?"

She laughed again, eyeing his neck, too. "Absolutely, because I'm starving."

Epilogue

"You don't have to do this," Mina told Sebastian.

"Yes, I do."

"But all of this is behind us."

"Not quite yet."

Sebastian held the door open and waited for Mina to enter before him.

"Let's just go home," she said. "Wouldn't you rather just make love all night?"

"And you call me the depraved one," he murmured, leaning down to place a quick kiss on the side of her neck. A place that she had learned was her favorite spot to be kissed. Well, one of them.

He caught her hand and pulled her into the room. Jane and Rhys and Christian and Jolee followed them in. Sebastian had called Christian to come from West Virginia for this. Mina hesitated as a few familiar faces turned toward her. She forced a smile as she led them to the back row. They all sat down and waited as Jackson Hallowell called the Society meeting to order.

Mina only half-listened as the board went through the official business. She was too aware of Sebastian beside her, his fingers linked with hers, his thumb stroking the top of her hand. But she certainly didn't want to be there. She realized now that the Society, even if some of the members did have good intentions, wasn't going about things the right way. After all, they couldn't have been more wrong about Sebastian.

Finally, Jackson asked the members if they had any business they wished to discuss, and Sebastian rose.

Mina stared up at him, waiting to hear what he could possibly want to say to these preternaturals.

"Hi," he greeted the room with one of his lopsided smiles that she loved so much. "I'm Sebastian Young."

Several members shifted uncomfortably in their seats.

Sebastian smiled again. "For those of you who may, or may not, recognize me, I'm the Society's third most dangerous vampire."

More awkward rustles. A cough. Silence.

"And before you go nuts and try to stake me or pelt me with garlic or something, I've actually come here to tell you that Mina—Wilhelmina Weiss has succeeded in her mission for the Society."

He looked down at her. She shook her head, not understanding what he was saying.

"Wilhelmina has stopped me from all my nefarious deeds. I'm reformed," he announced, then he pulled Mina to her feet. He took both her hands, so they were facing each other.

"What are you doing?" she asked him in a hushed voice, shaking her head, overwhelmed by this man.

"I'm telling them of your success," he whispered back with a proud smile. Then he returned his attention to the room.

"You see, I'm no longer a threat to humans," he told them.

"You never were," Mina murmured, and Sebastian shot her a glance designed to shush her.

"I'm no longer a threat because," he turned back to Mina, gazing into her eyes, "I only have fangs for you. I love you, baby."

He leaned forward and kissed her. Mina's arms came up

around his neck and she kissed him back, loving this crazy, outrageous man.

Then she realized that the whole room had erupted into applause. Mina broke the kiss to look around. Members of the Society clapped madly, grinning at Sebastian and at her. But mostly at Sebastian. She shook her head—leave it to Sebastian to go from villain to hero in just minutes.

The meeting then became a huge social event, members coming up to talk to Sebastian and Mina and all the Young family. Even Jude, who didn't warm to anyone, came over and clapped him on the back. Jude knew about Daniel/Donatello, although he'd said nothing to the other members. As far as the Society knew, Daniel just quit the group, a lie Mina hadn't agreed with. The Society should know that Sebastian Young had stopped the most dangerous vampire in New York. But to her surprise he'd been very humble about the whole thing. The only time he'd been humble about anything.

Mina shook her head again as she watched Sebastian work the crowd. Oh, he was still a flirt. He was definitely a charmer. And that was fine with Mina, because she knew he loved her with all his heart. She didn't doubt that in the least.

"Hey, Wil," Mina heard a voice call from behind her and she turned to see Lizzie entering the room in her usual leather and carrying her motorcycle helmet.

"These things are pretty crazy," Lizzie said, glancing around at the festive crowd.

Mina laughed, delighted to see her friend. "Well, you picked a good night finally to check out a meeting. Believe me, this one was a first. How did you know to find me here?"

"I happened to hear about it at Dr. Fowler's Institute, so I thought I'd come try to catch up with you. Since you are always with Super-Fang, I never see you."

Mina smiled at her friend, knowing that Lizzie was pleased for Mina's happiness with Sebastian. But it was true, they never did see each other since Mina had moved in with him.

"Come on," Mina said, taking Lizzie's arm. "Let me finally introduce you to Super-Fang. In fact his whole family is here."

Mina led her through the crowd to where Sebastian stood chatting with Vedette. The plump werefox practically glowed under Sebastian's attention.

"Sebastian," Mina said, touching his arm. "Meet Lizzie."

Sebastian turned, the smile on his face withering, his golden eyes widening in shock. Mina felt Lizzie freeze at her side. Mina glanced back and forth between them, confused by their stunned reactions to each other.

But before she could question them, it was Rhys who actually broke the silence.

"Elizabeth?" He stepped toward Lizzie, his features pale as if he was seeing a ghost. "Oh my God, Elizabeth."

"Rhys," Lizzie whispered, her eyes moving from one of the brothers to the next. "Sebastian. Oh my God, Christian."

The next thing Mina knew, all three Young brothers were encircling Lizzie. Then they were hugging her, lifting her in the air, asking her a million questions at once.

Suddenly Mina realized what was happening. Her old roommate was Elizabeth Young. Sebastian's sister. The one they believed dead. Mina looked at Jane and Jolee, who also watched the reunion in stunned amazement.

After many more hugs and laughter and tears, Lizzie turned to Mina. Through her tears, she stated in a wry way, so like all the other Youngs, "I guess I should have come to one of these meeting sooner, huh?"

Here's a look at Alison Kent's
scintillating new Brava,
BEYOND A SHADOW.
Available now!

She sighed heavily and shook her head. "What I wouldn't give for a real vacation. Christmas break is coming up, but I set aside that time to finish up the renovations to this place. I've been putting it off for too long."

He thought back to his earlier assessment that she wasn't happy with her life in Comfort Bay and knew he'd been right.

The fact that she put off such simple repairs as faulty wiring reflected her discontent. "If the upkeep is too much for you, why don't you share your place with a friend?"

"It's not that easy," she said, grabbing another screw. "The people here have roots. They grow up here. They marry here. They stay. I came for the peace and quiet and had my life turned upside down.

He understood roots. He understood tradition. He did not understand why she remained if being here made her unhappy and restless for change. She did not strike him as a woman to let a failed marriage stop her from living her life.

He watched the flex and roll of her shoulders as she worked to tighten the screw. "What keeps you here then if you don't have roots? Have you become that attached to the people and the town?"

She turned, angling her body into the shadows and hiding her face. "I told you this morning. My friends, my students. I adore my job."

The better part of valor demanded he let the subject drop.

"I can only hope mine will be equally satisfying. And that I don't disappoint the Maples."

"Well, you get points for being handy with a flashlight. There," she said, finishing with the final screw, "that will do until tomorrow."

"Is there no one in town to make such repairs?"

She nodded. "Dale Potter. But he's only one man in a small town that seems to be falling down around his ears with an unfortunate regularity."

"Then it seems I might be your best bet."

"Would you need access from inside?"

"I might."

She glanced over her shoulder at the window as if taking stock of her valuables. "I can leave the place unlocked, I guess. Or you can get the key from Molly."

"If you are not comfortable with me being here without you, I could wait until the evening when we are both finished with work for the day."

"I don't mind you being here, no. But I'll go ahead and call Potters to see when Dale can get out here. If it's going to be weeks, I'll take you up on the offer, okay?"

"Okay," he said, and reached up to help her down.

He had not intended to do anything more than offer his hand, but she turned to toss her screwdriver into the toolbox at his feet, and he grabbed for her as she leaned. It was an instinctive move, thinking she had misstepped and was going to fall, his hands going to her waist to steady her.

But she had not misstepped. And she did not fall. She remained standing where she was, where he held her on the ladder, his hands on her T-shirt beneath her open sweater, her abdomen inches from his face. The screwdriver clattered against the porch. He listened as it began to roll, knowing he needed to release her.

Instead, he slipped his hands lower, finding the small strip of skin where her shirt rose above her jeans and inching his thumbs along the hem, circling one around her navel and breathing her in. The feel of her flesh, her scent . . . it took nothing more. The moment ceased to be about discovering and exploiting any weaknesses in her loyalties. It became, instead, about wanting her.

But he would not force her; he would never force her. And so he bowed his head and prepared to step back. She stopped him. First with a small earthy whimper. Then by cupping one hand to the back of his head and pulling him near. He buried his face against her, gripping her waist, and she held him there as if her want mirrored his.

He felt her skin heat. He heard the rapid beat of her heart. He opened his mouth against her and tasted her on his tongue. His body tightened. His cock began to swell with the rush of his blood. And his reasons for being there vanished beyond the shadows.

You won't want to miss this peek
at Katherine Garbera's latest,
THE ULTIMATE ROMANTIC CHALLENGE.
Available now from Brava!

Sterling parked his car on the street and followed her up the walk to her town house. She glanced over her shoulder at him. He had a quiet intensity that made her more aware of her body; she could feel his gaze on her with each step she took.

"Nice neighborhood," he said as she unlocked her door and stepped inside.

It would have been easier if they'd been swept away with passion, kissing frantically and making out in her foyer, the way frenzied couples always seemed to mate in movies, but they weren't young impassioned lovers. They were mature—

Sterling caught her hand, drawing her into his arms as the door closed behind them. "Ah, that's better. No martini shaker to keep us apart."

He lowered his head, rubbing his lips lightly over hers as his hands slid lower on her back and drew her tightly against his body. She shifted against him, angling her head to a more comfortable position under his.

He teased her with nibbling kisses, but didn't kiss her full on the mouth. She waited for it, tensed each time he drew near but he always pulled away. And the anticipation was driving her wild. She sensed he was doing it on purpose, making damned sure that she knew he was in total control here.

She plunged her fingers into his hair and held his mouth still on hers. Inviting him to taste her, she opened her mouth. He thrust his tongue deep in her past the barrier of her teeth.

She was overwhelmed by Sterling. He held her in his strong arms, one hard around her waist and the other smoothing a trail up and down her back. His scent surrounded her. It was something raw and earthy and masculine with the salt from the sea breezes. She tunneled her fingers deeper into his hair, holding onto him as if that would let her control him. Keep control of him. Make this crazy night about nothing but hot and wild sex.

She pulled back from him, caressing his jaw as she trailed her hands down his neck to rest on his shoulders. Her lips tingled from contact with his. Her fingers rubbed over his stumbled jaw. His dark hair was tousled from her fingers; his lips swollen. He looked like a fallen angel ready for sin, and she wanted to be the one to lead him down the path.

"That was . . . unexpected."

"I wanted to make sure that you understood why I was here," he said after a few minutes.

She doubted she knew why he was here. Maybe he thought the way to get her cooperation with the merger was to seduce her. Or maybe experience had taught him that dinner automatically translated into an invitation into the lady's bedroom. She didn't care what his agenda was. She had her own and she wasn't afraid to go after what she wanted. What she needed.

She needed to figure out what made this man tick and then use it to drive him away. Away from Charleston, away from Haughton House, and most definitely away from her.

She was sure that Wes knew Cullen's last name. All she had to do was convince him to tell her. Holly hurried through the cool night and reached the bookstore just in time to see Wes come outside, turn around, and lock the door.

Slowing her pace, she walked up. "Hi." Damn, he was still sexy in that overbearing male way.

He pulled his key out of the lock, then turned his gaze to her. "Change your mind?" He glanced down at the book in her hand. "Want me to return Cullen's book?" He added a grin that should be labeled as dangerous.

Holly leaned against the side of the bookstore and shrugged. "I have time to kill. Thought I'd see if you still wanted to get a drink. Unless," she opened her eyes wide, "you really are afraid that I'm a stalker with murder on my mind."

A small smile tugged at his mouth as he shoved his keys into his pants pocket. "If not murder, then what—sex?"

Oh yeah. Wait, no! God, she was weak tonight. Maybe it was her bad week. She decided to change tactics. "I asked you out for a drink, Brockman. All you have to say is that you aren't interested." She turned and started to walk away.

"Does that work?" he called after her.

She'd only gone a couple of feet and turned back. "What?"

"The offensive. Does it work?"

She couldn't help smiling. "Usually. But then, I don't usually have to beg men for their company."

He directed his gaze in a slow examination down her body clad in a burgundy tank top and form-fitting jeans, then back to her face. His green eyes darkened. "Tell me more about this begging."

Down, girl. What was it about him? She shot back, "For that, you'd have to buy the drinks."

He stepped closer, throttling his voice down to a dangerous rumble. "Sex on the Beach?"

She swore the ocean roared in her head. Her hormones surged up into huge waves of longing, washing over her. "You're offering me sex on the beach?"

His grin widened, crinkling his gorgeous eyes. "The drink. What did you think I meant?"

Her thighs tightened in response. *Get a grip, Hillbay—it's just a reaction to a handsome man and a long dry spell of no sex.* Holly was all for sex but on her terms. She always kept her emotions in check. She was the cool one—the one that walked away when the relationship had played out. It was time to take back the power. She said, "That information will cost you more than the price of a drink."

He didn't hesitate. "Name your price."

"Steak." She was hungry. And food might keep her from thinking about sex.

"Done. You can follow me in your car."

She was practically dizzy from the pace he set. Or maybe that was pent-up lust breaking free. "Follow you where?"

"My house. On the beach. I'll make the drinks and we'll grill some steaks out on my deck and watch the waves. Or maybe listen to the waves since it's dark out." His grin suggested more than wave watching.

She thought about that, but in the end, Wes had what she wanted. Information on Cullen. *Not sex.*

She lifted her chin. "I'll follow you. I can spare an hour or so."

He nodded like it was no more than he expected.

Annoyed, she said, "I'm not sleeping with you."

He moved up to her until she felt the brush of his breath. "No?"

She felt a tremor in her belly that spread wet heat. *Keep control of the situation,* she reminded herself. "I don't go to bed on the first date."

He reached down and picked up her free hand in his larger one. "Kiss on the first date?"

She should put a stop to this. But the feel of his hand wrapped around hers was warm and sensual. She opened her mouth to tell him they weren't dating, but ended up saying, "If I like the man."

He ran his thumb over her palm. "You like me. Make out?"

Regaining her wits, she jerked her hand away. "Ain't gonna happen, book boy."

His face blanked at the nickname, then a grin spread out over his face. "Why don't we go to my house and take these rules of yours for a test drive?"

She was playing with fire. Holly knew it, but she couldn't stop herself. Wes was not the man she expected when she had walked into his bookstore. There was so much more, and she had a strange compulsion to peel back the layers and find out just who this man was.

Could she do that and keep her clothes on? Or maybe do it naked, but keep her emotions in check?

She was going to find out. "Lead on, book boy."